DEAD SPACE

"Three . . . two . . . one . . . ignition!"

Lt. Commander Jacob Enright checked the monitor directly in front of him on the control panel. Space Shuttle *Endeavor's* Payload Assist Module engine fired its 17,360-pound molten thrust at the lethal weapons satellite LACE on schedule to push it out of continuous orbit. In twenty-five minutes, it would hit the atmosphere in the middle of the Indian Ocean and hit the water as harmless debris soon after.

"Ignition plus twenty seconds. Range two miles, Skipper," Enright called out as he read the constantly changing computations. "One minute now. Still burning."

"Range below?" Colonel Parker asked.

"Four miles. Slant range two miles and counting."

The PAM's attitude thrusters were programmed to keep the PAM horizontal and to hold at a slight tilt. This off-center component pushed LACE down and away from the shuttle as it slowed her speed.

"Seventy seconds. Range six miles below."

"Prepare for shutdown," Parker barked, his eyes fixed on the chronometer. "Shutdown, now!"

The huge engine cut power and both men kept the shuttle on an even keel.

"She's slowed by 898 feet per second, Skip. She's on her way."

The death fall had begun . . .

BLOCKBUSTER FICTION FROM PINNACLE BOOKS!

THE FINAL VOYAGE OF THE S.S.N. SKATE   (17-157, $3.95)
by Stephen Cassell
The "leper" of the U.S. Pacific Fleet, SSN 578 nuclear attack sub SKATE, has one final mission to perform—an impossible act of piracy that will pit the underwater deathtrap and its inexperienced crew against the combined might of the Soviet Navy's finest!

QUEENS GATE RECKONING   (17-164, $3.95)
by Lewis Purdue
Only a wounded CIA operative and a defecting Soviet ballerina stand in the way of a vast consortium of treason that speeds toward the hour of mankind's ultimate reckoning! From the best-selling author of THE LINZ TESTAMENT.

FAREWELL TO RUSSIA   (17-165, $4.50)
by Richard Hugo
A KGB agent must race against time to infiltrate the confines of U.S. nuclear technology after a terrifying accident threatens to unleash unmitigated devastation!

THE NICODEMUS CODE   (17-133, $3.95)
by Graham N. Smith and Donna Smith
A two-thousand-year-old parchment has been unearthed, unleashing a terrifying conspiracy unlike any the world has previously known, one that threatens the life of the Pope himself, and the ultimate destruction of Christianity!

Available wherever paperbacks are sold, or order direct from the Publisher. Send cover price plus 50¢ per copy for mailing and handling to Pinnacle Books, Dept.17-459, 475 Park Avenue South, New York, N.Y. 10016. Residents of New York, New Jersey and Pennsylvania must include sales tax. DO NOT SEND CASH.

THE GLASS LADY

D. J. SAVAGE

PINNACLE BOOKS
WINDSOR PUBLISHING CORP.

For David L. Hall:
The Skipper

PINNACLE BOOKS

are published by

Windsor Publishing Corp.
475 Park Avenue South
New York, NY 10016

Copyright © 1985 by D. J. Savage. Published by arrangement with Daring Books.

First Pinnacle Books Printing: December, 1990

Printed in the United States of America

Acknowledgments

The detailed technical and engineering materials in this story would have been impossible without generous assistance from many sources. The Public Information Office of the Lyndon B. Johnson Space Center, Houston, Tx., and especially Mrs. I. L. Scott, were most generous with Space Transportation System documents, Crew Activity Plans, and shuttle mission profiles.

For detailed engineering descriptions of the space shuttle and of the LACE laser weapon system, the author is indebted to the editors of *Aviation Week and Space Technology* and particularly to Craig Covault, *Aviation Week*'s Space Technology editor.

The detailed descriptions of Shuttle's onboard systems would have been impossible without the long-suffering patience of Ms. Sue Cometa, Rockwell International, Space Operations Division.

The author cannot adequately thank Ms. Elizabeth Gasper for her time, trouble, and tea, in editing the final galleys of this story written in a foreign language. Even old Smokey had to wait.

The author assumes responsibility for inaccuracies in flight-deck procedures and protocols caused by failure to secure certain important checklists. When NASA or Rockwell declined to release to the author such cockpit checklists, the author attempted to compensate for such loss with the kind and generous counsel of project subcontractors.

Certain historical figures, living and dead, who have played a significant role in the United States and Soviet manned space programs are mentioned by name in this text. The author assumes full responsibility for offense taken by such figures and by others who, by coincidence, may resemble the otherwise fictional characters in this story.

1

December 12th

"Assbones. That's what it takes to be a real stick-and-rudder man: Assbones. What else does flying by the seat of your pants mean, anyway? Some got it, some don't."

The tall man's lips broke into a grin behind the microphone which crossed his stubbled cheek. William McKinley Parker looked through the cockpit windshield into the darkness.

"That mean we got 'em, Skipper?" smiled Jacob Enright from the right seat opposite the command pilot.

"And then some, Number One," the long man drawled in the left seat. "How's the EGT on APU Number Two?"

"A tad high, Skipper. No sweat." From the right seat, Enright's hands worked the flightdeck instrument displays to the right of three green television screens covered with numbers and graphs. The television screens blew their eerie green glow upon the two tired faces.

"Endeavor, Endeavor: Configure AOS, Houston remote, Yarradee local," the pilot's headphones crackled.

"Ah, rogo, Flight. Acquisition of signal by Australia." The pilot in command brought his boom microphone closer to his lips. "We have deorbit burn status report when you want it."

"Ready to copy, Endeavor."

"Okay, Flight: The GPC swallowed the re-entry state vectors whole; we have OPS-3 running in Major Mode 303; and we have three good APU's cranking away. Three water spray boilers are on line. Number One thinks the exhaust gas tem-

7

perature on APU Number Two is peaking a bit, but he says to fly with it. We burned on time, BT two minutes, 27 seconds, with two good OMS engines. Delta-V is minus 297 point 5. And we've pitched about to entry attitude. Alpha now 40 degrees and attitude hold in Y-POP."

"We copy that, Endeavor. We have Operations Sequence Three running in the GPC. Your auxiliary power units look fine. Backroom says to ignore the APU-2 EGT warning. We copy burn time of 02 plus 27, delta velocity minus 297 point 5. Understand entry attitude hold at forty degrees up, wings level."

"You got it, Flight. We're goin' over the edge here. See you over Guam in about six minutes. This is the AC."

"Roger, Aircraft Commander. Configure LOS Yarradee."

"Rog. Loss of signal, Australia."

"And we're about 15 from entry interface, Skip."

"Uh huh." The pilot shifted his weight in the tight seat as he stretched his long legs above the rudder pedals underneath the wide, forward instrument panel.

"Let's hear the Air Data Probe checklist, Left, one more time, Number One. Just to be sure."

"I think we've already danced that waltz, Skipper," sighed the pilot in the right seat who wiped beads of sweat from his chin.

In nature, there are certain looks which require no words. There is the look of an angry horse, the look of the twice wounded, and the look of a father at the birth of his firstborn. And then there is the captain's look which pierces the air, warming it as it passes. Jacob Enright felt his face singed.

"Air data probe, Left," the second in command recited as his moist fingers fumbled through his two-inch-thick Mission Procedures manual. As he recited the protocol, his captain laid a long index finger upon each switch and square pushbutton.

"ADTA, No. 1, circuit breaker, Main Bus A, panel Overhead Fourteen, Row E, closed. ADTA, No. 3, circuit breaker, Main dc Bus C, panel Overhead Sixteen, Row E, closed. Multiplexer-demultiplexer, Flight-forward One, panel Overhead Six, on. ADP, Left, panel Center Three, locked stow. And, ADP, Left Stow, panel Center Three, to enable." When he had finished as Colonel Parker gently touched the last switch on the center console between their seats, Enright nodded So There. But the tired command pilot had his face turned toward his side window over his left shoulder.

Six triple-pane flightdeck windows wrapped around the cockpit from the command pilot's left shoulder to the copilot's right shoulder. The night sky was the glossy and perfect blackness of space. One hundred thirty nautical miles below, the faint lights of Cape Londonderry on the north coastline of Australia's King Leopold Mountain Range passed over the western horizon behind the Shuttle Endeavor's white body. The two fliers rode heads up over the dark South Pacific.

"Thermal conditioning initiated," the thin pilot in the right seat called out. Working the triple hydraulic systems' switches two feet from his sweating face, the second in command directed warm hydraulic fluid through the spacecraft's wings and tail. Without sound or vibration, the four aileron-elevators at the back edge of the wings moved slightly as the warm hydraulic blood pulsed through aluminum veins.

"Okay, Jack. Payload bay vent doors coming closed."

Behind the roomy cockpit, the ship's four primary computers sealed eight vent doors in the 60-foot long payload bay of the shuttle.

"Check, Skipper. Confirm forward RCS propellant dump, radar altimeters, and TACAN to standby."

"Got it, Number One. Confirm TACAN landing beacon Number One mode select to receive and Number Two to mode GPC. And TACAN antenna select auto for One and Two, and upper for Number Three." The commander studied the green glow of the left television screen at the center of the front instrument panel. His long fingers reached for an array of switches. "Forward RCS purge complete . . . Helium pressure, Loops A and B, talk-back closed, manifold isolation Loops One through Five, talk-back closed, and items 12 through 19: All forward RCS Reaction Jet Drivers off on panels Overhead Fourteen, Fifteen, and Sixteen. Forward jets

9

configured safe."

"Endeavor, Endeavor: Configure AOS by Guam. You're Go at seven minutes to entry. We see you have trajectory plot One up on the CRT's. Your data dump is good. We show you 6,056 miles from landing, and velocity now 24,235 feet per second and rising."

"Ah, rogo, Flight. All three televisions are Go. We have attitude hold in plus Z, alpha at 40."

"Copy, Endeavor. Now you're flying right: Heads up, feet down. Your APU's are in the green. We'll be losing you momentarily. Entry interface in 4½ at 400K, 4390 miles range-to-go, at 24,446 feet per second over the water. Confirm CDR's entry roll mode select, Will."

"Rogee, Flight," the Colonel called. "We're right and tight in the sky. Lookin' for interface in about four minutes at 400,000 feet. My roll mode is lever-locked auto, Panel Left Four. Do you have a sunrise time for us?"

"Stand by, Endeavor . . . We show daylight in 15 minutes. We have S-band data dropout. Good . . ."

"And we're on our own, Skip . . . Just you, me and Mother."

"About that, Jack. Why 'Mother?' I've been meanin' to ask you about that for about six months."

"Easy: Calling it the General Purpose Computer is too damned cold and impersonal. The old GPC watches everything; it watches over us when we sleep, it tucks us in, it wakes us up, it monitors 3,000 parameters, it flushes the biffy; it does everything but wipe our noses . . . Only a Mother." The small pilot in the right seat gently patted the glareshield atop the broad instrument panel. "Mother," he smiled.

" 'Mother' says entry interface in 30 seconds at Mach 24 point 6, Number One. Major Mode 304 is running."

"I'm hangin' on, Skip. EI in 5, 4, 3, 2, and we've hit the wall!"

The cockpit shuddered as the uppermost wisps of the Earth's atmosphere 80 statute miles above the dark Pacific nipped at 100 tons of space glider. With all of her forward rocket thrusters shut down for re-entry, the shuttle is designed

10

to come home from space without engines, hot and heavy, gliding in at 25 times the speed of sound.

A pink glow outside the large windows bathed the cockpit in cherry light as air friction seared the black belly of the shuttle. Outside, the re-entry heating is twice as hot as the melting temperature of the shuttle's aluminum skin. Only the ship's 35,000 heat-absorbing tiles of 99 percent pure glass fibers insulate it from incineration at Mach 25.

Mounting deceleration forces pushed the crew forward and their chest straps tightened as the Earth sucked fiercely at the glass-covered starship riding 40 degrees nose high across the nighttime Pacific Ocean.

Outside, air friction generated its glowing heat at the temperature where steel burns white. The cocoon of roaring fire in the sky enveloped the heavy vessel in a molten plasma sheath through which radio beams will not penetrate. The digital autopilot, DAP, flew the ship steadily eastward to her landing at Edwards Air Force Base, California.

"EI plus three. Elevons enable." The airplane control surfaces on the broad wings were alive and flying along with shuttle's small jet thrusters in her tail section.

"I see it, Skip. We have aerosurface amplifiers on line. ASA is Go, Channel One."

Far behind the flightdeck, the great aileron-elevator surfaces at the rearmost edges of the wings were guiding the plummeting starship in concert with the Reaction Control System jets in the tail.

"EI plus 4 and 40. At Mach 24, out of 280,000 feet."

"Roger, Number One. Out of 280K. Roll jets inhibited aft. Dynamic pressure at ten."

"I see it. Lift over drag is a tad high, Skip. Traj One is right down the slot."

"Roger, Jack."

The blazing daylight outside turned from pink to apple red as the autopilot steered through the fiery shock waves.

A siren wailed mournfully through each pilot's headphones.

"Master Alarm! Flight Control System! I got it, Jack."

The commander pushed in the blinking Master Alarm light in front of his face to extinguish the alarm claxon.

"FCS Channel One to override . . . That's got her," the long pilot sighed deeply.

"Five minutes into the blackout, Skip. FCS has the con at Mach 24. Stand by for roll reversal."

The cockpit rolled slowly into a steep right turn laying the pilots on their sides.

"Out of 263K, Mach 22 point 3, 80 degrees of bank, Number One. Hang with it," drawled the tall commander lazily.

"Auto looks good in roll rate at five degrees per second, Skipper." The copilot scanned his winking green television screen as a tiny, bug-shaped shuttle chased a small, square box down the television screen's seven-inch-wide face. "Point 176 on G loading; drag at four; guidance internal. Range-to-go is 3,170 miles."

"Mother is really flying hands-on today, Number One. Traj One looks super. Confirming aft pitch jets inhibited at 6½. How do the APU's look?"

"All three purrin' along. We're running main pump pressure low on Number Two. They're burning 1 percent propellant per minute. Temps and speeds all green."

Outside, the brick-red glow ebbed to pink.

"Rog. At 12 minutes: Mach 21 out of 232,000. Standing by for equilibrium glide. Steady as she goes! Major Mode 305 is running."

The Mission Commander counted off the minutes since entry interface when Shuttle began her plunge into the inferno over the Pacific at daybreak far below.

"Go at 15 since interface, Skipper. Mach 18 out of 220K. Range-to-go: 1,000 even."

"Goin' to Trajectory Two on the left CRT. Auto roll reversal left. Velocity 18,450 feet per second . . . We're really hauling the mail, Number One."

"SM alert, Skipper!"

"Systems management. You got it, Jack. Find the stinker."

"Looks like the microwave landing system. Yeh, MLS. We popped breaker Main dc, Bus A on Number One receiver.

12

I'm taggin' the breaker, Row E, panel Overhead Fourteen. Bringing MLS Number Two up on the line . . . That's got it. Lights out, Skip."

"Out of 194K at Mach 16, Will. Constant Drag is initiated right down the slot. Profile at 33 feet per second. We're 715 miles from target, now out of 190,000 feet. Mach 15 at 17 minutes since entry."

As the ship rolled on her side to dissipate the energy of flight en route to landing in California, the pink glow outside gave way to a morning sunrise 35 miles above the blue-green, north Pacific. The shuttle's nose slowly dropped from her nose-high entry attitude of 40 degrees toward a target attitude of 14 degrees nose-high a few minutes closer to home.

"Endeavor, Endeavor. We copy your S-band modulation, out of the blackout at interface plus 18 and a half minutes. You're Go out of 188,000 feet at Mach 13 point 8. Your range-to-go now 497 nautical miles. Confirm AOS Houston remote, via Buckhorn."

"We have you, Flight. Real sweet ride inbound. We're right and tight here. Had a few alarms and FLT's, though. Showing Mach 10 point 5 out of 165K," drawled the AC.

"Copy that, Endeavor. Understand a few Funny Little Things on the way home. Confirm your TACAN acquisition. And you're Go for speed brakes at Mach 10."

"We have the TACAN beacon here, Flight. At Mach 9, we have auto roll reversal. Backin' her up with CSS."

"Roger, Endeavor. Control Stick Steering. Your stick inputs look real crisp from down here."

"Real tight, Flight."

"We see it, Endeavor. You're on track out of 154,000, making Mach 9 point 8."

"Copy, Flight. Trajectory Two is running. Out of 152,000 feet, Mach 8 point 8. Range-to-go-is 211."

"Roger, Endeavor. Confirm body flap enabled."

"This is the AC. Body flap is flappin'. Out of 151,000, at Mach 8 point 4."

Beneath Shuttle's tail, the single thick body flap automatically flexed up and down under the three, lifeless shuttle main engines. The four primary flight computers cycled the body flap to ease the crushing burden of the descent upon the wings and to adjust the ship's center of gravity for precision steering homeward.

"Endeavor: You're still full of Go from down here. Anticipate the coastline at Mach 6 point 6 out of 138,000 feet."

"And we have it! Big and beautiful, Flight. Amazing visual today!"

"Copy that, Shuttle. Standby to configure CSS."

"Roger, Flight. We're 200 miles out, 130K up, and makin' Mach 6 point 4."

"Copy, Endeavor. Telemetry modulation via Buckhorn is clean and clear. APU Number Two is still running hot and we're watching it. We see you 177 miles out, at Mach 6 even, descending through 124,000 feet."

"Okay, buddy. We see Mach 5 point 5 out of 119,000 . . . Flash evaporators off and ammonia boilers on. Now Mach 5 point 3 out of 115,000. Range-to-go: 148. And we have the San Joaquin Valley at 12 o'clock low!"

Inside Shuttle's long body, two freon coolant loops are the ship's sweat glands, absorbing heat from crew, air supplies, and warm black boxes. During the fiery descent above 140,000 feet into the sky, heat from the circulating freon coolant is dissipated overboard by the flash evaporators: complex pumps which turn heat into water steam for venting overboard. Below 120,000 feet, two ammonia boilers vaporize the freon circulation's heat.

"Roger, Endeavor. We show you 23 minutes since entry interface at Mach 5, out of 120,000 feet."

"Endeavor copies," the tall mission commander drawled. "I have manual roll reversal left. Your basic, standard rate turn at 3 degrees per second. Real crisp response from our glass lady this mornin'. We see Mach 4 point 5 out of 108,000. Range-to-go: 122 . . . Now 102,000 with 96 miles to go . . . Roll reversal damping out nicely out of 100,000 and Mach 3 point 6 . . . Rudder effective now at Mach 3 point 5. Very slight side slip here. No sweat."

Like any airliner, the ship's tall tail now coordinated the flying machine's turns left or right. Great jaws running the length of the tail's, 26-foot-long vertical rudder can open on each side of the tail fin. Opened, the rudder grabs the air stream to slow the vessel's forward speed. These are the speed brakes and they have the effect of the pilots hanging their feet out the door to drag in the dirt.

"Roger, Endeavor. Out of Mach 3 point 5, we see your Air Data Probes deployed. Digitals look good. At Mach 3, you're right down the slot coming through 90,000 feet."

On each side of Shuttle's nose, the iron finger of an Air Data Probe braved the vicious slipstream. The computerized probes send airspeed, drag, and angle of attack information to the ship's computers.

"Thanks, California. At Mach 2 point 8 out of 89,000 feet, we're watchin' the final auto roll reversal right with 73 miles to home."

"Copy, Endeavor," the voice from Earth called.

"Out of 82,000 making Mach 2 point 5. Alpha 13 point 5 degrees up bubble on the nose. We have vertical situation displays running on the CRT's. Goin' back to Autoland now."

The center Cathode Ray Tube, CRT, winked its green television graphics to the two airmen. With a tiny shuttle bug riding the vertical line of the television, the pilots marked their instrument approach at two and one half times the speed of sound to Edwards Air Force Base, California.

"Roger, right seat. You're Go from the ground."

"And at 51 minutes since deorbit burn, we are in TAEM out of Mach 2 point 4."

"Roger, AC. Terminal Area Energy Management. You're in the home stretch."

"Roger. We have Mach 2 point 2 now. Payload bay vents open . . . Now Mach 1 point 8 out of 70,000. Range: 42 miles Now 68K high, Mach 1 point 5. Range: 39 . . . Now, Mach 1 point 3 out of 54,000."

"You're right down the pike, Endeavor."

"Thanks, Flight."

"SM Alert, Flight !" Enright called from the right seat.

"We see it from here, right seat."

"Okay. We've popped the breaker on radar altimeter Number One, Main Bus A, panel 0-14. I've tagged it, and radar altimeter Two is on line and flying."

"Number One does it again for us, Flight," the AC smiled.

"Endeavor, we have you out of 53,000 at Mach 1 point 2. You're 270 seconds to mains on the ground. Confirm state vector transfer."

"Okay, Flight. We have state vectors loaded into the BFS," the command pilot called with his right hand upon the Rotational Hand Controller between his knees.

"Copy, Endeavor. Backup Flight System and Computer Five loaded."

"Endeavor is showing Mach One even, at 51,000 feet, 28 miles out." The voice from the ground filled the pilot's headsets.

"Copy, Flight. We're feelin' a bit of transonic buffet in the cockpit. Go at Mach point 8, at 22 miles out. We have alpha angle eight degrees. Manual control now. Aft RCS jets off out of 45,000 feet."

"Copy, Endeavor. You're 210 seconds from touchdown. We're seeing your speed brakes now. Expect HAC intercept at 320 knots passing 37,000."

"Roger, Flight. We have Leuhman Ridge dead ahead. Turning left base, 33 degrees of bank here makin' 265 knots. Body flap is full manual and we're 16 degrees nose down. Pullin' 1.3G. Nose Wheel Steering to direct, panel Left-2."

"Copy, Shuttle. Your EAS is a tad high at 290 knots. You're in the Heading Alignment Circle now."

"We have it, Flight. Pulling 1.6G in the turn. Have Saddleback Mountain ahead now." The pilot in the right seat briefly squinted outside into the early-morning sun before turning his attention to the instrument panels at his face and Endeavor's touchdown only ninety seconds away.

"Okay, California. We have MLS out of 18,000 feet; TACAN inhibit. Fifteen miles out. Anti-Skid is on, panel Left-2."

"Copy, Endeavor. We see you on Microwave Landing System. You're right down the slot for Runway 23. Wind is out of 240 at 05 knots, altimeter 29 point niner-five. We see you out of 15,000 feet and making 280 knots. Your attitude is nominal at minus 20 degrees. Now nine miles out at 13,000."

"Gotcha, Flight. We're comin' around to final out of 12K, six and a half uprange. H-dot is 200 down."

"Copy, Endeavor, descending at 200 feet per second. You're seventy-four seconds to wheels-on."

"And, Endeavor, Chase Two is with you," called a gleaming T-38 jet beside Shuttle's left wingtip. "We're at your nine o'clock and see your vent doors open in payload bay."

"Thanks, Chase," Colonel Parker acknowledged. "Out of 3,500, making 285 knots over the fence—a tad hot. Speed brakes deployed 80 percent."

Completing his turn to final approach and aligning his 100-ton glider with the runway centerline, the command pilot squinted through a six-inch square frame set into the forward windshield. Inside the black frame of his Kaiser Electronics Heads-Up Display, Will Parker could see the runway coming up quickly. The see-through HUD is clear glass like the windshield all around it. But on its glass face were numbers and symbols. Shuttle electronics and her humming black boxes projected critical flight information onto the small clear screen.

Along the left side of the HUD video image, a vertical column of numbers told the pilot his air speed. Another column of numbers on the right edge of the HUD face showed distance to the ground. And in the center of the glass screen, a white video "X" moved left or right of the centerline of the real runway below and half a minute away. By looking outside through the HUD frame on their windshields, both airmen could see exactly how their approach numbers looked without dropping their weary eyes inside the cockpit to the instruments above their knees. HUD keeps a pilot's eyeballs where they belong. The device first flew in space on Shuttle Six in April 1983. Will Parker flew it now.

"Endeavor: Chase One sees your speed brakes open wide."

"Thanks, Chase," the pilot in command called. "Flight: we're full manual CSS out here. Into the preflare at 1750 feet. Nose up bubble one point five degrees on inner glide slope

". . . Two miles out. Landing gear armed. We're sittin' fat."

"Copy, Endeavor. You're twenty-eight seconds out. Right down the pike."

"Thanks, Flight . . . Let me hear it, Number One!"

"Steady as you go, Skipper," Enright called. "Landing gear hydraulics valves One, Two, and Three, set GPC. Out of 250 feet at 270 knots. Three in motion . . . Three down and locked!"

The centerline of Runway 23 rose swiftly to stop Endeavor's descent. From their cozy office, the pilots could see the runway center line coming closer. But they could not see their ship's wings nor her down-and-locked wheels far behind them. They flew their flightseats toward the dry lakebed of Edwards Air Force Base.

"Chase Two confirming three gears down and six wheels in position. One hundred feet, eleven seconds out," the small chase plane called from beside the powerless glider.

"Okay, Skipper: 100 feet at 190 knots . . . 50 feet at 185 . . . 30, 20 . . . 10 at 170 . . . 5. Mains contact!"

"We're on the center line, Flight! Nose Wheel Steering ready. Nose wheel at 10 feet . . . 5 feet . . . 3 . . . and Flop! Speed brakes 100 percent. Looked like 160 knots at touchdown . . . And we're rollin' in the sunshine! Light braking here at 80 . . . 50 . . . 20 . . . And, all stop!"

"Roger, Endeavor. You're home and beautiful job all the way!"

"Yeh, Flight," the sweating and exhausted Aircraft Commander sighed.

"Endeavor, we're ready for closeout and safing procedures when you're ready."

"No thanks, Flight. We've been in this sweatbox for six hours. We blew up once on the pad, missed two OMS insertion targets, and bent our metal on two landings. And it smells like my old socks in here just now. You boys pull the plugs. Me and Number One are goin' for the beer. And right now."

When the Command Pilot yanked his microphone plug and laid his sweaty headset atop the forward glareshield, the second in command did likewise.

The Commander pushed his seat away from the instrument panel so he could lift his stiff, long legs over the low, center console between the two seats in the cockpit.

"Thought the Captain leaves last, Skip."

"Not when the Captain has to make tracks for the head, Jack," sighed William McKinley Parker.

The metal ladder swayed as Jacob Enright followed the commander out of the 60-million-dollar Shuttle Mission Simulator and into the cold fluorescent glare. In their sweat-soaked flightsuits, the two stooped airmen brushed past banks of computers and bleary-eyed technicians who conceive every possible failure, crisis, and catastrophic malfunction with which to torment the crew inside the lifelike simulator. Through the simulator's computer-controlled windows, even the view of Earth and space is perfectly accurate.

"Nice crash in the drink there, Colonel Parker," grinned a fat technician. The stoney glare from the flier's face froze the trainer in midthought.

"That, my friend, is why those two guys are called The Ice-men around here," laughed another engineer after Parker and Enright grimly strode past them into the austere halls of the Lyndon B. Johnson Space Center in Houston.

The two exhausted pilots stood side by side facing the wall in the JSC men's room, tending to business.

"Nine hours in that sweatbox, Jack!" the taller flier sighed.

"Yeah, Skipper. Least they can't generate a wing falling off," mumbled Jacob Enright.

"I'd call an FCS Saturation alarm and running clean out of elevon travel ten feet above the ground the next best thing, Jack."

The two fliers zipped in unison, reflecting months of training together as a back-up crew who had yet to get a flight of their own. At least they were finally on the manifest for a military mission next year.

"And always bridesmaids, but never brides," said the slow, down-home drawl of the taller, older man as he led his young copilot into the glare of the hallway.

19

"We'll get ours, Will. It won't be wasted. Not to worry." Jack Enright consoled his captain as they shuffled down the glassy corridors to the astronauts' office. They squinted against the cold glare of the hallway after spending half the night in the softly muted lights of the simulator's flightdeck.

Side by side, backs stooped, hands deep in sweaty flightsuit pockets, the tall man and the short man made their way onward. Flaccid faces of technicians watched the crew pass. Over coffee, night-shift technocrats commented often that Jacob Enright walked and talked more like Colonel Parker every day.

Inside a large, chilly conference room, Parker and Enright sipped hot coffee at a large table topped with tacky plastic wood. Across the table sat the Launch Vehicle Test Conductor, at his side sat FIDO, the Flight Dynamics Officer, and beside him sat the only woman in the room, the Lead Shuttle Simulation Instructor. In front of the room-long blackboard secured to the wall, the Flight Director paced anxiously.

"I know it's late," the Flight Director began as he glanced out the window into the dark, cool December night. "But I want to nail down the simulation on the Return To Launch Site Abort protocol." The director leaned over a pile of computer printouts and graphic time-lines spread upon the table.

"We had the Abort Region Determinator initiate the RTLS abort at 248 seconds into the launch. You carried trajectory lofting through 400,000 feet on two live main engines and one prematurely shutdown. No sweat there." The tall flight director squinted through his pipe smoke. "But then, men, you boys were out to lunch. Anne?"

Parker and Enright studied their steaming coffee mugs.

The young woman set her round glasses upon a pretty face. She sifted through her own stack of mission profiles before she addressed the tension.

"It fell apart right from the powered turn-around," she began dryly. "While burning the two remaining main engines after the center engine blew, you were late dumping 16,000 pounds of OMS pod fuel and 1,100 pounds of RCS propellant. You initiated powered pitch-around at 400,000 feet at five degrees per second, taking 32 seconds to reverse your track. That's 16 seconds too long. By the time you turned around to initiate guidance back to the Cape, you were 275 miles up-range — 50 miles too far from landing. Descending under power after the powered turn-around, you pulled 3 point 2 G's — that's one-tenth below crush level."

The two pilots grimaced together as the speaker continued her litany of flaming disaster.

"You initiated powered pitch-down late completing the PPD in 17 seconds instead of 15. Then at Main Engine Cut Off: MECO was late with zero instead of two percent fuel remaining in the external tank. You separated from the ET okay at the nominal 200,000 feet; but you were 375 miles up-range instead of the 325-mile target. ET separation was at Mach 7. That's okay. But your dynamic pressure on the vehicle was 12 pounds per square foot. That's 3 pounds too high. Then, during Alpha recovery . . ."

"Mea culpa," Enright whispered into his coffee as the mission commander smiled weakly.

"Then, *gentlemen,*" the woman droned on, "you were too fast recovering your angle of attack during load relief. You pulled up in 8 seconds instead of 10 and you pulled 2.8 G's instead of 2. And . . . you pulled up from 90,000 feet to 100K in six seconds instead of eight, at Mach 7 instead of Mach 6.7. You then overshot the target Alpha angle before your angle of attack stabilized at the 8-degree target. Finally," she sighed, removing her glasses, "you arrived inbound at the glide slope 175 miles up-range instead of 150. Somehow you were at 80,000 feet at Mach 4 instead of at Mach 5 out of 90K. And pulling 3.3 G's." She paused to catch her breath.

"And we broke her back and sixed in the drink four miles from the Cape runway," Parker interrupted. "We were there. Remember?" Parker looked up from his coffee for the first time during the midnight briefing. "We got our feet wet one lousy time. And that is why you have four shuttles in your hangar instead of one!"

"Listen . . ." an angry Enright added. "We've logged six hundred hours of dry flying in that mother. And we've only come home bent twice. Pretty fair average, I'd say." Jacob

Enright was fuming, a sight which made Colonel Parker the only onlooker to smile.

"You threw everything but a biffy backing up in mid-deck at us today," Enright raved softly. "And we hit the numbers every time today but once . . . Now I want to get some sleep. I'm whipped—and the skipper stinks." The second in command grinned feebly as he labored to recover his iceman composure.

"What say we gather over the cold, stiff bones in the mornin'," Colonel Parker offered sleepily. "I'll tuck in this here young buck if'n ya'll don't mind," the Colonel drawled in his finest, put-the-wagons-in-a-circle voice.

Sometimes, when hot, tired, and wrecked by ten hours of hangar-flying the simulator, Jacob Enright resented the Colonel's paternal intervention. Not tonight.

"Obliged," imitated the copilot.

"Not to mention it, Number One," the weary senior pilot smiled.

"Okay," the Flight Director sighed. "Tomorrow morning, say at 10 o'clock. You free, FIDO?"

"Ten's fine, Hutch."

"Then ten o'clock," said the bearded, youthful Flight Director who pounded his cold pipe on his palm.

Enright and Parker shuffled wearily toward deserted acres of parking lot. They stopped in a wintry drizzle at two wet vehicles parked side by side: Enright's gleaming sports car fit for any fighter jock, and Parker's delapidated pickup truck. They stood alone beneath harshly bright lights which grew on poles from the asphalt.

"About that RTLS abort, Jack?" Colonel Parker began.

Jack Enright looked at his wristwatch wet with rain. It read one o'clock in the morning.

"How about 7:30 at the simulator in about six hours, Will?"

"You got it, Number One. See you at O-dark-thirty." The tall colonel waved as he fought with his truck's crumpled door.

2

December 13th

It might be day, it might be night. It might be summer, it might be winter. There are no clues five stories below the living world in the Crystal Room locked in the concrete bowels of the Pentagon.

The Crystal Room is a huge glass box with clear acrylic plastic floor, clear plastic ceiling, four plastic walls — all transparent and the size of a corporate conference room. Nestled within a steel-and-concrete bunker, the Crystal Room sits upon a score of clear plastic blocks five feet above a bare concrete floor. In the bunker's ceiling of armor plate, rows of fluorescent lights rain their harsh, cold light down and through the Crystal Room's clear ceiling.

Even the thick ventilation and air-conditioning ducts which curl beneath the floor are clear plastic. Through the plumbing, air whines like a soft breeze of scentless, bottled atmosphere.

"Sorry to bring you here in the middle of the night. But we have something of a situation on our hands."

Admiral Michael T. Hauch spoke quietly to avoid the Crystal Room's unnerving echos. At his side, a ramrod-erect Marine sat beating the keys of the stenomachine between his knees. The young Marine was cut from the same lean and hard cloth as the two guards who stood rigidly outside the closed glass door of the Crystal Room. Around the long mahogany table, a dozen men and one small woman slouched sleepily. Half of the men wore the uniforms of each branch of the armed services. All of the military men were of flag rank, and the starchy light twinkled upon too many stars and gold sleeve echelons for the six civilians to count.

Admiral Hauch, in his blues and with his thick blond hair, glowed resplendently at the head of the table.

Four of the civilians sat gripping the edge of the massive table or the arms of their leather high-backed chairs.

"I know this place is a bit much for the senses until you've been in here a while," the Admiral smiled. "Especially the part about seeing your feet so far above the real floor. But you won't fall through."

The intense Marine stenographer did not open his eyes as he transcribed the Admiral's words. The silver wings upon the chest of an Air Force General bore the small triangle within a circle which marked Command Astronaut wings. His collar insignia carried the unfamiliar ensign of the North American Aerospace Defense Command.

"We learned long ago," continued the Admiral, "that debugging a security area is just about impossible. The other side is too clever. So we built this place, a glass greenhouse where burying a listening device would be impossible — unless they have invented a wired homing flea. Since we haven't, we assume they haven't."

A stifled chuckle simmered among the civilians in business suits. They sat gripping their chairs like passengers on their first airplane ride.

"I called you here. I am Admiral Michael Hauch, special counsel to the National Security Council and liaison to our Space Technology Center at Kirtland Air Force Base, New Mexico, which began operations in October 1982. For everyone's reference and for the record: around the table are our stenographer, three NSC members, and General John Gordon of the United States Space Command, Peterson Air Force Base, Colorado. John is with the Space Defense Operations Center created in September 1982. To his left is General Bruce Cochran, Air Force, Defense Department liaison to NASA's Office of Space Sciences, Houston. From the green branch, Army General Tommy Burns is with DARPA — the Defense Advanced Research Projects Agency, the boys with the billion-dollar erector sets.

24

"Beside Tom is General Ed Breyfogle of the Marines, liaison to DSRC — Defense Systems Review Council — and on temporary duty with the Strategic Defense Initiative Organization. On this side of the table are Commander Jack Wiegand, Navy, Project Sea Lite.

"Beside Commander Wiegand is Dr. Jaime Swisher from Lawrence Livermore Labs, Nevada. To Jaime's left is Dr. Kathleen Burtscher from Los Alamos Scientific Laboratory and liaison to the White Sands, New Mexico, High-Energy Laser Systems Test Facility."

The thin woman smiled and stroked dark wisps of hair from her healthy, tanned face.

"And at the end of the table is Dr. Joseph Vazzo from the Department of State, Soviet Technical Studies Group. Nice to see you, Joe."

The graying diplomat nodded.

"Well, to get down to business." Admiral Hauch, Annapolis 1954, shifted a pile of papers as he glanced up at the clocks along the wall: Two o'clock in the morning, Washington time. "It's LACE. And we have a problem."

The Admiral paused as his words cleaved the quiet air within the glass chamber. One dozen tired faces looked up from steaming coffee cups. Half a dozen cigarettes were smashed into pewter ashtrays engraved THE JOINT CHIEFS OF STAFF. The Admiral continued.

"It's TRIAD."

"But TRIAD doesn't fly, even boilerplate-experimental for five years at best, Admiral," the woman said with assurance.

"How familiar are you with TRIAD, Dr. Burtscher?" the Admiral inquired in a cordial tone.

"Same as everyone here. It's our spaceborne, laser weapons system with three elements: Alpha Project — a chemical laser, five megawatts, 2.7 microns in wave length. And LODE — Large Optics Demonstration Experiment by Hughes Aircraft — a four meter firing mirror. And Talon Gold — Lockheed's laser aiming-radar for tracking missile targets from space. I read the same technical reports as everyone else here. The laser satellite should fly in five years at the earli-

25

est."

"Very good, Kathy. Very thorough. One more detail, however: DARPA's laser, killer satellite *is* flying . . . in space . . . right now. General Burns?"

The youthful, sandy haired officer looked uncomfortable as he addressed the company.

"The orbiting laser platform was launched February 14, 1990, on a Delta-2 missile from Cape Canaveral. It was contained in the announced mission of the LACE/RME spacecraft flying in a 130 nautical mile circular orbit with orbital inclination of 38 degrees. We announced the mission as simply a benign test of the LACE and RME satellites publicized as laser target drones." General Burns shuffled through his stack of confidential documents. "LACE was to be only the Low-power Atmospheric Compensation Experiment: a flying target for ground-based lasers. The bird's 210 optical sensors were to monitor low-powered laser beams fired from the Air Force Maui Optical Station, Mount Haleakala, Maui, Hawaii. The Naval Research Lab built LACE for the public purpose of testing the distortion caused by the atmosphere to ground-based lasers firing into space.

"RME was announced as part of the McDomnell Douglas Delta-2's double payload. RME was billed in the press as the Relay Mirror Experiment: another drone with adjustable mirrors for testing whether or not a ground-based laser could bounce off of steerable, space-based mirrors for targeting on other satellites. RME was to carry twelve mirrors adjustable four thousand times every second."

General Burns looked uncomfortable and pained.

"The Alpha laser was carried live. It had been successfully test fired for the first time on April 7, 1989, at TRW's plant at San Juan Capistrano, California. And it did not carry the older Talon Gold aiming device. Talon Gold on LACE carried the working optics of Teal Ruby: the spacecraft AFP-888, infrared tracker by Rockwell. We announced in January of 1990 that the five-hundred-million-dollar Teal Ruby was being put into mothball storage at Norton Air Force Base, California. In actuality, Teal Ruby went to Canaveral's 6555th Aerospace

26

Test Group for integration with Talon Gold and mating to the LACE/RME spacecraft. Teal Ruby was further enhanced by combining it with certain parts of the CIRRIS infrared missile tracker which had been removed from the AFP-675, Lockheed satellite. You may remember that CIRRIS flew manned on the fourth space shuttle flight."

"Thanks, Tom. General Gordon, if you will fill in the blanks, please?"

"Admiral: The LACE test article was designed only for evaluation of the tracking optics. The Talon Gold sight was to be targeted on one of our three modified recon satellites, the Block 647 spacecraft built by TRW."

"And?" interrupted General Cochran from Defense. "I followed that mission. It did not carry a live killer laser, as far as I know. Only the ranging and aiming device with modified Teal Ruby electronics." The General looked hard at General Gordon. "Did it, John?"

General Gordon studied the grim face of the Admiral who nodded him on.

"It did . . . Alpha Project was carried hot: One hydrogen-fluoride, infrared, chemical laser at five megawatts."

"Mother of God," Joseph Vazzo of the State Department breathed as he rocked back in his tall chair.

"And it worked beyond our expectations — quite unplanned, I would hasten to add." The Admiral squirmed with discomfort.

"How unplanned?" demanded the gray-haired man from State.

The Admiral exhaled a long and tired breath as he looked his interrogator in the eye.

"Two days ago, the LACE spacecraft severely damaged and perhaps destroyed by a stray laser blast the Russian, Kvant-3 vehicle." Admiral Hauch spoke gravely. "The Kvant-3 module was on a five-day automatic rendezvous and docking mission to link up with the Soviet's Mir space station. Thank God Kvant-3 was unmanned! Kvant-3 is part of their Module-D program of sending up so-called building block units for attachment to Mir.

"LACE's Alpha laser literally got off one lucky shot. Mir flies in a much steeper, nearly polar orbital path, and higher than LACE. But Kvant-3 on its automatic way to Mir had a one-in-a-million nodal crossing where the orbits of LACE and Kvant-3 crossed. LACE simply looked sideways and let Kvant-3 have it broadside."

"John," General Cochran inquired, "do the Russians know that we have hit them?"

"We're not sure yet. They haven't said a word in two days. We're hoping they think it was internal damage, some kind of stray voltage spike. We are hoping . . . I can tell you this: Through the usual channels, the Russians have asked for a closed technical conference between our people and theirs in Vienna."

"When?" inquired Deputy Secretary of State Vazzo, more restrained.

"Later today, mid-morning our time, Joe."

Secretary Vazzo said nothing.

"Dr. Swisher?"

"How could it have happened, Admiral?"

"Don't know, Jaime. The LODE optics and Alpha Project laser are both designed fail-safe with triple redundancy in range safety. We know from the data over the last few weeks that we're not even close to the anti-missile, laser-aiming goal of accuracy to within two-tenths of one millionth of a degree on Talon Gold. And we still have quite a bit of jitter in the beam-focusing mechanism. Our best guess is that if LACE had actually aimed at Kvant-3 . . . she would have missed by a country mile. It just let one slip — at the wrong time, in the wrong corner of the sky." The Admiral looked very tired as he shook his head. "We're here at two o'clock in the morning to figure out how to disable LACE from the ground."

"Turn it *off*," demanded the man from State.

"Can't, Joe," responded General Gordon, who lived in a hole in the Denver mountains. "Can't. It's burned out her own encryptor. She will acknowledge an uplink telemetry signal from the ground, but she cannot seem to use her onboard encryptor to decode the signal.

"We expect a transient SGEMP. Let me explain: LACE is at the front, the very tip, of our avionics technology. Her innards are mostly what we call VHSIC—or very-high-speed integrated circuitry. These are tightly packed electronic modules, very sensitive to stray electrical fields. The laser energy of Alpha generates a low-level field of radiation within the spacecraft. This field can engulf a satellite in an SGEMP—system-generated electromagnetic pulse.

"That's what we think we have in LACE: a magnetic pulse from radiation creating a stream of electrons which are really electrical currents trickling down into our tightly packed electronics. This radiation drips down, the stream of electrons trickles inside LACE, and we have a short or some other electrical failure, like a burned-out code encryptor relay . . . LACE is crippled, but alive. Very much alive and on her own."

"Shot herself in the foot, aye, Admiral?" asked the man from State.

The Admiral nodded without words.

"I called you here at this outrageous hour of the night to ask for a real-time status report on all of your laser projects. The people upstairs want to know what we have on-line in our near-space laser arsenal to kill LACE." The Admiral did not turn his face toward the Deputy Secretary of State.

"Let's start with you, Commander Wiegand. How is Project Sea Lite?"

"One minute, Admiral," interrupted the Marine stenographer who opened his eyes blinking at the glare. "Have to replace the paper." Quickly, the young Marine threaded the end of a thick ream of steno paper into his machine. "Okay, Admiral. Sorry."

"Commander?"

"Admiral, the Navy's Project Sea Lite is a laser weapon in development since 1980. We have test fired TRW's, 2 point 2 megawatt, deuterium-fluoride laser at 3 point 8 microns wave length. But it's not operational. Our next step will be MIRACL, the Mid-Infrared Advanced Chemical Laser. It's pumped by a pulsed xenon lamp. We've already fired it at White Sands."

"Jack, can either system hit LACE from the ground?" asked General Breyfogle of the Marines.

"Maybe in about ten years, Ed."

"Thanks, Jack. Jaimie, what's cooking in your New Mexico projects?"

"Well, Admiral, we first fired the Dauphin Project laser in 1980. We're working with Lawrence Livermore labs on it. It's an X-ray-pumped laser using argon-flouride in a pulsed mode. It is designed to kill a missile by impulse — a lethal radiation shockwave . . . But we are maybe fifteen years from having anything operational. At Los Alamos, we're also working on the free electron laser, known as FEL. We've just developed a photoinjector device which can increase FEL beam brightness one hundred times and boost power output from twenty to forty megavolts. But for right now, no way, Admiral."

"Alright, Kathy, what about your excimer laser tests in the west?"

"In March 1988, we finally fired an eight-hundred megawatt, raman-shifted, excimer laser into the sky from Western Research Corporation's San Diego facility. Although it was our highest power excimer test to date, we can only sustain the beam for half a microsecond. We've also had some success with an iodine-pulsed laser, pumped by magnetic flux, compression generators. Anti-satellite radiation is created by a bleaching-wave effect. But, Admiral," the pretty scientist frowned, "we certainly are a decade away from knocking down something as big as the LACE spacecraft. Sorry."

"Thanks, Kathleen. General Burns, what about your two flying vehicles, Pegasus and BEAR? Can we disable LACE with either of your babies?"

All eyes focused sleepily upon the sandy-haired officer.

"Well, Admiral, BEAR is our Beam Experiment Aboard Rocket payload. It is our first flying neutral particle beam anti-missile weapon, as you know. But it was the most fundamental of early tests. She popped up to 126 miles on only a nine-minute flight. The particle beam was then cycled briefly through a firing sequence aimed at points up to only six miles away. The beam has a maximum power of one megavolt fired at five bursts per second. Just too primitive, Admiral." The General shrugged with visible disappointment.

"Okay, Tom. How about Pegasus? Could it be rigged to catch and destroy LACE?"

"Not likely, Admiral. Pegasus is an air-launched missile designed to orbit very small payloads, too small to carry the electronics needed to find LACE. And there aren't any explosive devices small enough to do the job if we could get them close enough to LACE. I just don't have anything for you."

"How about HOE, Tom?"

"Now that is a real breakthrough, Admiral. The Army's Homing Overlay Experiment succeeded in destroying an incoming drone missile in June 1984 during an all-up test of the Talon Gold tracking device. It was HOE's fourth test flight. We launched a Boeing Minuteman target missile from Vandenburg Air Force Base, California. Our interceptor missile was launched from Mech Island in the Pacific atoll of Kwajalein. One hundred miles up, our interceptor destroyed the Minuteman target . . . But, Admiral, HOE had three prior failures in February, March, and December 1983. HOE may be able to score on an incoming ballistic target 25 percent of the time, but it simply is not designed to pursue a target which is in orbit. Not enough energy. Sorry, Admiral."

"Okay, Tom. Thanks. B.C., what about ALL?"

"Also not powerful enough, Admiral. The Airborne Laser Laboratory has flown since 1981 in modified, conventional aircraft. As you know, ALL is a carbon dioxide, dynamic laser. But its 400 kilowatts of power and her one-meter optics won't even warm LACE's skin." The officer frowned. On General Cochran's shoulder, a lovely blue emblem read: "Airborne Laser Laboratory: PEACE THROUGH LIGHT."

"So," sighed Admiral Hauch as he pushed himself from the table. "No one has anything operational for shooting down our wayward bird after three and a half billion dollars funded for this research in 1990 alone?"

"*Your* wayward bird," counseled the man from State. "And you're only half correct."

One dozen exhausted faces studied Joseph Vazzo's strongly

31

lined face.

"There is a ground-based, anti-satellite laser which can vaporize LACE." The gray haired diplomat was grim. "And it's not ours . . ." He savored the dramatic pause. "Its code name is TORA and the laser weapon — I would call it a cannon — belongs to the Soviets. We've watched it for 10 years. We damn near have the wiring diagrams from our boys in trenchcoats. They've built it at Saryshagan, in Mother Russia: A flash-initiated, iodine-pulsed killer laser. It's the size of a football field: Twelve Pavlovski, magnetocumulative generators around one monster of a pulsed betatron."

"We estimate this facility can destroy our satellites up to 248 miles high, do damage to our satellites up to 744 miles, and at least disrupt our birds up to 25,000 miles."

"God," sighed the Admiral.

"Indeed. Its lethal range is only twenty-five thousand *miles*, give or take."

"Accuracy?"

"General Gordon: TORA has fried at least six Cosmos satellite drones. LACE could be obliterated by it — as everything else we put into orbit. You should have sent the Russians an invite to this coffee break, Admiral."

"I know, Joe. What else has Brother Ivan by way of operational, space laser weapons?"

"Near as we can tell, they have a free-electron, anti-satellite laser weapon at Troitsk and one at Chrernomorskoye. We don't know their lethal range or aiming ability — yet, Admiral."

Admiral Hauch looked at the clocks along the walls for a long moment.

"Then we cannot take LACE down ourselves. Is that the concensus here?"

"Not this year or next, Admiral," frowned the General from Cheyenne Mountain, Colorado.

"Question," said the young woman from the desert. "Can LACE do it again?"

"Even as we sit here," answered General Breyfogle.

"Well." The Admiral rose slowly with a great weight oppressing his sagging shoulders. "I'll let you all out of this glass cage.

We're in time for breakfast by now anyway. All we can do is hope the Russian's KGB-Ninth Department believes that their bird shorted herself out . . . I don't have to remind a one of you that not a word of this meeting is to be breathed to anyone. I shall brief the President in four hours . . . I'll get back with you."

"Each time is like the first. It is all so beautiful, Dimitri. Truly magnificent."

The black Mercedes wound its way southward from Vienna toward Wiener Neustadt thirty miles away. The two-lane highway made a circuitous course through Austria's lush mountains, low and rounded hills covered with new snow. Beneath a brilliantly blue noon sky, the road was burned dry by the dazzling sunshine.

"Yes, old friend. But you should see my Cheboksary, where the Vetluga flows into the Volga. In the spring . . . how do you say it: Your breath, it would go away."

"That's how I'd say it exactly." The American grinned with his face close to the exquisite countryside outside the heavily tinted windows of the backseat. "Maybe this spring, finally." The westerner in his gray three-piece suit turned his face toward the portly, middle-aged Russian at his side. "And the beautiful Lydia?"

"Very well, indeed," the Russian warmly smiled. He patted his round belly. "With number three due in June."

"I hope it's a fine, healthy Comrade," the American nodded to his friend. "Plump and happy, Dimitri — and with Lydia's blue eyes."

"Me, too," the Russian chuckled with genuine pleasure. "So what is the deal?"

"The deal?" the American asked with a smile.

"Where else can I practice speaking 'American?' " The Russian laughed loudly. "The British make me speak English. But with you," the beaming Russian slapped his American guest's knee. "With you, I talk 'Merican. What is up?"

"You tell me, Dimitri."

"You know how foolish I feel telling you American secrets

33

that you may not know yet."

"I'll keep it to myself."

Outside, the white snow sparkled on hillsides where patches of tall fir trees had been removed to clear fire breaks in the dense forest.

"Under your hat, right?" The Russian chuckled. "I would say — let me think — I would say your people have been caught holding up the bag, yes?"

The Russian's red, round face hardened as he studied the American's face, youthful compared to his own.

"Dimitri, you invited me, remember?"

"So I did. About the midnight meeting, your time, of your laser specialists with Admiral Hauch. Our Ninth Department is most with interest. Don't you know?"

The American sighed as he raised an eyebrow.

"Surprised? That's our job. Besides," the Russian showed his teeth with a knowing smile, "you can probably tell me what color necktie Marshall Kubosov wore at my meeting this morning."

The gleaming car rolled to a stop, turned around at Wiener Neustadt's outskirts, and then retraced its route northward toward Vienna.

"You people have a little trouble with a satellite. Yes? LACE is its name, is it not?"

"An accident, Dimitri. You would not have sent for me if your people thought otherwise."

The American cracked his window to the chilly, clean air. The weight of his diplomatic ballet made the roomy limousine close and warm.

"We would rather call it piracy." The Russian stated his last word carefully.

"I know the law, Dimitri. I helped write the space treaty between our governments." The American sounded tired.

"Our intelligence people tell us that your people cannot disable LACE. Is that correct?" The Russian's face was intense.

The American watched the sun-bleached snow pass beyond his fogged window.

"Well, my friend?"

The American's mind was awash with fatigue. He turned a weary face toward the Russian.

"We cannot disable LACE."

"An encryptor failure?"

"Yes."

"What about LACE's optics, Alpha Project. Tell me about its mirror."

"Dimitri, please!"

"The word is 'piracy.' "

"It is built by United Technologies Research Center. But you know that."

"Of course. Go on."

"Graphite fiber, reinforced glass. Matrix composite mirror. The mirror surface is vaporized silicon." The American's face showed physical pain.

"Graphite? Most impressive. Very clever indeed."

"Dimitri, what about your betatron at Saryshagan? Can you hit LACE from there?"

"Of course, my friend."

"And your anti-satellite homing spacecraft, Dimitri? You began operational tests in April 1981 when Cosmos 1,267 automatically docked in space with Salyut Six. It carried anti-satellite, mini-missiles did it not?"

"It did. Your people in Denver are quite good."

"And your anti-satellite, rendezvous-and-destroy missiles first flown with Cosmos 1,243 and 1,258 in February and March 1981? Is this system operational, Dimitri?"

"Perhaps."

"What about your latest air-to-air anti-missile interceptors, Dimitri?"

"Not likely, I am afraid. As you know, our SH-04 is designed to destroy incoming missiles before they enter the Earth's atmosphere. Our SH-08 missile gets to its target inside the atmosphere. Unfortunately, both Soviet missiles have nuclear warheads. Not very clean, to say the least. We are working on the SA-12 anti-missile weapon, which is not nuclear. But the SA-12 missile's maximum effective altitude is not more than 40,000 meters. These devices are of no help to Washington."

"But your betatron or your hunter-killer Cosmos vehicles could knock down LACE, couldn't they?" The American's face was pursed with anguish.

"Yes, they could."

"Will Moscow help us? There is unlimited grain in it if Moscow will help us. Or even the heavy equipment for the trans-European pipeline . . . Will your people help us?"

The Russian turned to his window, and he fogged it with his breath. The moment belonged completely to the silver-haired Soviet diplomat, an old street-fighter from the defense of Leningrad. He knew well the taste of war and of rat meat raw. He allowed that tense moment to linger as the "VIENNA 5 KM" sign sped rearward. He turned to face the glum American at his side.

"No, my friend. It will not be that easy. I am truly sorry."

The American studied his moist hands resting upon his gray wool knees. The car took the ramp toward the Vienna International Airport. On the airport apron, the American's unmarked jet sat idling its engines on the sunny concrete.

"My government has other plans." The Russian's words broke the silence as the brilliantly white jet grew larger in the limousine's windshield.

The car rocked to a stop at the jet's razor-thin wings. The whine of the jet engines filled the car as the Russian watched his old friend of many battles without bullets button his coat.

"Blue, Dimitri," the American called over the din of the jet engines.

"What?" the Russian squinted against the sunlight.

"Marshall Kubosov's tie this morning."

"But which blue tie?" The Russian pressed his round face toward the American's ear.

"The one with the gray stripes."

The Russian threw his head back with laughter when he slapped the American's knee. The tall American left the car for his ready aircraft and the long ride home.

3

December 14th

With a pie plate filled with motor oil between his legs, William McKinley Parker sat cross-legged on the sandy dune with Galveston Bay 20 yards from his left. He squinted into the brilliant sunshine from the cloudless western sky. Two hundred yards from the back porch of his home in a bedroom suburb 25 miles southeast of Houston, the Colonel balanced a heavy brass marine sextant in his large right hand. Holding the gleaming instrument's telescopic sight to his right eye, the gray-haired airman peered at the shaded image of the high sun reflected in the plate of oil between his dirty deck shoes. With his left hand upon the base of the triangular sextant, he gently moved the index arm until the two heavily shaded mirrors brought the real sun down upon the sun's reflection in the oil. The Colonel held his breath as he fine-tuned the sextant's vernier screw. The real sun above and the reflected sun between his feet merged into one image in the sight.

"Lost, Skipper?" smiled Jacob Enright, who walked through the ankle-deep sand toward the Colonel's bent back.

Colonel Parker looked over his shoulder and smiled at Enright's youthful face.

"Afternoon, Jack." The Colonel laid the sextant on its side in his lap. Immediately, he looked at the stopwatch hanging from his neck. Then, from the sextant, he read the sun's angular altitude above the motor oil's steady surface. On a pad of paper at his knee, with pencil the Colonel cut in half the angle read from the sextant. He circled this new figure. Beside it, he jotted down the time noted on the stopwatch.

As Jacob Enright stood silently aside, Will Parker made a black dot upon a pad of engineering graph paper set upon the sand. Across the sheet, a series of 20 dots formed a straight line from the paper's upper left corner down to the lower right corner. Sideways along the paper's left margin were penciled the words "sextant altitude." Across the bottom was written "time — gmt."

"Not lost, Number One," the Colonel drawled as he rose to his feet on the beach. "Just keepin' sharp." William Parker carefully loosened the alignment screws at each of the sextant's two mirrors before he carefully laid the instrument inside an elegantly waxed walnut box. He poured the motor oil from the plate into a plastic bottle.

Before he took a step, the tall colonel rubbed his right leg below the knee as if to work out a stiffness from sitting in the chilly sand.

"The old masters used to practice their sextant with a bowl of molasses for a horizon when they were ashore and away from the sea horizon."

Colonel Parker studied Enright's designer jeans, his Irish sweater, and his white Topsiders. "Country club closed today, Jack?" the taller man grinned.

"Nope. Thought I'd take you up on your invitation to see the old homestead after all this time."

Enright looked uncomfortable at his breach of the Colonel's zealously guarded privacy.

"You betcha, Jack," Parker beamed.

Relief filled Enright's clean, lean face.

"Great, Skipper."

"Come on up to the ranch, Jack. Pleased to have your company," the long flier smiled warmly.

Jacob Enright was pleased that finally he had chosen to visit his captain's beachfront home, although the two men should have had their fill of each other that morning. Two hours earlier, they had shot six hours of ascent aborts in the simulator.

You can train with a man, fly with him, sweat and swear with him over flightplans and checklists, and urinate into a plastic bag at his side in the cockpit. But you do not truly know your partner until you have stood in his home and have seen his toys.

Colonel Parker was an odd mixture of visual impressions. Standing, he was long and leggy. Although his short, graying hair ending at a farmer-red neck betrayed the wear of middle age, his lined face radiated the tightness of a four-stripe airman. Beneath his one long eyebrow which crossed the bridge of his angular nose, clear gray eyes twinkled at the world which he had fashioned carefully from his life. Fine lines creased from the corners of his eyes toward his too-large ears. These were perfect pilot's eyes: bright and clear and firmly anchored to the creases around them, borne of uncountable airman's sunrises at the top of the world. The firm leanness of his body and his long, veinous arms were ever covered by a baggy wardrobe of casual clothes and sweat-bleached flightsuits. His clothes hung loosely rumpled upon his spartan frame. He had the look of a man who wears his father's clothes.

At ease, the Colonel looked like a tall, almost gaunt man, who would most likely trip if he took a step. But he moved like a dancer with the agile grace and order of slowly flowing water. To watch his long and elegant stride was to watch a body moving onward to a place he longed to be.

Jacob Enright enjoyed watching his captain walk along the beach. The second in command took pleasure and comfort from the measured determination with which William McKinley Parker walked, flew, and steered his life. But Enright noticed the Colonel favoring his right leg as he walked.

"Too much handball for an old boy," Enright thought.

Genuine anticipation warmed Enright as he followed the Colonel toward the wooden back porch. The shorter pilot had often wondered what Parker's home would say of its owner. He had speculated whether he would find chrome-and-glass furnishings poised lightly upon thick carpet, or a dirt floor with a black kettle suspended above a firepit. For inside the slow-speaking colonel, whose twangy voice revealed his boyhood in the hollows of Kentucky, there lived both a brilliant electrical engineer and an honest-to-God, mud-on-his-spurs cowboy.

When the lights in the ceiling worked with the sunshine raining through the windows to reveal the room where he stood, Jack Enright was amazed. The Colonel's home was perfectly ordinary: well-worn furnishings, a few low bookcases, a stereo, and assorted junky easy chairs—all upon dirty carpet of no particular color.

"What ya think, Jack?" inquired the Colonel, who had laid his precious box and pads atop the sorely nicked table in the dining room. The table was cluttered with a day or two of dirty dishes.

"Homey, Skipper."

"Ya betcha, Number One."

Colonel Parker handed Enright a cold beer, still in the can, which the tall man had fetched from a kitchen cramped to the point of being crummy.

"Browse," Will Parker invited cheerfully with a wave of his own can of beer. He moved about and tidied up the single large room which had the back porch and dining room at one end and the living room at the other.

"Thanks, Will," Enright smiled. He could not find a single model airplane.

Enright moved about the airy little house. Along one

wall, broken by the arch leading to the tiny kitchen, was a line of framed photographs, large and institutional. They were the usual fare of squadron portraits with thin boys posing proudly before F-4 Phantom and A-6 fighter planes. In the background were rice paddies.

Turning to the long, unbroken wall opposite, Enright saw other framed images running the length of the long room. But these were dressed in finely crafted frames made from expertly mitred barn siding. And the colors were sparkling in the daylight of afternoon.

Jacob Enright sucked in his breath, warm with beer. He surveyed a dozen elegant photos and lithographs — every one a single lighthouse.

Against gray skies and frothy seas, each portrait was a solitary lighthouse growing from jagged and rocky shorelines.

"You still there, Jack?" called the Colonel as he walked from the kitchen.

"Skipper, these are magnificent. Magnificent."

Enright stepped sideways to study the long row of lighthouses. He shook his head slowly as he felt the tall man stand at his side in the afternoon sunshine.

The thin pilot turned his face to the older man at his side. Colonel Parker's neck was at Enright's eye level. The shaft of daylight swirling in from a window fell upon the Colonel's face. It accented the deep lines and hollow cheeks. The long face was firmly set in a strange weariness. The warm gray eyes within angular shadows were tranquil, even sad.

"Lighthouses, Skipper?" Enright said softly.

"Lighthouses, Jack . . . This one and that one are my favorites: Old Saybrook in Connecticut and Nubble Light at Cape Neddick, Maine."

The tall man paused and stared at his lighthouses. In the fragment of the Colonel's silence, Enright's beer-befuddled mind could hear the cruel sea breaking whitely at the feet of the stone towers before his face. He knew when

41

his command pilot was still in transit through a thought. So he waited with a copilot's studied patience.

"Lighthouses do their work without protest, without bending, come rain or sleet or high water. And they do it standing alone." William McKinley Parker glanced down at his ward and his closest friend. "That appeals to me."

"Our man in Vienna reported in an hour ago. No joy with the Russians." Admiral Hauch wiped his perspiring forehead with his large hand. "And they know—damn near down to the wiring schematics." The Admiral, in regulation shirtsleeves and open collar, sagged in his massive chair. "Bloody bastards."

The long table was huge in the chilly glass cage where only four weary men sat in the Admiral's council. Two men sat at each side of the conference table with the presiding Navy man at its head. Beside him, a young Marine sat at attention while his fingers rested poised upon his stenomachine's black keys. Disinfected, dehumidified, hypoallergenic, double-filtered air gushed rhythmically from the glass vents overhead and in the glass floor.

Commander Mike Rusinko of the Navy sat beside Colonel James Cerven of the Air Force. They looked tiredly across the broad table at Colonel Dale Stermer from the Air Force and Joseph Vazzo, the stoney-faced diplomat from State.

"For the record," the Admiral droned as the young Marine's fingers danced, "present are Commander Rusinko, Eastern Test Range; Colonel Cerven, Air Force, Western Test Range, Vandenberg; Colonel Stermer, Air Force Space Command; and Joe Vazzo of State.

"You have all been briefed on our LACE malfunction. At a session here yesterday, we ruled out disabling LACE with our own Earth-based laser weapons. Two hours ago, we concluded a conference between our people here and the anti-satellite operations people at Langley Air Force

42

Base, Virginia, and McCord Air Force Base, Washington. We reviewed the developmental integration of our experimental, miniature homing vehicle, anti-satellite system being tested at those bases. As you know, but for Joe's benefit, that device is a two-stage anti-satellite missile launched from an F-15 fighter plane. The missile is powered by a Boeing Short Range Attack Missile motor, or SCRAM, with a Vought Altair upper stage. The whole mini-missile device was first launched from an F-15 fighter in November 1984. The homing device sighted in on a star out over California. But nothing went into orbit and all we really tested was the infrared tracking optics. Our people say 'no way' as to hitting LACE."

The Admiral mopped his brow.

"What's up your sleeve, Michael?"

"One long shot, Joe. And only one."

The three officers leaned toward the Admiral.

"The space shuttle, gentlemen."

The Marine stenographer opened his eyes for a moment to study the Admiral's anxious face. The big Navy man looked feverish. The young Marine closed his eyes.

"We have one shuttle from the last mission on the ground at Edwards," Admiral Hauch continued. "If only we could do a quick turnout there and launch her from the Vandenburg shuttle launch facility. Unfortunately, as you know, that whole complex was shut down after the Challenger disaster. So all we have right now is Endeavor already on the pad at Cape Canaveral." The Admiral wiped perspiration from his face. "Commander Rusinko, can we go from Kennedy in a hurry?"

"Well, Michael, Endeavor is already stacked on Pad 39, as you know. If we had to, we could run a wet, plugs-out countdown test right now. However . . . if you're planning what I imagine — a rendezvous with LACE and going extravehicular with the shuttle crew — I'm concerned about the crew in line to fly the next Endeavor mission in six weeks."

"You're correct about the flight plan," interrupted Colonel Stermer of the Air Force Space Command. "The shuttle would rendezvous with LACE, stabilize it with an astronaut going EVA wearing the Manned Maneuvering Unit backpack, and the crew would use Shuttle's remote manipulator system to affix a rocket engine to LACE. We're thinking of the PAM—the Payload Assist Module motor. It would fire and drive LACE back into the atmosphere where re-entry heating would incinerate LACE."

"What about LACE getting a shot off at Shuttle, or at one of the astronauts?" Joseph Vazzo asked gravely.

"Dale?"

"To continue, Admiral: We would line the whole payload bay of Shuttle with a blanket of aluminized Mylar. In effect, we would create a mirror to deflect LACE's laser beam. Admittedly, the more serious problem would be protection of the rest of the shuttle which could not be blanketed. We believe, Admiral, that once we stabilize LACE with the manned maneuvering unit's thrusters and by precision attitude hold by Shuttle, we can keep LACE's optics off the unblanketed skin of Shuttle. We displayed that kind of attitude-hold accuracy—holding Shuttle steady to within five-hundredths of a degree—as early as Shuttle Three in March 1982. On STS-3, we needed that kind of precision position control for the payload of the Navy's X-ray, solar polarimeter experiment.

"We have flown the PAM rocket module since Shuttle 5 in November '82. Two of them were attached to satellites launched from the payload bay on that flight. And PAM motors have flown on shuttle payloads routinely." The officer shuffled through his documents. "We flew the PAM motor on Shuttles 7 and 8 in '83, Shuttle 12 in '84, Shuttles 16, 18, and 23, in 1985, and once in '86 on flight 24. In fact, 3 PAM boosters were flown on each of missions 18 and 23. Our only serious failure was on Shuttle 10 when both PAM boosters failed to ignite on satellites deployed from the bay. We would attach a PAM to LACE during a spacewalk.

"Specifically, our first EVA was done with the successful spacewalks of astronauts Musgrave and Peterson on Shuttle Six in April 1983. Neither pilot used the Manned Maneuvering Unit. We finally flew the MMU outside on Shuttle Ten in February 1984, when astronauts McCandless and Stewart flew the rocket-powered backpacks to distances up to 300 feet away from Shuttle. Before that flight, no American or Soviet pilot had gone EVA without a safety-line tether.

"And, as we all know, the whole ball of wax was done on Shuttle Eleven in April 1984, the Solar Maximum repair flight. The shuttle executed a rendezvous with the disabled, orbiting observatory, hooked it with the shuttle's mechanical arm, and astronauts Nelson and vanHoften went EVA to fix it in the payload bay. They also worked with the flying grapple fixture we hope to attach to LACE by hand so the remote arm can latch on to it. The grapple failed on Eleven, but we've worked the bugs out since then."

"But, Colonel Stermer, can the shuttle arm hang on to something as heavy as LACE?"

"Definitely, Mr. Secretary. On Eleven, the arm held the two-and-one-half ton Solar Max and also held the eleven-ton Long Duration Exposure Facility—a lab bench which was left behind in orbit with a year's worth of automated experiments inside. No sweat as to LACE or the PAM device."

"Well done, Dale. Commander Rusinko, what were you saying about the crew now flight-ready?"

"Yes, Admiral. Our next crew set to fly Endeavor has trained only to deploy two commercial satellites from the payload bay. They have no hard EVA training other than for emergency EVA to close the payload bay doors if the motors or latches hang up."

"Colonel Cerven, any thoughts?"

"Yes, Admiral. We cannot simply announce to the

world that we're going EVA from a shuttle with an inadequately trained crew to blow up a killer satellite. The problem is cosmetic in the extreme."

"Go on, Jim."

"Admiral, we need the right crew and the right cover story for the media if we are to avoid another damned feeding frenzy like we saw after we lost Challenger. I'm thinking about the Palapa-Westar operation. You will recall that we trained a four-man, one-woman crew for the Palapa-Westar rescue mission performed by Shuttle Fourteen, Mission 51-A in November 1984. Since that crew was successful, they are still rather well known to the press. But for the first time since Shuttle Two back in '81, we also trained a back-up crew to keep the insurance companies that underwrote the retrieval operation happy. Will Parker and Jack Enright, both of whom you know, were the back-up pilots. Trained with them were two mission specialists who would have done the spacewalks. That reserve crew would have gone only if the primary crew on Fourteen had failed.

"My people are proposing that we send only Parker and Enright to do the whole LACE operation—no other crewmen. First, eliminating the two mission specialists would cut our potential losses in half if the worst happens. Second, neither Parker nor Enright are well known to the media people. Parker flew in Gemini and in Apollo. But that's ancient history to the press. Enright has never flown. They don't have any friends in the press corps. These guys are real hard-asses. The Cape and Houston people call them 'the icemen.' Let Parker handle the ship while Enright goes outside. They both already have extensive EVA training for the Palapa-Westar rescue flight. In fact, they are still in active training for a shuttle military mission next year."

"Palapa and Westar," Secretary Vazzo inquired.

"Yes, Mr. Secretary," Colonel James Cerven continued with his fine Long Island accent showing just a trace of

North Carolina. "Palapa was the Indonesian communications satellite and Westar-6 the Western Union bird, both lost when their PAM boosters failed to light properly on Shuttle 10 in '84. They shot off into the wrong orbits, luckily low enough for another shuttle to get up to them. Shuttle 14 went after them. After a successful rendezvous in space, our two astronauts did a spacewalk—EVA—to bring them back into the shuttle payload bay for return to Earth.

"Here's our plan as of this moment: On March 14, 1990, a Titan-3 missile launched the Intelsat-6 spacecraft into space. Unfortunately, the rocket failed to get the satellite into the proper orbit. The 265-million-dollar bird is parked in a useless orbit of 220 by 140 miles.

"We propose to announce that sudden degradation of Intelsat's systems from prolonged exposure require an emergency shuttle mission to pick it up and return it to Earth for repairs. This is exactly what we did with Palapa and Westar. Astronauts Parker and Enright, under that cover, will rendezvous with LACE instead, attach the PAM, and blast LACE into the atmosphere. My people are confident of having the perfect cover with the perfect crew: absolutely trained but rather unknown."

Secretary Vazzo looked uncomfortable.

"What about security as far as radio communications with your Parker and Enright up there?" the Secretary demanded wearily.

"Good point, Mr. Secretary," the Colonel nodded. "If the Russians and the European Space Agency both agree to maintain our cover, then the only real security problem is worldwide monitoring of our air-to-ground communications. And we have a handle on that: Normally, we communicate with shuttles by the high-altitude, TDRS satellites—Tracking Data and Relay satellites. These birds give us virtually constant contact with shuttles. But they can also be listened to. So, we are now working around the clock to get crews into the old NASA network of ground-tracking stations. We began closing them down around the world in 1989, to replace them with TDRS satellites. We can communicate with Parker and Enright through these old ground stations and then relay the communications to Houston and NASA by landlines which are tap-proof. And we even have a perfect cover for this change: In February 1990, one of the TDRS birds went on the blink. Its Ku-band antenna broke so we could not get shuttle television pictures down. That TDRS had been sent up in September of '88. So, we will also be announcing with our Intelsat-6 press release that we may have to rely on the old NASA ground stations since we will need good television coverage of the Intelsat rendezvous and spacewalk. Perfect, gentlemen . . . Everything perfect." Colonel Cerven looked tired but pleased.

"Assuming," Secretary Vazzo sighed, "that you can work with Moscow's new Chief of Staff, Marshall Akhromeyev. Don't underestimate this new man." The diplomat's face showed the strain.

"We're working on that, Joe," the Admiral said with fatigue in his voice. "Our people agree with Colonel Cerven's proposal. Colonel Stermer, how soon can your people switch Parker and Enright to the LACE operation, install the mylar blankets in the shuttle's payload bay, and have Endeavor launch-ready from the Cape?"

"Just say the word, Admiral. We can pull Endeavor's chocks in thirty days." The Colonel from Canaveral was ecstatic.

"How about ninety-six hours . . . Four days."

The silence was intense.

"Admiral, we would barely have time for external tank chilldown and for installing Endeavor's pyrotechnics. Twenty days at the very best. And that's leaving a mess of screws untightened."

"Four days, Dale."

"Admiral. Forgive me. But it cannot be done." The man from Florida looked stricken.

"Dale, four days. That's the word from upstairs. The final word."

The Marine stenographer opened his eyes to join the little company looking at the harried officer from Cape Canaveral.

"Admiral: Four days. December 18th . . . Do you know what 'Palapa' means in Indonesia? It means 'Fruit of our Effort.' "

"Think we're going to get fired, Skipper?" Jacob Enright asked with a weak grin.

The two fliers slouched in their flightsuits soaked with sweat. They sat alone in the Johnson Center's conference room, the same sterile room where they had been humiliated the previous night.

"Wouldn't mind, Jack. This crap of flying the simulator at dawn or at midnight so the other crews can fly it in daylight is getting to me." Colonel Parker looked over his coffee mug to the cold darkness beyond the window. "Midnight again, Jack. Going to forget how to fly in daylight." When angry, the Colonel's voice lost its down-home drawl.

"I know. At least, Will, we didn't bend our metal today . . . All damn morning shooting launch aborts, and half the night doing workarounds in the cockpit on electrical glitches . . . Was it this afternoon we tipped a few at your place, or was it last week?" Enright sighed, slouched deeper into his chair, and with closed eyes he sipped his cold coffee.

The conference-room door opened and the tall, bearded flight director entered, followed by his wake of pipe smoke. His face was grim as Parker and Enright looked up with bleary and dark eyes. The fliers waited for the rest of the director's entourage for another simulator, postmortem at midnight.

The Flight Director turned his face to the door, which

he pulled closed behind him. The two seated airmen looked quickly at each other as their sleepy minds registered that the Flight Director was alone.

"Git them resumés ready, Number One," Colonel Parker whispered to Enright as the youthful engineer in a cloud of pipe smoke sat down opposite the exhausted pilots.

Parker and Enright sat up as the Director intently studied the ashen-faced astronauts. The pilots looked back at the Director's face, an anguished face, thought Parker.

"Jack. Will," the Director said, laying his pipe upon the bare table.

"Hutch," greeted the Colonel with what was left of his strained good cheer.

The airmen waited impatiently while the Director studied his own hands upon the table.

"The next mission is yours."

That was it. The Flight Director's facial muscles did not move.

"Oh," offered William Parker from his dry throat. He whispered, but his brain did handstands.

The Flight Director's words rattled around behind Enright's heavy eyes. The full thought did not root in Enright's mind before the Director continued his monologue.

"Does the LACE mean anything to either of you?"

"Don't know, Hutch," Jack Enright smiled. "I've never been married."

"Hot damn, Skipper!" Jacob Enright sang beneath the blinding arc lights of the midnight parking lot. He fairly danced in the cold, black drizzle between his sensuous driving machine and the Colonel's battered truck.

"Four days?" the Colonel asked blankly with his worn-out face pressed against the rain-streaked side window of his pickup. With his large hand cupped to the sides of his wet face to shield his eyes from the glare of the floodlights, he surveyed the puddle of water growing on the front seat of his flatbed relic.

"Come on, Will," Enright pleaded, unable to restrain his pleasure. "The LPS can get her off in four days. We've run fully automatic countdowns since Eight."

Colonel Parker turned to his young partner in the light rain. He envied his copilot for his passion and his vigor. The Colonel had been that way—20 years earlier when he had posed thin and proud beside a sleek jet amid the rice paddies. He had saved the picture.

"Maybe the Launch Processing System can push us off well enough. But I need a little time to kick the tires before cranking up."

"We'll make time, Skipper. Unless we have pneumonia. Let's get out of the rain."

Enright led his captain to his little treasure, a shining chassy tightly wrapped around a monster engine. Enright squeezed in behind the wood steering wheel.

Inside Enright's four-wheeled cockpit, Colonel Parker looked at his knees pulled up to his sweat- and rain-soaked chest. The array of battery and engine dials gave the illusion of a jet cockpit idling on the apron, aching for the purple sky. The low midnight sky leaked softly upon the windows.

"Look at it this way, Will," Enright counseled as his breath fogged the windshield close to his face. "We've trained for Palapa-Westar Six and for flying the MMU. And we're already working on next year's rendezvous and recovery flight to retrieve a fused-out, recon satellite for the Defense Department. The Manipulator Arm has flown successfully since STS-2. The Plasma Diagnostics Package checked out perfectly on Three in '82. It'll sniff out any radiation or flux leaks from LACE just fine. This thing is exactly what we are trained to do: First-orbit rendezvous with a target, go outside with the MMU, stabilize LACE with the manned maneuvering unit and the flying grapple fixture, attach the pyro package with the RMS,

51

and push 'er off. All in a good day's work, Will." Enright was still euphoric, itching for his first ride Out There. He looked longingly at the black and rainy sky, his sky at last.

This would be Colonel Parker's fourth flight into the blackness. Another day at the office was all.

"What do you know about LACE, Jack?" Will Parker asked with his face looking over his right shoulder toward his truck. He could hear it rusting in the rain.

"Only what I read in *Aviation Week*."

"Well, buddy. Whatever is in *Aviation Week* must be the truth." The Colonel smiled at his truck.

"Then, Skipper, let's do it!" Jacob Enright beamed, filling his youthful face with teeth.

The weary Colonel thought about tomorrow, which was already two hours old. In only six hours, they would again get their feet wet in the Johnson Center's huge, neutral buoyancy pool to simulate working upon their deadly target in watery weightlessness. With his mind full of slow-moving, exhaustion-numbed thoughts, the Colonel faced his excited partner. Jack Enright's boyish grin infected the Colonel's deeply lined, pilot's face.

"You betcha, Number One," the Colonel smiled as he pried his long body from the cold, damp cockpit.

4

December 15th

"Moscow wants its piece of the pie." Admiral Hauch shrugged wearily. Three nights of midnight meetings were darkly written upon his face. "Joe, would you, please?"

Joseph Vazzo extracted a notebook from his briefcase. Opening the binder inscribed "Confidential Cables," he addressed the midnight assembly of officers and diplomats.

The ventilators filled the plastic cave with the chill, scentless sigh of filtered air. The man from State adjusted his bifocals.

"Following our Vienna connection, the Soviets informed us through direct communications that they are agreed to maintaining a secrecy lid on LACE, but at a price."

Even the somnolent Marine stenographer opened his eyes to hear what his fingers were tapping as the diplomat continued.

"The Russians will observe a news quarantine only if they are permitted to have a cosmonaut crew on-station in space for the Intelsat-6 operation. I am advised that a Soyuz, Block-TM spacecraft is already stacked and ready for launch . . ."

"Do the bastards understand the risk to their crew, Mr. Secretary?" demanded a Colonel in shirtsleeves.

"May I suggest, sir, that our colleagues behind the Kremlin wall understand the risks of LACE, and that they did even before your special projects people." The

53

graying diplomat glared coldly over his glasses toward the officer. "We believe that's also why Moscow is sending their people up in the Soyuz-TM spacecraft. The TM version is new, but the basic Soyuz design is old, reliable — and expendable. They are not risking their new, more efficient, but radically more expensive Buran space shuttle."

"Thanks, Joe. The new crew of Parker and Enright received their initial briefing earlier this evening. Our people here and at NASA's Office of Space Science in Houston are confident that our substitute crew is the likely choice and in need of virtually no retraining. After all," said the Admiral as he lifted a coffee mug to his round face, "Parker and Enright have trained for months for this precise mission. We're only changing their target and the applications package to be attached to it on-orbit . . ."

"Not to mention that your mislaid communications satellites could only have winked at them," Deputy Under Secretary Vazzo offered dryly. "LACE can crisp them . . . and the Shuttle Endeavor . . . and the Soviets in Soyuz."

"Joe, Joe," muttered the tired admiral, pleading from the head of the table.

"Admiral," interrupted a gray-suited National Security Council representative.

"Pete?"

"NSC remains curious about Endeavor's extraordinary turnaround schedule. How confident are you about going up in three and one-half days?"

"I think the KSC people are better informed than I on that one. Colonel Stermer?"

"Sir: as Commander Rusinko pointed out last night, Endeavor is already rolled out to Pad 39-A at Kennedy. With a fully automated checkout and countdown, the LPS — that's Launch Processing System — can get her off in 80 hours. That's not our critical weakness. Let me be specific."

As the liaison officer between NASA and Defense shuffled through his stack of papers, a dozen hands raised coffee mugs toward faces sagging with midnight fatigue.

"Systems integration is a serious constraint on our timeline. Endeavor's payload bay is stuffed with the communication satellite payload. We must get the bird out of Shuttle and lay in the Mylar reflector blankets. Also, the Payload Assist Module and an OSS pallet with a plasma diagnostics package must be mated, connected, integrated, and checked out in the payload bay . . ." The speaker paused to catch his breath. "Ordinarily, this complex operation would be executed with Shuttle in the horizontal position in the Orbiter Processing Facility. To go in three days, this operation must be done with the system stacked vertically on the pad. We are pushing the time-line, pushing the structural limitations, and pushing the launch team."

"Dale, will your people be configured for vehicle close-out in time?"

"In time and on time. Barely."

"Good. Joe, what about integration with the Russians once Endeavor is airborne?"

"The Soviets will launch a little after midnight our time the morning of the 18th. As I understand it, Shuttle will launch at 10 o'clock that morning Eastern Time. Soyuz should arrive at the target about 90 minutes later, just before Shuttle's rendezvous with LACE. Because the Soyuz-TM has rather limited, orbital maneuvering capabilities due to her small fuel reserves, they will need the whole eleven hours to shoot their rendezvous with LACE. Their rendezvous will require just less than eight orbits."

"What about air-to-air communications with the Russians?"

"General Breyfogle, there probably will not be any Soviet comm with our ground stations. They use very different radio frequencies from our FM channels, as you know. Soyuz and Endeavor may have air-to-air voice contact by UHF radio, normally only used by Shuttle for the last minutes of the approach and landing sequence. Am I correct, Admiral?"

"As always, Joe."

"What about the risk to Soyuz from LACE? Can Soyuz be damaged by another lucky shot by LACE, Mr. Secretary?"

"We don't know for certain, Major. Our best intelligence suggests that all Soviet offensive missiles and military satellites are 'hardened,' as we say, against laser attack. We estimate their offensive missiles for the last few years have been hardened against laser radiation along the lines of two-tenths kilojoules per square centimeter. That is a measurement of laser focusing energy. Their warheads are hardened against seven kilojoules per square centimeter. That may insulate Soyuz sufficiently if it is also hardened to the warhead range of protection. As most Soyuz and Salyut space station missions are military in nature, we can only presume that they are hardened. That kind of armor may account for their limited maneuverability. We are not sure."

"Seems you are not sure about a lot of things, Mr. Secretary."

"That may be, Commander Rusinko . . . But our people have never shot down a Russian satellite with an offensive weapon which was not supposed to be there in the first place."

Joseph Vazzo spoke through clenched teeth at the silent Navy officer. The Admiral shuffled his papers and all eyes were on him.

"Gentlemen, it's two o'clock in the morning and we're all a little tired and short on patience . . . One more detail: What about handling the press on this one—a joint space flight out of the blue and a bumped Shuttle crew, all in three days? How are we going to ice the cake? Mr. Young?"

"Admiral, we've worked out this scenario at the Cape.

Tomorrow morning, we will issue to the wire services a routine statement announcing an emergency repair mission to the lost Intelsat-6 satellite. No press conference, no hoopla. We'll announce the mission on the premise of a sudden degradation of the Intelsat's orbit. We will analogize the situation to the unexpected re-entry of our Skylab space station over Australia in '79. We're still smarting from that one. The Soviet participation will be announced by stating they will be there to confirm that Intelsat does not re-enter the atmosphere over Soviet air-space. We'll thank the Russians for their rapid, international cooperation. A true handshake in space equal to the joint Apollo-Soyuz Test Project flown in 1975. All quite tidy."

"About tidiness. How is it that the Russians are ready to go so quickly, and with an English-speaking crew?"

"Maybe Joe can respond to that one?"

"We've wondered about that, too, General. Our theory is that Soyuz was already set to go, probably to back up a ferry Cosmos, such as Cosmos 1267, which is their killer-satellite series. They were probably already targeted for LACE. As for their English-speaking crew, they may have changed crews just as we have."

"They wouldn't dare go after LACE alone . . ."

"Dare what, Colonel? Wouldn't dare attempt to take down a rogue satellite? Do I have to remind you of the applicable law of the sea here?" Joseph Vazzo rubbed his tired eyes. "Our crime here is nothing less than space piracy . . ."

"Piracy, Mr. Secretary?"

"Complete with the black flag, as far as our space treaty with the Russians is concerned, Admiral."

"Early for a swim, isn't it, Jack?"

The brawny technician smiled at Jacob Enright, who was raising his fish-bowl helmet to his head. The clock above them on the wall read 7 a.m., Houston time.

"You know that the Colonel and I work the swing shift, Chief," Enright grinned.

"From the poop I hear upstairs, I'd say your night-shift days are about over. What say?" The big man fiddled with a hose connection on Enright's bulky white pressure suit.

"Think so?"

"Poop has it you 'n' Colonel are flying, and soon. Somethin' hush-hush." The smiling deck-crew chief spoke toward Parker, who stood in his faded flightsuit beside Enright. "You boys must know *someone*."

"Reckon so," the Colonel drawled.

With his helmet secured to his full suit, Jacob Enright balanced on the wire basket at the side of the Johnson Center's neutral buoyancy pool. Submerged 40 feet deep in the 1.3-million-gallon pool, a full-size mockup of an open Shuttle payload bay shimmered. Both Enright and Parker felt an eerie twinge reminding them of Monday's simulated landing which ended in the drink, at least on paper.

Strapped to Enright's back was a full-size model of the Martin Marietta Manned Maneuvering Unit, the MMU.

Ordinarily, shuttle crews train in watery, simulated weightlessness in the pool at the Marshall Space Flight Center at Huntsville. But there was no time to fly from Houston to Alabama.

"Tell you boys another thing," the technician said as he gave Enright a cheery thumbs-up. "That ain't no Intelsat down there, either."

The engineer regarded the cylindrical black hulk which floated 10 yards to the side and slightly above the sunken payload bay's sill, near where the open bay door would be in space.

Neither pilot replied.

"Basement, please, ladies' intimate apparel." The voice crackling from the wall-mounted loudspeaker belonged to the space-suited Enright, who perched ankle-deep in water upon the grating of the steel elevator at poolside.

The lift groaned and descended into the clear water. Enright's helmet just cut the surface as a Navy safety diver below the surface reached up for the weights fastened to the ankles of Enright's bulky EVA suit. Two divers on either side of Enright steered him from the submerged lift toward the Shuttle payload bay. With one diver holding each of Enright's legs, they guided his feet into the foot restraints bolted to the bay's floor.

"Don't make a wish," Enright's voice laughed over the wall speaker as each diver held one of his legs.

Behind the neckring of the suit, a few bubbles percolated upward from the MMU's air supply. Quickly, the bubbles stopped. As in space, the cumbersome manned maneuvering unit on the pilot's back did not vent his breath overboard.

With weights precisely positioned about his ankles, thighs, wrists, and lower back, Enright's air-filled space suit was perfectly balanced in the water. He was, in fact, weightless, as he would be 130 nautical miles into the airless sky.

With his feet wedged into the foot restraints, Enright let his body float backward until he was nearly horizontal in the open bay. His heavily gloved hands floated before his helmet. The two safety divers floated at his elbows. Behind them, two NASA utility divers straddled each ledge of the 15-foot-wide shuttle bay.

"Okay, Chief. All set down here." Enright peered over his neckring at the dials and controls strapped to his small chestpack. As with the helmet he would wear in space during extravehicular activity, the bottom portion of his clear faceplate on the helmet was optically ground to magnify the chestpack dials under his chin. "Air at 28 PSI, suit inlet temp at 65, outlet at 75 degrees, nitrogen at 2500 PSI each tank. Don't feel any fish inside the suit. Real snug here, Chief, and ready to engage the MMU."

"Copy, Jack," the deck chief replied into his microphone headset from behind his poolside console. "Go for MMU activation."

At the chief's side, Colonel Parker scanned the console's digital numerics relaying Enright's pulse and suit temperatures from the water.

In space, the MMU maneuvers about by 24 compressed nitrogen jets. But in the water simulation, the MMU scoots around propelled by water jets. Enright's nitrogen gauge on the chestpack was one more simulation, one more meter to read too high or too low, one more caution-and-warning light to flash in simulated catastrophe.

" 'Kay, Chief," the speaker crackled. "Powering up."

Strapping the 300-pound MMU to one's back, a pilot nestles his behind into it. Like sitting in Grandfather's great chair, the pilot becomes part of the MMU.

A boxy wing projected from the upper corners of the MMU outward along each side of Enright's helmet. Each of the eye-level booms contained forward-shining work lights. A tiny thruster nozzle was positioned on each wing, level with the pilot's jaw. In space, each small jet fires nitrogen gas with one and a half pounds of thrust to maneuver the pilot in a backflip. Two similar nozzles faced outward from the side of each neck-level projection. These thrusters maneuvered the pilot either sideways or in a slow roll, clockwise or counter-clockwise. At the outside of each of Enright's knees, two matching wings projected from the base of the MMU backpack. Each of these pods contains one knee-level, forward-thrusting jet and two outside-thrusting jets. One jet in each of the head wings and in each of the knee-level wings points backward.

"Telescoping arms deployed," Enright called from 35 feet under water. From beneath each armpit, he adjusted an arm-length boom which locked into place under each of his arms. These booms fit the length of the space suit's arms. The pilot cradled each of his forearms upon the white arms of the MMU which projected nearly perpendicular from the backpack. At the end of each arm,

Enright grabbed a T-shaped control handle between his gloved fingers.

"Rotation Hand Controller engaged." Enright's right hand flicked the switch, energizing the MMU's right-arm control handle. This handle would control his in-place attitude. By firing the water jets with the handle in his right hand, his wrist movements would "pitch" him forward or backward, "roll" him clockwise or counter-clockwise, or "yaw" his heels sideways left or right.

"THC engaged," Enright called topside.

"Understand Translational Hand Controller activated," the chief confirmed. In his gloved left hand, Enright gripped the translational T-handle which would activate the MMU's jets to shove him through the water upward or downward, left or right, and forward or backward.

One of the divers slowly circled Enright and carefully touched the pilot's helmet neckring and hoses locked to the suit from the PLSS—the Portable Life Support System backpack permanently attached to the suit's upper torso. The PLSS pack was nestled inside the MMU backpack as it would be in space. The diver gave Enright a wet thumbs-up sign.

"Ready, Chief," Enright radioed over his single umbilical line, which reached to the surface and to the deck chief's console. There would be no such safety tether in space. Colonel Parker's face moved from the console's dials and caution lights to the shimmering image of his sunken partner.

"Go to secure the flying grapple fixture, Jack."

"Rogo, Chief."

The four watchful divers gave Enright room to twist his cumbersome body attached to the bay's foot restraints.

Gently, the submerged astronaut leaned toward a breadbox-sized fixture mounted on a tubular brace in front of his position. Facing the chest-high structure, the pilot carefully grabbed the grapple device in his gloves. He pulled his body toward it until he aligned his chestpack

61

with the device's corners. The grapple fixture snapped into place upon Enright's chestpack brackets.

"Grapple fixture secured," Enright called. "Coming free."

Enright pushed a release lever atop the grapple unit, and the fixture parted from its bay support stand.

"See you free, Jack," the chief confirmed.

Flexing his weighted ankles, Enright straightened his body. Each of his weighted arms found the MMU's forearm cradles. Each of his gloved hands clutched a T-handle.

"And we're flying," Enright called as his left hand moved the THC handle. Water jets squirted from the base of the MMU.

"TVC direct, Chief."

"Copy, Thrust Vector Control to direct, Jack."

The jets thrusted upward as long as Enright pushed the left-hand T-handle upward. The pilot rose. Ten feet above the open bay's floor, Enright fired downward-shooting jets behind his ears. The flier stopped and floated near two windows in the submerged simulated flightdeck.

"You're a tad out of my field, Jack," the wall speaker crackled with a garbled, water-filled voice. The diver behind the windows in the rear of the boilerplate shuttle flightdeck peered through the window which faced aft into the open bay. "Only have your feet, Jack."

"Okay. Comin' down." With a downward push on the THC handle, Enright dropped 12 inches and arrested his descent with a brief burst from the downward-thrusting jets beside his knees.

"Gotcha now, Jack," the diver gurgled behind his window.

"RHC checkout," Enright called. Topside, the deck chief touched the digital readout of Enright's pulse. Colonel Parker followed the chief's fingers. The numbers read 80.

"Copy, Jack. Stay cool."

The pilot twisted the T-handle to the right. Two water jets beside his left ear and two jets beside his right knee squirted outward. Slowly, without moving off, Enright's body rotated counter-clockwise as viewed from the window he faced.

"RHC Go in roll."

"Got it, Jack," the chief radioed.

Moving his right hand in the opposite direction, Enright's rotation stopped. He was upside down in the water and motionless.

Pushing his right-hand T-handle sideways, Enright executed a half circle and ended up standing on his head.

"You're upside down," the pilot radioed to the diver he could see behind the aft flightdeck window.

"No. You are, Jack" came a garbled voice with a stream of shimmering bubbles.

"Roger that. Rollin' aft." The white space suit rotated on its head until the pilot faced the shuttle's submerged tail at the far end of the open bay. He stopped his rotation and then pitched rightside up with small movements of his right hand on the T-handle.

"RCS real tight, Chief."

"Copy, Jack. Reaction Control Systems Go. Clear to translate to the target, Jack."

The black object floating beside the open payload bay hung by cables reaching out of the water to an overhead derrick. Silently, on the deck chief's command, the support cables flexed and the sunken cylinder began a slow rotation in place beside the shuttle mockup.

"Got the target, range ten meters. Slight rotation, maybe a quarter revolution per minute. Moving out."

Pushing his left hand forward upon the handle of the MMU's translational hand controller, the pilot moved forward, slowly approaching the black, suspended canister.

Jacob Enright was dwarfed by the black drone rotating slowly in the water. Propelled by his water jets at his backside, Enright arrived at the floating target. He hovered beside the shuttle bay. At his waist level, a narrow ledge protruded around the circumference of the target,

63

10 feet long and 4 feet thick.

"Ready to snatch it, Chief."

Four divers formed a safety ring around Enright and his slowly spinning target above and to the side of the sunken Shuttle.

"You got him, flightdeck?" the deck chief radioed.

Behind the shuttle windows, the diver eased his body sideways until he could look from the rear window across the payload bay. He saw Enright floating beside the target.

"Got 'im, Chief." The diver's voice was full of water as it came over the wall speaker by hydrophone.

"Go to make contact, Jack. Easy does it."

Taking his right hand from the MMU's arm, the pilot touched the boxy grapple fixture suspended from his chestpack. At the front of the unit, alligator jaws opened wide.

"Flying grapple fixture open, Chief. Movin' on in."

"Carefully, Jack." As the chief spoke, Colonel Parker looked over the edge of the pool.

The pilot in the water pressed his left hand forward on the T-handle. Jets fired in the MMU and Enright edged toward the rotating seam around the midline of the target. The projecting ledge rotated between the grapple fixture's open jaws.

With his left hand, the pilot touched the top of the grapple unit. The metallic jaws closed tightly around the lip of the target's middle skirt. Instantly, Enright's body rotated around with the revolving target.

"Hard contact, Chief."

"You're clear to null the rates, Jack."

As the safety divers looked on, Enright pushed his left hand on the T-handle in the direction opposite the direction in which the target rotated. Four water jets on the side of the MMU thrusted continuously in the direction his body rotated. The jets fired against the movement of the slowly spinning target which rotated on its narrow end. Gradually, the target, with Enright riding its tall side, came to a stop under the influence of the steady-firing MMU jets.

"Stable one, Chief. All stop."

"Roger, Jack. Flightdeck, clear for RMS."

"Okay," the voice gurgled behind the flightdeck's rear windows. "Coming forward with the RMS, Jack."

"Don't bite me, buddy."

From the right ledge of the open payload bay, as viewed from the aft-facing rear windows of the flightdeck, the boilerplate remote manipulator system arm lifted slowly from its cradle on the bay's portside sill. The three-jointed, 50-foot-long arm slowly tracked toward the suspended pilot, who floated to the side and above the opposite starboard side of the payload bay. The arm's far tip, the End Effector Unit, stopped on command beside Enright's shoulder. The pilot hung motionlessly, still attached to the target by the grapple fixture locked to his chestpack.

"I'm eyeball to eyeball with the end effector."

"Understand, Jack," the watery voice called from the flightdeck thirty feet from Enright. "Got us, Chief?"

"With you. Clear to disengage, Jack. Watch the tail and OMS pod close behind you."

Five feet behind Enright, the simulated Shuttle's tail, 26 feet high, broke the surface of the water. On either side of the vertical tail fin, a bulbous orbital maneuvering system pod protruded from the rear of the Shuttle.

" 'Kay. Comin' free, Chief. Flightdeck?"

"With you, Jack."

When the pilot touched the top of the grapple unit with his gloved hand, the unit separated from the brackets on Enright's chestpack. With his left hand on the hand controller, the pilot slowly backed away from the grapple fixture attached to the target cylinder. Enright stopped three feet from the target with a burst from his MMU jets.

"Left just a tad," Enright directed. The remote arm

drifted between Enright and the target on command from the diver in the sunken flightdeck.

"Plus Y," Enright called inside his suit as he spotted for the diver steering the RMS arm. The arm drifted on command over the starboard sill of the open bay.

"Okay. Minus Z, you're high . . . Good. Right, right. Hold it! You got her now."

"Thanks, Jack," the voice gurgled.

The arm's wire-snare jaws within the end effector yawned and encircled a spiked target probe jutting from the grapple fixture secured to the side of the target. The EEU snare closed like a camera iris around the grapple-fixture probe.

"Rigidize, Jack." The diver on the flightdeck confirmed his contact with the suspended target.

"And we see it topside," the chief called. "Come on up for lunch, Jack."

"I'm ready, Chief."

Jacob Enright flew the MMU's water jets to the lift waiting beside the shuttle mockup.

"Topside, cabby," Enright called from the lift. He raised an arm free from the MMU and waved to the half-dozen divers beneath him. "See you after lunch, guys."

The divers waved back as the space suit cleared the surface.

"No sweat, Skipper," Enright smiled at poolside as a suit technician lifted off his plastic bubble helmet. With the MMU fastened to the side of the lift, as it would be stored in space on an outside bracket in the shuttle bay, Enright disconnected his PLSS backpack from the MMU. He stepped forward off the lift and felt the ground beneath his feet for the first time in four hours.

"Just like the real thing, aye, Will?"

The Colonel smiled. He knew the real thing well enough.

"Could sure use a few burritos about now. How 'bout it, Skip?"

"No thanks, Number One. You go on and taco up. I have a little errand to run during lunch. Be back in ninety minutes."

"Okay."

Jack Enright walked slightly stooped under the suit's weight, 75 pounds more than his own. He headed for the suitup room as the Colonel walked in the opposite direction out of the new pool area.

"Quite a break, Colonel," a pretty secretary smiled cheerfully as Colonel Parker passed her in the long JSC hallway. He stopped and looked down at the youthful face.

"The crew assignment, I mean. And all in three days. It's really something." She shook her head.

The tall, tired pilot looked down into the clean face. Her bright cheeks made her appear very young indeed. Gently, the Colonel with the deeply lined pilot's face touched the soft chin before him. The young woman blushed.

"Something indeed," the long airman smiled warmly.

"Dr. Casey. Dr. Cleanne Casey. Please call the operator."

William McKinley Parker stood in the spacious lobby of the huge hospital complex. He squinted toward the windows into the brilliant sunshine of a Texas winter afternoon. The tall pilot hid behind sunglasses and his officer's dress coat.

"Operator. Yes, Dr. Casey. There's a man here at the front desk for you. Says he's from the Houston Health Department, Venereal Disease Division. Says he needs to get some names from you. I think he said of all your boyfriends . . . I'll tell him."

"Sir? Dr. Casey will be right down. You may have a seat."

"Thank you kindly," drawled the man in the long coat. He stood for five minutes looking into the harsh daylight outside.

"Thanks a lot, Will," said a laughing voice at the Colonel's back. He turned to the small, sandy-haired woman in white.

"Not to mention it, C.C.," the tall man grinned.

"You just ended my social life in this hospital, you know."

"Oh, the fleet'll be in soon. You can make new friends."

With his long arm around the thin woman's shoulders, the pair walked down the long corridor to an airy, plant-filled lounge marked HOUSE STAFF ONLY. They sat in a corner warmed by sunlight surging upon them from a nearby window. Her brown eyes sparkled as the sun delighted her short blond hair. The airman at her side folded his bridge coat across his legs and he stuffed his sunglasses into a sleeve pocket of his faded flightsuit. A small plastic badge with his photo on it dangled from his chest pocket.

"Radio said you and Jack are doing the Intelsat-6 flight after all." The woman was serious and thoughtful.

"Just another day at the office, Cleanne," the flier offered with cheery assurance.

"Maybe for you, Will."

"Come on, C.C. The triple bypasses you people do every day are more difficult than a little junket up and down."

"But we don't do surgery on three days' notice."

"Me, neither. Jack and I have trained for months to do this. We're sick of training for it."

"Oh."

"And, besides, young Jack is A-1. Think you two would make a handsome couple." The lines in the weary pilot's face creased into a smile at the young woman twenty years his junior.

"Thanks, Will. But worrying about one space-type is my limit. Anyway, I am glad to see you. Been a month."

The woman touched the big man's hand. He squeezed her fingers gently.

"I need you for a housecall, C.C."

"A professional visit, is it? Another sore throat? I feel like your flight surgeon sometimes."

"You know pilots and air medics—natural enemies. Every time a pilot visits a flight surgeon, he stands a 50/50 chance of having his ticket pulled. So why risk it? You know how I am: I stay up all night and cram just to turn my head and cough before every flight physical."

The pair chuckled in the bright lounge.

The pilot withdrew his hand from the young woman's. His face darkened.

"Where can I go to drop trou, C.C.?" The pilot was grim.

"No dinner first? No soft music, wine?" The blond woman grinned.

"Cleanne, I'm serious."

"I thought you told me long ago that I could doctor you anywhere—so long as what ails you is below your knees or above your belt." She could not hold her throaty laugh. Intense young physicians around the room severely regarded the pair by the window.

"Now, C.C. I have to be getting back after lunch . . . Please."

"All right, Will." Her face was very serious. "This way."

They walked silently down the long hallway. The woman pushed open a windowless door and the tall colonel followed her into a narrow examination room.

"Well?" she asked with her hands inside her deep white pockets.

"I feel silly," the tall flier said softly.

"I should hope so. I haven't seen your knees in all the years I've known you."

"Hell." The big man sighed as he pulled the zipper of his faded blue flightsuit from his Adam's apple down to his crotch. He stepped out of his coveralls as he felt heat rising into his gaunt face and large ears.

"Damn, William . . ." The woman's smile disappeared

69

as the physician within her small body instantly took over.

Cleanne Casey's face is angular and her brown eyes are ever darkly tired. Her beauty comes richly and warmly from within, from the depth of her capacity to care, and from her abiding gentleness. Cleanne's dark beauty and her wondrous, throaty laughter are revealed to those upon whom her light falls warmly and gently. Standing sheepishly, the tall airman loved the woman who laid her cool hand upon his swollen right leg above his knee.

"I can feel the heat, Will."

"So what do you think, Doc?"

"I think that my piano has better legs." She smiled. "How'd you do that?"

"About three weeks ago, when I had that damned earache you fixed for me. I bumped the bejesus out of my shin going through the door on the shuttle simulator. The pain in my calf and knee started two days later. Been runnin' a fever, 99, 101, off and on since. At least two weeks. I've been chugging aspirin every few hours every day . . . I can't have a fever for our pre-flight physicals!" The Colonel heaved his long body up to the examination table. His long, knobby legs dangled over the side.

"I can't imagine how you've walked around on it . . . We'll have to shoot an X ray and run a blood test. I want to drain that for a culture, too."

"Osteomyelitis, C.C.?"

The woman raised an eyebrow.

"I read too much, you know."

The woman in white nodded.

"I still don't know how that thing hasn't crippled you."

"My trusty vet."

"Your horse doctor!"

"You betcha." The tall man smiled victoriously. "Told him my old salt had a hoof abscess. Gave me a jug of equine erythromycin . . ."

"And you've been popping horse pills for two weeks?"

"We cowboys are a hardy lot."

"Tell me about it—after we put you to bed upstairs."

"No way, Cleanne. I fly in sixty-nine hours."

"I want you in bed, Will."

The long man grinned broadly.

"I must confess, Doctor, the thought has crossed my mind once or twice."

The woman did not smile.

"If we do not treat that, and right now, you can lose it. You'll be a one-legged cowboy, William Parker. Do you hear what I'm saying?"

"Five-by, C.C. Work your way with me. But I'm not goin' to be admitted. You can drill me and douche it out. The book says antibiotic effusion of the bum knee. Fine. I can come over again tonight about 10 o'clock. But . . ." The drawn and tired face was stoney. William McKinley Parker flashed his Iceman glare. "But if I can breathe, I can fly."

"All right. I'll draw a culture and shoot you up now."

"Penicillin?"

"Enough that you'll not be sitting down for the rest of the afternoon." She glanced at the wall clock, which read 1 p.m. "All of your lady friends will thank me. Your old six-shooter, cowboy, will be squeaky clean."

The tired woman forced a soft smile to her face.

"In my way, C.C., without touching you, I love you. Greatly."

"I know."

71

5

December 16th

"Dr. Casey, please," the big man said at the front desk.

"It's 12:30 in the morning, sir."

"She's expecting me."

"Your name, please?"

"Colonel . . . Colonel Sanders. Her chicken is ready."

"One moment, please . . . Dr. Casey, Dr. Casey. Please call the operator."

The tall man in baggy slacks and rumpled sweater listened to the loudspeaker fill the deserted corridors with echoes.

"Operator. Yes, Doctor. A Colonel Sanders at the front desk to see you. About your chickens . . . Thank you."

The man with the tired face swallowed his grin. Have to tell this one to Number One, he thought.

"If you'll have a seat, please. Dr. Casey will be down in about twenty minutes. She is with a patient."

"Thank you very much."

The pilot rode his long legs to a secluded corner of the large, empty lobby. He sat down gingerly beside a huge plastic fern. When his pants hit the couch, he grimaced as his wallet tormented the wound in his hip where 6 million units of long-acting bicillin ate away the meat of his backside. He squirmed to remove his wallet from his throbbing thigh.

Ten yards away, the Colonel could see an elderly man sitting with a young woman not much past her teens. Her face was bloated and her cheeks were wet. She rocked back and forth in the arms of the old man.

Parker loathed hospitals. His bowels knotted in the morbid austerity of hospital hallways, where there is room for everything except dignity and privacy. He closed his dark, weary eyes. The distant sobs of the tortured young woman rolled over his mind at midnight.

When ordinary men close their eyes, there is only darkness. When fliers close their eyes, they see white sun against purple sky or August clouds which from above appear firm enough to support a pilot's body in solitary peace. Such reverie makes the daily risk of incineration a small price to pay.

The tall man's chin with its gray stubble touched his chest, which rose and fell with a steady, even rhythm. Behind his eyelids, Will Parker flew. It is the pilot's way.

"MMU is set. Ready, Chief."

"Okay, Jack. Clear to affix the PAM to the target." The deck chief and Colonel Parker studied the poolside instrumentation console. The submerged pilot's heart rate showed 95 after two hours under water. "Stay cool, Jack."

" 'Kay. Keepin' clear."

Enright twisted his weighted ankles while three safety divers hovered above the top of his bulky backpack.

Inside the flightdeck of the submerged shuttle mockup, a diver directed the remote manipulator system's 50-foot arm out of its cradle on Shuttle's portside sill in the open payload bay. The diver carefully steered the dummy arm's three joints toward the payload assist module nestled in the rear of the sunken bay. The arm's far end, the end effector unit, EEU, snared the grapple post atop the PAM package.

"PAM in motion, Chief." Enright flexed his ankles, secured to the bay-floor restraints. He faced the rear of the open bay. The pilot, in pressurized flightsuit, helmet, chestpack, and large MMU backpack, stood stooped under the weight of his gear. Beside the boilerplate vertical tail, the PAM cylinder rose secured to the deployed RMS arm, which had hoisted the garbage-can size PAM from its pallet in the bay.

"At pilot's discretion, Jack."

Enright's left hand jockeyed the hand controller with an upward motion.

"And man can fly, Chief."

The divers in the huge pool gave way for the cumbersome white space suit which slowly floated upward and forward to the dangling PAM at the end of the remote arm.

"Watch the plasma package, Jack," the diver behind the aft flightdeck windows gurgled.

"Gear up." Enright lifted his boots as he floated over and past the canister secured in the midsection of the payload bay.

"Clear of the plasma sniffer, Chief."

"We see it, Jack. When you're on station aft, take a breather. Suit outlet temp is eighty. Don't want you to fog your visor, Jack."

" 'Kay, Chief."

Four divers followed the pilot to the tail section.

The pilot moved his left hand forward, a water jet squirted from the manned maneuvering unit's wing beside each of the pilot's ears and beside each of his thickly suited knees.

"All Stop."

The pilot flicked the control handle in his right hand. He rotated to his left and stopped, facing the black target which hung suspended beside the Shuttle three feet from the PAM package fastened to the deployed RMS arm. Beneath Enright's boots, the shuttle's orbital maneuvering system, OMS, pods protruded long and round, one on each side of the base of the nearly three-stories-high-tail fin.

"Watch the OMS pod, Jack," the spotter diver gargled by hydrophone near the floating pilot.

"See it. I'll catch my breath here for a minute."

"Take your time," the deck chief radioed with his hairy fingers touching the pilot's pulse monitor, which read 110. "No rush, Jack."

"Yeah," the pilot blew into his two lip microphones underneath his sweating nose.

"Colonel there, Chief?"

"Right beside me."

"Let's take the burritos out of Endeavor's pantry, Skipper."

The Colonel waved at Enright's upturned face within his fishbowl helmet 30 feet under water. A lame chuckle rolled out of the wall loudspeaker.

"How we lookin', Chief?"

"Eighty on heart rate. Suit outlet temp down to seventy. Carry on, Jack."

"Okay. Take her in."

Enright flicked his left hand on the translational hand controller's T-handle. He jetted closer to the large black target motionless beside the shuttle.

Carefully, the simulated RMS arm was maneuvered closer to the target. The PAM rocket package hung from the end effector unit at the arm's end. The PAM stopped six inches from the target's midsection seam where the small flying grapple fixture was still attached from Enright's "space walk" in the water before lunch.

"To your left . . . easy. Plus Z . . . 'Kay." Enright beside the huge target spotted for the diver who flew the remote arm. "Another four inches . . . Steady . . . Okay. Clear to go in."

The RMS arm moved the PAM unit until it touched the 10-foot-long, 4-foot-thick target. Four grapple latches on the side of the PAM unit engaged the grapple fixture secured to the long target's side. "You got it! Rigidize." The PAM firmly gripped the target's middle.

"Ready to arm the PAM, Chief," Enright called close to the simulated rocket motor.

Colonel Parker pointed to a checklist clipped to the deck chief's console.

"Challenge and read back, Shuttle," the chief radioed with his fingers touching the checklist.

"I hear the skipper coaching, Chief," Enright chuckled. "Waiting."

The submerged pilot floated beside the target where the PAM unit gripped it still attached to the deployed RMS arm.

When the Chief read each item from his checklist, the flier between two safety divers listened to the gargled words repeated by the diver behind the aft flightdeck windows.

"Encryptor alpha, enable."

"Encryptor bravo, enable."

"Ku-band tracking beacon to auto."

"Master pyro alpha, armed."

"Master pyro bravo, armed."

"Squibs one, two and three to command enable."

"Master Sequencer, locked command and double-locked."

"Interlever set."

"Checklist completed, Chief," the man in the sunken flightdeck called.

"Okay, Jack. Clear for PAM release."

Firing his MMU water jets, Enright backed away from the target toward Shuttle's 26-foot high tail fin.

The diver in the Shuttle cabin cycled the End Effector snare wires wrapped around PAM's grapple post. He attempted to separate the RMS arm from the PAM unit affixed to the target.

The wire snare did not open at the arm's end. The PAM package did not separate from the remote arm.

"Negative jettison, Chief," the diver in Shuttle radioed. "Going to Loop Two."

Two divers converged to Enright's side above the payload bay.

In the cockpit behind the two windows opening into the payload bay, the diver again cycled the arm's electronics.

The end effector's wire fingers budged only slightly. Topside, Colonel Parker leaned over the water's edge.

"Looks like it's loose on one clamp, but not free on the other," Enright radioed over his umbilical line.

"We're with you, Jack. Maneuver clear of the target."

The pilot's left hand jerked backward and four jets squirted a high pressure burst of water. The pilot beside the target lurched backward. With another push on the THC T-handle, he stopped and floated between the target secured to the RMS arm and Shuttle's tail.

"No joy, Chief. It's still attached."

The high tail fin stood 2 feet from the MMU's backside, where two long nitrogen tanks protruded. In the watery simulation, the tanks carried only ballast.

An instant after the pilot stopped with his feet 3 yards above the sill of the shuttle's payload bay, the manipulator arm pivoted inboard. The arm carried the 10-foot-long target cylinder and the attached PAM unit smack into Enright's body. The arm forced the pilot over the bay's wall as it slapped a safety diver off the bay's sill.

"I'm on it! Brakes direct!" the voice shouted from the submerged flightdeck as the arm made a slow swing across the open bay toward the tail fin with Jacob Enright in between.

"Full manual!" the chief called loudly. "Nulling rates from up here with brake drive direct!"

As the manipulator arm swung slowly out of control toward Shuttle's tail, Enright's left hand commanded the MMU backpack jets to thrust long and hard toward the tail which the RMS boom, the target, the PAM, and Enright slowly approached.

"We have oscillation building, Jack," the chief shouted. "Pull him out, Number Four!"

Immediately, a NASA safety diver built like an Olympic wrestler reached for the space suit's ankles. He jerked Jacob Enright down, but not fast enough. The swaying target slowly ground the pilot into Shuttle's thick tail plane.

A burst of bubbles exploded from the top of the MMU, totally obscuring Enright's helmet. The grotesque gurgle of a man spitting water bubbled over the wall speaker.

On his hands and knees at water's edge, Will Parker labored to peer through the foam gushing to the surface.

Thirty feet below, the pressure of two atmospheres pushed a wall of ice water into the EVA suit's torso and limbs.

With Enright on his back in a cloud of bubbles upon the floor of the payload bay, a diver straddled the pilot. The diver pulled hard on a wire ring at the pilot's crotch. The foaming, heavy MMU backpack dropped away from the limp pilot's backside. A diver at each of Enright's arms pried his gloved hands from the MMU's handles.

At the pilot's head, the fourth diver carefully pulled the flier's fishbowl helmet from his pale face. A rush of bubbles rose from the inverted helmet as it sank quickly to the floor of the Shuttle bay.

The diver at Enright's head forced the mouthpiece from his scuba air tank into Enright's open lips. Bubbles percolated from the tank on the diver's back. While bubbles rose from the neckring of Enright's suit, the diver squeezed Enright's nostrils closed.

The pilot opened his eyes and thrashed his thick white arms at the mask of the diver leaning over his face.

A second diver restrained the pilot's arms.

Jacob Enright inhaled deeply from the mouthpiece in his face and he relaxed his arms. He opened his eyes wide and he nodded on his back. The diver straddling the pilot's waist released Enright's arms.

Jack Enright gave a thumbs-up sign into the face of the diver beside him, who held his breath. Enright touched the mouthpiece between his teeth and pointed to the diver with the purple, bulging cheeks.

Enright took the tube from his mouth and he handed it bubbling to the diver kneeling over him. The diver put the mouthpiece into his mouth as Enright flexed his body and floated to his feet in the bay. His hair swayed in the chilly water.

The diver at the pilot's side handed the mouthpiece to Enright, who took a long drag of air before he handed it back. Buddy-breathing with the pilot, the diver put his hands under Enright's armpits as two other divers held each of the pilot's elbows.

Slowly, Jacob Enright and the four divers clinging to him rose toward daylight.

The five men surfaced at the pool's edge beneath Colonel Parker's crouching body. Behind Parker, six anxious men leaned over his shoulders.

Jacob Enright spit out a mouthful of water. Colonel Parker ran his long, bony fingers through his partner's wet and matted hair.

The pilot in the water choked out a soggy cough.

"So how'd we do, Skipper?" Jack Enright grinned weakly.

"You alright, sir?" asked a distant voice as warm fingers firmly grasped the shoulder of the dozing man in the corner.

Will Parker opened his eyes wide as he gasped for air like a drowning man. His eyes focused upon a young, bearded physician close to his face.

"Excuse me?" the tall man said groggily.

"You okay?" repeated the young intern.

"Yes . . . Yes. Thank you. A dream, I guess . . . What time is it?"

The intern straightened and looked at his watch.

"One-thirty in the morning."

"Oh," the Colonel mumbled as he ran his fingers through his short, graying hair.

The sitting man looked past the physician standing before him. He searched for the young woman who had been seated nearby. She and the old man had gone.

"I'm waiting for Dr. Casey."

"Trauma Room One. That way." The Colonel followed the young man's arm down the dim hallway.

"Thanks." The Colonel rose a head taller than the thin man in white. "Thanks."

By the time William McKinley Parker reached the windowless door enscribed TR-1, he had fully recovered his bearings. His right leg at the knee throbbed as did each of his sore hips inside his baggy trousers.

"Damn," he whispered rubbing his backside where he had been recently shot.

He leaned with his back propped against the tile wall in the hall beside the closed, heavy door.

"Help you?" inquired a fragile nurse at his elbow.

"Dr. Casey."

"In there. You a doctor?"

The weary pilot's mind mulled over his two doctorates in electrical engineering.

"Yeh."

"Then you may go in."

"Dr. Casey isn't with a patient, is she?"

"No. Don't think so. A staff meeting, I think. An M and M."

"Thanks."

Colonel Parker pushed open the massive door. He entered the bright examination room and found Dr. Casey and four men in white huddled around the exam table.

The tall airman blinked at a delicate young woman who sat upon the table. Her legs dangled barefoot over the table and a paper gown was crumpled about her sides.

From her small waist upward, she was naked in the harsh glare.

Colonel Parker shrank into a corner. Dr. Cleanne Casey stared coldly at his haggard face. He could not retire with honor.

"You the consult?" asked an elderly man in a long white coat. The Colonel recognized the old physician as the figure who had comforted another young woman in the lobby 60 minutes earlier.

"Guess so."

"Well . . . Your patient, Doctor," the old man ordered as he and his colleagues in white backed away from the examination table.

With two long strides, the tall flier stood beside the naked young woman. He avoided Dr. Casey's dark brown eyes heavy with the night. She said nothing.

William McKinley Parker laid a large, warm hand upon the girl's bare shoulder. The girl blinked enormous and clear blue eyes. He had not seen such blue for over 20 years. Then, he had pressed his younger face to the small window of a two-man Gemini spacecraft 150 miles above Bermuda's azure reefs.

When the tall man's face creased into a warm and genteel smile, the crimson flush left the young woman's neck and cheeks. She had a face like Truth.

"Have you a name, child?" the Colonel whispered softly.

"Maria."

The Colonel smiled as his hard hand hid her bare shoulder.

With his large right hand, the sad-eyed pilot engulfed completely her small left breast.

"Breathe deeply," Parker said softly. The girl's narrow chest pressed warmly against his large hand.

"Again, child." Her other breast disappeared completely into his palm.

Colonel Parker blinked a wetness from his gray eyes. He turned to the old physician who stood with his mouth open.

"Carry on, Doctor," Will Parker commanded firmly.

"Live long, and be happy, Maria," Colonel Parker said softly over his broad shoulder as the heavy door closed behind him.

The long airman resumed his vigil in the hallway where he slouched against the wall beside Trauma Room One.

He shook his head. What a day, he thought. His mind returned to an afternoon press conference an hour after Jack Enright had nearly drowned. A wire-service reporter asked the reigning Iceman how he would approach his unprecedented rapid countdown and dangerous Intelsat-6 repair mission. Colonel Parker had glanced at Jacob Enright with his hair still wet. Enright's eyes were still red. "Get it up. Get it done. Get it down," the Colonel had replied soberly as a NASA technocrat gasped behind him and Enright stifled a roaring laugh. I could go on the road with this act, the pilot thought with a broad grin as his back held up the hospital wall.

"A few more midnight meetings, and we'll all become mushroom people who shrivel up in daylight."

Admiral Hauch smiled weakly. The large man was beyond exhaustion. He was spent and used up inside, like a smoking shell coughed from its white hot breech and dumped into a pile of useless brass. Above him, beyond the glass walls, the clock on the bunker wall read 2 a.m. in the morning, Eastern Time.

"There will be no stenographer tonight. No official record. Any officer here who ever breathes a word, a syllable, of our discussion here will find himself spending the rest of his career as latrine orderly at our weather station on the Dibole Iceberg Tongue. That's within two hundred miles of the South Pole, if anyone has need to make travel plans. You civilians who feel the need to impress some cowgirl at Gilley's with all you know will have ample opportunity to impress the locals from our embassy at Liberville in Rio Muni, a West African country too small to be in your edition of *The Statesman's Handbook*."

As the Admiral mopped his face, six grim and tired men squirmed in the Crystal Room's chill and tasteless air.

"What I have to say comes from upstairs . . . Even the President knows nothing of this meeting or its contents."

The blurry-eyed seaman studied each face, each pair of blank eyes, until those eyes turned away from the cold wind of the Admiral's glare.

"Brother Ivan has demanded a contingency plan in the event, God forbid, that Soyuz is fatally disabled by LACE."

"I would hope so," Commander Mike Rusinko offered with a voice tired and strained from fatigue.

"Be patient, Mike," the Admiral cautioned abruptly.

"We are here to discuss the Sleep Tight alternative to destroy Shuttle in the terrible exigency of the fatal loss of Soyuz."

The big man sighed deeply. Six sagging faces heavy with midnight examined the perspiring, round face at the head of the table.

"Gentlemen: if Soyuz is lost to LACE, Sleep Tight will be initiated—for the sacrifice of Shuttle Endeavor with extreme prejudice . . ."

"You cannot be serious, Admiral."

"As I could possibly be, Dale. If Soyuz goes in, Shuttle goes in . . . Four men in place of everything which lives and breathes on our sorry little planet."

"My God, Admiral."

"I know, Dale. I know," the Admiral said to Colonel Stermer from Cape Canaveral and the U.S. Space Command.

"But, Admiral—"

"Parker and Enright are both officers," the big man interrupted. "Their duty includes biting the big one. That is one of the reasons their choice for this crew is so perfect."

"And the other reasons, Admiral?"

The Admiral hesitated for an instant.

"Neither man has family, Mike. The people upstairs have thought of everything, so it would seem. Just too late."

No one responded.

"Now, Dr. Pritchard, you have been briefed thoroughly. I understand you speak HAL/S, the program language of the shuttle's five on-board computers."

"Fluently," the small, bespectacled engineer gloated.

"You have analyzed your assignment, Doctor?"

"Yes. In every detail, I might add."

"Can a termination program be implanted into Endeavor's computer banks, Doctor, without detection?"

"Excuse me, Admiral. We are talking assassination here, murder—and of our own people!"

"Colonel, I know that!" The harried Admiral sagged in his great chair. With his elbows upon the shining table, his hands rubbed his face.

"I know that, Colonel. May I remind you that when you were a light colonel taking daily health checks on your senior officers in hopes of an opening so you could go silver, I was working and drinking with these two men, Parker and Enright. I was eating in their homes. Don't tell me what we are about here! We are here to avert a space war, nothing less than global suicide . . . Let's get on with it. Please, Doctor?"

"Thank you, Admiral. May I lay out for everyone the system we're discussing? The shuttle's on-board data-processing systems."

"Can you do it without putting the rest of us into a coma?"

"I'll try, Colonel Stermer. If I may continue . . ."

The thin engineer bore the pursed and sallow features behind his thick glasses of a man with too much bile circulating through his translucent skin. His hollow cheeks had a sickly yellow pallor.

"First, the nuts and bolts. The general purpose computers, or GPC, five in all, are exquisitely complex, utterly beautiful. Almost sensuous."

As the little wizard prattled on in his engineering reverie, the five listeners with half-closed eyes squirmed in discomfort.

"Imagine: each of the five computers—four primary and one backup—has as its heart a central processing unit. This CPU can perform 450,000 functions every *second*. The CPU's talk to thirty-eight Shuttle systems. The link between the CPU's and Shuttle's subsystems are electronic relays called multiplexer-demultiplexers, or MDM's. The computers speak to Shuttle over the MDM's. The CPU's think forty times faster than the computers used in the Apollo moon-landing spacecraft!

"The four, primary shuttle computers are completely isolated from the fifth computer. This fifth GPC is reserved for the backup computer system. The four primary GPC's compare electronic notes among themselves. They actually vote on major flight-control decisions at least once every second. They synchronize themselves with each other three hundred times every *second*. And, they speak their computer language at the rate of 787,000 words per *second*.

"Now, here is my plan: The GPC's have an internal separate Control Application Program. This is the computer program, about 400,000 written lines of it, which flies the shuttle's re-entry profile into the atmosphere.

"Now, the programs and the re-entry trajectories are physically stored in two tape-recorder type, mass memory units, MMU's. Shuttle's operations sequences programs are stored in the MMU's. The program software is subdivided into smaller core programs called major modes. The actual re-entry into the first fringes of the atmosphere is Major Mode 304 . . ."

"Doctor, please!" the Admiral pleaded with his face in

his large hands. "Get to it."

"Well, all I have to do is tinker with this Major Mode 304. Put in a programmed sequence of re-entry flight maneuvers—put it into both the primary and the backup flight control systems, the BFS. Such maneuvers would subject Endeavor to lethal structural loads. Break the ship's back, as it were . . ."

Five men grimaced.

"You see, re-entry is profoundly delicate for Shuttle, which comes home from orbit as a 100-ton glider without main engine power. It is flown with a maximum of three G's. A load of only 3 and three-tenths G's will fatally overload the wings and body of the shuttle. Program in a sudden dip of the nose from the normal, forty-degree, nose-up attitude down to say twenty degrees . . . and it is done. We call this maneuver an 'alpha sweep.' Takes only a few seconds. I figure an automatic, computer-induced pitch-over to twenty degrees would take two seconds, at most. The crew takes another second or two to realize that they have a flight-control system failure. Then another two or three second pull-up manually commanded by either pilot—it will be a reflexive pilot response. The high G load in the pull-up will do the job."

The thin engineer paused. His exhausted observers scrutinized his yellow face. A smile?

"So, Dr. Pritchard. You just saunter on over to Pad 39-A with your little screwdriver and a few key-punch cards?"

"Not at all, Colonel. The automatic, computer-controlled countdown by the Launch Sequence Processor can be instructed to insert my computer programs into the five flight computers over the pre-launch Ground Command Interface Logic software. This is a normal pre-launch computer and navigation up-date always done on a shuttle launch about twenty minutes before lift-off . . ."

"And our crew just quietly incinerates themselves?"

"Not quite, Major. We simply tell the crew that we intend to fly an automatic test of the re-entry flight systems.

86

It's called a Programmed Test Input. These PTI's, sets of up to seventeen of them, were routinely flown on the first six shuttle missions. Tell the crew we need another PTI sequence to check out the flight systems and they won't raise an eyebrow.

"Just before the re-entry, we advise the pilots either to execute the PTI or not to run it as part of Major Mode 304. We only use the lethal PTI if it is necessary."

"That's it, Doctor?"

"In full, Admiral: Clean, quick, and buried within 400,000 lines of computer programs. And the final beauty of my plan: If the go-ahead is given to the crew for my PTI, it will be run during the early re-entry, during the normal communications blackout caused by the initial heat pulse. Endeavor will go into the blackout, but she will not come out of it."

The Admiral felt his bowels twisting.

"You can do all that between tonight and launch in fifty-six hours?"

"Admiral, that is my job."

"Tell you one thing, Jack, give me a good old truck stop over a dinner jacket joint anytime."

"I'll buy that, Skipper."

With morning sunshine warming their faces by the window of a truckers' diner along Interstate 45 just north of Houston, the newly anointed prime crew for the Intelsat-6 rescue mission relished bacon and eggs laced with greasy hashbrowns and the scent of diesel fuel.

"The best, Number One," the big man drawled. His face looked uncommonly drawn to his junior partner.

"Look tired, Will," Jacob Enright offered cautiously over his black coffee. He braced for a captain's look to warm his face at 8 o'clock in the morning.

"Just worked late and too early to the office, Jack. A mornin' off before we fly to the Cape should restoke the old furnace."

Enright was surprised by the Colonel's benign response. The long pilot had not raised his face from his eggs.

"Yeh, Skip. I'm lookin' forward to a few hours off. No simulator, no briefings, no Stoney, no Hutch, no Tommy. May take my cycle for a spin."

"You be careful, buddy . . . Does feel good, don't it?" The command pilot smiled a tired grin.

"About this morning's briefing, Will. I'm still surprised about running a PTI this late in the game. We're pretty much routine since the first few flights after the Challenger stand-down. Maybe they're still learning how she flies? Strange, though."

"Oh, I don't know, Jack. We'll be there anyway. Might as well give the backroom its money's worth. Just push a button and let Mother fly us home. No sweat."

"I suppose. What you gonna do with your whole hour of R and R?"

"Got a visit I want to make. See a friend up north. Drive from here."

"Got a girl, Skipper?" the thin pilot smiled.

The gray-haired airman thought for a long moment. Enright attended to his eggs. He thought the older flier had forgotten his question.

"Yeh, Jack. A girl."

Hastings Manor sprawled majestically across the sun-drenched hills an hour from Houston. White stucco buildings glowed in the clear, chill air. A relic from the Mexican heritage of Texas, the old mansion was elegant as Colonel Parker walked with a limp along a pathway between cottages.

Staff members in street clothes waved cheery good-mornings at the familiar, long-legged visitor. "Have a safe trip, Colonel," they called and smiled. The tall man nodded and returned the cheer of the glorious winter's morning.

Colonel Parker stopped outside a large, single-story cottage, white and ancient, with clay arches over a red tile veranda.

"Morning, Colonel," smiled an older woman with a plastic name tag upon her chest.

"And to you, Sister."

"You are well, Colonel?"

"As any old salt can hope to be, Sister."

"I shall pray for you and that other young man tomorrow." She looked worried in the sunshine.

"I would be very grateful, Sister." The Colonel did not smile. His face was thin and tired. A slight flush burned his hollow face.

"Emily is in her room, Colonel."

"Thank you." The tall man nodded as he limped past the large woman to enter the cool, clean building made of clay baked starchy white by two centuries of Texas suns.

Inside, young adults laughed with pleasure when the Colonel in his faded blue flightsuit entered the large room. They ran or hobbled or wheeled themselves toward him.

Parker coaxed each muscle of his lean face, one neuron at a time, to open into a warm, familiar greeting. He touched many hands, many happy faces. As the Colonel greeted the grown men and women with the childlike faces, he could taste his heart.

The Colonel steered through the throng toward a long hallway. On the walls hung framed lithographs of oceans and mountains.

At a closed door marked "Emily Parker," the doorknob disappeared into his large hand.

"Daddy!" cried the young woman inside who ran to embrace the big man. She buried her clear face into his chest. The airman held her thin shoulders and he laid his chin upon her auburn hair.

"How's my Emily girl?" the Colonel smiled, pushing the

woman to arm's length.

"Awful fine! How's my daddy?"

"Awful fine. Awful fine . . . Come sit beside me."

The Colonel backed into a large chair which filled a corner of the small but airy room filled with a girl's peculiar softness: stuffed animals, thick books full of pictures with bright colors, and a flowered bedspread upon a single bed.

The woman in her late twenties sat cross-legged at his feet, resting her lovely face upon his left leg above his knee. She held his hard, left hand to her face in both of her small hands. For a long time, they sat in silence. The low morning sun shone orange upon her hair, which was askew upon her forehead.

"I'm sorry I have not come for four days, Emily girl."

"That's okay," she smiled with a child's face. "You have to be a colonel. I know."

He squeezed her face gently with the hand cradling its softness.

"Emily, I have to go flying tomorrow with Mr. Enright. I've told you about him. Remember?"

The woman pursed her eyebrows in thought.

"Very far?" She became serious.

"Yes, Emily. But only for two days."

The woman opened the fingers on one hand and she counted off two with her other hand.

"Yes. You are very good." He smiled.

"I am very good," she giggled.

"Emily, while I am away, Dr. Casey will visit you. Is that okay?"

"Sure. I like her lots. She reads to me and we take walks. She knows all about animals and sailboats . . . Do you like her, Daddy?"

"Yes."

"Well, does she like you?"

"I think so."

"Then can she be my mom, and take care of you and

me?"

The big man turned his face from the child-woman in his hands.

"I don't know, Emily," he said toward the dazzling daylight beyond the single window.

"That's okay," Emily smiled.

For many minutes, he stroked her hair. Her gray eyes closed.

"Tell me about it again, Daddy. About the black sky even when the sun shines. Please?" Emily adjusted her face upon his lap. She cuddled his firm hand to her smooth cheek.

William McKinley Parker closed his heavy eyes. The morning sun was warm and crimson behind his eyelids. He listened to Emily's gentle breath, warm upon his left hand. With his right fist, he rubbed the throbbing heat above his right knee.

"Just as on the Earth," he began, "in space, there is a daytime sky and there is a nighttime sky. Only, both skies are black way up where there is no wind blowing and no bird singing.

"When the sun is shining, the sky is still black. But it is a dull black. And even though the sky is black, there are no stars in it. From way up there, the sun shining upon the blue Earth is more than daylight. The Earth glows like a shining blue jewel. The clouds which closely touch the seas and the mountains are the Earth's warm breath. The warm Earth with her blue water and green land and red deserts reflects the daylight sun back into the black sky. This warm and breathing dayglow washes out all but the brightest stars, all but maybe Sirius in the North and Canopus in the South. Up there in the daytime, only these two stars and Venus and Jupiter shine against the black sky.

"But at night when the sun is gone, the sky is more than black. It is blacker and starrier than the sky over a meadow far from the city. The space sky without the sun is a shiny black, a wet blackness. It is like the midnight sky seen by looking down into a glass smooth lake with a midnight sky above it.

"And the stars at night: More than can be counted, more than could be named, more than one star for every person alive in the world, more than one star for every person who ever did live in the world. The stars are forever. The same white stars and red ones and blue ones that Moses looked at and that Jesus looked at.

"At night, the Earth way down below is not perfectly dark. It never is. The living Earth at night always glows with the faint lights of cities, and of towns with their white churches and an old courthouse at their centers.

"The nighttime stars never twinkle up there.

"At the edge of the world, the stars which do not twinkle move down toward the west. Only when they touch the thin, chill breath of the glowing dark Earth do they twinkle. But only for a minute. At the hazy corners of the Earth, the stars become misty and dim, like a light under water. And then they go out when they fall swiftly, silently, over the edge. At the place far, far below a starship, where the stars go out, there it is nighttime. Nighttime for all of the people, the farmers, the factory workers, the children, everyone.

"Just like down here, the sun comes up in the East, but very fast.

"At morning, from a spaceship sailing round and round, morning and night come eighteen times every day, once every forty-five minutes.

"First the Earth's hazy, black edges in the east become red. A ribbon of red is no thicker than your little finger held out as far as you can. And the red ribbon after a minute gets redder and redder until it becomes orange. And with the orange, the sun peeps up over the edge of the world, a burning white globe no bigger than a quarter held out at the end of your arm. But it is too hot and too white bright to look at. The new sun is a white fire in the black sky which burns away the shadows on the Earth below.

"From a whirling spaceship that goes all the way around our little world every ninety minutes, the sun moves upward and across the sky so fast that you can see it moving, rising and setting.

"When the white sun climbs all the way up and over and then starts down toward the western edge, it stops at the edge of the world for the blink of an eye, maybe two.

"The setting sun stops right at the edge, barely touching the far corner of the world. But instead of going white and full over the edge, the sun first becomes flat. Imagine holding a half-dollar so you can see it all round in your fingers held way out. Now, very slowly turn it over on its side until it is flat, just a straight line. The sun does this before it falls over the world's western corner to where it is evening far below. The flat sun makes the Earth's far corner burn orange and red. And all of the little white church steeples are red and all of the old courthouses, and the trees and the blue mountains, too.

"With a final burst of white and red, the flat sun is gone, gone over the edge to where it is daytime somewhere very far away . . .

"When a body so high and so far away has seen the sun go flat up there, and has seen the black sky go all moist in its starry fullness, he is not the same ever again . . . Never."

For many minutes the bright eyes peculiar to airmen blinked as they watched the brilliant daylight swirl in through the window. He could feel upon his left hand the warm, wet breath of his life which nuzzled his fingers.

The woman did not stir, not even when a distant lunch bell chimed in the hallway and the walls rang with the clamor of those who would be forever children. William McKinley Parker wondered if Emily slept at his feet.

"Daddy?"

"Emily."

"Will Mister Enright take care of you up there?"

The tall flier thought and he blinked hard until he could find his throat.

"I believe that he will."

6

December 17th

"Finally, ladies and gentlemen, we now want to end this pre-flight press conference. Our crew, Colonel Parker and Lt. Commander Enright, are probably a little tired after flying here from Houston an hour ago. We will break for lunch after which the crew will go over to Pad 39-A to observe the fueling of the Shuttle Endeavor. At this time, we have loaded Endeavor's cryogenic liquid oxygen and liquid hydrogen tanks in the orbiter. These super-cold fuels power the onboard electrical system and the cabin's air systems. The liquid oxygen and liquid hydrogen for the main engines will be loaded into the external tank later tonight. Although it may look rushed, our count-down is essentially quite routine as we rely on the auto-matic Launch Process Sequencer.

"The Shuttle Transportation System was designed from the beginning for rapid turn-around. On this, the In-telsat-6 rescue mission, we are doing nothing with this system which is more than it was designed to do. "Every-thing we have to do on the Intelsat rendezvous has been done on Shuttle 11's Solar Max repair, the Palapa-Westar retrieval on Fourteen, and the LDEF recovery on Thirty-two in January '90.

"We remind you that the terminal countdown begins at 3 o'clock tomorrow morning, aiming for lift-off of Endeavor at 10 a.m., Eastern Time. We will rendezvous with the Intelsat-6 satellite during Endeavor's first orbit. We have already fired Intelsat-6's onboard rocket to lower its orbit to the 130 nautical mile height where Endeavor can get to it. Our Soviet colleagues will launch tonight at midnight, our time.

"Our crew will get to sleep by 8:00 tonight due to their early wake-up call. We will entertain one final question for either crewman . . . ?"

"Lieutenant Commander Enright: Today, December 17th, is the anniversary of the Wright Brothers' first flight of a powered aircraft. Your mission tomorrow to refurbish a failed satellite is some kind of monument to Kitty Hawk. As the junior member of this crew making your first flight into space, how do you want to be remembered for this special flight?"

"Well, that's quite a question. I have given a lot of thought to the mission." Jacob Enright cast a sideways glance at Parker's twinkling eyes. He weighed his words to make them truly worthy of The Icemen. "When people look back on this space rescue assignment, I want them to think of me and say . . ." No one breathed as the intense, young airman framed his thoughts for posterity. "I want people to think of me and say, 'Who was that masked man? We didn't even have a chance to thank him.' " Jack Enright's thin face was stone-cold serious.

No one moved. Enright dared not look at the NASA brass surrounding him with wide eyes. But he did turn to face Colonel Parker at his elbow.

When William McKinley Parker nodded his genuine pleasure, his smiling partner felt knighted. At long last, Jacob Enright knew that he had arrived. He was one of The Icemen.

* * *

"You put Neil Armstrong's 'one small step' to shame, Number One!" the tall pilot laughed with his arm around Enright's shoulders. "Or should I say 'Tonto?' "

" 'Number One' still sounds just fine to me, Skipper," Enright smiled. The chicken-wire elevator bounced to a stop 180 feet above the concrete base of launch pad 39-A. The pair in blue flightsuits stepped into the White Room wrapped tightly around the nose section of the erect Shuttle Endeavor.

Only the side of the vertical starship could be seen in the White Room's sterile, surgical atmosphere. The side hatch through which they would crawl tomorrow was open wide. Thick covers protected the one-foot wide, round window in the center of the thick, crew-access hatch. One story higher in the 20-story-high tower, engineers in airtight helmeted safety suits serviced the Reaction Control System's sixteen jet thrusters in Endeavor's black tiled nose. As soon as Parker and Enright leave the White Room, the two RCS tanks in Endeavor's nose will be topped with 930 pounds of monomethl-hydrazine fuel in one tank and 1488 pounds of nitrogentetroxide oxidizer in the other tank. The two small helium tanks in the nose RCS pod which pressurize the two propellant tanks were already full of gas.

"A work of art, Number One," the pilot in command said as he touched the ship's heat-absorbing, pure glass tiles around the open side hatch. The glass brick felt like a styrofoam coffee cup. After other flights into space by Endeavor, the coded fabrication numbers etched into each brick of silica remained clearly readable.

Beyond the White Room's walls, technicians were installing the many explosive charges which power the inflight separation mechanism on the two Solid Rocket Boosters. Each SRB, 149 feet long and 12 feet thick, each packed with one million pounds of rubbery, high explosive fuel, would do their work tomorrow for 122 seconds before being cast off into the sea. Strapped to Endeavor's belly, also unseen beyond the gantry wall, the empty external tank, 155 feet long and 28 feet wide, with 36,000 inches of welds, was being serviced. The ET would be filled during the pre-dawn darkness with 1,337,358 pounds of liquid oxygen oxidizer and 224,458 pounds of liquid hydrogen fuel, each super-cold at nearly 250 degrees Fahrenheit below zero.

"Always awesome, Will."

The taller pilot nodded.

"When you boys are done with your fifty-cent tour, after you've kicked the tires, we can taxi up to the pumps to fill 'em up." The closeout chief smiled warmly at his crew. One hundred feet below, technicians prepared to fill each of the maneuvering rocket engine pods on either side of Endeavor's tail with 9,000 pounds of fuel and 14,866 pounds of oxidizer for each of the two Orbital Maneuvering System engines. These OMS motors, one in each tail cone, each generating three tons of rocket thrust, would push Shuttle into orbit after the three Space Shuttle Main Engines, SSME's, have burned up their fuel in the external tank after 8½ minutes of powered flight. Each rear pod also must be topped with another 2,418 pounds of fuel and oxidizer to drive each OMS pod's 14 reaction control system jets used to maintain Shuttle's attitude in space.

"Sure, Chief. Fill 'er up."

"Will do, Colonel. My boys have been hanging by their feet for 48 hours inside there, refitting the payload bay for you. She'll be achin' to fly come mornin'. The PAM is already on board."

"For sure, Chief," Enright smiled. "Right and tight."

"In the bank, Jack," the chief waved as he crawled into the ship's open, round hatch.

"So what do you think, Skipper?" Enright inquired as the pad elevator creaked toward the ground. The refurbished Pad 39-A had been used for the manned Apollo moon flights.

"She'll rise to it. We're goin' to do it, Jack," the Colonel drawled with cheery resolve.

"Right and tight, Skipper."

In the Kennedy Space Center van which carried the new prime crew to the Cape's three-mile runway built for shuttle landings, the two fliers were joined by the Launch Vehicle Test Conductor.

"I half thought we couldn't pull this one off, you know."

"And now, Rob?"

"We're going to do it," Robert Meckler said with resolution. "Four days of rewriting the text book, and we're really going to do it. Even I'm amazed. What do you boys call her, the Glass Lady? Your bird is some lady. We gutted her innards in two days and ran a full plugs-out, dry countdown yesterday. All she did was purr along without a whimper."

"All you got to do is talk sweetly to her iron heart, buddy," the Colonel said warmly. Sitting by the window, his tired face was revived with red life by the brilliant and warm Florida sunshine.

"What about you two? You both look tired. You've got a real workload up there tomorrow—and with the Russians right beside you breathing down your necks."

"Oh, we're up for it," Enright bubbled. "It's just the night before the big game. Team is bound to look antsy. We're ready. Ready and then some. Aye, Skipper?"

"You betcha, Number One." The tall man soaking in the afternoon sunshine meant it. The clear sky, the clean salty air, the pad crew doing double-duty, the firing room tension before going Up There again, all were cathartic for Will Parker. In the humid air full of Go, the command pilot felt reborn, ready to be about doing a pilot's business. The gray-eyed colonel with the sun in his weathered face was the young airman framed on his living-room wall. He could feel the hairs on the back of his furrowed neck. "Right and tight, Jack."

"LACE won't be any picnic, Will. Hear about last night?"

"What about, Rob?" the Colonel asked the white sun.

"Picked off one of our earth resources, imaging satellites about two o'clock this morning," the engineer recited grimly.

The two pilots beside him said nothing. The purple sky was too full of Can-Do for talk.

"Everything out and dirty," Colonel Parker called from the left seat of the Cape's Gulfstream jet. The sleek corporate aircraft is the shuttle approach and landing trainer. Heavily modified for generating shuttlelike landings, the Gulfstream had a shuttle instrument panel in front of the command pilot's left seat. Wing flaps and slats provided so much drag that the jet comes in for landing with her nose 20 degrees below the horizon, the aerobatic approach angle of the returning shuttle. The approach glide path is seven times steeper than for an unmodified jet.

With wheels down and locked, with everything but the crew's laundry hanging down from the wings, and with her two jets generating 91 percent *reverse* thrust, the Gulfstream's descent was unnervingly steep and rapid.

"Looks good, Aircraft Commander."

"Roger, Flight," the Colonel drawled as he manipulated the Shuttle control stick between his knees. "CSS real crisp."

"Copy positive control stick steering."

"MLS centered, Flight."

"Copy you tracking inbound, front course, on the microwave landing system. Cross wind off your left, Will. Altimeter 30 point 01; wind 240 at 07."

"Rog, Flight. A perfect winter's day."

With Jack Enright watching the earth rise quickly from his jump seat between and behind the shoulders of Parker and their NASA instructor pilot, the command pilot slightly dropped his left wingtip into the wind to compensate for the wind blowing him to the right of the approaching runway's centerline. In his final descent, to simulate the handling of a 100-ton and engineless shuttle, the jet trainer plummeted 1,000 feet every three seconds.

"Little bit 'o slip is holdin' right on, Flight."

"Roger, NASA 356. Go out of 2,000."

"Okay . . . Preflare out of 1750, Flight."

The 30-ton jet leveled off as her nose came up toward the hazy Florida horizon. In her empty passenger cabin, two large Sperry 1819-B and Rolm 1666 computers drove the airplane to feel exactly like the deadstick shuttle in the pilot's hands.

"Two degrees up bubble at 900 feet."

"Looking good, Gulfstream."

To compensate for the wind blowing from his left, Colonel Parker first eased the left main wheel onto the concrete. Rolling down the runway on one wheel, the pilot kept the white centerline fixed beneath his seat.

With a squeal, the right landing gear kissed the ground with the nose wheel following three seconds later. Pilots would call it a "greaser."

"Do that with Endeavor, Will," the ground radioed.

"You got it, buddy," the tall airman laughed.

"Gulfstream NASA 356 cleared for take-off. Maintain runway heading. No delay on the active."

Before he had used up 8,000 feet of concrete, the pilot's large right hand eased twin throttles forward. Without stopping his rollout, the AC pointed the glistening jet into the clear blue sky.

"And we have wings!" the Colonel called happily. Will Parker was home.

"The Russians went up ninety minutes ago, ten minutes before midnight, Washington time. Our people are in

101

contact with Soviet controllers at the Kalinin Control Center near Moscow. To our surprise, they went from Baikonur Cosmodrome in Kazakhstan, on the Aral Sea."

"But, Admiral, how can they possibly shoot a rendezvous with LACE and Shuttle from there . . ."

"That was our first impression, Colonel. The Baikonur site sets them up for their usual Soyuz-T orbital inclination of around 51 degrees. LACE, as everyone here knows, is at a more equatorial inclination of 38 degrees. The power and maneuvering impulse required for a thirteen degree orbital plane change is huge—roughly 5,760 feet per second delta-V. It is beyond our capability to execute an orbital plane change of a side-step of 780 nautical miles. Soyuz alone could never do it . . ."

"How do they plan to do it?"

"They have done it, Colonel. They shot a monster burn during their first crossing of the Equator."

"Energia? My God," the tired Colonel argued.

"That would be our best guess from what we know. The only way they could have done such a massive orbital plane change to get close to LACE would be launching Soyuz atop Energia. They must have kept Soyuz attached to the booster and relit it for the maneuver. There is simply no way Soyuz could have done it alone. Must have left off the strap-on boosters and just flown with the Energia core vehicle. Its first manned launch until they fly their Shuttle Buran manned."

Energia stands 197 feet high and is the world's largest rocket. The size of America's long-gone Saturn-V moon rocket, Energia was designed to launch the Soviet space shuttles. Energia's 5.4 million pounds of thrust can put 110 tons into Earth orbit or send 32 tons to the Moon or 28 tons off to Mars or Venus. Like most Russian boosters, including the normal Soyuz rocket, Energia is modular with strap-on, liquid-fueled booster rockets for heavier payloads. Its first test flight occurred in May of 1987 and its second flight in November of 1988 launched the Russian shuttle Buran on its unmanned, maiden voyage.

"So, Admiral. They really can get to LACE?"

"With bells on, Colonel."

"Have Parker and Enright been briefed on the Soyuz launch?"

"No, Joe. They went to bed two hours ago at the Cape."

"Cleanne? Hope I didn't wake you."

"Real fine, both of us. Just tucked Jack in for the third time. It's real comfortable up here. Can see Shuttle from here under her arc lights . . . Breathtaking! Like chains of white light holding her down. She is aching to fly, and the light holds her tail in the sand. A sight to remember!"

"Oh, he'll be awake again in an hour. Like trying to put the children to bed the night before the fair."

"Better, thanks. The pain isn't so bad now. More like numbness on the inside of my calf, from my knee to my ankle. But swelling's down. Been shootin' up real reg'lar, as ordered. Those damn penicillin cartridges really bite."

"Okay. Saw Emily before we flew down here. Seems more like last week. You'll check in on her? Thanks . . . We had a really good day today. They've started the chilldown of the external tank already. They'll top it off about four o'clock this morning."

"C.C.?"

"I want you to listen real careful. Don't want you to say anything when I'm done. 'Kay? . . . Jack and I are going to do this thing. I really think so now. The Intelsat-6 repair is goin' to come off like clockwork. And we'll have Brother Ivan up there to hand us the screwdriver. But . . . Cleanne. You remember meeting my old flight instructor from home? Well, he has this place out East. By the sea . . . If we don't make it, if we bend our metal and

103

they can get to us, I want my ashes laid upon the gray water up there. Upon the morning tide as it goes out. Please. I don't want my friends to think of me when they stand beside a hole in the ground, all cold and dark. I want my friends to think of me only when they feel the salt wind of the sea washing cool and clean over their faces. I want my flight instructor to take me there, and to let me go . . . He knows the way."

"Don't, Cleanne. You promised."

The tall flier sitting in the dark at the side of his bed laid the phone down gently. Jacob Enright on the far side of the little room did not stir.

Parker picked up the telephone again. He laid his long fingers upon the lighted buttons. But after a long sigh, he returned the receiver to its plastic cradle. The tiny lights went out.

For many minutes he sat in the darkness. He rubbed the heat from his sore leg.

In the stillness, he reached again for the telephone. His fingers moved slowly. Then he waited.

"Hello. It's me, Willie . . . Willie Parker."

"I know. Sorry. I know it's late."

"What can I tell you about hearing your voice again? Your sleepy voice . . . My God, how long has it been?"

"That long?"

"I have to hurry. Please. Tell me of your children. How old are they now?"

"You've had a third?"

"Tell me: Do they have your green eyes?"

"Oh, that's good. So very, very good."

"I have to ask you. I have to know: After all these years, do you think . . . Do you think of me? Ever?"

The big man blinked hard.

"Thank you. I remember you . . . I remember you. Good night."

The large hand laid the telephone down without a sound. He reached behind to open the curtains above his bed in the crew quarters.

Laying upon his back with his hands clasped behind his head, William McKinley Parker lay by the open window. A distant white light touched the deep lines carved into his pilot's face.

7

December 18

"Seems we've made our mark in the world, Number One," Will Parker laughed through his open faceplate. Jacob Enright at his side clapped his thickly gloved hands together.

As the pilots walked in pressure suits down the hallway of the crew quarters, the hall was lined with two dozen female technicians, engineers, and secretaries. The women were pleasingly flattered by tight red, white and blue T-shirts enscribed "GET IT UP—GET IT DONE—GET IT DOWN."

"We're a hit, Skipper!" Enright laughed, saluting the melonosity along the corridor.

"Let's play this town again, Jack," the Colonel replied through his white helmet's open visor.

The chief suit technician led the two joyful airmen into a small conference room. Inside, they left the launch morning bustle outside the closed door.

The pilots stood slightly stooped by the awkward weight of their pressure suits. They faced two suit technicians and one dower-faced Colonel. Shuttle crews had not worn pressure suits for launch since Shuttle Four in July 1982. The destruction of Challenger changed all that confidence in the shirt-sleeves, "operational" shuttle. Beginning with Shuttle 26 when flights resumed, all crews now wear the heavy blue pressure suits for the launch and return to Earth. Parker and Enright wore the bulkier suits worn during Shuttle's first flights in 1981 and 1982. If LACE punctured Endeavor's glass-covered haul, these pilots would have some protection against suffocation in the lethal vacuum of space. Parker and Enright wore the U.S. Navy orange pressure suits worn by the first four shuttle crews when the Shuttle Columbia had been fitted with emergency ejection seats. These were not the white, massive, extravehicular activity suits used for spacewalks. The EVA suits were already stored inside Endeavor.

"Will. Jack," the lead suit man smiled.

"Colonel," Enright greeted.

"I have new faceplate visors for you both," the Colonel said as he carefully removed two flat bundles from his briefcase.

The two pilots glanced sideways at each other.

"Oh?"

"They're new but thoroughly tested, Will. Made by Hughes Radar Systems Group for the Navy. They're designed to reflect laser light. The visors should protect your eyes in the vicinity of LACE on-orbit. We'll replace your sunshade visors with these. We've already put one on Jack's EVA suit in the ship."

The new helmet visors were phosphate glass coated with special dye for absorbing laser beams before they can penetrate a pilot's eyes. Until the dye loses its effectiveness after three weeks' exposure to air, the visors would be 18 times stronger than normal sunglasses for eye protection.

Before the pilots could respond, the man in blue was fiddling with the neckring of Colonel Parker's helmet. In an instant, the officer had lifted Parker's white helmet from his head. Another technician helped Enright doff his helmet. An Air Force man pulled two, nickel-size circular patches from his pocket.

"Gonna blindfold us?" Parker asked with a grin.

"Not quite. These patches are soaked with a new drug for motion sickness. All past shuttle crews have experienced Day One motion sickness when they started moving around the cabin too soon after launch. These patches are made by Ciba and are laced with Transderm-V Scopalamine. Your skin will absorb the medication for at least two days from the patch. You should be able to get out of the seats fairly quickly. Here."

The officer unwrapped one of the patches and laid its adhesive side to the back of Parker's ear. The suit technician took the second patch and stuck it behind Enright's ear.

Next, the DOD man and his colleagues in white coveralls began working on the two white helmets. They worked to disconnect the helmets' normal sun visors attached above the clear faceplate atop each helmet. The sun visors on each helmet were removed and anti-laser visors protected within a blue cloth wrap were snapped into place on each helmet.

"There you go," the Colonel from the Department of Defense smiled as he took a step backward to admire his work. "Just what everyone is wearing these days."

"Or should be," Enright grinned. Only his partner shared his chuckle.

"We thank you," Parker said as he eased his head into the helmet. Each pilot twist-locked his helmet to his suit's neckring.

"Do good work, boys," the Defense Department man said firmly.

"The best, Colonel," the pilot in command replied with words full of Can-Do.

Returning to the crowded hallway, the new prime crew pressed toward the brilliant sunshine at the hall's double doors. With a turn to the group in the hallway and a wave from each flier, the two airmen climbed the steps into the transfer van for the ride to the base of Pad 39-A. Only Enright noticed Colonel Parker grimace as he lifted his right leg to the steps.

Parker and Enright were silent in the van as it rode the causeway from the crew quarters. Their faces were happy in the warm sunshine bursting through the van's tinted windows. The milk-truck van was full of Go. As they drove toward their ship, Colonel Parker thought about his dawn, pre-flight medical examination. Silently, he smiled into the morning sunshine.

"You know you can't fly with that leg, Will." The physician from the Aeromedical Certification Branch looked angry. "How the hell could you keep that leg to yourself for a month without telling us?"

"I know, Mike, I'm sorry. But I knew you would pull my ticket."

"Consider it pulled, Will." Michael Gottwalt looked sadly at his old friend in the examination room of the Cape's crew quarters at daybreak. "You simply cannot go with that leg. I'll inform the Flight Director."

"Mike, you owe me. Just one. Damn, we've known each other since Genesis. In 20 years, you've seen places on me my wife never saw. I'm asking you for one final mission. Two days up there won't kill me. I've been hopped up on antibiotics for the last week. Swelling is down. And I can live with the pain . . . Please."

Dr. Gottwalt stuffed his hands into the pockets of his white coat, well rumpled and coffee stained. He looked intently at his patient and his friend.

"We just about go back, you and me, to wooden wings and iron men, Will." Michael Gottwalt smiled. "We came onboard together with Gemini in '62. We grew up together here . . . Tell me about the fever, Will."

"None for two days, maybe three."

"You're a tough old cowboy, Will Parker." The physician with the good face smiled at his friend. "You always did aim high."

"Perhaps." The tall flier hopped down from the examination table. He pulled on his fishnet woolies worn under the heavy orange pressure suit. "Well, Mike?"

"I suppose they'll jerk both our tickets . . . I'll sign you off . . . But I tell you this: You damn well better come home in one piece, you and Jack." The physician did not smile.

"Haven't bent one yet, Mike. I have a supply of medication already stashed in Endeavor. We'll be fine."

The physician only nodded. He watched his old friend open the heavy door to the hallway. With one foot outside the narrow examination room, Will Parker looked back over his shoulder.

"It's funny, Mike, looking back. I guess I have aimed high. But you know, in all the years, I can still remember the highest ambition of them all: All I ever really wanted from this life was to walk Kathy Turner home from high school. Even once." The tall command pilot smiled with a gentle, faraway look in his gray pilot's eyes.

"Did you ever do it, Willie?"

"Nope . . . Never got the nerve to ask. Be seeing you, Mike."

The physician stood quietly and for a long time he studied the closed door through which his friend had passed with the slightest limp.

Along the beach, people waited in the humid morning sun to celebrate Endeavor's launch.

When the little caravan of NASA vehicles stopped at Pad 39-A, Parker and Enright emerged into the sun. Each pilot carried a portable air conditioner plumbed into his cumbersome suit.

With 90 minutes to go, the two airmen stood quietly beneath the purple and cloudless sky. The fliers were in no hurry to end the peculiar brotherhood of their hectic training. They stood side by side and they looked upward to the white starship, their bird, their Glass Lady. From her tail, plumes of white liquid hydrogen vapors, 250 degrees Fahrenheit below zero, swirled in the sunshine at the black nozzles of Endeavor's three Rocketdyne main engines.

Colonel Parker looked hard at his main engines. Before Challenger's first flight on Shuttle Six in April 1983, the ship had been grounded for four months when all three of her main engines were found to have cracked fuel lines. Five years before that setback, a report by the National Research Council Assembly of Engineers had warned NASA about shuttle engine weaknesses. But their warning had gotten lost in the shuffle of federal paper. And in June 1984, the STS-12 countdown for Shuttle Discovery's maiden flight had ticked down flawlessly to minus six seconds from lift-off when her main engines ignited for 2½ seconds and then burped stone-cold dead—four seconds before the solid rocket boosters were to fire. Shuttle Discovery went nowhere. Had Discovery's main engines failed on Shuttle's twelfth mission only five seconds later—after the solids had ignited—Discovery and her ship's complement of five men and one beautiful dark-eyed woman very likely would have become one great grease spot.

Standing at Endeavor's tail, Parker and Enright took the communion of their ship, whose black tiled nose pointed skyward. Standing quietly, with their pilots' eyes and hearts they kicked the tires.

A ship of the line poised to rip open the sky is a living thing, a breathing thing, a pregnant thing. Like a roundly pregnant mare searching for her private meadow in which to foal, a fueled starship fumes potently, anxious to leave

111

behind in her white-hot wake the probing fingers of her keepers.

There is an urgent noise about a spacebound vessel at the ready. Pipes whine and clank like a pot-bellied stove as super-cold propellants settle and flow in tankage and plumbing. Vents and purge ducts belch frothy steam and icy vapors as the coldest cold sends plumes percolating into the humid air.

To describe Shuttle as weights and measures is to describe birth as only ganglia, neurons, and synapses. The shuttle, like the human organism which birthed her, is greater than the sum of her parts.

Two solid rocket boosters, the SRB's, strapped to Shuttle's external tank, stand silently. Each of these 149-foot-long silos holds 1 million pounds of explosive. Once lighted, each SRB spits 2,700,000 pounds of thrust for 122 seconds from the largest solid rocket motor ever built, the largest moveable rocket nozzle ever fired, at nozzle temperatures in flight of 5,600 degrees Fahrenheit. Words pale. The energy of the two SRB's is known only by their vibration, which starts in the heels of an observer standing five miles away and travels up his body until the teeth ache.

The great external tank sweats frost from its 66,809 pounds of metal pores, where 140,000 gallons of super-cold liquid oxygen sit atop 380,000 gallons of super-cold liquid hydrogen. Inside, some 1,561,816 pounds of propellant churn with the same energy with which God fashioned heaven's first molecule of water.

The scent of Go excreted from Shuttle's glands, like deer musk in November, rides the still, humid air. Go is in the wind, it clamors in the ears, it penetrates the steel launch tower, and it reverberates into the earth and into the hearts of Shuttle's stewards. The Go engulfs a body until it sweats out moistly on the palms.

With their eyes and their legs, Parker and Enright felt

112

the presence of their ship enter their bodies, surge through their plasma, and tingle their nerve endings.

"Let's do it, Number One," Colonel Parker, Astronaut, said firmly through his open faceplate as he led Enright into the gantry elevator.

"Right behind you, Skipper."

Atop the launch tower in the White Room, 147 feet above the sand, Parker and Enright were met at the catwalk leading to Endeavor by the former prime crew of the mission.

The two suited fliers stood awkwardly before the dispossessed crew who had emerged from Endeavor's flightdeck.

"We're ahead of the timeline on the flightdeck, switch position protocol," the bumped command pilot smiled lamely.

"Thanks, buddy," Colonel Parker nodded.

"This is from us 'cause you and Jack need it." The displaced mission commander reached behind toward his own crewmate. The pilot handed Parker and Enright a new, yard-long, toilet plunger with a bright bow festooning its wooden handle.

Colonel Parker held the offering as he and Jack Enright studied it with mock gravity and dignity.

"I know just the place for this," Parker said with sober resolve through his open faceplate.

"Knew you would, Will," the pilot in coveralls replied, unable to restrain his broad grin.

The momentary tension evaporated with a four-way laugh among brothers in the humid morning air.

Enright on his hands and knees crouched through Endeavor's open side hatch. Parker followed him along the narrow Crew Access Arm which reached from the White Room to Endeavor's glass side. The former crew followed and stopped outside the open hatch.

As Parker bent low to squeeze on all fours through the hatch, his colleague, whose seat had been pirated, reached to Parker to retrieve his non-flight-rated gift, the be-ribboned Plumbers' Friend.

Colonel Parker did not hand it back through the hatch. Instead, he pushed the plunger inside to Enright.

"This is mine," Will Parker smiled warmly.

The serious pilot outside on the catwalk nodded as he peered into the hatch where Endeavor's mid-deck basement cabin was crowded with her two pilots and two closeout technicians anxious to see the crew take their seats upstairs on the flightdeck.

With the two astronauts and their technicians standing in the mid-deck with Endeavor sitting vertical on Pad 39, the four men actually stood on the mid-deck's back wall: the "floor" of the upright shuttle. Secured to the wall of the mid-deck, which will be the ceiling when Endeavor is right-side up, was a 280-pound canister pointed toward the open hatchway. The canister contained the shuttle escape pole dreamed up after the Challenger explosion. Should any shuttle experience serious trouble and if the pilots could wrestle the ship into a normal glide toward the ground, the pole would allow the desperate crew to bail out. At least that is what the advertisement says.

As the crippled shuttle coasted toward the ground, the crew would use the pole on the mid-deck ceiling to abandon ship. First, the pilot would have to get his glider down to 40,000 feet. There, the crew would depressurize the cabin which is now allowed since everyone since Challenger wears the heavy pressurized suits. At 31,000 feet, 70 explosive bolts in the mid-deck hatch would be blown and the hatch jettisoned. The spring-loaded escape pole would then be released to extend nine feet outside the hatch-way. When Shuttle reached 20,000 feet, the commander would put her on automatic pilot with instructions to the black boxes to keep Shuttle level at 200 knots flying speed. Each crew member would then hook on to the pole like a telephone man's safety belt along a telephone pole. They would then jump at 15-second intervals. By scooting down the pole, the pole would steer the evacuating fliers away from the massive wing, missing the wing by 18 feet. The astronauts would then parachute to Earth, arriving about one mile apart.

Parker and Enright grinned at the dubious escape pole installed more for the press after Challenger than for the Shuttle. Some say the astronaut corps calls the nine-foot escape pole "Big Johnson."

"Bring her back alive, Will," the displaced pilot called into the open hatch.

"You betcha," the Colonel smiled as he grasped the man's forearm firmly for a long, quiet moment across the hatch sill.

Within 10 minutes the crew was strapped into their seats in Endeavor's nose. Mission Commander Parker lay on his back in the left seat with Enright next to him in the right seat. The closeout engineers carefully recited their checklists as they connected air hoses, restraint harnesses, communications cables and aeromedical sensor cables. Before the technicians left the flightdeck with a firm pat upon each flier's shoulder, the pilots were busy confirming switch positions from Ascent Book checklists. The cabin was warm in the brilliant sunshine pouring in through the six forward windows and the two overhead windows in the ceiling of the aft crew station five feet behind the pilots' seats.

"Endeavor: Comm check."

"With you five-by, Flight," the pilot in command answered.

"Copy, Endeavor. At T minus 70 minutes, we have hatch closed and sealed. We'll run the cabin pressure integrity tests by hardwire from here."

"Okay, Flight. Thanks," the Mission Commander drawled slowly.

Shuttle is pressurized with a normal air mixture of one

115

part oxygen to four parts nitrogen. This mixture is maintained at sea level pressure of 14.7 pounds per square inch on the ground and in space. Cabin air is supplied by the ship's Atmosphere Revitalization System, the ARS.

Shuttle's environmental control system is a maze of plumbing, pipes, heat exchangers, and space radiators, all manufactured by Hamilton Standard.

The ARS is the lungs and the sweat glands of Shuttle. Like the hands which created her, Shuttle keeps her iron bowels cool by sweating water from her aluminum pores. Heat from Shuttle's vital organs and black boxes, and from the bodies and the breath of her crew, is absorbed by two water loops. Water circulates through each loop, picking up heat along the way. That heat is transferred to twin freon coolant loops. The freon refrigeration fluid carries the heat to tubular radiators attached to the inside of each of the two, 60-foot long doors of the payload bay. In space, when the doors are opened, the radiators in the shade of Shuttle's wings radiate the freon's heat into the cold of space, like a perspiring athlete spreading his wet arms wide to a cool breeze.

During launch and the fiery re-entry from orbit, heat is sweated out as steam by two flash evaporator units inside Shuttle's tail section. During the last minutes of re-entry and landing, two ammonia boilers sweat out the heat load from the freon loops.

"Endeavor: At T-51 minutes, we'll be aligning the IMU's at this time. And you can crank up the water boilers now."

"Rogo, Flight," Parker replied.

In Shuttle's nose, three Inertial Measurement Units, IMU's, were being fine-tuned to feel the ship's way into space. Each IMU is a complex array of motion and acceleration sensors which "feel" Shuttle's position and where she is going. Just as a child's spinning top wobbles as it winds down, so the IMU's wobble from precession and

116

must be realigned to proper positions. The IMU alignment is a computer-generated order which tells the IMU gyroscopes where Shuttle sits at Pad 39 and where she is bound: A tiny needle's eye in space 800 miles to the east. "Where am I now?" the sealed black boxes in Endeavor's avionics bay demand. And the computers reply: "You stand with your tail feathers in the sand at Cape Canaveral, Florida, 28 degrees, 36½ minutes north latitude by 80 degrees, 36¼ minutes west longitude. When you leave the ground, you must twist your tail, which now points southeast, until it points northeast so you will cross the Equator half a world away at an angle of thirty-eight degrees." And a world away, ninety minutes from lift-off, the IMU's must find their whirling target, LACE: Hitting a bullet with a bullet, each traveling at a velocity over the Earth of 25,460 feet per second.

"Okay, Flight," Parker confirmed. "GPC and BFC have accepted the IMU alignment."

Each of the three IMU's was aligned to a slightly different reference point so each unit could be cross-checked against the other two.

"We see it, Endeavor. Main computers One through Four have the state vectors. Your GPC Mode Five is stand-by. Execute Item 25. Then proceed with ARS routine."

"Roger, Flight. Challenge and readback, Number One."

Enright, flat on his back, consulted his thick Procedures Manual open in his lap. He recited the checklist.

"Cabin Atmosphere breakers closed, Main Bus B, Overhead Panel Fifteen, Row D: Cabin delta pressure and delta temp, nitrogen supply Number Two, oxygen-nitrogen controller Two, oxygen crossover valve Two, nitrogen regulator inlet Number Two, and, cabin relief A. All closed, Skipper."

"Confirmed, Jack."

"Atmosphere pressure control breakers, Main Bus A,

Overhead Panel Fourteen, Row D: Nitrogen supply Number One, oxygen-nitrogen controller One, oxygen crossover Number One, nitrogen regulator inlet One, cabin vent and isolated cabin vent, all breakers closed, Skipper."

"Okay, Number One. Confirm emergency oxygen and cabin relief valve Bravo breakers closed, Overhead Panel Sixteen, Main Bus Charlie."

"Confirmed, Skipper."

"And on my side, Jack: Flash evaporator feedline heater running alpha supply Number One and bravo supply Number Two, Panel Left-Two. On my Panel Left-One: Humidity separator alpha on, bravo off; cabin fans A and B on; water pump Loop One to GPC with Loop Two off; Loop One bypass to auto; water Loop Two to auto; and, flash evaporator controllers, Primary A and B to GPC." The command pilot followed the checklist in his lap.

"Confirmed, Skipper."

"Okay, Flight. ARS is powered up and full of Go."

"Roger, left seat. We're Go at T-30 minutes. We are now updating the SRB guidance for winds aloft."

The ground computers spoke to the black boxes within each of the two solid rocket boosters strapped to the sides of the external tank. Final steering commands told the SRB computers how best to cleave the high altitude, winds aloft encountered during the first 60 seconds of launch. So vicious were these winds during the launch of STS-5 in November 1982 that Mission Control nearly canceled the Veterans Day launch.

"Endeavor: We'll be pressurizing the OMS and RCS pods in a moment."

"We'll watch it, Flight," Enright called into the twin microphones inside his helmet.

In Endeavor's tail, gaseous nitrogen pressure increased in each of the two orbital maneuvering system pods.

One OMS pod, 22 feet long and 12 feet wide, protrudes from each side of Endeavor's vertical tail fin. The rocket engine, ignition system in each pod fires the single, large rocket at the back end of each OMS pod. Each of the two OMS engines drives Shuttle with 6,000 pounds of thrust after the three Shuttle main engines have finished their work during the launch. Gaseous nitrogen opens the pneumatic activation valves which send fuel and oxidizer to the thrust chambers of each OMS engine. Without 360 pounds of gas pressure in the ignition valves, the OMS engines cannot fire to give Shuttle its final push into orbit, to provide power for large maneuvers in space, and to slow Shuttle so she falls from orbit at journey's end.

"We see 2,500 pounds in the main GN_2 tanks, Flight," Enright called from the copilot's right seat.

"We confirm, Jack."

In the three reaction control system units, one in Endeavor's nose and one in each OMS pod, gaseous helium pressure increased in the two helium tanks carried within each RCS module. The helium pressurized each RCS unit's fuel tank topped with 930 pounds of monomethylhydrazine and one oxidizer tank filled with 1,488 pounds of nitrogen tetroxide.

"We have gas pressure in RCS forward and aft left and right, and in OMS left and OMS right, Flight."

"Roger, Endeavor. At T-22 minutes, your primary avionics are on line."

Throughout Endeavor, black boxes warmed to life. Navigation beacons prepared to steer Shuttle back to an emergency landing at Cape Canaveral's concrete, three-mile-long runway if a launch malfunction during the first 265 seconds of powered flight dictated a high-speed turnaround for a perilous Return To Launch Site abort, or RTLS. In the mission simulator, Parker and Enright had bent their metal and had gotten their feet wet more than once.

"Copy, Flight. Configured for RTLS steering . . . Let's hope not," the AC sighed.

"Endeavor: At T-20 minutes, configure GPC to ascent OPS-1."

"This is the AC. We're running computer Operations Sequence One outbound. Cabin vents comin' closed now."

"Roger, Aircraft Commander."

Endeavor's four primary General Purpose Computers concentrated on the OPS-1 launch program for steering the powered launch phase. In the fifth back-up GPC, a separate ascent program ticked away, ready to fly Shuttle aloft if computers One through Four should fail. Trajectory graphs blinked upon the front instrument panel's three television screens on the flightdeck.

"Endeavor: You're Go at T-19 minutes and counting. Configure computer Error Logic to RESET position, and configure GPC to MM-101 and OPS-9."

"Copy, Flight," the AC called. "Major Mode 101 is running." With Operations Sequence Nine, the on-board Shuttle computers were taking Endeavor's pulse as her own black boxes monitored the computerized, pre-launch checkout. Shuttle is America's first manned spacecraft designed to automatically launch itself with its own, on-board computers.

"Endeavor: You're Go at fifteen minutes and counting. We're now conducting the nitrogen purge of the SRB skirts. Configure OMS and RCS crossfeed valves for launch."

"Okay, Flight," Parker replied lazily. The command pilot was relaxed and ready to fly. With his legs elevated above his reclining body, the throbbing in his right leg ceased and he was comfortable.

"Okay, Number One. Panel Overhead Seven: Left, aft RCS pod, crossfeed lines One and Two configured GPC talk-back closed, and crossfeed lines Three, Four, and Five, configured GPC talk-back closed. Right, aft RCS crossover lines One and Two to GPC talk-back closed. Lines right Three, Four, and Five, to GPC talk-back closed. And, master RCS crossfeed locked off."

"Okay, Flight. Our RCS crossfeed is ready to go."

"Copy that, right seat. We're listening."

"Ready for OMS, Skipper."

"With you, Jack. Panel Overhead Eight: Left OMS crossfeed Loop A and Loop B to GPC talk-back closed. Left OMS engine, lever-locked armed, Panel Center Three. OMS right: Crossfeed Loops A and B to GPC talk-back closed. Right engine lever-locked armed, Panel Center Three . . . OMS primed and ready, Flight."

"We copy, Endeavor. At ten minutes and counting, we see cabin vents are sealed."

"Roger, Flight. Vents closed."

Fifteen hundred miles to the north, an exhausted Admiral nodded his sagging face. A Colonel at his side spoke into a red telephone in a glass room where no sun ever shines. The haggard Colonel laid the phone down gently and he wiped his hands upon his thighs as if the instrument were unclean.

"Endeavor: You are Go at T-9 minutes. Start your event timers at this time. The Ground Launch Sequencer now has the con."

"We see it here, Flight."

The countdown was now fully automatic. The master launch computer could either let the count go to zero or could stop the countdown at any moment.

"And, Endeavor, we are now feeding you the new PTI-7 routine for re-entry."

The two pilots flat on their backs glanced sideways at each other. Five on-board computers swallowed the Programmed Test Input Number Seven to be engaged during re-entry.

"Alright, Flight," the Colonel shrugged high atop Pad 39-A. "We see lox tank in the ET topping off now."

Inside the silo-size external tank bolted to Endeavor's belly, the liquid oxygen, or LOX, tank had been continu-

121

ously venting out frigid vapors into the clear morning air. As the super-cold gas vaporized, the ET's supply of 140,000 gallons of liquid oxygen was steadily replenished through lines running from the launch tower. Now the replenishing and venting of oxygen stopped so the sealed tank could build up flight pressure.

Twenty-seven hundred miles away, over California, the killer satellite LACE crossed the American coastline at its ground speed of 300 miles per minute. The silent, slowly tumbling bird whirled eastward toward Florida. LACE would soar directly over Cape Canaveral at the instant Shuttle rode the fire into the sky.

"At seven minutes and counting, Endeavor, the access arm is in motion. You're on your own, guys."

Outside, the catwalk from Pad 39-A jerked away from Endeavor's closed side hatch. The long arm would require one minute to swing back to its locked position next to the tall gantry well clear of Shuttle.

As the crew access arm left Shuttle's glass side, Endeavor at last stood naked and white in the dazzling daylight. Portions of her round nose and the forward parts of the two OMS pods showed slightly dark scorch marks from her past re-entries from orbit.

Along Cocoa Beach and the Kennedy Space Center's Merritt Island sands a thousand eyes squinted into the sun as hearts beat faster in time to the two hearts strapped within Endeavor's aluminum soul.

"Endeavor: At six and counting, confirm faceplate visors closed and locked. Configure APU for startup."

"Roger, Flight," the command pilot called as he and Enright pulled their clear faceplates down over their faces. As each pilot locked his faceplate into position on his helmet, the pilots' nostrils inhaled the spaceman's blend of bottled air laced with the smell of rubber hoses and sweat.

"Ready for APU checklist, Will," Enright called through the flightdeck intercom. His voice was anxious.

When the three auxiliary power units were lit to supply pressurized hydraulic fluid to Shuttle's wings and tail and to the steering motors which swing the three space shuttle main engines, the ship would be committed to fly within five minutes. Failure to go would mean shutting down the APU's and returning to the T-20 minute point in the countdown to give the APU's time to cool. Enright was tense. Like a pilot's first solo flight from a long-ago grass field, like a body's first wet kiss, to practice for a lifetime cannot dilute the gut's tension at the event. Enright raised his right gloved hand to the instrument panel above his right elbow. He had done so a thousand times before, in the mission simulator and in his sleep. But this was the first time he did it with his hands sweating.

As his captain recited the checklist for the APU's, Enright's right hand waited for each command before his fingers threw the silver toggle switches.

"Okay, Number One, this one's a keeper. On Panel Right-Two: APU Numbers One, Two, and Three, controller power lever-locked on."

Enright flipped three switches.

"Fuel tank valves One, Two, and Three lever-locked open."

"And, APU's One, Two and Three barber-poled as ready, Skipper."

"Okay, Jack. Speed select to normal One, Two and Three."

"Speed normal, all three APU's, Will."

"All hydraulic main pump pressures to normal."

"Normal, normal and normal, Skipper."

"And, automatic shutdown to enable, Jack."

"Enable."

"Fuel pump valve coolant, Loops A and B, to auto."

"Auto, auto and auto." Enright returned his clammy hand to his lap.

"Endeavor: At five minutes and counting, your flight recorders are running. You're cleared to crank up the APU's."

"Rogo, Flight," Enright called. "Number One, lever-locked start! Number Two, start! Number Three, lever-locked start! And, we have APU ignition times three. Hydraulic pressure is up and in the green. Three water spray boilers also on-line and green all values. Hydraulic fluid at 220 degrees with APU lube oil at 270 degrees."

"We see it, right seat. Looks fine. And configure Caution and Warning to ascent mode."

In Endeavor's tail section, the three auxiliary power units hummed and their small engines pumped warm hydraulic fluid through Endeavor's veins. The wings and tall tail were now alive for flying like any airplane with elevons on the wings and the rudder fin on the tail. These control surfaces would fly the Return To Launch Site abort if necessary during the first four-and-a-half minutes of launch. Hydraulic fluid also surged at flight pressures within the three Space Shuttle Main Engines, SSME's, to power the engines' gimbal motors which will pivot the SSME nozzles to steer the rising ship.

As the countdown passed the five-minute mark, the automatic launch sequencer armed the ship's explosive, self-destruction mechanism which would annihilate the solid boosters and would fatally rupture the external tank's seams if the vessel flew off course.

"Range safety is hot, Endeavor. At four and a half, configure Main Propulsion Systems and ATVC."

"Rogo, Flight. On your side, Jack, Panel Right-Two. Main engines: Helium isolation Loop A to GPC; helium Loop B to GPC; helium interconnect to GPC; liquid oxygen prevalves to lever-locked GPC; and, liquid hydrogen prevalves lever-locked GPC. Engine Interface Units: Main center, main left, and main right to on. Center engine, power source select to bus AC-1; left main engine, power source to AC-2; and, right main, power source to AC-3."

"With you all the way, Skipper. She's hot and ready to fly!" Enright's hand swept the instrument panel at his right side.

"Okay, Jack. Your side: Helium crossover to GPC. On Panel Right-Four: Liquid oxygen feedline relief, lever-locked GPC; liquid hydrogen feedline relief, lever-locked GPC; liquid oxygen manifold pressure, lever-locked GPC; and, liquid hydrogen manifold pressure, lever-locked GPC."

"She's primed now, Skip!" Enright shouted into his glass faceplate. The hairs on the back of his neck tingled.

"And my side, Jack, Panel Center-Three: Main Propulsion System, limit shutdown to auto, and, vibration shutdown to auto . . . Okay, Flight: The Glass Lady is ready to roll."

"Copy, AC. At T-4 minutes, your SSME helium purge is complete."

"Mains purged, copy."

"T-3 minutes and 45 seconds, Endeavor. We see your aero surfaces cycling."

The elevons, combination elevator-ailerons at the back edges of Shuttle's wings, flexed automatically in preparation for flight.

"And we see ASA cycling," Enright confirmed as he scanned the rectangular indicator of control surface positions above the center, green television screen. The indicator's pointers moved left and right as the elevons, vertical rudder, and the body flap beneath the three main engines moved briefly.

"This is the right seat. We have TVC hydraulics lever-locked neutral, systems One, Two, and Three, on Panel Right-Four. And on Panel Overhead-17, we have ATVC Channel Two. Solid booster separation, mode select is auto on Panel Center-Three. External tank separation lever-locked auto on Panel C-3. External tank umbilical doors, latch select lever-locked auto on Panel Right-Two."

"Copy, Jack. Ascent Thrust Vector Control is set. At T-three-and-a-half minutes, you are on internal power."

Shuttle was now self-sufficient, cut off from ground electricity, and running on her own electrical fuel cells.

In her three fuel cells, liquid oxygen and liquid hydrogen join to form electricity, heat, and water beneath the floor of the closed payload bay. The fuel cells generate seven pounds of waste water each hour for the drinking water tanks and for the coolant systems.

The automatic launch sequencer swung the engine nozzles from side to side on the three, main engines to ready them to steer Endeavor by their shifting positions.

"At 3 minutes, Endeavor, SSME gimbal test complete."

"We watched it, Flight."

"Roger, AC. At 2 minutes and 55 seconds, ET LOX tank is sealed and coming up to flight pressure."

In the massive external tank, glinting brown without paint to save weight in the sunshine, the liquid oxygen stopped venting vapors as the tank sealed for launch.

"Flight: We see the LOX vent arm leaving us."

"Roger, AC, at 2 minutes 50 seconds."

The launch tower's hollow arm was attached to the nose of the external tank for replenishing the ET's liquid oxygen as it boiled away. The fueling pipe pulled back from the ready starship.

High over Texas, a black laser gunship was streaking eastward as it rolled slowly in the airless, piercing sunshine. Following LACE, two Russians in their round Soyuz vessel soared over Nevada in pursuit 10 hours into their long day. The Soviet craft's twin arrays of solar panels, like glass and silicon wings, sucked in the fierce daylight to generate electricity.

"At 2 minutes 45 seconds, Endeavor, your fuel cell ground supply is off."

"Roger, Flight."

126

Endeavor's fuel cells now lapped at Shuttle's own four tanks of liquid oxygen and four of liquid hydrogen beneath the floor of the payload bay with its blankets of silvered, plastic mylar.

"At two minutes and fifteen seconds, SSME gimbals are set."

"We saw it, Flight."

The shuttle's three main engines swiveled into launch position to push Shuttle upward and slightly sideways at the instant of ignition. Like any winged airplane, the shuttle's flight out of the atmosphere will generate lift from her massive wings. The direction of lift, perpendicular to Shuttle's belly, would rip her backward away from the external tank if the main engines in Endeavor's tail did not thrust forward in the direction of the external tank to counter the wings' lifting forces.

"At one minute, fifty-seven seconds, the ET is flight-pressurized, Endeavor."

"Thanks, Flight. Let's light this candle!" Enright nearly shouted. He was ready and his temples pounded with the Go which surged breathlessly through his veins. Along the beach, faces were riveted on Endeavor and many lungs dared not breathe. Half a country away, a child-woman kissed a television screen, where her daddy lay on his back atop 4½ million pounds of iron and frothing explosives. Above the clear blue sky, LACE looked down upon Alabama.

"At one minute, sound suppression system is armed. Your OPS-1 looks clean."

"Roger, Flight. Thank you."

The launch tower was ready to deluge the base of Pad 39 with 300,000 gallons of water to carry away the teeth-rattling shock wave generated by the ignited solid boosters. The two SRB's would light three seconds after Shuttle's three main engines ignite.

"T-40 seconds."

"Okay, Flight. We're ready here. SRB flight recorders are on. Payload bay vents are open."

"Copy, Jack. At minus 25 seconds, Shuttle GPC has the con. SRB hydraulics on-line and SRB gimbals activated."

Endeavor's own on-board computers, four primary and one in reserve, conducted the final seconds of the countdown. LACE watched as it crossed the gulf coast of Florida 130 nautical miles below. The Russians watched the red clay of Georgia. At the tail of each of the two solid boosters, the largest solid rocket motors ever built pivoted into launch position.

"T-18 seconds. SRB gimbals set." The Spacecraft Communicator's voice rose in pitch. A bird was ready to go.

". . . T minus 16 seconds. Pyros armed!"

Explosive charges primed to cast off the spent solid boosters and the empty external tank were alive.

". . . IMU internal at 12 seconds. God speed, old friends."

Endeavor's three inertial measurement units now steered the ship's five internal computers. "Which way?" the computers demanded over miles of wire to warm black boxes. "Up," the inertial sensors replied.

". . . 11 seconds. Water start."

The floodgates beneath Shuttle opened and flooded the pad's buried flame deflector channels.

". . . 10 . . ."

Inside the two solid boosters, the armed self-destruct sensors flipped on as the main engines' prevalves opened sending liquid oxygen and liquid hydrogen toward the ignition valves which are the last stop before the engines' combustion chambers.

". . . 9, 8, 7 . . ."

The armed, self-annihilating range-safety destruction sensors in the external tank and in the solid boosters switched on to listen for the suicide command.

Directly overhead, LACE looked down and sped on to

open water.

"...6!..."

Shuttle's center main engine exploded to life with a clean blue flame which sent boiling steam into the air above the water flooded base of Pad 39-A.

Along the beaches, no one breathed.

"...5, 4, 3..."

Main engines left and right fumed into blue hot life.

"...2, 1, Ignition!"

The twin solid rocket boosters exploded into white flames. The whole vehicle flexed a full yard in the direction of the external tank when the pad's hold-down clamps yawned open.

Endeavor had the sky.

"You have lift-off!" the ground radioed.

The Glass Lady, riding white fire, inched skyward. A blizzard of ice and frost from the freezing external tank sprayed the flightdeck's six windows. Major Mode 102 ticked through Endeavor's computers programmed to tear a fiery hole in the purple sky seven days before Christmas.

"And we have wings!" William McKinley Parker shouted from his sky.

8

A thunderclap of fire swirled from Endeavor's tail and 2,237 tons of aluminum, fuel, men, and bricks of purest glass shuddered.

One million, one hundred thousand pounds of rubbery explosive in each solid booster fired out 3 million pounds of thrust into the sand at each side of the starship as powdered aluminum and aluminum perchlorate incinerated. From Endeavor's three main engines, each generated 490,000 pounds of thrust with a clean blue flame. A ton of ice cakes and frost flakes vibrated free from the chilled external tank's sides and pummelled the forward windows of the flightdeck.

Inside the warm heart of each of Endeavor's five flight computers, 400,000 mathematical operations every second pulsed within Shuttle's wire neurons over 24 serial data buses, the spinal cord of the living starship. Inside her two magnetic tape mass memory units, 34 million data bits were being sorted, interpreted, and flown. Nineteen multiplexer-dimultiplexer black boxes acted as traffic cops—like nerve bundles in living ganglia—directing the instantaneous computer-talk. Three engine unterface units on each Shuttle main engine listened for the flight computers' steering commands. Thirteen signal conditioners converted Endeavor's pulse, pressures, temperatures, and inertial measurements into computer chatter which traveled at the speed of light along 1,200 data channels to Shuttle's two pulse code modulation master units. These PCMMU's ready the ship's vital signs for digestion by her Network Signal Processor which beeps the vitals to the ground's tracking stations by FM telemetry beacons.

"And we have wings!" an excited bass voice thick with Kentucky twang called. "102 is running!"

Riding white fire, the glass-covered starship with five iron brains and two human hearts, nudged back the clear sky.

"Tower clear!" the ground called as Endeavor's tail climbed past Pad 39-A's launch tower. Seven seconds out, the ship was 200 feet aloft making 75 miles per hour through the humid morning air.

Eight seconds into the sky, 400 feet high, Endeavor slightly dropped her black nose toward the blue-green sea.

"Roll program," the Mission Commander radioed. "And pitch program initiated."

Shuttle was slowly twisting her body atop white, rolling thunder to align herself with the proper flight heading. As the nose dipped closer to the sea and the ship rolled into a slow wing-over, the two pilots flat on their backs flew heads down toward the sea with their feet skyward.

"Roll complete," a slow voice drawled from the sky.

"Copy, Endeavor," the ground called. "Go at thirty seconds. You're 8,000 feet high making 675 feet per second."

Half a minute out, the solid rocket boosters shuddered and vibrated like a rutted country road. A distant buzzing from the high-pitched vibration filled the flightdeck cockpit.

To ease the stress on Shuttle of punching through the shock-wave wall of the sound barrier, Shuttle's three main engines automatically throttled down from 104 percent power to only 68 percent power.

"MPL at 32."

"Copy, Jack. Minimum power level at 32 seconds. You have a Go at 40 seconds."

Shuttle's nose pierced the sound barrier with a slight shudder of transonic buffet 52 seconds into the sky, 5 miles high. Outside air forces pressed the ship with 700 pounds per square foot of glass-covered skin.

"Throttles up, 100 percent, Flight. PC at 2,960 all three."

"Roger, left seat. Chamber pressures 2960 psi on the mains. Configure control surfaces neutral."

Shuttle's body flap beneath the blue flames of the main engines and her wings' elevons had been flexing automatically to ease the strain of air pressure as the ship cleaved the morning sky. Their job was done.

"Go at 1 minute fifty-three seconds, Endeavor."

"Thanks, Flight. We're right and tight in the sky!" the firm voice drawled confidently as Endeavor's nose dropped to 39 degrees below vertical 120,000 feet high at three times the speed of sound.

"Go at 2 minutes, Will. Mach 4 out of 136,000 feet. Go for SRB separation."

"Rogo, Flight. Flash evaporators on. And we see PC less than 50 at 2 plus 06."

Inside Shuttle's fuming tail, the heat dissipating flash evaporators began sweating out the heat from Endeavor's systems. The green television screens on the flightdeck told the two airmen that the thrust level in each solid booster was trailing off to lessen the shock of an abrupt burn-out when their fuel was exhausted. Sensors felt each booster's engine pressure drop to 50 pounds per square inch.

"BECO! And booster away."

"Roger, Will. Booster engine cut-off. Looks good."

"And it's much smoother now, Flight, at 2 plus 15."

"Copy, that, Jack."

Spent and dry, the two dead solid boosters shut down simultaneously. Four small rockets in the nose of each SRB and four rockets in the tail of each, burst with 22,500 pounds of thrust each for seven-tenths of a second to shove the lifeless boosters clear of Endeavor and the external tank at four and one-half times the speed of sound, 30 nautical miles high. At 2,891 knots true airspeed, the ship climbed past the separated SRB's.

The two discarded solid boosters will continue to coast

upward by their own momentum until they reach 200,000 feet high. From there, they will arc down toward the ocean. Riding parachutes manufactured in Manchester, Connecticut, by Pioneer Parachute Company, the SRB's will glide into the warm sea 140 miles east of the Cape. Landing and floating only one mile apart, the empty silos will be plucked from the sea, refitted, recharged, and reused.

"Real smooth ride at 2 plus 26. Guidance is now closed loop, Flight. Center television showing second-stage trajectory."

"Copy, Jack. You're right down the slot at two and one-half minutes out. We see Major Mode 103 now running in the GPC. Your flash evaporator is Go."

Against the purple sky, the faint blue flames of the three main engines could no longer be seen from the ground. Only a grotesquely contorted contrail from the spent SRB's marred the sky where high altitude winds tied the SRB exhaust plumes into a knot.

Between the third and fourth minutes of powered flight, Endeavor, riding heads down beneath her half-dry external tank, accelerated from 4.6 to 6.3 times the speed of sound as she climbed from 43 to 63 nautical miles high. Her nose slowly dropped toward the sea, a clearly curved blue line when viewed upside down by the two fliers behind their six windows.

"Endeavor is press to MECO at four minutes."

"Thanks, Flight. Go in the sky."

The ship now carried sufficient energy to reach her main engine cut-off goal should one main engine fail early. Endeavor screamed past 65 nautical miles in altitude, where her gray carbon-carbon composite nose cap glowed a dull red from the intense heat of high speed air friction.

"Press to ATO at 4 plus 20."

"Copy that, Flight. Pulling three G's and we're real tight up here."

"And from the ground too, Will."

Should Shuttle lose an engine now, she could still struggle upward to execute an Abort to Orbit, or ATO.

"Negative return at 04 plus 26."

"Roger, Flight. Then we'll *go forward!*"

"Do that, Jack."

Endeavor was now too high and too far out to sea to turn around to shoot an emergency landing on Cape Canaveral's runway.

For the next several seconds, the crew rode the most dangerous part of their ascent in terms of abort options. An engine failure during this brief period leaves them too far out over the Atlantic to return to the Cape and too slow to coast to an emergency landing in Europe. Main engine failure now would reduce the 1.2 billion-dollar ship to only a banner headline in the morning newspaper.

"And you're press to Rota, Endeavor."

Leaving behind them the momentary No Man's Land of their abort options, Shuttle can now make an emergency landing if she blows only one main engine. She could use two surviving engines to reach the U.S. Navy air station at Rota, Spain, on the far side of the Atlantic.

Endeavor rode her blue flames into the black, airless sky. Only blue ocean, upside down, can be seen outside the flightdeck windows. The pilots are pressed into their seats by forces which triple their body weight.

"At 06 plus 05, Endeavor is single-engine Rota."

"Copy, Flight. We're Go at six minutes five seconds."

Even with a failure in two of her three main engines, Shuttle now carried enough speed to reach an emergency landing in Rota, Spain, without getting her feet wet.

In the cockpit of white lights and three green television screens on the forward instrument panel, there is absolutely no noise, no vibration, and no feeling of movement. Only the acceleration load of 3 G's tells the inverted crew that they are in motion hanging by their lap belts.

"Single engine press to MECO at 06 plus 50, Endeavor."

"Roger, Flight. Good news!"

Shuttle could now make a fragile orbit even if she should lose two of her three main engines. Endeavor pressed onward, upside down, 68 nautical miles above the mid-Atlantic.

Far below and behind, 7 minutes and 13 seconds into the flight, the two SRB's splashed into the chill sea close to the booster recovery ship USS *Mercury*.

"Throttles down!" the Aircraft Commander called.

"Copy, AC. You're Go from here."

The flight computers automatically reduced the power on each main engine from 104 percent to 68 percent for the final sprint into space. This would reduce the structural strain of an abrupt burn-out when the SSME's completed their eight and one-half minutes of furious work.

The inertial measurement units sought out their keyhole in the velvet black sky. The primary, on-board computers found their invisible target.

"MECO at 08 plus 33!"

"We see it, Endeavor. Main engine cut-off. Energy state looks right on, Endeavor."

Instantly, the engines stopped and the fliers floated weightlessly against their seat belts. Jacob Enright immediately grabbed the glareshield on the dashboard before his face. He was seized by the pilots' somatogravic illusion of pitching forward, head-over-heels, when the forward acceleration suddenly stopped with main engine burn-out.

Riding straight and level upside down, 900 statute miles east of Pad 39-A, 70 nautical miles into the black sky, Endeavor's engines are quiet. Eight and one-half minutes aloft, the 100-ton bird with the nearly empty external tank attached to her belly coasts bottoms-up at the velocity of five miles per second. Even with her engines stilled, Endeavor still climbed upward at a rate of 220 feet per second. The two pilots were weightless in Zero-G and they could feel their faces become puffy and swollen as blood begins to pool in their cheeks. Their earth-borne circulatory systems did not know what to do with their blood when heart and veins do not have to work against gravity's pull. Tiny pools of blood collected within the hair-fine capillaries of the crew's faces. Weightlessness also increased the fluid pressure inside their eyeballs by 25 percent: an unsolved problem which could mean blindness on long flights to the planets.

In the excruciating sunlight of the black sky, where no stars shine in daytime, Endeavor glided silently, nose forward, wings level and belly up. The brown external tank was still bolted to Shuttle's underside.

"Major Mode 104 now running. Mother likes it. We're looking at digitals of 80 by 13."

"Copy, Jack. We see 104 in the computers and we concur with an orbit of 80 by 13 nautical miles. LOS momentarily at Bermuda. AOS Madrid in ten minutes. You are Go for OMS-1 burn at 10 plus 34. First sunset at 32 minutes out . . . Configure LOS Bermuda . . ."

Nine minutes from the still hot and steaming Pad 39, almost 1,000 miles behind them, Endeavor coasted out of radio range with the Bermuda Island tracking station.

Endeavor's preliminary orbit with a high point of 80 nautical miles and a low point of 13 miles was an illusion of orbital physics. Shuttle carried sufficient energy to whirl around the blue planet in this lopsided orbit for years before gravity's immutable tug cracks the delicate balance between the ship's velocity and her 100-ton mass. But in reality, the planet's gossamer envelope of air would wrench Endeavor from an orbit so low within an hour. More kinetic energy must be added to Endeavor to hoist her higher if she is to keep her aluminum toes from tripping over the atmosphere's fiery fingers. With the external tank nearly dry and the three main engines quiet and cooling, Endeavor must ignite her two powerful OMS engines tucked in her tail to raise the orbit to a survivable energy state. The OMS-1 rocket maneuver would loft Shuttle into a slightly safer, higher orbit 10½ minutes into the flight, in mid-Atlantic out of earshot of any tracking station. Another OMS firing, OMS-2, in half an hour would finish the job of inserting Endeavor into a safe orbit. But first, Shuttle must cast off the external tank which glistens with frost in the burning daylight under the ship's inverted belly. The flight computers are programmed to disconnect the ET.

"Attitude hold, Skipper," Enright called 8 minutes 50 seconds into his first ride into space.

"Mother has it, Number One," the command pilot replied. "Auto sep . . . ET away!"

Automatically, explosive charges detonated without sound in the airless blackness. The three support brackets holding the ET to Shuttle ruptured. As the brown tank drifted upward into the sky away from the belly-up Shuttle, Endeavor's reaction control system's small jets fired automatically for five seconds. The little jets pushed Endeavor downward and away from the freed external tank.

"ET free. Evasive maneuver complete. Delta-V at 4 feet per second, Jack."

The upside-down pilots could not see the ET rise away from Endeavor as Shuttle slipped downward at a rate of four feet per second. The green television screen read out confirmation of ET separation.

"Goin' to normal on the Caution and Warning, Jack."

As the ET drifted away, a valve in its frosted nose popped open automatically. Unburned fuel vapors shot from the open valve like a small rocket engine. The programmed release of gas will cause the tank to tumble end over end to assure that it will incinerate when it plows into the atmosphere over the Indian Ocean. Since Shuttle had yet to perform the OMS-1 rocket burn, the jettisoned tank's lonesome orbit is fatally low.

"Mother has our OMS-1 targets, Jack. Inertial attitude, deadbands are 3.5 degrees attitude, 0.3 degrees per second in rate, and 0.2 degrees per second in discrete rate." The command pilot scanned the left of three television screens at the center of the forward instrument panel. "TIG at 10 plus 32; BT 01 plus 27; Delta-V 165; Alpha plus 05 degrees by DAP in Vernier mode."

"Watching, Skipper."

Mother's green face told her pilots that the first burn of the orbital maneuvering system's two rockets would occur automatically if given the go-ahead at 10 minutes 32 seconds into the flight and would ignite for 1½ minutes until Endeavor had picked up another 165 feet per second forward velocity to add to her speed over the sea of 25,668 feet per second. The digital autopilot, the DAP, and Mother set Endeavor's upside-down nose five degrees above the sea's blue horizon. Shuttle coasted toward Spain with the ship flying belly-up, wings level, nose pointed toward Europe.

The Colonel pressed his PROCEED computer key on the small keyboard by his gloved right hand.

"TIG minus 5, 4, 3, 2, 1. Ignition!" the AC called out.

Eighty-five feet behind the pilots, each OMS rocket in Endeavor's tail thundered to life with each engine pounding away with three tons of thrust. As the two engines fired, the flight computers automatically began to dump overboard the unburned propellants trapped in Shuttle's internal fuel lines from the quiet main engines. First, 3,700 pounds of liquid oxygen spewed out through the cooling center main engine. When this was completed, 1,700 pounds of unused liquid hydrogen would be dumped into space through the umbilical vent on the starboard side of Endeavor's tail. Helium gas would then flood the frigid fuel lines to drive out any traces of unburned propellants to avert an explosion in Shuttle's bowels.

"Shutdown!" the AC called as Mother pulled the plug on the two OMS rockets after 87 seconds. "Looks good, Jack. Delta-V right on at 165 for an orbit of 132 by 57 nautical miles. On our way now, Buddy!"

Endeavor, well clear of the tumbling external tank, climbed toward her higher, safer orbit in pursuit of LACE. Their new orbit's low point of 57 nautical miles was still fatally low. But the OMS-2 burn in 28 minutes would fix that.

"MPS inerting routine is continuing, Skipper. Major Mode 105 now running."

"Roger, Number One. Douche 'er out, Jack."

The cleansing of the Main Propulsion System would continue for another ten minutes.

"Close your doors, Jack."

The copilot anxiously watched five lights on the cluttered instrument panels at his right side.

138

"ET umbilical doors closed and latched, Skipper."

Enright pushed five lighted pushbuttons which confirmed that two large doors had closed and sealed on the underside of the rear of Endeavor's black wings. Through these two doors in the ship's belly, the ET's 17-inch-wide pipes had passed into Shuttle's insides to feed propellants from the ET into Shuttle's three main engines, which remain permanently attached to the ship's square tail section. Failure to seal the doors, each four feet square, would spell doom during re-entry's searing heat.

"OPS-2, Major Mode 205, running in the GPC."

" 'Kay, Skipper."

"And at 15 minutes out, let's secure the APU's, Jack."

Endeavor coasted silently on her back above the middle of the cold North Atlantic. From this height, the hazy blue horizon of the sea was 957 statute miles distant from the forward cockpit's six large triple-paned windows. Creeping toward them over the far eastern horizon, the islands of the Azores emerged from the planet's fuzzy, curved edge. The upside-down crew could have seen the small islands but for the haze at the Earth's distant corner and the achingly white sun directly overhead where it was noon in mid-Atlantic.

"APU shutdown, Skipper. My side, Panel Right-Two: APU coolant pumps, Loops A and B, off. APU automatic shutdown to inhibit. Hydraulic circulation pumps One, Two, and Three, off. Ignition switches lever-locked off, off and off. Fuel tank valves lever-locked close, close and close. APU controller power One, Two, and Three, lever-locked off. Okay, Skip, three auxiliary power units secured."

With Endeavor's three main engines cooling, and with the wings' elevons and the tail's rudder not needed until re-entry and landing, the ship's three hydraulic systems were put to bed for two days.

Directly beneath Endeavor, the seven small islands of the Azores glowed blue-green in a sparkling sea.

"God! Looky there, Skipper!" Enright pressed his helmet to his side window. The tiny islands glistened in sunlight, where under Shuttle it was 2 p.m. on a sunny winter day.

Shuttle's clocks set on Houston time read 9:15 a.m.

"Endeavor, Endeavor: Houston remote, Madrid local. We have solid S-band lockup at sixteen minutes. How do you read?"

Enright started as his reverie was broken by the crackling radio in his ears. After crossing the Atlantic from one end to the other in 16 minutes without radio traffic from Earth, it was easy to forget that a legion of technicians far below were anxious to invade Endeavor's weightless privacy as the ship hurtled eastward and crossed a new time zone every four minutes.

"With you, Houston," a Kentucky voice drawled 780 miles west of the Spanish coastline, a distance to be flown in only 2½ minutes.

"Okay, Endeavor. We're getting a good solid downlink from you. We see Major Mode 202 running for rendezvous with your target. You're clear to run GPC Number One for GNC functions, GPC Two for rendezvous, and GPC Three for systems maintenance in Major Mode 801. Computers Four and Five to standby in Major Mode 106. We show your target at range 206 miles and closing. Slight out-of-plane error of point 0-0-7-5 degree. Your OMS-2 burn will therefore be a combination mid-course correction with the programmed Delta-V and a plane change. No need to induce a nodal crossing with the target vehicle. Your OMS-2 burn pad follows: TIG at 40 minutes 51 seconds; Delta velocity plus 151 point 9 and 03 feet per second plus Y; BT of 91 seconds. Backroom boys are Go for a closed loop solution for an 'M equals One' rendezvous. And we have some SM data for you when you're ready."

"Okay, Houston," the Mission Commander called. Both pilots flew headsdown over the North Atlantic toward the west coast of Morocco. They rode in their bulky orange pressure suits but without their gloves. Inside their helmets with the laser-proof visors in position, two microphone booms reached to their slightly swollen lips, puffy from only 18 minutes of weightless spaceflight.

" 'Kay, Houston. Understand Go for on-board rendezvous solution. Super. Copy OMS-2 burn at 40 minutes plus 51 seconds; burn time 91 seconds; velocity change 151 point niner feet per second with half a mile plane adjustment. What do you have for systems management?"

"Endeavor: Houston by Madrid. We want you to go to Loop Mode on the signal processor. And we recommend going to water Loop One on the ARS. Inhibit water Loop 2. We show you carrying a tad excess heat in the freon loop. Keep an eye on flash evaporators. We don't see any problem at this time in keeping the bay doors closed until your first pass Stateside. But we may have you initiate PTC over Australia."

"Understand, Flight. Water Loop One up, Two down. Let us know about the passive thermal control. We would rather not be in rotisserie mode when we shoot the TPI."

Rotisserie mode referred to having to put the ship into a very slow roll, wing over wing, to even out the shuttle's exposure to the sun's ferocious heat in airless space. This would prevent one side of the vessel from baking while the other side remains frozen in the hot side's shadow.

"Rog, AC. We concur on remaining in stable minus-Z during your terminal phase initiation. We're looking for TPI and rendezvous over the states at about ninety-nine minutes, MET."

"Mother agrees, Flight. We should be closing on the target at mission elapsed time of ninety-seven and one-half minutes."

"Thanks, Jack. So how's the ride, right seat?"

Enright turned his face from the right television screen to the three windows wrapped around his helmeted face.

"Incredible simulation, Flight! This is just breathtaking. Nineteen minutes out of KSC and I'm looking down on Rabat, Morocco! The old clock on the wall here says 9:20 in the mornin' Houston Time, and we're flying upside down over Morocco where it's 3 o'clock in the afternoon. Truly amazing! The terrain is pretty hazy. With the sun's subpoint about forty-five degrees west of us, the sun angle is too shallow for very much detail below. But there is no doubt that Morocco is very pink, red almost. It's just bizarre to sit here heads-down with Rabat out my forward window and Casablanca just over my right shoulder. Casablanca! 'Of all the gin joints in all the towns in all the world . . . What a morning, Flight! And I can see the eastern shadows off the Atlas Mountains extending into Algeria!"

"Sorry to interrupt the tour, Jack, but we're going to lose you in about two minutes over Algeria. You're about eleven minutes from first sunset. We're hoping that'll cool you off enough for the flash evaporators to carry the heat load. Next comm by IOS when you cross Kenya in fourteen minutes."

"Okay, Flight. Next AOS by Indian Ocean Ship in fourteen."

"And, Endeavor, for your burn pad, we have Day Zero de-orbit burn times for Edwards: De-orbit Rev One, BT at 00:52:18; Rev Two, burn in at 2 hours, 25 minutes, 18 seconds; Rev Three, BT at 03:59:08; Rev Four, burn at 05:33:12; Rev Five burn in at 07:06:44; and Rev Six, BT at 08:41:21. Your de-orbit burn times for landing at Kennedy, Day Zero follow: Revolution One, BT 58 minutes plus 51 seconds; Rev Two, at 02:33:17; Rev Three at 04:07:49; Rev Four, BT at 05:42:17; Revolution Five at 07:14:49. Then KSC de-orbit Rev 15 at ignition time of 21 hours, 39 minutes 04 seconds; and Rev 16, BT at 23:11:58."

"We got it, Flight. You getting our PM downlink in doppler tracking?"

"Affirmative, AC. Solid lock. Starting to breakup slightly as you go over the edge at twenty-two minutes."

"Roger, Houston. Catch you by IOS. Endeavor is right and tight up here."

"Copy, AC. Configure LOS Madrid at . . ."

"And we're on our own again, Number One."

The copilot nodded as he watched the mountainous border between Morocco and Algeria pass overhead beneath his upside-down office.

"MPS inerting and purge is complete, Will." Enright studied his green television which told him that Shuttle's three main engines were safed and clean of explosive fuel vapors.

Two and a half minutes from Morocco, Endeavor coasted silently over the Fazzan Oasis in Libya. A glance out the thick window revealed a lush speck of green the size of a fingernail far below, which tracked its 25-second transit across the window. Shuttle sped at 17,500 miles per hour over the arid pink wastes of central Africa, over Libya and Chad, bound for the Sudan only 150 seconds southeast of the Libyan oasis. Chad's 11,000-foot-high Tibesti Massif pointed snowy peaks toward Endeavor's white body.

Both pilots startled when a Caution and Warning siren wailed in their earphones. At the center top of the main forward instrument panel, a yellow caution light glowed at one of the 40 annunciator lamps. In front of each pilot on the glareshield overhanging the instrument panel, a Master Alarm light flashed red. Parker pushed his Master Alarm pushbutton light, which extinguished the alert tone but not the RGA yellow caution light on the annunciator's second row of eight lights.

"Rate gyro assembly!" Enright called.

"Run it down, Jack."

Enright scanned the system failure checklists which he called up on the right television screen. He summoned the proper checklist by tapping a coded sequence of numbers into his computer keyboard unit on the right side of the center console by his left thigh. The wide console separated his seat from Parker's.

"Looks like RGA Number Three, Skipper. Damn."

"Take 'er out, Number One."

"Rate gyro assembly Number Three, Overhead Panel-16, off. RGA secured."

The yellow caution light went out.

"One down, three to go," the AC said dryly as Endeavor skimmed over the Sudan's deserts 100 miles west of Khartoum, only 30 minutes away from Pad 39-A, now more than 8,000 miles behind Endeavor.

Shuttle's four Rate Gyroscope Assemblies, now reduced

143

to three, work together with the ship's inertial measurement units to feel Endeavor's position and attitude in space. One rate gyro disabled was a serious but not critical failure. Two lost would be dangerous; three down would dictate an emergency landing at the first opportunity. And four out of four lost would be all she wrote as a doomed crew struggled to bring home a 200,000-pound glider by the most basic of scarf and goggles flying by the old turn-coordinator and air-speed indicator.

"Take a minute outside, Jack," the AC said calmly to break the tension. "Reckon we can spare the gas to crank her around for a minute."

The Colonel powered up the Rotational Hand Controller between his knees and set the ship's Reaction Control Systems to Pulse Mode.

Nudging the control stick toward his right knee, the command pilot fired a minuscule, pre-programmed burst from the RCS jets in the right OMS pod in Shuttle's tail. Two RCS jets popped loudly like cannon and shot a 30-foot flame past the ship's tail section.

Endeavor's upside-down nose rotated smoothly clockwise as she would be viewed from the ground. She made a half circle flat on her back. As the nose swung toward 180 degrees after 60 seconds, another pulse from the two RCS thrusters fired with 870 pounds of thrust from each jet. Endeavor's slow rotation stopped as the starship came about flying tail-first. With her nose looking back across Africa along the track already covered, Endeavor's cockpit faced west toward the rapidly setting sun. Thirty-two minutes out, Shuttle rode backward over the 13,000 foot peak of Mount Amba Farit in Ethiopia 75 miles northeast of the capital Addis Ababa.

From the upside-down flightdeck, the crew had a 200-degree panoramic view through the six forward windows of their first sunset in space.

"Take a look, Jack."

"God, Skipper," Enright breathed with his face and open mouth close to the wide windshield.

Below, the arid mountains of Africa's east coast were already in darkness. Far to the west, the sun sat blindingly white just at the hazy blue horizon above the Sudanese desert. Within half a minute, the white globe sank into the horizon's ribbon of pale atmosphere. The sun flattened as if its upper and lower limbs were squeezing out the middle of the solar disk. The Earth's far western corner exploded into gold and orange. And after a final dazzling burst: darkness, the moist and star-filled blackness of nighttime in heaven.

"Remember that to tell your grandchildren, Jacob."

The copilot of Endeavor could not speak.

"Endeavor, Endeavor. Greetings from the Seychelles Islands. We have solid downlink. How you read by IOS?"

"Ah, with you Indian Ocean. Jack and I are fine at thirty-four minutes. Blew an RGA a while back."

"Copy, Endeavor, we'll look at it. You're over Mogadiscio in Somali. You cross the Equator in two minutes. We see you flying in minus-Z, tail first. Be with you six minutes this pass. We show you thirty-five miles behind the target and 40 below it."

"Roger, IOS."

"Your OMS-2 will be as planned at MET 00:40:51. At OMS shutdown, you'll be twenty-three miles behind target and closing at an R-dot of 178 feet per second. We'll lose you about one minute into the burn . . . Your temps are coming down nicely in the dark. You may inhibit Loop One and go to Loop Two on the freon for the night pass. LOS this station at forty-two minutes out, with AOS Australia at fifty-one minutes. As soon as you null the residuals after the OMS burn, we want you to roll upright to align the platforms with star trackers and COAS."

"Okay, Flight. Yawing about now."

The computers on command from the AC brought Shuttle's tail around until the ship was flying upside down and nose first.

"Got you in Y-POP now, heads down in OMS-2 attitude, Endeavor. We're watching your downlink. OI playback looks a bit noisy."

"Understand. Operational instrumentation data dump noisy," Enright replied. "Want us to switch quads?"

"Negative, Jack. Leave the antennas as they are. We may have you change signal processors later for the phase-modulated downlink. Backroom thinks you're just breaking up a bit over the mountains. Should clear up when you're over water momentarily."

" 'Kay." Enright brought the second OMS firing numbers up on the right and center televisions called CRT's for cathode ray tubes. The center screen showed the OMS-2 checklists. "CRT's on-line with OPS-2 and Major Mode 205 running."

"Copy, Jack. Operational Sequence Two. We'll leave you alone with your burn prep. Configure data dump to high bit rate, please."

"You're looking at it, Flight."

"Data real clean now, Jack. Thanks."

As Endeavor coasted southeast over the nighttime shoreline of East Africa, the two fliers readied each of the two OMS pods in Shuttle's tail for the upcoming rocket burn. The firing of the two engines for a minute and a half would change Shuttle's lopsided orbit, 132 by 57 nautical miles, to a near circular orbit of 130 nautical miles all around, synchronized with LACE ahead.

The crewmen directed their attention in the cabin's floodlights to Overhead Panel-Eight located on the flightdeck ceiling above Enright's left shoulder. The AC read the preburn checklist printed on the center CRT as Enright touched each switch.

"Helium pressure, Loop A, left and right, talk-back open; Loop B, left and right, to GPC; propellant tank isolation, Loop A, left and right, talk-back open; Loop B, left and right, to GPC; left and right crossfeeds, Loops A and B, to GPC; engine valves, left and right, on, at Panels Overhead-14 and -16. And, engine arm, left and right, Panel Center-Three, lever-locked arm."

"OMS ready, Will."

"Okay, Flight. We're cranked up and ready for OMS-2 in

two minutes on my mark . . . MARK! Two minutes. We're in inertial attitude mode with attitude deadband of 3 point 5 degrees, rate deadband of three-tenths degree per second, and discrete rate at two-tenths degree per second. DAP in automatic."

"Copy, Endeavor. We'll have a work-around for the RGA failure this afternoon. Expect sunrise over Samoa at seventy-four minutes MET. We remind you to keep a close watch on coolant loops when you hit daylight. We see you flying flight control channel Two."

"Roger, Indian Ocean. Running FC channel Two. I have the con with CSS fly-by-wire in attitude hold in Roll-Yaw. Mother is steering the alpha angle and OMS TVC."

"Copy, Will, as to control stick steering and GPC thrust vector control. You're fifteen seconds to OMS ignition, 1 minute 12 seconds to loss of signal . . . 5, 4, 3, 2, 1 . . ."

"Auto ignition, Flight! Fire in the hole, left and right. Good solid thump from the OMS." The AC carefully studied the "eight ball," the round attitude indicator above his knees in the center of the forward instrument panel at his station. He watched three orange course-deviation needles to make certain that Mother held her ground without wobbling during the OMS firing.

Although the slight acceleration of the OMS-1 burn 20 minutes earlier was barely perceptible after the 3-G load of launch, both pilots could feel their backs solidly contact their flight seats during this OMS burn. Their bodies were already oversensitive to gravity after a quarter hour of weightlessness.

"Go at thirty seconds into the burn, Flight." Enright called. "Feels like we're going flat out to Australia!"

"Roger, Endeavor. Pressures and chamber temps are all green. LOS in thirty seconds. Hang on, Jack."

Far behind them, the two OMS engines, each 45 inches wide at their nozzles, burned furiously. Each engine's nozzle swiveled slightly through seven degrees of freedom to steer the ship as the OMS rockets pushed Shuttle higher.

"Good burn at forty-five seconds, Flight. Mixture ratio at

1 point 65 left, and 1 point 63 right. Chamber pressure 124 left and 127 right. Fuel flow is 4 point 13 pounds per foot of Delta-V."

"Copy, Endeavor. Losing you now. Configure LOS, see you over . . ."

"And it's on to kangaroo land," Enright said as the Indian Ocean tracking ship went over the Earth's far western edge as Shuttle sped eastward at 5 miles per second.

"360 psi in the GN_2 accumulators. And GN_2 tanks at 2,400 psi. Sixty feet per second to go," the AC called. In the cozy flightdeck, there was no sound nor vibration from the OMS engines. Only the cabin fans broke the stillness.

"Shutdown!" both fliers called as Mother automatically stopped each OMS engine when she felt that the proper speed had been reached. "Auto trim," Parker called as Endeavor's RCS jets in her nose and tail popped loudly to clean up the OMS burn's residual guidance errors. Outside their windows, the loud 870-pound jets in Endeavor's nose RCS unit lit the night with 30-foot plumes of yellow flame.

"Good burn. Residuals nulled," Enright said over the intercom. "Major Mode 106 now running. Going to 10 degrees attitude deadband. DAP logic select to Mode A, and RCS to normal."

Immediately, the command pilot punched the CSS/PITCH and the CSS/ROLL-YAW, lit pushbuttons on the panel glareshield in front of his face. With full manual control of his ship, the AC moved the control stick between his knees. As he commanded the RCS thrusters to roll Shuttle rightside up, the computers chose the best thruster combination to accomplish the wing-over. Neither pilot knew which of the thirty-eight primary RCS thrusters were selected for firing by Mother. All that mattered was Endeavor's slow three-degrees-per-second roll which stopped after one minute with Shuttle coasting right-side up.

"Now we're flyin' right!" Enright smiled as he flew in space heads-up for the first time. He had utterly no sense of speed or of up and down.

Outside, the windows were full of black sky with the

nighttime Earth's black horizon obscuring half of the starlit sky. Due to the cabin's harsh lighting, only the few brightest stars were visible outside.

"OMS safing," the copilot said as he threw the switches to put the two OMS rockets to bed. As he worked the instrument panels above his head, the AC began the checklist for deploying the two small star-trackers tucked inside Shuttle's nose. Parker looked up at Overhead Panel-Six directly above his helmeted face.

"Star tracker door controls, System One, to open. Power: Y-axis on; Z-axis on. And we got stars aplenty, Jack. Crank two in and see which way is up."

In Endeavor's broad, tiled nose beneath the windshield, two small doors opened without sound. The doors were just under the left window at the Colonel's left shoulder. Inside the open ports, two telescopic sights, each weighing barely fifteen pounds, scanned the night sky over the dark, southern Indian Ocean 2,000 miles south of the Equator. Each of the shoebox-size trackers searched the black sky for stars chosen by Mother. The Y-axis tracker eyeballed a point of white light to the left of the rightside-up flightdeck. A single star directly overhead was locked in the five-element glass eye of the upward-scanning Z-axis tracker. Automatically, Mother read the angular separation between the two stars and compared that angle to the astronomical ephemeris stored in Endeavor's mass memory units. Mother reduced the stellar sights to a reading of true local-vertical. Each spherical, attitude indicator in front of each pilot rolled slightly as the ship's gyroscopes were fine-tuned by the computer conversions taking place at the speed of light among the computers and the two star-trackers built in Boulder, Colorado. The ship's data processors directed the computer talk.

"P-52 completed, Jack. We have our REFSMAT."

"Okay. Crankin' reference stable member matrix into IMU Number Two. So, Skipper, which way is up?"

Will Parker raised a thumbs-up above the center console between their seats. He smiled and deep creases cracked around his eyes. "That way, Jack."

"Pretty technical stuff," Enright laughed 100 nautical miles above the black sea 48 minutes from home and 1,500 nautical miles west of Australia.

The crew's momentary respite from work ended abruptly when a square light labeled SM ALERT lighted with a warning tone beneath the left CRT screen above the center console.

"Systems management!" the AC called as he pushed the alert-light pushbutton to kill the audio alarm. Above the center television, on the 40-light annunciator unit, the rectangular warning light labeled FUEL CELL REAC glowed ominously red.

"Running it down," Enright said as he tapped out a sequence of numbers on his small keyboard on the center console by his left thigh. A fuel cell malfunction checklist blinked onto the right CRT screen.

Endeavor carries three independent electrical systems, each fed by the super-cold liquid oxygen and liquid hydrogen tanks nestled beneath the floor of the still-closed, payload bay. Each fuel cell contains 64 stacks, or chambers, where preheated liquid oxygen and hydrogen meet to form electricity and waste water. The water overflow is filtered and decontaminated with iodine for crew drinking. Each fuel cell generates direct-current electricity for one of three DC circuits: Main A, Main B, and Main C. Each DC bus is routed to three inverters which convert the direct current power into alternating current used by Shuttle's systems. Fuel cell Number One feeds DC circuit Main A, which is converted to AC line AC-1. Fuel Cell Two feeds DC Main B and AC-2, while fuel cell Three powers DC Main C and AC-3.

"Looks like Main B, Skipper. Running it down. . ."

The electricity output meters and all electrical distribution controls are the domain of the copilot in the right seat. Enright followed the video checklist as he managed the bulky fuel cell by the switches and meters located in front of his face and next to his right arm on Panel Right-One on the cabin wall.

Enright first checked the temperatures in fuel cell Two's twin stacks of electricity-generating cells.

"A hundred ninety degrees and two hundred ten degrees. Stack temps okay."

The copilot examined the three round meters above his right knee on the forward panel. He turned a large, round knob until it pointed to Cell Two.

"Two kilowatts at 31 point 5 volts DC; 60 amps. Looks okay, Will."

Then Enright asked the green CRT about cell Two's water output.

"Damn. There it is, Skipper. Six pounds per hour water production. That's two pounds too high. Got room? She's barfin' water."

"Let's see," the Colonel drawled. "Plenty of room in potable water Tank B. Tune her down if you can and we can manage the damn thing later . . . I hope."

Shuttle carries five potable water tanks for collecting water generated by the three fuel cells.

"Crankin' her down, Skip. Okay. Lights out."

The red Caution and Warning light flickered and winked out.

"We'll let Mother in systems management mode keep an eye on that baby, Number One. Meanwhile, let's go on down the routine."

As the crew interrogated the computers, Mother put her finger on the fuel cell Two vitals, like any mother laying her face against a feverish brow. Enright followed his bloated baby out loud.

"Power controller assembly, check . . . load controller assembly, check . . . mid-power controller, check . . . forward load controller, check . . . aft load controller, check. Looks stable, Skipper. Three essential bus lines—1BC, 2CA, and 3AB—all look healthy. Strange glitch in there some'eres."

"Fine, Jack. At least we won't have to light the candles. Don't want to repeat STS-2!"

Both fliers had thought of Shuttle Two in November

1981, which was brought home early after only half a mission when a whole fuel cell threw up and drowned in its own water.

The headphones crackled in the south sea night.

"Endeavor, Endeavor. Yarradee has downlink at fifty-one minutes. Be with you for six. We're looking at a fuel-cell saturation C-and-W."

"Mornin', Australia. Rogo on the caution and warning," the command pilot called to Australia's western coastline, which Shuttle would not cross this pass as she coasted heads-up past and under Australia's southern shore. "Number Two fuel cell burped up but Jack got a blue bag on her in time. Keepin' an eye on it. We've aligned the platforms and everything is right and tight. How do we look by PM downlink?"

"Real fine, Will. Telemetry is coming in crisp and clean. You are in plane and closing on your target now fifteen miles ahead of you and ten above you. R and R-dot are right on. You have a Go for closed loop rendezvous."

"Roger, buddy. Understand we can run with on-board range and range-rate digitals. How's Brother Ivan?"

"Ah, we show Soyuz now in daylight just south of Norfolk Island, about 170 degrees east by 30 south. They're radio silent within two miles of the target. They should be braking very soon. No comm with them at all so far."

"Copy, Yarradee. We're ready for Terminal Phase Initiate up here. Jack's called up our MCC-3 digitals which you should be lookin' at now."

"We see it, Will. Mid-course correction three looks fine, well within your propellant budget. After you lose contact with Orrora, we want you to roll minus-Z well before sunrise which will be at seventy-six minutes, MET."

"Got it, Flight."

"Endeavor: Let's see PCMMU Number Two for a while, please. Your downlink data still looks a bit noisy."

"You got it, Flight."

Endeavor's Pulse Code Modulation Master Unit controls the flow of on-board operational instrumentation data from

Shuttle's systems by way of 13 signal conditioners. The signal conditioners convert Shuttle's vital signs to computer talk which one of two PCMMU black boxes routes to a Frequency Division Multiplexer for telemetry broadcasting to the ground through the Network Signal Processor.

"And your TM data now looks real clean. Much better, Endeavor."

"Fine, Flight," the pilot in command radioed.

"Yeah, Will. We were afraid you had a quad glitch."

Endeavor speaks to the ground over seven, S-band antennae: Four "quad" antennae surround the rear cockpit bulkhead; there is one "hemispheric" antenna in the cockpit ceiling and another on the underside of Shuttle's nose behind the nose wheel well; and, the seventh antenna is located on Endeavor's back just ahead of the closed payload bay doors. Mother chooses which antenna is the best for a direct shot to the ground stations. The crew can also pick the best antenna combination should the computers get lazy. In all, Shuttle carries 19 different antennae built by Watkins-Johnson in San Jose, California.

"Before you lose us by Yarradee, Endeavor, we'd like you to run a COAS shot as soon as you can. Let us know how it flies before you lose Orrora. Your S-band is breaking up at . . ."

"So long, Yarradee . . . Okay, Jack. I'll take a shot here with the COAS. We'll have Orrora contact in two minutes."

" 'Kay, Skipper." Enright was busy fiddling with his electrical controls and meters.

As Endeavor skirted Australia's southern coastline, Parker reached overhead to instrument Panel Overhead-One, where he turned on the COAS power. To the left of a four-inch-square panel containing 25 white computer status lights above the AC's forehead, the eight-inch-long tubular sight of the space sextant, the Crew Optical Alignment Sight, came to life.

"COAS alive," the AC said to himself. "Manual CSS."

Parker peered into a small mirror at the base of the COAS periscope. Several stars were visible on a circular

153

grid on the mirror. Using control stick steering, the AC commanded the tail thrusters to slowly move Endeavor's nose until a single bright star moved to the center of the recticle grid on the palm-size mirror.

"Mark!" the AC called as a star momentarily centered on the mirror. As he spoke, he punched the attitude reference pushbutton to the left of his round attitude indicator at the upper left corner of the forward instrument panel. Mother instantly logged the angle between Shuttle and the star which the pilot had first identified for the computers. He twisted the control stick between his thighs until another bright star crossed the COAS sight as Endeavor's nose moved sideways among the stars of the southern hemisphere.

"And, mark!" the pilot said as he pushed the ATT REF button again. With two identified stars in the hopper, Mother compared their angles and the information reduced with the attitude information coming through the two-star-trackers working automatically outside.

"And Mother says the COAS and the trackers are in agreement, Jack."

"Super, Skipper. Glad we don't have to go VFR On Top today." Enright looked outside as they passed within 180 miles of Kangaroo Island on Australia's southern coast. No town lights could be seen from 125 miles above the pitch darkness. "Sure can't see any kangaroos down there, Skip."

Endeavor coasted wings level, heads-up, toward Australia's southeast land mass. The ship would glide between Melbourne and the island of Tasmania.

"Endeavor: Configure AOS by Orrora."

"Howdy, Canberra. With you loud and clear. We shot a good COAS sight. We're doin' fine."

"Copy, AC. Downlink is real solid at 61 minutes MET. So how goes your first hour in the sky, Endeavor?"

"Havin' a ball, Flight. Target is four miles ahead and seven above us," Enright called. He greatly enjoyed the sensation of weightlessness, although the puffy flush in his face was warm and uncomfortable.

154

"You're two minutes from open water, Endeavor. We'll be with you another four minutes."

"Okay, Flight," the AC drawled. "Jack is up to his eyeballs with our little fuel cell boil-over. I'm configuring the ARS for sunrise. Give us a minute, Flight."

"Sure, Will. Take your time."

The Colonel worked Panel Left-One beside his left shoulder in preparation for the 270 degrees Fahrenheit heat which would come with sunup.

"Secondary flash evaporator, high load evaporator on, duct B. Cabin fans A and B to on and water loop One bypass to manual, Two bypass to auto. And we'll cool the cabin air a bit here."

The AC worked his switches at his left.

"Okay, Canberra. With you now."

"Roger, Will. At sixty-three minutes, you're crossing the coastline. Can you see Sidney about 180 miles to your left?"

"Ah, lookin', Flight," a Kentucky twang drawled in the black sky above Australia's eastern shoreline where everyone slept at 2 o'clock in the morning.

"Just barely, Flight. Some cloud cover down there." The AC squinted down toward a hazy patch of light, like a light bulb wrapped in cotton.

"Say, Flight, is it really summer down there?"

"Eighty in the shade, Jack."

"Surely is dark down there."

"Roger that, right seat. Happens every night about this time. Losing you in about ten seconds. Keep an eye on your freon loop temps after daybreak. You're Go at sixty-five minutes."

"Bye, Australia . . . Ready to roll, Will."

The AC commanded the computers to roll Shuttle onto her white backside. Tail and nose RCS thrusters worked together as Endeavor executed a slow wing-over. After a minute of rolling, the RCS jets popped to arrest the roll bringing Endeavor to a stop upside down. Coasting nose forward, Shuttle's black glass belly faced the starry sky where a billion white, red and blue stars shone without

155

twinkling.

Without sound, Endeavor coasted across the black South Pacific. Six hundred miles and two flying minutes behind the ship's inverted tail, Australia rolled over the edge of the dark, sleeping planet as the white speck against the sky hurtled across the sea.

Like six white birds flying in tight formation across a black sky, the illuminated windows of the lighted flightdeck moved against the stars. Jacob Enright looked over his right shoulder and looked upward toward the sea below his upside-down office.

"Look at that!" Enright exclaimed into his triple pane window.

Far below, the black Pacific glowed a faint fluorescent green like phosphorescent paint spilled into a well. The sea glowed in a ribbon 50 miles long.

"Plankton, Jack. Glows when seawater disturbs it. A school of fish will light it up. Only dolphins won't light it. A dolphin can swim at thirty knots without generating a twitch of vortex turbulence. The perfect airfoil . . . If we could fly dolphins, we would be on Mars by now."

The Aircraft Commander spoke into his window. He spoke softly, prayerfully.

Two and a half minutes after losing contact with Orrora, Australia, Endeavor crossed latitude 30 degrees south, 120 miles southeast of Norfolk Island. Just at the Earth's invisible horizon, 750 nautical miles to the northeast, the mystic Fiji Islands lay in a tropical summer's night. An hour from home where it was the dead of winter, Endeavor flew in the airless silence of a South Pacific night.

An hour and twelve minutes aloft, Shuttle coasted above the Tongatapu Islands, 1,500 nautical miles south of the Equator.

"Looks like a contact, Skipper."

Flying nose first, upside down, Endeavor's radar beacons had been searching the nighttime sky for the radar footprint of LACE. But the beacons had wandered aimlessly at the speed of light to bend toward the very edge of the universe.

156

Until now.

"Got a MAP, Jack?" The Colonel squinted at the green CRT before him where print and a graphic, three-dimensional box slowly rotated like a teenager's video game.

"Looks like we have a message acceptance pulse, Will."

"Soyuz?"

"Don't think so. Not in this radio spectrum, Skipper . . . There."

The video graphic cube steadied as the two pilots with their heads nearly touching peered into the open graphic box on the television.

"LACE?" the command pilot inquired gravely.

"I'm interrogating it again."

Enright's left hand worked his computer keyboard and Mother instantly sent her encrypted electromagnetic waves of greeting out to the planet's far corner.

"And we have our baby, Skip. Solid lockup. Range five thousand meters." The hairs on Enright's neck tingled.

Both fliers jumped into their shoulder harnesses when one of Endeavor's nose jets barked out a plume of orange flame into the darkness just eight feet in front of their faces. Mother was automatically maintaining their even keel upside down. Each pilot smiled sheepishly.

"Might close in here, buddy."

Jack Enright nodded at his captain.

"Best tell Mother, Jack."

Without words, the copilot in the right seat which his floating body barely touched tapped at the keyboard's black keys. The computers reached out into the black vacuum with electronic fingers which wrapped around LACE'S black body.

"See anything, Jack?" Both men peered into the darkness.

"Can't even see the stars with these floodlights in here."

Seventy-six minutes out, Endeavor glided 720 miles east of Samoa toward the Equator 900 miles to the north. At the Earth's far eastern corner, the curvature of the horizon was visible as a hair-thin band of pink with blackness above and below. Because Shuttle flew bottoms-up, the curving pink

157

lines of their South Pacific sunrise looked from the flight-deck like an airy smile with the Earth's reddening limb curving up at its edges.

"Mornin', Skipper."

"And to you, Number One, 'Bout time to go out to fetch the newspaper from the front porch."

"Watch that first step, Will."

Both pilots chuckled 14 minutes from their next ground station contact. They watched the upside-down horizon turn quickly from pink to red to orange as the sun's white disk erupted over the edge of the world with an explosion of blinding daylight like a magnesium flare.

From the top of their helmets, the pilots pulled a tinted visor down over their closed faceplates advertised as laser-proof.

Far below, the sea was still black and colorless as the ship raced in daylight toward the sun. On the South Pacific islands beneath Endeavor's white backside, the horizon was only three miles away and the new sun had a long way to go before it climbed over the edge to awaken the gold-skinned islanders. For Shuttle, the horizon where the sun sat was a thousand miles distant. Endeavor flew in daylight which the palm trees below would not feel for another hour.

Two minutes after the dazzling sunrise 720 miles northwest of Tahiti, the black glass bricks on the underside of Endeavor's wings and body were baked by full daylight. The flash evaporators sweated profusely as the freon in Shuttle's veins warmed to the blinding sunlight.

Flying upside down and racing over the gray sea 80 minutes from home, Enright's window faced north and the left seat pointed toward the south. The copilot squinted outside to search for Christmas Island 750 miles to the northwest. He could see only endless green sea in morning twilight. Wisps of clouds dotted tiny islands where turtles and crabs were the only life stretching in the morning sunshine. The clouds covered the islands but not the ocean. Two minutes and 600 miles from crossing the Equator, the upside-down command pilot squinted east toward the dozens of cloud-covered islands of French Polynesia.

The pilots watched their green television screens, which depicted their target ahead of them and moving eastward with Endeavor. The shuttle was lower than LACE, which gave the pilots a faster orbital speed than their target. As their range closed, the glass starship would catch LACE from below and would move steadily upward toward the laser satellite. During the final moments of the chase, during Terminal Phase Initiate, Shuttle would pass underneath LACE and would end the game of space tag by coming up east of LACE and ahead of it. The final rendezvous would then be shot from a position in front of LACE in a matched tandem orbit.

"Rev Two, Skipper," Enright called as Endeavor crossed the Equator northbound 82 minutes into the mission.

Unlike prior American manned spacecraft whose orbits were numbered from the west longitude meridian of Cape Canaveral, Shuttle orbits, or revolutions, are counted from the point where Shuttle crosses the Equator while flying from south to north. As Endeavor sped over the Equator, she began her second Earth revolution, although her position along the orbital track was still 4,000 nautical miles west of Cape Canaveral. Her second revolution thus began after only five-sixths of a complete orbit around the earth.

"Eight minutes to acquisition of California voice, Jack." Endeavor would travel 2,400 miles during that eight minutes over open water before hearing from the ground. They pursued LACE alone with Mother's warm black boxes at the helm. Their first United States landfall would be Texas in thirteen more minutes after a pass over northern Mexico.

The white sun was low in the eastern sky. On the blue-green sea 128 nautical miles beneath the inverted shuttle, it was 7:30 in the morning. With Endeavor's nose and black belly between the cockpit and the morning sun, the flight-deck went dark gray, just dark enough to make reading impossible. The center annunciator panel's forty lights illuminated white, yellow, and red for an instant. Then the warning lights and all of the cabin floodlights went out.

159

There was only the gray gloom and a silence absolute as the lights and the three televisions and the cabin fans went dead.

The two pilots sat quietly in the silent semi-darkness. To keep their weightless arms from floating against the instrument panels, the pilots tucked their hands into their chest straps. There were no simulations for Mother suffering a stroke.

"So I was jest wond'rin', Jacob," the AC drawled calmly, like any old farmer talking over the back fence with his cousin from 'cross the creek.

"Yeah, Skipper," the copilot asked with his very best, downhome "so how's your old mare?" voice.

"Meant to mention it: Did you pay the 'lectric bill 'fore we left this mornin'?"

"Didn't have time, Skipper. Do it when we get home."

"Reckon that explains it," said the Colonel in the half darkness.

"Think we could mail it in?"

"Think you can find the mailbox, Number One?"

Both airmen chuckled in the air which was quickly becoming stuffy without cabin and suit fans.

"Think Mother's state vectors are off the line, too?"

"Don't even *think* it, Will."

The two pilots abandoned their gallows humor. Parker reached over his head to Panel Overhead-13.

"Let's see, Jack. Circuit breakers, Essential Bus 1BC are all closed, rows A and B. Essential Bus 2CA, breakers closed. And Essential Bus 3AB, also all closed. She's alive here. Try your side, Jack."

Enright felt for the long instrument panel, Right-1, by his right elbow. He tried to get his face closer to the barely visible array of 96 switches, pushbuttons, and circuit breakers on the single 12-by-32-inch electrical systems panel braced to the cockpit wall.

"Okay, Skipper. AC controller, all nine breakers, still closed. Let's put AC bus sensors One, Two, and Three, from auto-trip to off. Inverter AC-1 to on, AC-2 to on, and

160

AC-3 to on. Let's try control bus power, DC Main A to reset, DC Main Bravo to reset, and Main Charlie to reset."

"Damn" was all Parker said when the cabin lights blinked on, along with the three green televisions. The hum of the cabin fans filled the stale flightdeck.

"How can air from a bottle taste so sweet, Skip?"

"Amen, Brother Jacob."

"What about Mother?"

The command pilot watched his attitude indicator ball swing upside down as the ship's three inertial measurement units caught their electronic breath. The digital numbers on the Mission Elapsed Time clock located just above the forward windows blinked on showing 00:01:29:30 and counting up. The pilot in the right seat checked his wristwatch sewn into the sleeve of his pressure suit. His watch read 10:29 Houston time, in agreement with the MET clock. Mother had not missed a beat.

Enright pulled a clipboard from beneath his seat. On it were a complex series of graphs and square grids full of numbers. The pilots called it a Buzz Board in honor of retired, Apollo astronaut Edwin "Buzz" Aldrin, the man who followed Neil Armstrong down the ladder of the lunar lander Eagle at Tranquility Base, the Moon. On Aldrin's first spaceflight on board the two-man spacecraft Gemini-12 back in 1966, Astronaut Aldrin had concocted his own, long-hand tables for executing a space rendezvous with an Agena target satellite by eyeball-only. The other astronauts laughed and dubbed the quiet, intense airman, "Doctor Rendezvous." But on Gemini-12, the ship's rendezvous radar failed before astronauts James Lovell and Buzz Aldrin could catch their Agena target in the heavens. Aldrin pulled out his home-grown charts, and with them, Twelve shot a perfect rendezvous and docking without radar help. No one laughed after that performance.

"What's the Buzz Board say, Jack?" the Colonel asked impatiently as they coasted northeast, headsdown, over blue water halfway between Hawaii and Mexico City.

"It says: Range to target 1 point 2 miles, R-dot 30 feet

per second and closing. Does Mother agree, Will?" It was Enright's turn to sound anxious.

The AC tapped his computer keyboard beside his right leg. On the center television, Mother's green face printed "1.2 R . . . 28.3 R."

"Seems we're still in business, Number One!"

"Neither rain nor sleet nor dark of night, Skipper."

"Endeavor, Endeavor: GDS listening at 90 minutes."

"Greetings, California," the AC drawled from a thousand miles due west of Guadalajara, Mexico.

"Bet you boys are just sitting up there, hands folded, looking out the window while everyone down here has to work for a living."

The two upside-down pilots looked at each other across the twenty-inch-wide center console separating their seats.

"You got that right, Goldstone," Enright replied without smiling.

"Thought so, Endeavor. Your temps look fine. When we get a good hard lockup on your uplink, we'll update your state vectors via GDX."

The two great dish antennae at the Goldstone tracking station in southern California carry the designators GDS and GDX.

" 'Kay," a Kentucky voice called from the black sky full of sun.

"You're 2½ from Baja. We show you 1 point 2 behind your target and closing at R-dot of 26 feet per second. Soyuz is station-keeping two hundred meters from the target and they remain radio-silent. Backroom wants you to roll plus Z throughout TPI. You should have no problem using the COAS for the final approach alignment."

"Roger, California. Understand attitude-hold in headsup. We're still anxious about our temperatures with the doors closed in the bay."

"We're watching it for you, Shuttle. Your next sunset will be at two hours, two minutes. No problem with your heat load till then."

"Flight, you got a time hack on opening the bay doors?

Don't want to rely on the flash evaps one minute longer than necessary."

"We hear you, AC. We're hoping to have you on station with the target on this revolution by the time you lose Bermuda. We should be able to cycle the bay doors and engage the radiators during your BDA contact."

"Okay, Houston. We'll plan on getting the doors open before we lose Bermuda. How's that timewise?"

"Ah, standby one, Jack . . . You're AOS Bermuda at 01 hours, 49 minutes. Then your LOS seven minutes."

"Roger, Flight. It's already warmin' up in here . . . And we're now rollin' to plus-Z."

"We see you rolling over. The evaporators should be able to handle the heat load another ten minutes, no problem. We show you now crossing Baja California, at 01 hours, 02 minutes, MET. See it?"

"Sure do from the right seat, Flight. It's very clear, very reddish."

"Believe that, Jack. And we show your range to target one mile even. We'd like to try a COAS shot here. AC: Your target should be about sixty-seven degrees above the horizon. Sun now about forty-five degrees high in the east, well below the Celestial Equator. Target should be in motion ahead and above you and rising against the stars Vega, low, and Alphecca, high, both northeast."

The command pilot riding headsup squinted against the sun burning through his center, side window. His face was close to the small mirror of his COAS alignment sight.

"Lookin' . . . Lookin'. Have stars Altair very low in the east, and Antares about forty degrees high southeast."

The command pilot gently nudged Endeavor's nose from side to side with pre-programmed, one-tenth-second bursts of Shuttle's two small vernier thrusters one on each side of Endeavor's nose. Each tiny thruster popped with only 24 pounds of thrust for very fine attitude adjustments. The pilot fine-tuned his ship's position with his control stick as he searched near the faint star Rasalhague in the equatorial constellation Ophiuchus nearly invisible against the sun in the east.

"Good star field, Flight. Wait one . . . One of 'em is moving . . . moving upward. Jack is checking on it."

The copilot tapped his computer keys asking Mother to resolve the Crew Optical Alignment Sight observation with the vector to LACE by the rendezvous-radar. Mother's green face blinked at her pilots.

"Visual contact confirmed, Flight. Range one mile, and R-dot of sixteen feet per second. Angle 71 point three degrees high and increasing as we pass under the target. Have a very bright Soyuz in the starfield ahead."

"We hear you, Jack. You're Go for braking maneuver your discretion. KSC will remind you via MLX to confirm Hughes, anti-laser visors down and locked."

"No need, Flight. They're in place and secured."

"Copy that, Endeavor. And welcome home! You are over Texas now at 95 minutes out. Configure LOS Goldstone. With you by Merritt Island."

"Mornin', Florida. See you later, California, thanks. Our range-to-go now zero point niner miles, and Jack and I both have a real visual dead ahead. Brightest thing I've seen out here. Brighter than approaching an Apollo CSM for sure. Sun angles must be just right."

"Copy, Will. You're four and one-half minutes from Bermuda acquisition which will occur over Georgia. And put Jack on the day watch; backroom says his eyeballs are sharper than yours, Will."

"Thanks, Flight. Just don't call me Gramps yet . . . You heard the man, Number One. Into the crow's nest with you!" the AC grinned with his very best Wallace Beery voice which always convulsed Jack Enright.

"Aye, Captain Bligh," the copilot laughed, flying headsup, 130 nautical miles above southern Texas 180 miles west of Houston.

"Step lively, Mister Christian," drawled Wallace Beery with a touch of Blue Grass country in his raspy voice.

"You guys all right up there or what?" the headphones crackled as Shuttle over Texas spoke with Cape Canaveral's antennae.

"Too much sun, I reckon," the AC grinned.

"Sounds like it, Will. Make Jacob wear his hat."

"Roger, Flight."

"And, Endeavor, we see you really close now. Advise when braking."

Endeavor approached LACE from below. In her lower orbit, Shuttle sped over the ground slightly faster than her target.

"Range half a mile; R-dot down to 12 feet per second. Target is right in the COAS field, dead center and 83 degrees high. Great visual out the windows. And there's Brother Ivan five degrees below the target. I can just make out the new window in the work-station module. Must be a Soyuz-TM alright."

"Real fine, Will. Your freon loop temps still look good from here."

"A real traffic jam up here, Houston."

"Roger that, Jack. Don't run over anyone."

"Try not to. Skipper is now on the THC for final approach."

"Copy, Jack. Understand Will is braking manually."

The Aircraft Commander had powered up the translational hand controller, a square handle with four spokes forming a fist-size cross at the lower left side of the forward instrument panel. With the THC in his left hand, Parker called upon the RCS thrusters which fire fore-aft, up-down, and left-right, to nudge Endeavor into minutely different orbits en route to LACE. With the rotational hand controller, RHC, in his right hand between his knees, the Command Pilot adjusted the attitude of Shuttle's rightside-up body. Both pilots had an RHC control stick between his thighs, but only the pilot in command had the translational controller for moving the ship through space under rocket power. Pushing the THC into the instrument panel fired two RCS jets in each of the tail's OMS pods. These pushed Shuttle forward. Pulling back on the THC handle fired three 870-pound-thrust jets in the nose for slowing Endeav-

165

or's forward velocity.

Squinting into the tubular COAS sextant and out the window, the AC had his hands full of starship. He had to slow their closing speed with exacting precision to stop right at LACE in an orbit perfectly matching LACE's orbit. Any alignment or velocity error would send Shuttle silently above or below their target, an error grossly costly in propellant. Such an overshoot, called a "wifferdil," would require enormous amounts of precious RCS fuel to fix.

In close pursuit of LACE over the heartland of the Old Confederacy, the command pilot flew his terminal approach while his copilot read out the numbers of the chase.

"At 99 minutes, Endeavor, you are due north of Atlanta."

"Thanks, Flight," the Skipper called. " 'Old times there are not forgotten' . . ."

" 'Look away, look away,' " Jacob Enright sang inside his helmet over the hiss of the air rushing into his face from the suit's sealed neckring.

"Think your frog got loose, Will," the voice from Earth chuckled.

"Hard to argue with that, Flight."

"Fifty seconds to AOS by Bermuda."

"Thanks, Houston."

Endeavor flew 130 nautical miles above the Appalachian Mountains of east Tennessee and western North Carolina. Below, where it was 11:40 in the morning Eastern Time, the mid-day sun of winter was well below the Equator. The white sun cast soft shadows from the northern flanks of the Great Smokey Mountains browned by winter chill. As the mountains slid beneath Shuttle at five miles per second, the ship was almost vertical. The command pilot paused in his final approach to study the bright landscape of his youth. In the high sun angle, terrain features were fuzzy and were washed out by the sun's glare. Behind his eyes, William McKinley Parker filled in the details of mountain hollows along the Cumberland Plateau dotted with little clapboard houses from whose chimneys smoke would be rising, and of paintless old churches beside ancient graveyards. Behind the

166

battered fences, letters etched into coarsely hewn stones had been erased by wind and weather over the generations. Riding with his head pointed toward the black but starless sky, the Colonel intently searched the holes in the clouds for Kentucky's white rail fences and old smokehouses.

"Endeavor: At 100 minutes, we have you by Bermuda. You're two minutes from the coast and three minutes from LOS by Merritt Island. You lose Bermuda in 8 minutes. Target now 300 meters, R-dot at 08 feet per second. Downlink looks fine; Freon temps look fine."

"Thanks, Flight," the pilot in command responded. "Looks like a real solid lockup with the target."

"Copy, AC. We'll be quiet while you shoot the approach. Still not a word from Soyuz now 400 meters from the target. If Ivan is talking with his own stations, Network is not hearing it. We do have their C-band beacon though."

" 'Kay, Flight. You watch the store for us, especially the water loop temps . . . What you see, Jack?"

"Climbing right up the slot, Skipper." Enright repeatedly queried the green television about LACE's position. Ordinarily, Shuttle crews pilot a space rendezvous from the flight station in the rear of the flightdeck. But Shuttle's first-revolution rendezvous with a crew of two instead of the normal operational complement of four astronauts made a front-seat rendezvous necessary. Enright flew the computer keyboard and the televisions while the AC handflew the starship.

"Easy, Will. R-dot down to 6 FPS. We're 280 meters out and 300 meters below. Steady as she goes . . ."

Endeavor rose toward LACE, twinkling like a black jewel in the blinding sunshine.

"Now 200 behind, 250 below . . . Left just a tad, Skip."

The AC jerked the translational hand controller in his left hand toward the cabin wall. A pulse toward the right stopped the portside drift as Shuttle crossed directly beneath LACE 150 meters away.

"Easy does it, Will . . . Braking . . . Braking."

Forward pulses from Endeavor's nose jets slowed Shuttle

as she climbed out ahead of LACE.

"Null your plus-Z residuals . . . Now! Real fine, Skip."

Lifting the THC handle fired the thrusters in the top of the two tail pods and the upward-firing jets in Shuttle's nose. The ship matched LACE's altitude perfectly.

"Combination braking, Skip."

With the computers choosing the best RCS thrusters to accomplish the commander's orders from his two control sticks, the pilot halted Endeavor's drift out ahead of and eastward of LACE. But slowing Endeavor to allow LACE to close their separation distance would actually drop Shuttle back into a lower orbit which would defeat the delicate physics of a space rendezvous. So with each retrograde thrust to slow Shuttle, Mother chose a combination of upward-firing jets to hold Endeavor in line with her target.

"Thirty meters, Skipper. Nail her down."

With a rapid series of thruster pops, Endeavor stopped ahead of LACE and slightly to the side of Soyuz.

As all three ships flew in precisely matched orbits, 130 nautical miles into the brilliant sky, each vessel was perfectly motionless relative to the others. In coming up and under LACE, Endeavor had kept her glass nose pointing toward LACE. As a result, Shuttle had pitched fully over backward when she came up ahead of LACE at the eastern limit of the range of the tracking station on Bermuda Island.

"Flight: We're all stop," a weary Kentucky voice sighed. "Tell the boys in the backroom that M equals one."

"Good news, Endeavor! We're about to lose you here. Everyone is breathing easier down here. After you catch your breath, you're Go to get the payload bay doors open. Well done, Endeavor. Configure . . ."

9

The white sun burned fiercely upon the black belly of Endeavor as the upside-down starship coasted across the Atlantic.

Eighteen hundred miles of blue sea, out of contact with ground stations, would be crossed in six minutes.

Thirty yards from Shuttle, the cylindrical black hulk of LACE rotated very slowly in the blinding daylight of what was mid-afternoon at sea. Twenty-five yards beyond that, Soyuz floated with her antennae bristling and her twin solar wings glistening in the sun. Energia, the world's mightiest rocket, had hurled Soyuz aloft twelve hours earlier. Since then, not a single word had been monitored from the Russians by American ground stations.

"And best take a barf bag with you, Jack. Try not to turn your head too abruptly."

"One blue bag, Skipper. Check."

Enright prepared to leave his seat. He grinned broadly in anticipation of his first free-flight in weightlessness an hour and fifty minutes since leaving Pad 39-A. He still wore his bulky pressure suit and its white helmet with the anti-laser visor opened so he could breathe cabin air.

"Okay, Number One: Gloves stowed; lap belt and shoulder harness disconnect; comm power off; O_2 hoses disconnect; biomedical cables and vent hose disconnect. And, don't kick me, buddy."

As the command pilot read off the seat egress checklist, the second in command's ungloved hands moved swiftly to free himself from his web of hoses, cables, and seat belts.

Gingerly, Enright floated up from his seat in the harsh glare of the cabin floodlights. The copilot pushed his seat backward along its floor tracks as he tucked his legs up into his middle. He heaved his weightless body over the broad center console between his seat and the Colonel, who remained strapped to the left seat.

The copilot's boots did not touch the flightdeck floor as he rose very slowly to face the forward windshield. He balanced in mid-air with a hand resting upon the back of each of the front seats. Everything in Enright's body longed to do a Zero-G backflip as he floated toward the back end of the cockpit only five feet from his empty seat. But fear of the pervasive, early-mission, spacesickness which plagued all previous Shuttle missions restrained his impulse to soar.

With his spacesickness medication, an ear-patch stuck to his head, Enright turned slowly to face rearward. Very gently, he pushed off from the forward seats. His body floated the 60 inches to the instrument displays at the back of the flightdeck which is barely 80 inches long from the front windows to the aft bulkhead.

"Man *can* fly, Skipper!" the copilot called through his open faceplate as he floated over the two 2-foot square, open hatchways which open into the roomy mid-deck beneath the flightdeck. There is one access hole behind each of the two forward flight seats. The lower mid-deck, Shuttle's basement, contains the ship's kitchen, sleeping hammocks, airlock leading into the payload bay, storage lockers, and the zero-gravity latrine.

Enright stopped his flight by grabbing the handrails along the ceiling when he reached the aft crew station. He floated with his back toward the command pilot and he faced the aft wall-to-wall and floor-to-ceiling instrument panels.

Enright locked his feet into the foot restraints secured to the floor. Then he plugged into his suit the communications cable for Endeavor's intercom. Into his waist, he locked two air hoses from a hastily rigged duct installed for the mission. Ordinarily, the rear flight controls are worked in unpressurized flight overalls, the intravehicular-activity flightsuits. There is no aft outlet for space suit air hoses. Before his helmetted face, two large windows looked into the dark and sealed payload bay through the aft bulkhead.

Raising his face to the aft ceiling, Enright looked out the 20-inch square overhead window directly above his head. There were two such aft windows overhead.

"Got me, Will?" Enright called into his lip mikes.

"Loud and clear, Jack."

"Wish you could see the view from Window Seven. Breathtaking!" Enright craned his neck upward.

"Believe that, Number One."

The two aft ceiling windows looked down from the upside-down Shuttle to the blue ocean 130 nautical miles below. The copilot wanted to play tourist for a while. But there was too much work to do if the huge doors of the payload bay were to be opened to expose the space-radiators to the cooling vacuum in the inverted ship's shadow.

"Okay, Will," Enright radioed by intercom as he turned to face the rear instrument arrays along the wall beneath the starboard ceiling window. "At Panel Aft Right-15: Circuit breakers for payload bay lighting, and PS floods, OS floods and MS floods, all closed this side."

171

Enright floated across the aft crew station to the panels along the side wall directly behind the Colonel's back.

"And, Panel Aft Left-9: Payload Station flood lights on." As Enright threw a toggle switch, the banks of instruments behind the command pilot were bathed in harsh white light. Enright turned and floated back to the aft starboard panels behind his empty seat. There, he threw another switch which filled the right side of the rear station with light. "Panel Aft Right-10: Mission Specialist station floods on. And, Panel Aft-6, Orbit Station floods on," he called as he flipped a toggle switch below the payload bay window at eye level looking rearward. The center of the rear instrument clusters illuminated.

The floating copilot faced the rear of the flightdeck. He took a half step to his right so he stood between the two large windows in the rear bulkhead which looked into the black payload bay. Above his head, the middle of the North Atlantic glowed brilliantly beyond the two ceiling windows. In the flightdeck's lights, the two windows into the closed bay were flat black.

"Ready to light the bay, Jack?" the intercom crackled inside Enright's helmet.

"Ready back here, Skip. And it's showtime . . . At Aft Panel-7, payload bay lighting: Aft starboard lights on; portside aft, on; lights amidships starboard, on; mid-section portside, on; and, forward bay section, starboard lights on and portside lights on . . . And it's daylight inside the bay, Skipper."

"How's it look in there, Number One?" Parker asked from the left front seat.

Enright looked into the rear window directly behind his empty seat. Although the bay doors were tightly closed, the six floodlights created glaring daylight on the far side of the double-paned 11-by-14-inch aft window.

"Okay, Will, lookin' out Window Nine into the bay. Everything is still nailed down in there. Thermal blankets

172

in place. Don't see any exposed areas of floor or walls. I can see the remote manipulator arm in its cradle, lookin' secure. Quite a few bits of debris floating around in there. Looks like a few pieces of the blankets or flakes of aluminum film off the thermal blankets. Nothin' much."

"Okay, Jack. We're about two minutes from AOS Dakar. Let's get the doors open and the radiators outside."

Into its second daytime, almost two hours since riding the fire into the sky, the ship's heat control systems were sweating from the freon coolant loops and the flash evaporators. It would soon be imperative to open the bay doors. Opening the long double doors would expose the space radiators mounted on the doors to the icy cold of space in the shadow of Shuttle's wings as the ship flew upside down.

Endeavor sped toward the Canary Islands 400 miles west of North Africa where it was 5 o'clock on a winter's evening. As the planet turns upon her axis once each day, the Earth turns a new face to each of Shuttle's orbits. Each revolution around the globe by Shuttle, which takes 90 minutes, will pass over a stretch of Earth which was not there on an earlier revolution. As Shuttle completed one Earth orbit every 90 minutes, the planet has turned through one-sixteenth of a day.

Jacob Enright raised his feet from the flightdeck floor. With his knees flexed, he hovered motionless in mid-air. With a tug on a wall handhold, he turned sideways without touching the cabin floor. He stopped at the rear displays mounted on the side wall behind his forward seat. Over his right shoulder, the payload bay lights illuminated the two rear windows. Over the copilot's head, the ceiling window was filled with blue ocean and the brown specks of the seven Canary Islands. Las Palmas on Grand Canary Island began its twenty seconds of crossing the overhead window. The pilot, still seated in the left front seat, glanced over his right shoulder toward Enright, who floated at the cabin's far diagonal corner.

"Ready to cycle the bay doors, Skipper."

"You got it, Number One."

"Okay, Cap'n. At Panel Aft Right-13A2 . . . Mechanical power, System One to on, System Two off. And, doors lever-locked open."

Enright looked over his right shoulder. The center roof seam of the bay split open silently. An explosion of dazzling sunlight streamed into the bay as the two 60-foot-long doors spread slowly like white wings.

"Two in motion."

"Got it, Jack."

Slowly, each door swung open on its 13 electric hinges driven by 6 motors. The doors are not aluminum like the rest of Endeavor's skin. Instead, each door is composed of five sections manufactured from superlight, superstrong, graphite-epoxy composite.

The two doors gaped wide as each opened so far that it dropped out of sight over the sill on each wall of the bay. As the doors came to an automatic halt fully open, they stopped fifty inches from the upper surface of the ship's five-foot-thick wings.

Jack Enright consulted CRT Number Four, the green television screen mounted on the aft crew station. The CRT graphically displayed the track of the doors as they opened and locked into place outside.

"Doors stopped, Will."

"Endeavor, Endeavor," the pilot's headphones crackled. "Configure AOS via Dakar at 01 Hours 54 Minutes. Be with you about 5 minutes. Backroom wants to know the bay-door status."

In the late afternoon twilight, Endeavor crossed the bleached terrain of the Western Sahara on the west corner of North Africa between Morocco's arid Atlas Mountains to Shuttle's north and Mauritania far to the south. The West African tracking station at Dakar, Senegal, does not

174

have telemetry-receiving facilities but only crackling, UHF radio capabilities. The voice of Mission Control from Houston arrived in a wave of static.

"With you, Houston. Jack has the doors open and locked. No problems on cycling the doors. We have a small amount of debris in the bay; nothin' serious. Give us a minute to get the radiators outside, please."

"Copy, Endeavor. We'll listen while you work."

"Thanks, Flight . . . Ready on the radiators, Jack?"

Enright steadied his floating body at the side console across the cabin diagonal from the command pilot's back.

"At Panel Aft-13A2, Skipper: Radiator deploy System Alpha to deploy and System Bravo to deploy . . . Lights on, talk-back open."

Outside in the open bay, two flat rectangular radiator panels swung outward over each side of the bay. Two radiator panels on the forward half of each open door rose over the bay sill and moved slowly toward the open doors.

In the eternal silence of space high above West Africa, the radiator panels moved out and downward toward the door. Each of the four radiators is 126 inches wide and 320 inches long and moved outward by six motors.

"And all stop . . . Latch control to latch on System A and System B . . . Okay, Skipper, we have four radiators deployed and latched open." Enright tapped the 32 black keys of the computer keyboard just below the side console's television. To his coded inquiry, the CRT displayed the pictorial display of each of the four radiators. "And each radiator is latched 35 point 5 degrees above the bay doors. You can crank 'em up, Will."

"You got that, Dakar?"

"Every word, Will. Lose you in two minutes. Let's get the ATCS on-line before you go over the edge if we can."

"Okay, Flight. Powering up the Active Thermal Control System."

The Aircraft Commander strapped into the left front

seat reached over his helmeted head to touch the rows of round, black circuit breakers on the ceiling of the forward flightdeck.

"Main DC bus A, Overhead Panel-14, freon radiator controllers One and Two, breakers closed. Overhead Panel-15, radiator controllers One and Two, Main bus B, closed and closed." The command pilot turned to the panel bristling with 134 circuit breakers behind his left shoulder.

"And, Panel Left-4, bus AC-1: Breakers freon Loop One, pump A, closed, closed and closed; freon Loop Two, pump B, all three breakers closed. Bus AC-2: Loop One, pump B, three breakers closed. And, AC-3: freon Loop Two, pump A, closed, closed and closed. freon signal conditioners AC-2 closed and AC-3 closed. Radiator controllers 1B and 2B, bus AC-1, both closed. On bus AC-2, rad controller 1A, closed. And bus AC-3, rad controller 2A closed . . . Okay, Flight, moving to Panel Left-3." The pilot studied the panel for the Atmosphere Revitalization System on the cabin wall at his left elbow. "freon pumps set to pump A, Loops One and Two; radiator controllers, Loops One and Two, set auto; outlet temperature to normal. And, bypass valves, Loops One and Two, set auto . . . And we're lookin' at four good radiators. Loop One outlet temp is 34 degrees Fahrenheit and Loop Two at 36 degrees."

Outside, freon refrigerant carried Endeavor's body heat from the cabin and equipment water circulation lines to the freon lines, where the refrigerant flowed through the radiators latched to the open bay doors. There, the freon bled the heat into space. The heat from freon coolant Loop One is carried to the two radiators on the portside bay door behind the command pilot. Loop Two flows into the twin radiators on the starboard side behind the copilot's empty seat.

"Good news, Endeavor. You're going over the edge

176

here. Expect to contact Indian Ocean Ship in fourteen minutes. Next sunset in three minutes . . ."

The ground's voice broke up into static as the silent Soyuz, the slowly rolling LACE, and the upside-down Endeavor, crossed the Prime Meridian of Greenwich for Shuttle's second time at MET 01 Hours and 59 Minutes aloft. No ground station would be within earshot of Shuttle until the ship reached the Indian Ocean in a quarter of an hour.

"Only three minutes of daylight left, Jack. Let's set up our attitude-hold while we can still see the target."

"Want me to do it, Will?" Enright radioed from the rear station. Shuttle can be flown from either the forward seat or from the center of the rear crew station.

"I might as well fly her . . . Important to keep busy at my age." The seated, tall flier smiled.

"Glad I didn't say that," Enright chuckled over the intercom.

"Okay," the AC said to himself. "We'll ask Mother to hold us with the payload bay facing the target. Mode select on the autopilot in LVLH with reference X-POP and minus Y."

Working the eighteen pushbuttons on the digital autopilot control panel by his right thigh and the black keys of his computer keyboard, the AC ordered the computers to yaw the ship sideways until Endeavor rode with her body perpendicular to their orbital path with the open bay facing LACE. In the Local Vertical-Local Horizontal reference matrix, Mother chose the best combination of Shuttle's 19 Z-axis, RCS thrusters which control the ship's roll and pitch rotation, to crank Endeavor over on her side until the open bay faced LACE. When Mother stopped the ship's slow twist, Shuttle floated on her side with the open bay door behind the command pilot pointing toward dusky Africa. The open door behind Enright's empty right seat pointed skyward. Over Africa, the ship's

177

nose faced north as Endeavor coasted lying on her left side.

"Maneuver complete, Jack, with one minute of daylight to spare. I can see the target out the top of my center window. You got her back there?"

Enright floated 5 feet behind his empty seat. He raised his helmeted face to the starboard, overhead window. The large portal faced west along their track already flown. The white sun hung just above the western horizon with excruciating brightness.

"Nothin' but sun out here, Skipper. I'll have her after sunset in twilight."

Crossing the border between Nigeria and Niger, just north of Kano, Nigeria, 2 hours and 2 minutes aloft, Shuttle flew into twilight as the sun fell rapidly toward the western horizon. At Endeavor's speed of 300 miles per minute, the sun set quickly with its explosion of bright colors all along the hazy blue band of the Earth's film of air.

"Got her now," Enright called as the sun slipped below the planet's far corner. The final moments of twilight bathed the black, shining sides of LACE in orange flame. And then it was night. Only the steady white glow of the running lights on Soyuz could be seen on LACE's far side.

Suddenly and silently, a pair of piercing arc lights illuminated on Soyuz in the darkness absolute. The two white beacons fell brightly upon LACE now clearly visible. Without air to scatter the light, no beam corridors reached between Soyuz and the fully illuminated, gently rolling LACE.

"A little help from Brother Ivan, Skipper."

"Seems so, Jack."

As Endeavor on her side sped into the shadow of her second African night, the rear crew station was bright with its interior lights and with the six floodlights in the

178

payload bay filling the two large windows at eye level on the rear bulkhead wall.

"Let's crank up the CCTV for power up of the RMS, Jack. How you feelin' back there, buddy?"

Enright assumed the astronauts' crouched position behind the seated command pilot. With his feet secured to the flightdeck floor's boot restraints, Enright stood with his knees well bent. His arms within his bulky suit floated before his face. Above his head, outside the twin ceiling windows, LACE rolled slowly, bathed in the light from the open payload bay and in the arc lights from Soyuz flying in tight formation without a word.

"So far so good, Will. My face really feels full though. Maybe just a tad of lightheadedness. But I'm fine for sure. Tryin' not to move my head too much."

"Super, Jack," the intercom crackled over the small African nation of Cameroon which slept in pitch darkness. "Be right with you."

Up front, Parker extricated himself from the hoses and cables rising from beneath his seat and from between his long legs. He raised the anti-laser visor on his helmet and the faceplate under it so he could breathe the cool, dry air of the flightdeck. Heaving his long legs from under the forward instrument panel, the AC floated out of his seat and over the center console. As he straightened his legs for the first time in three hours, a searing pain squeezed his right leg below the knee. Enright saw the tall flier's grimace.

Hovering with his legs flexed in mid-air, Parker floated between the two open hatchways in the floor behind the front seats. The desire to cartwheel back to Enright seized the tall pilot and he grinned broadly.

Enright instantly read his captain's deeply lined pilot's face.

"You wouldn't let *me*, Skipper!" Enright shouted with a laugh through his open faceplate. The Colonel heard him and he floated slowly toward Enright in the rear.

The command pilot stopped his flight at the Mission Specialist station on the starboard side of the rear flight-deck. He locked his boots into the floor restraints before he knelt to pick up two of the jerry-rigged air hoses which he twist-locked into the belly valves of his orange pressure suit. He plugged into the biomedical jack and intercom jack on Panel Aft-11 at the left lower level of the side wall's displays. He looked up to the overhead window full of night and the illuminated LACE between Shuttle and Soyuz. Ahead of Parker at eye level, the lighted payload bay looked like daylight. On Panel Aft-13, at knee level, the AC flipped the microphone power switch and he turned the audio knob to its PTT/VOX position which activated the push-to-talk switch for air-ground communication and set the inner-ship intercom to voice-activation.

"Got me, Jack?"

"Loud and clear," Enright radioed from the Payload Specialist station at Parker's right side. The two pilots lowered and sealed their laser-proof faceplates.

"Let's do it, Number One," the AC called as Endeavor flew upon her side across the Equator 2 hours, 7 minutes out. They flew 130 nautical miles above the black Congo River in Zaire, Central Africa.

Parker crouched to his left to reach the knee level Panel Aft Right-15 on the rear starboard wall behind the copilot's empty seat. The two hoses leading to his suit and the two communications and biomedical cables tangled in Parker's long legs.

"Lots of snakes back here, Jack!"

"Don't feed 'em, Skipper."

"Not me . . . Okay, Panel Aft Right-15, circuit breakers: Main DC bus A, aft bay television camera pan-tilt, and camera heaters, and pan-tilt heater, and control unit, all closed. Main bus B, forward bay TV: Camera pan-tilt, closed; camera heater, closed; pan-tilt heater, closed; and control unit and monitor, closed. Portside RMS television: Pan-tilt, heater, and pan-tilt heater, all closed. And, Main bus C, all three breakers, EVA television, closed . . . Do it, Jack."

Standing against the resistance of the legs of his stiff suit, the tall man winced as pain wracked his right calf.

"Say somethin', Will?"

"Nah . . ."

Both fliers stood shoulder-to-shoulder, looking out the rear window before each of their faces. Enright floated at Parker's right side.

At the center of the chest-high, rearmost instrument arrays the aft rotational hand controller protruded from the wall like a fist-size pistol grip. With it, either pilot could command Endeavor's RCS thrusters to change Shuttle's attitude as she coasted belly-forward, one-wing-down. Parker could work the aft RHC with his right hand, Enright with his left. Just to the right of the aft attitude control stick, fifteen toggle switches and twenty-seven lighted pushbuttons controlled the television cameras mounted inside the payload bay. Enright worked the TV controls with his ungloved left hand. At the aft flightdeck's portside corner, by Enright's right shoulder, two television screens came to life as the copilot activated Endeavor's closed-circuit television.

"CCTV alive, Will."

"They told you the service would teach you a trade, Number One!" the tall flier chuckled at Enright's left. Both men looked into the open bay through the window before each face.

Working the CCTV controls with his left hand, Enright called upon each bay camera to make a close survey of the open bay. For six minutes while Endeavor, Soyuz, and LACE, sped over two thousand miles of southeast Africa, Enright steered the moveable zoom lens of the television cameras until a complete and careful scan of the entire

181

bay was performed. The wall-to-wall reflective anti-laser blankets were meticulously examined. Two hours and eleven minutes aloft, Shuttle crossed Tanzania just east of Lake Nyasa lost below in the inky darkness.

Enright powered up the television camera mounted on the wrist joint and on the elbow joint of the 50-foot long, 900-pound, three-segment, remote manipulator system arm. The arm still cradled on the port sill of the open bay in front of Enright's window would be a critical element of Enright's forthcoming trek outside.

"Endeavor, Endeavor," the earphones crackled. "Configure AOS via IOS at 02 hours 13 minutes . . . Colorado Springs is now controlling."

During Shuttle's pass across sleeping Africa, NASA controllers in Houston had handed off Shuttle control to the Air Force Space Command's new Consolidated Space Operations Facility in the Rocky Mountains from which satelite missions are monitored. The sophisticated equipment there allowed the facility to manage Endeavor's voice communications, television broadcasts out the windows, and telemetry beacons.

"Copy, Flight," Parker called as he pushed his microphone button dangling from the cable locked to his chest. "How you mountain men doin' down there?"

Endeavor and the Air Force center communicated through the Indian Ocean Ship of the NASA network as Shuttle shot across the Mozambique Channel off southeast Africa between mainland Africa and the island of Madagascar. As Shuttle made for the large island just coming over the eastern horizon, the ship traveled ten times faster than a 150-grain bullet leaving the muzzle of a .30-06 rifle.

"Real fine down here, Will. We see your temps all looking in the green. We would like you to go from Power One to Power Two on your encryptor without delay, please."

The command pilot threw a toggle switch on Panel Aft-3 with his left hand at waist level. The ship's encryptor coded Endeavor's operational instrumentation telemetry beacon before the data beamed Earthward.

"That looks much cleaner, Endeavor. We're going to be with you only two minutes by IOS this pass. After we lose you here, your next network contact will be Australia in eleven minutes. How's the CCTV test?"

"About done," Enright called as he depressed his push-to-talk mike button. "Bay looks real clean. Blankets all secure. The RMS cameras, wrist and elbow, are functioning. The wrist camera is a bit grainy but should be usable."

"Copy, Jack. Before you go over the edge, give us a hack on RMS power-up. And we want you to begin cabin-depress routine when able."

"Just gettin' to the RMS qualification runs, Colorado. Should be well into the manipulator test by Australia. And we copy on the delta-P."

The earphones crackled high above sleeping Madagascar two and one-fourth hours into the mission.

"Colorado?" the AC called into the darkness.

"Guess they're out chasin' mountain women, Skipper."

"Can't blame 'em."

"I'm about ready for RMS power-up, Skip."

" 'Kay. Let me cruise up front to pop the cabin vents while you're breakin' out the RMS checklist. Holler if you have any ear trouble when I bleed the pressure."

" 'Kay . . . And no handstands," Enright called over his left shoulder as the AC disconnected his hoses and cables.

Free of the beta cloth-covered air hoses, the AC shoved off from the aft station. He floated with his arms and legs parallel to the floor. He swam to his left seat forward.

" 'It's a bird, it's a plane . . . ' " the horizontal floating pilot called through his open faceplate. Enright could not hear his captain's pleasure.

183

The AC floated sideways into his seat. He did not connect his lap belt but held his position with his right hand upon the glareshield overhanging the forward instrument panel.

"Got me, Jack?" the AC called after plugging in his communication cable.

"Five by, Skip."

Parker's body did not touch his seat as his left hand rested upon a triangular instrument array beneath his left forearm.

"Okay, Jack . . . Cabin relief enable . . . Now!" As the AC flipped and held down two spring-loaded toggle switches, air hissed out of the flightdeck. The AC felt his ears pop and he swallowed to equalize the pressure inside his head. As he depressed the two switches, the Colonel watched the fourth from the left of eleven vertical meters set into the ceiling just above the center windows. The meter's vertical tape slowly moved beside its fixed pointer. As he read the cabin pressure gauge, air pressure in the flightdeck dropped from its normal 15 pounds down to 10.2 pounds per square inch.

At both ends of the flightdeck, the two crewmen cleared their ears by yawning and by swallowing as the cabin pressure bled down.

The cabin relief maneuver was essential to Enright's planned walk in space to attach the grapple fixture to LACE. The object of lowering cabin pressure by one-third was to protect Enright from the "bends" during his extravehicular activity, EVA, outside. Since the EVA suit would be pressurized with pure oxygen at only 4.3 pounds per square inch, nitrogen gas from the cabin air mixture would bubble out into Enright's blood if he went from sea level pressure into the low pressure of the EVA space suit which was stowed in the mid-deck airlock. Such a bloodstream bubble in Enright's brain or lungs would mean an agonizing and convulsing death in space. To avoid the normal Shuttle EVA preparation of pre-breathing pure oxygen for three hours before going outside, the lowering of the pressure in the cabin's oxygen-nitrogen mixture for several hours would remove most of the nitrogen from Enright's blood. Such was hoped. The Shuttle program had abandoned the cabin-pressure-reduction routine in 1982 as only marginally reliable. The program adopted the more reliable three hours of oxygen pre-breathing before the EVA scheduled for Shuttle Five in November 1982. A whole day at the lower pressure was called for by the manual. That much time is required to wash most of the dissolved nitrogen from astronauts' blood. Now, Parker and Enright did not have time to wait and to do things by the numbers.

"Ten point two and holding," the AC called as he tightly held his nose while blowing hard through sealed nostrils to clear his ears. He ordered Mother to hold that level of cabin pressure.

"Okay back here, Will. Ready for RMS routine."

"Comin' back, Jack."

Parker swam back to Enright's side where he plugged into his hoses and cables.

Two hours and twenty minutes out, Endeavor flew over the black sea toward Australia now six minutes and 2,000 miles away.

Jacob Enright at the port side of the rear flightdeck had the inch-thick checklists for the RMS arm lashed to the aft instrument consoles. The pilots prepared to bring the remote manipulator system to life in preparation for capturing LACE with the wire snare at the arm's far end.

Standing shoulder-to-shoulder and facing rearward, the fliers raced the clock to begin the manipulator tests before interruption by Mission Control in Colorado.

The RMS built by Spar Aerospace in Toronto is a 100-million-dollar gift to the American space program from Canada. The exquisitely complex manipulator arm is the single piece of equipment in the billion-dollar starship which cost the American taxpayers nothing.

Enright flexed his knees to reach Panel Aft-14 below his waist. He crouched to read the controls for an emergency jettison of the whole 50-foot-long arm into space.

"RMS jettison pyros, lever-locked safe; jettison command lever-locked safe; retention latches jettison forward, lever-locked safe; midships latch, lever-locked safe; and, aft latch jettison, lever-locked safe . . . She's not goin' anyplace, Skipper."

"Let's do it then, Jack."

"Roger," Enright said over the voice-activated intercom behind his closed, laser-reflecting faceplate. The copilot worked the chest-high control panels: "At Panel-A8A2: Primary power on; command switch to deploy; RMS latches from latch to off to set release."

Two black-and-white television screens beside Enright's right shoulder blinked "RMS released." The 905-pound arm was free and resting upon its open triple-latch rests on the portside sill of the payload bay. "And heater switch to auto."

Inside the 15-inch-thick arm, 26 automatic heaters and thermostats came to life to keep the motors in the arm's shoulder, elbow, and wrist joints no colder than 14 degrees Fahrenheit when Endeavor sped through nighttime's cold of 250 degrees Fahrenheit below zero.

Enright laid his ungloved left hand upon Panel A8A1 at chest level. On the console's lower left corner, a small, red and white maple-leaf Canadian flag flew 130 nautical miles over the southernmost reaches of the Indian Ocean.

"Safing to auto," Enright called as he went down his thick checklist. "Brakes lever-locked off. Shoulder brace, lever-locked release." The launch phase, support strut secured to the arm's shoulder joint detached from the RMS arm outside Enright's rear window. "End effector switch to auto; end effector barber-poled derigidize, open, and cap-

186

ture snare extend."

Fifty feet away from the arm's shoulder joint, the arm's end effector is its electronic fingers, a tubular complex with three wire snares which close around the arm's target when a trigger is squeezed on the arm's pistol-grip rotational hand controller beside Enright's right hand. With the end effector unit's wire snare, the RMS can grab and deploy from the payload bay a 65,000-pound package. The same snare can retrieve from space and stow in the bay a 32,000-pound object.

"Parameter select to POSITION."

Enright turned a round knob on the Canadian instrument console. He stopped the six-position knob at its POSITION mark. Above the knob, three glass windows with digital numbers blinked to life.

With the setting knob, the pilot of the RMS selects the information to be displayed in the three two-inch-long windows. The display shows one of three dimensions on each dial face. The meters can display the end effector's position in an X-Y-Z coordinate axis, or its attitude in degrees of pitch, roll, and yaw. Or, the knob can direct the three windows to display the angle of bend in the arm's shoulder, elbow, and wrist joints, or the speed of the end effector through space, or the rate of angular change of the moving joints, or the meters can be commanded to show three sets of arm temperatures.

"Okay, position select, Jack."

The digital numerics on the console's three small meters flashed to life. The dials displayed the X-Y-Z axes of the end effector at the far end of the arm, about 55 feet away from Enright's rear window. The arm remained just touching its three open latches on the port sill of the bay illuminated in the darkness by the bay's six floodlights.

The X-Y-Z coordinate system is a means to identify a point on Shuttle or a place in space close to Shuttle. In the airless vacuum and zero-gravity, the concepts of up, down, left, and right have no meaning without some kind of benchmark for a fixed reference. For Shuttle aloft, that reference is the X-Y-Z coordinate system, a three-dimensional grid akin to the X-Y-Z system drawn on graph paper in high school geometry. The X-axis runs the length of Shuttle from nose to tail down the ship's long axis. Locations along the X-axis are either in front of or behind the zero point on the X-axis. The Y-axis is "horizontal" to Shuttle, passing from one wingtip through the ship to the other wingtip. It is perpendicular to the X-axis. The X- and Y-axis intersect to form a cross within the same flat plane. The Z-axis is vertical. Points along the Z-axis are "above" or "below" the point where the vertical Z-axis intersects the intersection of the X- and Y-axes.

To provide an immovable reference point, the three-way intersection of the X- Y-, and Z-axes must be fixed somewhere in space or in Shuttle. This Zero Point datum is fixed outside of the shuttle. It is located precisely 236 inches ahead of Endeavor's nose tip and 400 inches below the tip of the ship's nose. This is the location fixed in space and memorized within all of Shuttle's computers. From this Zero Point beyond Shuttle's nose, all points within and without Shuttle are measured. It is the permanent, fixed benchmark for labeling up, down, left, right, fore, and aft. From this Zero Point, all directions toward Shuttle along the lengthwise, X-axis are positive. To a crewperson standing on the flightdeck and looking forward, points left along the sideways, Y-axis are negative and points right are positive. And, along the Z-axis from the Zero Point ahead of and below the nose, the direction "upward" toward Shuttle is positive.

With the RMS parameter knob set in the POSITION mode, the end effector's position in space, and the locations of outside targets, are measured in inches from this Zero Point. These measurements in inches are shown in the three meters on the RMS console at the aft crew station.

The RMS is built to function like the human arm. Its shoulder joint and shoulder-joint motor are attached to Shuttle on the portside sill of the payload bay beneath the rear window. The shoulder joint is mounted on the bay sill at a point $679\frac{1}{2}$ inches from the X-Y-Z axis Zero Point. This puts the shoulder joint 37 feet behind Endeavor's nose tip. The 251-inch-long "upper arm" is attached to the RMS shoulder joint. At the far end of the upper arm is the elbow joint, its motor, and the elbow television camera. The 278-inch-long "forearm" stretches aft from the elbow joint. Like the human arm, the shoulder joint flexes left and right, and up and down. The elbow joint flexes up and down. At the aft end of the forearm, the RMS "wrist" is 74 inches long and includes two joint motors. These two motors flex the lower arm up and down, left and right. At the far rear end of the wrist is the end effector unit with its three wire snares which are the arm's fingers for grabbing targets. Mounted atop the forward end of the forearm is the elbow's closed-circuit television camera. Another CCTV camera is mounted on the top of the aft end of the wrist, just on the near side of the end effector. These two cameras feed their black-and-white images to the two wall-mounted screens.

"Ready to run in auto, Skipper."

"You got the con, Jack."

"Okay."

Enright switched on the arm-mounted television cameras and the two CCTV screens to his right.

"Auto one and run. Ready light is on." A white light illuminated on the Canadian console.

The RMS arm has five different modes for steering the arm through space. In the automatic mode, Mother steers the arm by memory from her computers. Mother has memorized two dozen programs for guiding the end effector to pre-determined destinations outside. Four of these

Programmed Automatic Sequences can be called up instantly by turning the RMS mode selector knob to position auto 1, auto 2, auto 3, or auto 4.

Enright chose automatic trajectory Number One. To ask Mother to fly the end effector on a memorized path other than these four routes, Enright must call up a coded, automatic sequence using his computer keyboard in the Command Automatic Sequence mode.

"Lights on," Enright said as a white IN PROGRESS light illuminated with the arm's first movement out of its cradle.

Mother's computer spoke to the arm's two-joint power conditioners, one manipulator controller interface unit, six motor module/signal conditioners, and six servo power amplifiers. The whole arm rose at the shoulder joint until the arm was straight and rigid, with the end effector suspended two feet above the bay wall. The arm stopped at this position at an automatic, pre-programmed pause point. In Mother's memory are 100 automatic pause points where the arm stops until the pilot tells Mother to advance the RMS arm to the next memorized pause point.

Enright studied the three sets of numbers in the small meters by his chest. He glanced at the two televisions at his right shoulder. He saw the bird's-eye view of the lighted bay as seen from the cameras on the arm's elbow and wrist. Satisfied that the arm would not strike a shuttle structure en route to the next pause point, he pushed a spring-loaded toggle switch upon which he rested his left thumb. On its own, the switch would return to its center, neutral position.

"In motion," Enright said as he pushed the proceed switch. The arm's joints flexed as the arm bent inward across the open bay. As the end effector moved silently at a programmed speed of two feet per second, the arm stopped at a pause point every few seconds so Enright

190

could consult his televisions before he sent the next proceed command.

"Endeavor: Configure AOS Yarradee at 02 hours, 26 minutes. We have solid downlink from you and your temperatures look fine. We see you depressed to 10 point 2 in the cabin. How's the RMS shakedown going?"

"We're runnin' auto-1 now, Australia. Jack is about to his auto-1 point of resolution at keel Number Two."

Mother was busy flexing all three of the arm's joints as she flew the end effector through the inside of the payload bay. Each time the joint motors in their "safing" mode brought the arm to a halt without using the mechanical brakes, Enright directed the arm onward. The end effector finally stopped with the far end of the arm in the rear half of the open bay. The end effector stopped two inches above the floor of the bay just to the side of the floor's centerline. Enright consulted his control console before calling the sleeping Australian continent.

"Okay, Flight. We're stopped at keel Two. Showing end effector parameters at X equals 902 inches, Y at minus 4, and Z at 410 inches . . . Right on. Mother flew it the whole way."

"Good news, Endeavor. We'll be with you six minutes. Colorado will listen quietly as you run the RMS through its paces."

" 'Kay, Colorado. I'm takin' the arm up to keel Number One in mode manual-augmented now."

"We're listening, Jack. And we're getting a super view down here through the arm's elbow camera."

"Real fine, Australia. We're running manual-augmented, using orbiter-unloaded coordinates . . . Joint angle is up on the parameter display . . . And we've powered up the RHC and the THC."

"Copy, Endeavor. Rotational hand controller and translational hand controller on in manual-augmented—orbiter dry."

The remote arm's manual-augmented mode for flying the RMS is a semi-automatic routine. Although Mother flies the entire arm system in the automatic mode, Mother and the arm's pilot work together in manual-augmented.

In the manual-augmented mode, the arm pilot steers only the arm's far end, the end effector unit. The astronaut standing behind the command pilot's empty seat steers the end effector with a gearshift-style stick protruding from its box housing between the two aft windows facing into the payload bay. This is the translational hand controller, THC. The THC directs the end effector in motion through space. Pushing the THC's knobby handle forward toward the rear wall moves the end effector unit, EEU, toward Shuttle's tail. Pulling on the THC directs the EEU backward toward the flightdeck. Pushing the THC left or right, up or down, moves the EEU in the same direction. Where Enright stood at Parker's right, the copilot's right hand can squeeze the pistol grip of the rotational hand controller, RHC. Located in the port corner of the aft flightdeck station, the RHC beneath the two CCTV screens directs the rotation of the EEU about the arm's wrist joint. As the RHC handle is rocked, the end effector moves in the corresponding direction at its stationary position.

Although the pilot flies the EEU with the THC in his left hand and the RHC in his right hand, the arm is actually moved by the ship's computers in manual-augmented mode. The pilot's hand controllers do not directly steer either the arm or its end effector. The hand controllers tell Mother where the pilot wants the EEU to move and the computer makes every decision about which arm joint to flex to accomplish the assignment.

To steer the EEU by the pilot's hand commands in manual-augmented operation, the RMS computer must know which coordinate axis with which to tell up from

192

down, left from right. By selection of the orbiter-unloaded position on his control knob, Enright told Mother to fly the arm with reference to an empty payload bay using the X-Y-Z axis system. The computer can also be instructed to think in terms of the EEU's own three-axis coordinate system, or to think with an orbiter-loaded coordinate system, or to think in terms of the coordinate references of an outside payload with the arm in the payload mode of operation.

"Hand controller alive," Enright called. His left hand touched the THC between the aft windows, and his right hand held the RHC grip. Slowly, he commanded the arm to come toward the aft windows in the forward end of the payload bay. He pulled the THC and the arm's computer flexed all of the arm's joints as he asked Mother to fly the EEU toward him. The arm responded as the EEU low inside the bay moved up the open bay's floor. The flexed arm's elbow rose 25 feet into the black sky above Endeavor which cruised eastward over nighttime Australia.

"Go in Man-Aug all the way, Colorado."

"Copy, Jack. Looks good from here," the voice from Australia responded.

"Rogo, Colorado. Goin' back to POSITION on the parameters."

Enright took his left hand from the THC and the arm stopped dead. He twisted the knob by his chest to call up the inches-from-datum numerics in the three small windows on his console. Returning his left hand to the THC, he flew the EEU with Mother's help to a point 214 inches from his window facing the bay.

"All stop at keel One." Enright checked his position indicator meters. "We're at 790 inches in X0, minus 4 in Y0, and on the floor in Z0. Real fine in manual-augmented."

With his right hand, Enright rotated the end effector

193

with the arm's main joints stopped.

Enright used the THC to raise the EEU to the level of the shoulder joint on the bay sill.

"EEU to Z0 of 444 point 8 inches. All stop."

"Copy, Jack. We see it from down here."

The EEU at the end of the wrist joint hung from the arm above the open bay's centerline 83 inches from each side of the payload bay.

"Goin' now to manual single-joint drive, Colorado."

"Take your time, Jack."

"We'll try not to bend anything back there, Flight," the command pilot radioed from Enright's left side.

Single-joint drive is one of three manual modes for handflying the remote arm. The RMS pilot directs each of the arm's joints one at a time. The two hand controllers are not used. Instead, the astronaut selects which of the arm's segments is to be flown and he drives that joint alone by a spring-loaded toggle switch. The switch is pressed to either its positive position or its negative direction. When released, the switch returns to its neutral stop position.

Enright turned the large circular knob at the upper left corner of the Canadian console to SINGLE. At the console's lower center, he turned the parameter selector knob to ATTITUDE so the three meters would display in degrees of pitch, roll, and yaw, the attitude of the single joint selected for movement.

The arm had stopped with the upper arm reaching upward and outward over the bay's sill at the shoulder. The forearm flexed at its elbow joint high in the black sky. And the wrist section drooped at the centerline of the bay's floor.

"Endeavor: Colorado is about to lose you via Yarradee. Acquire Orrorra in one minute. Sunup in fifteen . . ."

The two pilots floating at the rear of the flightdeck ignored the ground's transmission lost in static as the station at Yarradee went out of radio range a thousand miles behind Shuttle. The nighttime horizon over central Australia blocked the FM radio signal from the ground limited to line-of-sight range.

Rushing to test each arm mode as quickly as possible, the fliers crammed into less than an hour the RMS shakedown which took four to six hours on earlier missions.

With the arm's elbow hanging over Endeavor's port side, Enright powered up the yaw axis of the wrist, one of that joint's three axes of freedom. Flicking the command toggle switch to the spring-loaded negative direction, Enright asked Mother to raise only the vertical wrist joint just beyond the crew's aft windows.

Slowly, the computer swung the wrist joint upward until the joint was perpendicular with the level of the aft station windows. When Enright removed his thumb from the switch, the wrist stopped, pointing the wrist camera and the end effector at the lower edge of Enright's rear-facing window.

Jacob Enright turned the joint selector knob to SHOULDER-YAW. A momentary flick of the command toggle switch in the negative direction swung the upper arm further over Endeavor's port side in front of the copilot. This one-second movement of the upper arm brought the end effector to the lower corner of Enright's window. He turned the knob to ELBOW. Another brief touch of the command toggle in its positive direction flexed the elbow and raised the wrist and its camera to the center of Enright's window.

Both fliers looked into the top of the two CCTV monitors by Enright's right shoulder. In the screen was Jack Enright's helmet behind the aft window's two layers of glass.

The copilot stuffed his hand into the bulging pocket in the thigh of his deflated pressure suit. He retrieved a rumpled cloth pennant from the pocket. He carefully stretched the small, square banner across the window before his helmeted face.

Parker leaned toward Enright's shoulder so he could read the sign's lettering. The brilliant floodlights in the open bay shone through the pennant and made the letters readable from behind, although the letters were backward as seen inside the flightdeck. The two pilots consulted the wall-mounted television screen to confirm that the arm's wrist camera was focused on Enright's window and its little banner.

"Merry Christmas," Parker read from the monitor screen over his partner's shoulder. Far below, Christmas was seven days away.

"And God bless us everyone," the radio crackled. "Colorado with you through Orrorra at 02 hours, 33 minutes. Good morning again, Endeavor."

"And to you, Australia. But it's afternoon up here," the AC drawled, pressing his mike button on his chest. "How's our downlink?"

"Real crisp, Endeavor. With you four minutes this pass. The CCTV from the wrist looks super from here. Continue with the RMS tests. We'd like you to run the arm to the end of its reach envelope aft in direct-drive, please. When you reach singularity, bring it back to keel Number Two in manual-backup. You'll be on your own by then for going on to PDP deployment."

"Gotcha, Flight," Enright called, pressing his mike button. "Goin' to direct-drive now."

The arm's fourth manual mode of operation is one of two fully manual systems. In direct-drive, the arm is flown one joint at a time by the joint-selector knob and the command toggle switch. But unlike the three modes already tested, the direct-drive system has no computer assistance from Mother. It is strictly an eyeball operation with the pilots' aids limited to the aft and overhead windows and the arm's own television cameras. The steering commands bypass Mother and run by hard wire from the instrument panel to each joint motor. The only usable electronic aids to the crew are the three position meters in front of Enright which were set to show the end effector's position in inches from the zero datum point.

"Runnin' in direct, Flight," Enright called as he switched first to SHOULDER-YAW.

Enright steered the upper arm which slowly moved from its shoulder joint affixed to Shuttle in the direction of the far diagonal end of the cargo bay on the starboard side. Parker at Enright's left watched the drooping wrist move outside his aft window.

"Two feet per second, Flight."

"We see it, Jack. Super view down here of the thermal blankets from the wrist camera."

"EEU at X0 equals 941 inches," Enright radioed as the parameter dial confirmed that the end effector was at the center point of the bay's length.

Switching to ELBOW, Enright flicked the toggle switch which commanded the forearm of the RMS to reach toward the bay's far end. As Endeavor sped over eastern Australia in pre-dawn darkness, the 278-inch-long forearm slowly maneuvered toward the aft bay area outside Parker's window.

When a tail thruster automatically thumped once to hold Shuttle's attitude, the arm oscillated very slightly. The joint motors in their safing mode momentarily locked the arm in place until the vibration through the arm stopped.

With the upper arm and forearm nearly horizontal, Enright switched to WRIST-PITCH and the toggle switch sent the EEU reaching for the bay's far corner.

A yellow SINGULARITY caution light flashed on the control panel. The arm could reach no further.

"Okay, Flight," Enright radioed. "We're at reach envelope. The EEU is stopped at X_0 equals plus 1,159 inches,

Y_0 at plus 82 point 5, and Z_0 is at plus 444 inches. Good clearance around the OSS pallet back there."

"We see it, Jack. We're looking via the wrist camera right into the eye of the aft bulkhead TV camera. Get on to approaching the PDP package. Forget about keel Two. We're only with you another minute."

"Rog. Goin' to manual backup."

The fifth and final RMS steering mode is the totally manual, eyeballs-only mechanism. The arm is flown by an entirely separate hard wire system isolated from all other arm circuits. There is no computer help, not even from the digital position meters. It is a pilot's job.

"Backup engaged," Enright advised as he used his left hand to control the joint-selector knob and the command toggle switch. Although the other semi-manual modes all use the same joint-selector knob and command toggle switch, manual backup operation has its own of both, totally separate from any other RMS circuitry. The isolated controls are at the lower left corner of the chest-high Canadian console.

Steering the arm one joint at a time, Enright guided it toward the payload package in the rear third of the bay. He steered the arm toward the Office of Space Science (OSS) pallet bolted to the bay's floor as Parker spotted for him out his starboard window. "Up . . . Up . . . Easy, Jack . . . Wrist left . . . Elbow down . . . Easy." As the command pilot called out the steering commands, Enright's busy hands complied. His eyes darted from window to television to window.

"You're about over the edge, guys, at 02 plus 37. Next contact in 18 minutes via Hawaii. Sunrise in 10. Good . . ."

"Copy, Australia," the taller airman drawled. "Peace and quiet at last, Number One," he sighed into the voice-activated intercom.

"With you on that one, Skipper. Goin' to manual-augmented . . . Let Mother help."

"Okay, Jack."

Endeavor, Soyuz ever silent, and LACE rolling peacefully in the glare of the lights from Soyuz, all crossed the Australian eastern coastline at Brisbane for the dark South Pacific. "Looky there, Skip," Enright called with excitement as he pointed out his window toward Endeavor's tail. "Think I saw the glow. Let's kill the bay floods, just for a second."

"Think so? Okay, Jack."

Enright's left hand threw the six switches which extinguished the bay's floodlights. The payload bay went black, the perfect moist blackness of the nighttime South Pacific. The RMS arm was parked a foot above the OSS pallet.

"Gawd," Parker breathed. "Good eye, Jack. Incredible."

The fliers were transfixed at their aft windows.

Outside, Endeavor's tail and the bulbous protrusions of the OMS pods glowed orange. A fluorescent orange glow, like a neon sign flashing "eat" bathed Shuttle's back end. The strange glow was first reported by Shuttle Three in April 1982. On Shuttle's body, high altitude atoms of oxygen struck the ship in the nearly perfect vacuum of near-Earth space. At Shuttle's velocity of 17,500 miles per hour, the occasional stray atoms of oxygen 130 nautical miles aloft hit the vehicle so hard that their energy caused the ionic orange glow visible only in darkness. The tail shimmered in the eerie and ghostly glow. A crusty old sailor before the mast would have called it St. Elmo's Fire.

"Amazing, Number One. But let's hit the floods and get the PDP out. Wanna see what LACE is sweating out."

Enright nodded and revived the bay's arc lights one at a time. The arm still hung motionless where it had been parked.

As Endeavor sped over the dark South Pacific toward the New Hebrides Islands 1,200 miles and four flying minutes away, Colonel Parker floated at Enright's left side. The AC's left boot was anchored to a foot restraint on the flightdeck floor. His right foot was cocked behind his left ankle. With his weightless legs flexed at the knees, Parker had assumed the resting position of horses. Without thought, Parker stroked his painful and throbbing right leg. The knee pain radiated upward into his thigh across his groin and into his right hip. His sigh of anguish rode sufficient breath to trigger his voice-activated microphone at his lips.

"You okay, Will?" Enright queried with both of his hands full of RMS controls.

"Huh? . . . Right and tight, Number One . . . While you fly the arm to the plasma package, I'm goin' to visit the biffy."

"Don't fall in, Will. It's a long way down! . . . And don't flush until the train leaves the station." Enright grinned behind his closed visor toward the tall pilot's back. The AC had already pulled his plugs and floated toward the forward cockpit.

Drifting slowly, the command pilot floated horizontally toward the six dark front windows of the cockpit. With a push from his hand upon the back of his empty front seat, Parker did a half somersault and sank headfirst down the hatchway in the floor behind his left seat.

The weightless airman entered the dark mid-deck. He did a momentary handstand before twisting rightside up with a gentle kick on the ceiling by the square hole through which he had just floated headfirst.

Parker steadied himself with his fingers gripping a handhold on the mid-deck wall. The glare of the flight-deck lights topside of the access hole bathed him in white light. He hovered beside the locked and sealed, side door-way of the mid-deck. Through that circular hatch, Enright and Parker had entered Endeavor three and one-half hours earlier.

At Will Parker's side, the hatch's 12-inch-wide, triple-pane round window was dark behind its sun filter. He braced his back against the mid-deck airlock, a floor-to-ceiling cylinder five feet wide. The airlock filled the rear section of the mid-deck. Beyond the airlock wide enough to hold two pilots was the payload bay's lethal vacuum.

The AC reached over his head to the instrument panel on the ceiling by the access hole. On mid-deck, Overhead Panel-MO13Q, Parker flipped eight toggle switches which filled the cramped lower deck with floodlights.

Pushing off from the airlock, Parker floated to the front end of Shuttle's basement. On the flightdeck above, Jacob Enright still worked the RMS arm.

At the front of the mid-deck, the AC stopped his weightless flight at the floor-to-ceiling stacks of small lockers resembling a wall of large post office boxes. He opened his personal box and peered in at floating combs, toothbrushes, toothpaste, and a safety razor. He retrieved a small brown bag before he closed the locker box.

Twisting his pressure-suited body, he turned toward the rear airlock and pushed off the wall of lockers. He floated back toward the portside hatch and the ceiling hole above.

At the portside, rear corner of the mid-deck, wedged tightly between the cylindrical airlock and the wall, is the waste collection system compartment—the zero gravity latrine.

The zero-gravity biffy resembles a tiny stall from a bus station washroom.

Parker opened the narrow metal door which revealed the unisex commode. From the open door of the small stall, Parker could have unraveled the privacy curtain which stretches from the vertical edge of the open biffy door to the galley which faces the latrine. The curtain encloses the area of the side hatch. Another curtain can be pulled from the top edge of the open stall door to be stretched overhead to block out the view from the flight-

201

deck into the biffy from the gaping access hole in the ceiling. What the hell, Parker thought.

Parker backed into the stall and forced his floating body down onto the commode's saddle. He pulled a lap belt across his waist. His feet found the foot restraints which secured his boots to the floor. With Parker wearing his bulky pressure suit, the fit in the stall was tight.

The Colonel opened the small paper sack which he had retrieved from his personal locker. A finger-size plastic hypodermic syringe floated out beside a small amber vial of fluid. He pulled off the guard cap from an inch-long, 20-gauge needle.

Parker caught the syringe before it could float with the cabin air currents up through the ceiling hole toward the flightdeck. The sitting pilot pulled the syringe plunger out, almost to the end of the plastic syringe. With the plunger retracted, he thrust the needle into the vial's rubber stopper. After depressing the plunger to fill the vial with air, he withdrew into the syringe an equal volume of fluid. The needle squeaked as he pulled it from the vial. He read the vial before he returned it to the crumpled sack: "Carbocaine 2% Mepivacaine HCL, *veterinary equine use only.*"

Looking at the syringe, the tall airman smiled. Many times, he had trusted his life and comfort to an old, sweating horse. Now he would again. A man should ride a tall horse, he mused. Good old salt.

After unzipping the suit's horizontal belly zipper, he forced his hand into the bulky suit until it touched his right thigh as far as the suit would let him reach. Even through his long woolies, he could feel the heat which throbbed through his right leg from the shin upward through his groin. With his eyes closed, Parker pulled out his hand and he returned it to his thigh with the syringe.

Parker grimaced as the needle penetrated his long johns and his thigh. He slowly injected the horse painkiller into

202

his body.

The sitting pilot capped the needle and returned the emptied hypo and the vial to the little sack which he stuffed into his suit pocket.

Parker sat quietly, fully suited, secured by his seat belt to a multimillion-dollar toilet which hurtled through space at a velocity of 300 miles per minute. He removed his stuffy helmet which he parked in midair before his face.

Slowly, the grinding pain in Parker's right leg drew away from the airman who slouched at his post in the stall. His eyes closed lightly and the synaptic distance between the tall man and his inflamed leg grew. In a minute, his long legs were gone and his hip was gone and his lower back was gone. The lower half of the flier had gone to sleep seduced by his injection. Without thought, he hugged the handrails on either side of his hips to keep from flying away with his numb legs left behind.

Without his helmet, the command pilot could now listen to his ship.

As Shuttle lives, so does she breathe. The warm, dry air from liquid oxygen bottles carried the low hum of cabin fans and ducts. Hot black boxes in floors, bulkheads, and equipment bays hummed softly. From his painless and cozy metal corner, the drowsy airman imagined himself in a submarine, an iron lady sheltering his fragile manform with her warm metal heart.

A dazzling ring of piercing white light burst around the circular frame of the hatchway's window shade just beyond the biffy's open door. Nine minutes and 3,000 miles past Australia's midnight darkness, Endeavor was coasting into sunrise high above the Tokelau Islands in a dawn South Pacific. Within the starship where everything floated without weight, there was utterly no sense of motion.

With wisps of daylight from the shaded hatch touching his numb legs, Parker opened his eyes. He looked into the sweat-stained interior of his helmet, which floated a foot from his face. He licked his strangely dry mouth and his lips which faintly tingled from the horse medicine flowing in his veins with narcotic tranquility.

Parker locked his helmet to his suit's neckring before he unstrapped himself from the seat which he could not feel. He pushed his weightless body from the tiny stall and he closed the metal door behind him.

With his legs free from heat and pain, but useless, he placed his fingers on the sill of the ceiling hole and lifted himself toward the flightdeck. His left hand hit the eight switches on the mid-deck ceiling as he flew up through the hatchway. With the lights exinguished, the mid-deck was illuminated by the ring of blinding daylight leaking around the edges of the sunshade secured to the porthole in the side door.

The faceplate on Parker's helmet was open for breathing when he floated up into the harsh daylight of morning on the upstairs flightdeck. His legs trailed limply behind him as he slowly flew to Enright's side at the rear of the cockpit. In zero gravity, he did not need his legs anyway.

The copilot was busy with his manipulator controls when the AC reached his side. Enright did not notice that his captain had to crouch and use his hands to steer his feet into the floor's foot restraints. Parker rose, connected his two air hoses to his suit, and plugged into the aft station intercom. When the AC felt the suit's air supply against his face from the neckring vents, he closed his faceplate and visor to breathe air laced with the scent of rubber hoses and sweat.

"About ready to send out the dogs for you, Skipper," Enright said without moving his face from the large rear window now filled with morning daylight, LACE glinting in the ferocious sunshine, and the bulbous Soyuz.

"Feel much better, Jack. Ready to deploy the PDP?"

The AC glanced at the mission clock between the two square windows in the aft bulkhead adjacent the payload bay. It read "Day 00: 02 Hours: 47 Minutes: 30 Seconds, Mission Elapsed Time."

"Got the end effector secured to the grapple probe on the plasma package. About ready."

"Super, Jack."

Parker glanced over Enright's right shoulder at the twin television monitors. The top screen was full of the grapple rod at the top of the package which was locked to the floor of the bay within its protective pallet.

"Ready to deploy the PDP, Will."

"It's your baby, Number One."

Enright rechecked the RMS panel before his chest. The small lighted windows at the upper right corner confirmed the secure capture by the end effector of the grapple handle atop the plasma diagnostics package.

With his left hand, Enright turned the RMS mode knob to auto sequence Three and the AUTO-3 light illuminated white. The AC threw a switch to release the hold-down clamps at the base of the PDP housing. Enright flicked the spring-loaded, proceed toggle switch and Mother slowly flew the RMS arm upward.

The 353-pound, 26-inch-long, 42-inch-diameter cylinder, built by the University of Iowa, slowly lifted out of the OSS pallet which held it. The PDP stopped at the arm's first, automatic pause point five feet above the bay floor.

"Looks real clean, Jack."

"And Mother likes it . . . Let's fly with it, Skip. Goin' to manual-augmented."

As Endeavor dashed in daylight across the Equator northeastward to begin Revolution Three at 02 hours, 51 minutes out, Enright powered up the translational hand controller for his left hand and the rotational hand controller for his right hand.

The Aircraft Commander busied himself with the aft console for the digital autopilot making certain that the

RCS thrusters held Shuttle's trim with the nose pointing northward, perpendicular to their ground track, and with Endeavor's belly facing east toward the rising sun. The DAP held the ship's left wing pointed straight down toward the brilliant sea.

Enright, with Mother's help, steered the end effector with the PDP attached at the far end of the 50-foot-long RMS arm. The computer raised the PDP over the bay's left side toward LACE which rolled slowly in the blinding sunlight 30 yards away. With the RMS mode selector in manual-augmented-orbiter-loaded, the RMS gently steered the PDP toward LACE.

"Zero point two feet per second," Enright called as his hands worked with Mother's silicon brain to fly the plasma-sensing package toward LACE where the PDP would sniff for LACE's wake of radiation and electrical fields.

The arm hoisted the plasma sensor 40 feet above the open bay. The two pilots could only watch it through the two overhead windows above their rear work station. When the arm stopped at a pause point, Enright commanded the EEU to maneuver slowly outboard until the package had been waved in the direction of the end of Shuttle's port wingtip. From there, the arm would ferry the package over the open bay doors toward the opposite wingtip. Outside their windows and on the television screen, the pilots watched the PDP canister.

"Endeavor, Endeavor: Colorado with you by Hawaii at 02 hours, 53 minutes. With you four minutes. Your temperatures are Go. And we're looking at PDP data coming downlink."

"Mornin', Hawaii," the tall flier called. "What do you see from the PDP?"

"Backroom says you're plowing through a wall of electromagnetic garbage . . . Drop your visors immediately if they're up."

206

The two airmen looked at each other through their laser-proof visors.

"Garbage, Flight?" Enright inquired, pressing his mike button.

"Like boating down the Cuyahoga in Cleveland, buddy," the radio crackled.

10

"What about a magnetic wake? Why is that serious, as problems go?"

"The best we had hoped for, Colonel, was a simple mechanical failure with LACE." Admiral Hauch's large frame was rumpled and exhausted. Behind him, the clock on the wall of the basement bunker read 53 minutes past noon Washington time. Beside it, a second clock face read 02:53. Beneath that clock hung the words "MISSION ELAPSED TIME, SHUTTLE."

"A breakdown in LACE's flux generator is leaking a wake of magnetic energy." The Admiral slouched in his high-backed chair. He fumbled with his thick fingers and looked at his sweating hands instead of at the ten grim faces around the large table set upon the glass floor. "Any other problem with LACE would have meant that we only had to bring her down at a reasonable opportunity — hopefully before she takes a pot shot at Endeavor, or God forbid at Soyuz. But magnetic problems mean that now we are on a deadline, an absolute deadline. General Gordon, you should take it from here . . ."

The General from the Air Force and commander of the new U.S. Air Force Space Command from Colorado Springs nodded from across the table.

"Admiral, a magnetic disturbance inside LACE means that the bird is greatly susceptible to external magnetic influences. Any sudden magnetic disturbance in space could trigger another round of stray firings of the laser . . ."

"Can these magnetic disturbances be predicted—disturbances from space, I mean?"

"Not from space, no, Colonel . . . But from Earth, yes, and predicted to the second."

"From Earth, General?"

"Yes. Michael, what do you have?"

"General." A tall engineer in civilian clothes took over. Group Captain Michael Dzurovcin looked tired from his dawn flight to Washington from the Air Force Geophysics Laboratory at Hanscom Air Force Base, Massachusetts. "We can predict a serious—very serious—magnetic perturbance when the vehicles cross the SAA . . ."

"The SAA?"

"Yes. The South Atlantic Anomaly—a huge area due east of South America which is the center of gigantic magnetic storms. At Endeavor's present altitude, the SAA stretches from Uruguay in South America all the way across the Atlantic to Cape Town, South Africa. And it's a thousand nautical miles wide, from latitude 30 degrees South down to 48 degrees South. It was the South Atlantic Anomaly which caused one of the early failures on the Hubble Space Telescope. By June 1990, after only five weeks in space, NASA figured out that the Anomaly's intense radiation interference was actually destroying computer memory on board the telescope. Memory bits which were supposed to be off were switched on, and on-bits were switched off by the radiation fields . . .

"When LACE rides into that area, it will be like she hit a wall—a wall of magnetic interference. Our guess is that when LACE enters the region, no ship close to her will come out of it."

"When does LACE cross this area of the South Atlantic?"

"Our vehicles, and Soyuz, squarely enter the SAA for the first time during Shuttle's sixth revolution at mission elapsed time of 8 hours and 16 minutes. They'll all be inside the Anomaly on that pass for nine minutes. They cross again on Shuttle's seventh revolution at 9 hours and 43 minutes. On that transit, they are inside for a very long 14 minutes. These are actual entries into the zone. But they also make a very close brush alongside the SAA, within 75 miles, on Shuttle's rev five at 6 hours and 47 minutes mission elapsed time. That proximity pass lasts only about one minute."

"Tell us, Michael, is there any way LACE could pass over the Anomaly on rev seven for a quarter of an hour without being activated?"

"Admiral, in our judgment at Hanscom, she won't survive the rev six transit without the laser very likely to fire. And just grazing the zone on rev five for 70 seconds has us worried. Very worried."

The weary engineer studied the clock on the wall behind the Admiral, who had not lifted his face.

"Admiral, we have another five hours and eleven minutes till that rev six direct entry into the Anomaly for Shuttle to disable LACE. After that, in our best guess, LACE will probably vaporize anything within fifty miles of her . . . And that assumes we can survive the close pass on rev five in about four hours from now. Going to be real tight."

The glass greenhouse was silent. The Admiral's tired face looked upward through the glass roof, and with his mind's eye, through the concrete ceiling, through the hundreds of feet of earth, through the Pentagon above, into the early-winter afternoon a week before Christmas, and through the tranquil, coldly blue sky to where a winged starship pursued her deadly target.

210

"How's the view, buddy?"

"CAVU everywhere, California," Parker called from his place at Enright's left side in the rear of the flightdeck. He peered into the open payload bay through the rear window at his face. As Endeavor flew on her side, over the sill of the bay the coast of southern California passed with brilliant clarity: what airmen call CAVU for "ceiling and visibility, unlimited." Raising his face to the aft overhead window, the AC could see LACE tumbling slowly with a dazzling blue Pacific beneath it.

"Magnificent, Buckhorn. Real pretty down there. Sure doesn't look like winter."

"Never does here, Will. You're directly over San Diego right now. Coming up on 03 hours, 05 minutes, 30 seconds, MET. And your next sunset is in 27 minutes."

"Copy that, Colorado," the floating AC drawled.

"Your vitals look stable, Endeavor. We'll be with you Stateside for another sixteen minutes. We're looking at a real good data dump downlink. Your OI telemetry is very clean . . . Ah, the backroom boys want you to pace yourselves to get out to the target, secure the grapple fixture, affix the PAM, and maneuver clear of the target well before 08 hours, 16 minutes at the very latest. If possible, they want the job done and you guys out of there before 06 plus 47. Copy?"

"Copy, Flight, eight and a quarter for sure, and 07 hours if able . . . What's the deal?"

"Backroom wants the target safed before you enter the South Atlantic Anomaly on rev six, at eight and a quarter. You're going to pass within 80 miles of it though on rev five at 06 plus 47."

The two airmen who floated at the aft station looked at each other.

"Okay," Enright cut in as Endeavor shot over New Mexico's San Jose River and 11,300-foot high Mount Taylor

211

three minutes east of San Diego.

In a moment of silence over the air-to-ground link, the pilots returned to steering the Plasma Diagnostics Package at the end of the manipulator. They waved the arm over Endeavor's open backside.

"Good data coming down from the PDP, Will," the Spacecraft Communicator in the mountains of Colorado Springs radioed. His voice traveled at the speed of light over land wire to California for transmission to Shuttle by the huge dish antenna at Goldstone, California.

Endeavor coasted on her side over the eastern horizon at her speed of five miles per second. She left Goldstone out of radio range in her dust at 3 hours 9 minutes into the flight. Endeavor had already traveled 53,000 miles since leaving the ground.

"With you by Northrop," the ground called as Endeavor passed 130 nautical miles above Roy, New Mexico, and the southern Rockies. Ordinarily, the White Sands Missile Range in New Mexico only talked with Shuttle flights during a landing at Northrop's sandy runway.

Deep within the bowels of the Rocky Mountain bunkers of the U. S. Space Command, a computer's silicon heart twitched and television screens blinked with the curved plot lines of orbital paths. Across a row of television monitors, three small dots moved in single-file formation over an outline of the southwestern United States. The blip farthest west was slowly gaining on the two images ahead of it. The lead dot crossed the screens from west to east directly over Galena, Kansas. Two American fliers piloted the small, lead blip. In the upper corner of the screen, numerics ticked past 03 hours, 11 minutes. Beside the numbers was the word "Shuttle."

"Endeavor, Colorado via White Sands. We show Soyuz maneuvering up there. What can you see? Standing by . . ."

The two fliers in the sky raised their helmeted faces to

212

he two overhead windows of the aft flightdeck. As Endeavor flew on her port side with her nose pointing northward, the overhead windows, one above each crewman, faced west toward the ground track already flown. The ship was directly beneath the white sun which bathed the three vehicles in blinding, painful daylight.

"Flight," Enright called, with his face floating close to the portside ceiling portal. "We're pretty much subsolar here. Quite a bit of washout in the high sun angle. But Soyuz is approaching from the target's far side. Yeh, there goes one of her thrusters. She's braking, I'd say. Call her range maybe 50 meters from the target. Puts Brother Ivan about 100 meters from us. She's stopped now."

"We confirm, Jack. Thank you."

As the three ships in tight formation sped over the Midwest just south of St. Louis, only 6½ flying minutes past San Diego, Endeavor passed out of radio range with White Sands.

"Endeavor: Mission Control Colorado with you now by MLX."

"Afternoon, Florida," Parker called to the Cape Canaveral antenna.

"Copy, Will. With you another 10 minutes. If you can do it, please keep one eyeball on the payload bay and the other on Soyuz."

"No sweat, Flight. We're trained to do *anything* the job requires," the AC drawled. His mouth was still dry from his inoculation and his legs remained very far away. The command pilot was as high as his lofty office and his twangy voice brimmed with "can do."

"We believe that, AC. Thanks." The voice from below did not carry the AC's exuberance.

Ninety seconds east of the Mississippi River, Endeavor silently buzzed Moorehead, Kentucky. Parker peered intently over the centerline sill of his overhead window. He scanned the blindingly white, thin snowcover upon the

213

Blue Grass country. He imagined the white fences surrounding fields of plump Thoroughbred mares, all in the seventh month of their pregnancies and anxious to foal come May. He saw only barren earth, but his sweating nostrils flared with the sweetly musty smells of freshly brushed horses. He could taste it. It was enough to know that they were surely down there.

As the three ships flew across the southeastern states, Parker and Enright concentrated on flying the manipulator arm and its cumbersome payload. Loaded, the arm moved slowly at two-tenths foot per second. They steered the arm outward where the arm reached 50 feet into space above Shuttle's cockpit. The Plasma Diagnostics Package pointed westward toward LACE and Soyuz on the target's far side.

"Endeavor, we just got a spike of energy through your PDP downlink. Check your target. Do it *now*."

The ground's voice was full of business as the three vessels coasted over Chesapeake Bay just south of Pocomoke City, Virginia. Shuttle left the American coastline behind at 03 hours, 15 minutes into the mission, barely ten minutes east of California.

"Don't see anything unusual out of Window Seven, Flight. Sun still too high for seeing any real detail." Parker studied the two ships beyond his overhead window.

"Nothing unusual out Window Ten, either," Enright called as he looked through the window in the rear wall which overlooks the payload bay. He could see their company beyond the open sill on Shuttle's port side.

"Okay, Endeavor. Keep an eye outside for anything from Soyuz. Anything at all . . ."

"Like what, Flight?"

"We don't know, Jack . . . LOS via Florida in fifty-five seconds. Continue with the PDP survey. See if you can map the center of the target's wake. We're watching it closely down here. With you another six through Ber-

214

muda network. We lost the flux spike, whatever it was."

The two weightless airmen busied themselves with the RMS arm which dangled above Endeavor's flightdeck. The end effector hung above Shuttle's white nose. The arm's wrist camera drooped toward Shuttle and sent a picture of the six forward windows to the television monitor beside Enright.

"LOS by Kennedy, Endeavor. With you via Bermuda at 03 plus 17. LOS Bermuda in 5 and a half."

"Gotcha, BDA," Parker called as he worked the RMS computer keyboard at waist level to Enright's left.

Two minutes east of the Virginia coastline, Endeavor was 600 miles out to sea. The blue-green terrain of the American coast was lost at the hazy line of the western horizon. Only the brilliant ocean filled the flightdeck's thick windows.

"Another voltage spike, Endeavor," the headphones crackled. "Please give another look outside. See any outgasing from either the target or Soyuz?"

"Stand by one, Bermuda," replied an exasperated Enright, who had both ungloved hands full of RMS.

"Let me, Jack," the AC offered over his voice-activated intercom which the ground could not hear. He pressed his mike button to address the sparkling planet.

"AC here, Colorado. Real sorry, but with the sun west of us and smack in our field of view, I can barely see the target or Soyuz through all the glare. Real sorry, buddy."

"Thanks, AC. First thing after sunset . . . in twelve minutes . . . give another look, please. You're AOS by Dakar five minutes before sunset and with DKR for two minutes after sunset. Try to get a visual report in darkness by Dakar. You lose DKR at 03 plus thirty-four. You are then out of network contact for ten minutes."

"Will do, Flight," the tall flier drawled as he fiddled with the autopilot pushbuttons.

"Good enough, Will."

215

Above the bright Atlantic, Soyuz drifted with its round nose only three Shuttle lengths away from Endeavor's open payload bay. The bay faced LACE and the Soviet ship. With the blinding sun behind Soyuz, the shuttle crew could not see the thin blue-green beam of light which radiated from the belly of Soyuz toward the sea. At the far end of the beam, a Russian tracking ship pitched slowly in light seas. The trawler's banks of optical antennae sucked in the beam of light from space. Burning through the humid afternoon air, the beam was as secure as a buried telephone cable which could not be tapped. As Soyuz coasted eastward, the optical antennae aboard the trawler tilted toward its target unseen in the purple sky. The laser beam from Soyuz could carry telemetry and voice in either direction over a medium unseen and unheard by Shuttle's black boxes tuned to radio frequencies.

"Another field spike on the PDP, Endeavor. See anything? Hurry before we lose you here . . ."

"Say again, Flight. You're breaking up." The AC squinted out his overhead window.

The AC's headphones were silent as Endeavor, LACE and Soyuz, careened over the horizon out of earshot with the Bermuda Island tracking station at 03 hours, 22½ minutes out.

"Peace and quiet at last," Enright grumbled. The command pilot at his left nodded as he fine-tuned Mother's autopilot. Endeavor would require only another eight minutes to reach the west coast of Africa.

The rugged old engine of the *Jennifer Lee* chugged loudly in the little fishing boat which puffed into Chesapeake Bay under gray, winter skies. The cold salt air stung the hard face of the *Jennifer Lee's* captain, the fishing boat's crew of one. And the air was painful against the

216

skin of the fisherman's only passenger dressed in a business suit.

Ahead loomed the Hampton Roads Bridge linking Hampton, Virginia, off the right side to Norfolk off the left side. The boat made a foaming wake as she plowed northwestward into the mouth of the great bay.

"You picked the perfect spot to go fishing," the queasy visitor stammered to the middle-aged captain. "Can't say much for the weather, though."

"You're not used to the little boat and the big waves, that's all," the man at the tiller said dryly.

"Guess not. Too many years at a desk, I suppose."

"CIA, Langley?" the burly seaman asked gravely.

"No, Nikolai, Defense Intelligence Agency."

"Oh. My friends down here call me Nick. Not for much longer, it would seem." The boatman steered his boat across whitecaps which broke over the low bow of the thirty-foot trawler.

Hampton Roads Bridge cast its faint shadow in the gray weather upon the *Jennifer Lee* making her tossing way into the bay.

"It is the perfect place to fish, though," the sailor called over the noise of wind and waves. "Langley is just off to the right and the Norfolk navy yard is just south of the bridge."

Langley Air Force Base and the headquarters of the Central Intelligence Agency were on the north side of the towering bridge overhead. Norfolk Naval Air Station was on the south side. The two air bases were hardly 12 miles apart.

The *Jennifer Lee* was pointed under the bridge toward the James River. Just off the boat's right side, old Fortress Monroe passed under the northern piles of Hampton Roads Bridge. A young army engineer had built the ancient fort in the 1830's: Lt. Robert E. Lee, fresh out of West Point. Three decades later during the holocaust of

217

brother killing brother, Lee's son was a prisoner of war in the Yankee fort.

"Nikolai, I haven't much time. Our shuttle flight is running into trouble. That's why I'm here." The man from Washington looked sicker with each wave.

"Your runaway LACE spacecraft?"

The greening man beside the tall fisherman raised his eyebrows.

"My job is to know about such things, you know," the captain said with no trace of Russian in his perfect, Tidewater, Virginia, accent.

"Oh. Well, I am told that you can tell us about your Soyuz-TM spacecraft. Our people haven't monitored a word of communications with it in 13 hours. And the shuttle astronauts have monitored electronic fields in the vicinity of Soyuz. I need to know if those impulses are from Soyuz?"

"Don't know about that. The disturbances, that is. I do know that Soyuz is a military version of the spacecraft. So she must be using a laser beam of her own to communicate with our ground stations and tracking ships. It's like your submarine laser."

"You have done your job well, Nikolai," the seasick guest said weakly.

"Yes."

The two men rolled on rough seas for a long silence. They cruised past Willoughby Bay just past the navy yard on the *Jennifer Lee*'s left.

"I shall miss it here," the fisherman sighed loudly. "These people are like my own kind: hungry, poor, and hard. Their handshakes have always been good."

The man from Washington said nothing. His hand covered his mouth on his ashen face.

"Yes, I like it here. How strange, now: my country is losing the Balkans, and I shall lose your beautiful Chesapeake Bay. Oh well, the shellfish are almost all gone now.

218

And what's left are poison."

The *Jennifer Lee* steered toward a row of wharves where dozens of little boats were moored. The air was heavy with the stench of rotted fish in freezing salt air.

"Can you make a living fishing, Nikolai?" the nauseous man inquired between stomach convulsions in the rough sea close to the docks.

"Yes," the boatman said firmly. "I certainly can't do my other job after today."

Just shy of the clapboard dock, the big seaman turned to face his sickly passenger who had been dropped off 15 minutes earlier by a Coast Guard cutter.

"What will you do, Nikolai, when the oyster beds run dry?"

On the dock, two black cars with government plates waited.

"Fish for something else. My people have always been fishermen."

The *Jennifer Lee* banged gently into the dock.

"I wish you luck . . . next year on the water, Nikolai."

The big man blinked moist eyes at the back of the bilious bureaucrat who stumbled toward his dark car.

"With you, Endeavor, at 03 plus 27. Your downlink is clean and crisp."

"Thanks, Flight," the AC answered from his command seat in the front of the flightdeck. As Shuttle had approached the western edge of the listening range of the Dakar station in Senegal, the command pilot had strapped himself into his front left seat. There, he was powering up the ship's celestial sextant, the Crew Optical Alignment Sight. The COAS would back up the two star trackers in Shuttle's nose for aligning the inertial measurement units' platforms by a star sight.

"COAS warmin' up, Flight," the AC reported from his

seat over blue sea 800 miles west of Africa. With Enright standing at the aft station where he handflew the remote arm, the AC forward had to make the slowest possible attitude maneuvers to track his stars after sundown five minutes away. Only instantaneous firings from Endeavor's smallest RCS thrusters would protect the outstretched manipulator arm from dangerous strain during maneuvers.

At the aft crew station, Enright steered the deployed RMS arm back toward Shuttle's tall tail fin. Stretching the arm outright such that none of the joints were flexed would lessen the swaying moments induced in the 50-foot-long arm as Endeavor changed positions to search for navigation stars for the COAS sight. The tubular COAS periscope mounted before Parker's face was fixed in Shuttle and could not move to search the sky. The two startrackers gimbaled about in their shoe-box-size containers to search on their own for bright stars.

"Endeavor: Colorado via Dakar. Backroom says the field spikes recorded by the PDP may be from a communications laser on board Soyuz. Probably a blue-green laser similar to our submarine laser communications."

"Oh," the AC mumbled as he worked Mother's black keyboard. His mind befuddled by horse tranquilizer, he failed to press his mike button.

"You copy that, Endeavor?"

"Gotcha, Flight," Enright called from the rear station.

"Roger, Jack," the voice called remoted through the African coastal station near the already-darkening eastern horizon. Evening twilight came to the starship sixteen times faster than as seen from Earth.

Three and one-half hours into the mission on Shuttle's third revolution, Endeavor crossed the west coast of Africa. In four minutes, the ship would lead LACE and Soyuz back out over open sea as they left Africa's western bulge for the Atlantic west of Africa-proper. For the blink of an eye, Endeavor was directly over the tracking station at Dakar 150 statute miles below. Then she was gone.

"Endeavor, we have another word for you from the backroom boys: One of our recon survey satellites in synchronous orbit 23,000 miles above you is getting some kind of ultra-light, molecular out-gassing near Luanda, Angola. Could very well be a missile venting hydrogen vapors. No word from our guys in trenchcoats on this. We want you to execute a roll maneuver using DAP in vernier-B to take a quick look when you overfly the area at 03 plus 39 plus 40. You should be wrapping up your P-52 alignment by then. Copy the time?"

"Got it, Flight," the AC drawled from his left seat in the forward cockpit. "Copy that way-point and we'll roll after the IMU sights. Shadows really getting longer down there."

The command pilot's visored head was close to the two side windows over his left shoulder. With Endeavor flying on her port side with her nose pointing north, the pilot looked over his left shoulder straight down to the dusky African countryside. Shuttle cruised into the veil of evening twilight and sunset over Guinea. The small nation Ivory Coast drifted silently into view in the waning daylight at a speed of 300 miles per minute.

Not more than four feet behind Parker, Enright stood at his station at the portside rear bulkhead, where he stabilized the remote arm for the Colonel's navigation maneuvers. The copilot floated erect with his knees bent and his boots locked to the floor. He strained his neck muscles against his helmet's neckring to raise his face to the square window above his body.

Peering into the darkness beyond the overhead window, Enright watched the sun flatten upon the far western horizon. Between the twilight horizon's band of orange-and-blue ribbons at sunset, he could see clearly the black and slowly rolling hulk of LACE. On the death ship's far side, the silent Soyuz glowed orange as the dying sun lapped at

221

the long wings of solar electrical cells along the flanks of Soyuz.

As Shuttle flew into the darkness of the planet's night-time shadow, the AC ordered Mother and the digital autopilot to roll Endeavor rightside-up.

Just beyond Parker's triple-pane, forward windows, the two star-trackers scanned the moist blackness of heaven for navigation stars memorized by Mother. "Where are we by the eternal stars?" beeped Mother at the speed of light over her wire ganglia. And the mass memory unit replied: "Ten degrees north latitude by eleven degrees west longitude at 03 hours and 32 minutes since leaving home." Armed with her dead-reckoning bearings guessed by memory, Mother commanded the minus-Z tracker to look straight up for the faint star Markab in the sprawling constellation Pegasus. The star-tracker found the pinpoint of light overhead. The minus-Y tracker just ahead of Parker's left shoulder looked sideways toward the black western sky as Endeavor flew heads-up with her nose pointed to the north. Mother ordered this tracker to look for the star Altair halfway to the horizon in the constellation Aquila.

Mother chose her stars based upon her electronic dialogue with her three inertial measurement units, which felt where Shuttle ought to be. Mother found her stars in the corners of the black sky where her magnetic memory told her to look. This meant that the uncorrected IMU alignment was within half a degree of true.

Working his computer keyboard, Parker gave Mother permission to convert her star sights into torque angles which command the IMU gyroscopes' gimbals to swing just enough to sense true local vertical and local horizontal. Each IMU was aligned with a slightly different bearing to allow cross-checks among them until the next IMU alignment.

"P-52 complete, Jack," the AC called by intercom to Enright behind him. "Right on, Number One. No need to recompute the reference stable member matrix."

"Roger, Skip," Enright said. "So where are we?"

"Right here," the AC chuckled.

"That's a comfort, Will," Enright laughed.

"Ah, Flight? The IMU is aligned all balls."

"Copy, Endeavor. Real fine. LOS Dakar momentarily. We remind you to roll heads down before Angola in six minutes to check on their activities down there. You're Go to stow the RMS and to begin EVA prep to get Jack outside by the States. At 03 plus 34, you look fine all vitals . . ."

The ground's voice broke up in a wave of static as Shuttle sped over the horizon.

Shuttle coasted out over open water after passing Abdijan, the capital of Ivory Coast, West Africa. Leaving Africa's western bulge behind, the ship would cross open sea for six minutes and 1,800 miles before returning to the land mass of central Africa. Radio silence would last ten minutes before acquisition of signal, AOS, through the NASA station in Botswana near the city of Gaborone, 190 miles northwest of Johannesburg, South Africa.

With Endeavor flying rightside-up, Parker peered into the COAS periscope recticle before his face. He had raised his helmet faceplate to get his eye closer to the small mirror at the base of the Crew Optical Alignment Sight. As an old sailor, the AC could not resist consulting his space sextant. Gently nudging Shuttle's nose among the stars, he found the star overhead which Mother had shot. Since the COAS can only look overhead, he could only use it to check the minus-Z startracker which also looks only upward. Working his computer keyboard, he fed his eyeball sighting from the COAS to the computer's navigation and control programs. The left of the three green televisions on the center forward instrument panel blinked and confirmed that Mother's sight was reliable. "Man in the loop," the real pilots in the astronaut corps called it. Parker inserted an airman's eyeball into the loop at every opportunity.

Behind the AC, Enright steered the heavy plasma diagnostics package at the end of the RMS arm. He directed the PDP toward its berth in the open bay.

Flying the arm in manual-augmented mode, Enright eased the PDP into its latches on the OSS pallet in the stern of the bay. When the RMS panel and the shoulder-high television monitor confirmed to Enright the security of the stowed package, Enright squeezed the pistol-grip trigger in his right hand. The arm's end effector unit released the wire snares holding the PDP's grapple probe. The EEU backed away from the berthed PDP canister.

"PDP secured, Skip."

"Sweet music, Number One. Advise when you've put the arm to bed."

Enright steered the arm's joints until the arm was stretched out straight. He directed the arm toward the cradle and latches on the bay's portside sill. Gently, the copilot aligned the arm with its three latch posts. All three latches grabbed and held the 900-pound arm.

"Manipulator secured; all latches rigidized, Will." The small windows on the RMS console showed the end effector coordinates at $X_0$1195 inches, $Z_0$44.77 inches, and Y_0 108.0 inches from the datum zero point.

"Super, Jack. Catch your breath, buddy."

"Right on that one," Enright sighed into his voice-activated intercom. His face, new to zero-gravity, felt swollen and warm. His suit ventilation bathed his flushed face with the scents of rubber and sweat. "Mind if I stroll downstairs a minute, Will?"

"Take a magazine with you, Jack."

"Just so it ain't *Aviation Week!*" Enright sighed as he pulled his plugs and thick hoses from his hot suit. He opened his faceplate to breathe the flightdeck's cool, dry air. Even the cabin's sterile, bottled atmosphere smelled like morning by the sea after the stuffy suit's humid breath.

Enright slowly flew without weight, head-first, down the floor hatchway behind the front seat where Parker floated against his lap belt.

In mid-air, Enright somersaulted to his feet beside the dark and curtained window in the wall hatch of Shuttle's mid-deck basement. Holding his body steady with one hand on a wall handrail, he hit the row of light switches for the mid-deck compartment.

In darkness, after 03 hours and 36 minutes, Shuttle flew over the Equator southbound 200 miles northwest of and 130 nautical miles above the Pagula Islands.

Enright's empty, bulky suit stood rigidly like a third crewman beside the sealed side hatch. Wearing only his white, long woolies, Enright backed into the cramped stall of the zero-gravity biffy. He strapped his seat belt to his waist and he eased his stocking feet into the foot restraints.

Powering up the electric biffy raised the sound of a cake mixer. At his crotch, ballast air sucked the copilot's urine into the plastic cup between his bare thighs. The rush of air countered the weightlessness which would have sent yellow globules upward to the flightdeck were it not for the little cup's air suction. Beneath the commode's seat, Enright's breakfast rode a rush of ballast air suction deep into the biffy. Under the seat, the knife blades of hinged slinger tines spun at 1,500 revolutions per minute. The flying blades are designed to shred solid waste and spread it as a gruel on the walls of the inner commode. To Enright, the space pot sounded like he rode a kitchen blender. Each crew member of Shuttle is officially allotted 0.12 kilograms (0.27 pound) of solid body waste per day. The sitting copilot wondered if he had just blown his daily quota. The noisy system of rushing air current and whirring blades tormented Enright's throbbing head. But he

225

retained sufficient energy to smile at the vision of his female astro colleagues riding the little cold cup between his naked legs.

With his right hand, Enright felt for the commode's control panel beside his right knee. Squeezing out of the narrow stall, he was momentarily unnerved by the presence of his empty suit, which still hovered at attention beside the latrine. Cabin air currents had raised the suit's empty right sleeve up past the round neckring. The headless suit appeared to salute the skivvy-clad airman.

Enright tumbled slowly as he wrestled with the suit to climb back into the rubbery cocoon. After he closed the long belly zipper, he fetched his helmet from the corner where the wall meets the ceiling. The inside cheekpads of the helmet felt coldly wet with perspiration where it covered the pilot's face.

Enright adjusted his helmet as he rose through the ceiling hole to the upstairs flightdeck. He floated up behind Parker. Floating over the center forward console, Enright carefully eased into his right seat beside the command pilot. After pulling his lap belt across his middle, Enright plugged into his communications jacks and his two air hoses.

"Feel better, buddy?" the AC drawled.

"Much. Thanks." Behind his closed faceplate, a revived Enright grinned. "I'm an evil man, Skipper," Enright said with mock gravity in his voice.

"Thought about little Sally riding the million-dollar, house-outback, aye, Number One?"

For an instant, Enright looked with surprise at his captain. Both pilots laughed out loud over the voice-activated intercom.

The square face of the mission timer before their faces ticked past 03 hours, 40 minutes. While Enright had been below, Parker had rolled Endeavor and had pitched her nose toward the Earth. They flew upside down over the

226

dark coastline of Angola. The faint lights of the capital city of Luanda marked the sea's edge far below in the darkness.

They flew heads down four minutes before contact with Endeavor's next ground station.

The two airmen still chuckled at their private humor. The laughter stopped when the darkness below erupted into a momentary flash of intensely white light just east of Luanda.

11

"With you, Endeavor, by Botswana, at 03 plus 44. How do you read?"

"Gotcha, Colorado. We're just sittin' and catchin' our breath up here. For a while there, young Jack looked like he got rode hard and put away wet. But we're both right and tight now."

The AC's bouncy voice reflected his newly acquired space legs. To his weightless body and his anesthetized leg, Endeavor was growing roomier and homier even in the narrow forward flightdeck. Enright's rooky wings also felt more like flying as Shuttle cruised over sleeping Zimbabwe. Far below in the darkness, the clocks on the walls read 8:45 as the two pilots flew on their left sides above Africa.

"Super, Will."

"And we had a real display of pyrotechnics five minutes back over Angola." The AC's ungloved hand worked the mike button floating close to his chest and his two hose fittings. Mother and the autopilot held trim with Shuttle flying on her port side with her nose pointing northward toward the Equator 1,200 nautical miles away in the darkness.

"Backroom would like some details, Endeavor. Only

with you on this station for another four minutes."

Parker did not reach for the floating Push-To-Talk switch when he saw Enright reach for his.

"Right seat here. Looked like daylight down there just for a few seconds. After the initial burst of light, we followed a brilliant contrail for a good minute. Lost it when Soyuz crossed the field of view behind us. No mistaking a missile, Flight. Be under us somewhere. Eastern trajectory for sure. You got anything from your eyes in the sky?"

"Nothing yet, Jack. We hope to get a skin track via Yarradee station in fifteen. Could you see any staging activities from whatever it was?"

"Negative on that," the second in command answered.

"Copy, Jack. We'd like you to begin your EVA activities when you can. You can grab a bite first if you want. This rev, we lose you by Botswana in two minutes. You're with Australia twelve minutes later. LOS Australia by Yarradee after eight minutes of contact. Sunrise 04 minutes later at 04 plus 12 MET. From LOS Yarradee to Hawaii acquisition is twenty minutes. Stateside contact is for twenty minutes. We'd like to have Jack close to going outside over the States . . . Got all that?"

"Sure," the AC said casually. He took no notes.

"And when you go downstairs with Jack, Will, we remind you to do your first CO_2 absorber insertion."

"Got it, Flight."

"Roger, AC. Don't forget to plug in downstairs."

"You betcha, Colorado. Leavin' you for a minute here."

Both pilots slid their seats back along their floor tracks. After opening their visors to breathe cabin air, they pulled their biomedical and radio plugs, and unlocked their belly air hoses. The two hoses in front of each seat floated upward like snakes.

Parker eased himself feetfirst into the hole behind his seat. Enright floated helmet first down the access hole behind his own seat.

In the floodlighted mid-deck, Parker's boots hovered above the floor in the 2,625 cubic-foot compartment. Enright did a zero gravity handstand with his feet braced upon the ceiling which was 7 feet above the floor in the 16-foot long mid-deck.

"You're upside down, buddy," Enright grinned through his open faceplate.

"One of us is, Jack."

Enright cartwheeled in the air until his boots against the floor stopped his flip.

"Show off," the taller pilot laughed.

"Was nothing really," Enright smiled, feeling his new wings.

As Endeavor, Soyuz and LACE coasted over the night-time terrain of southern Africa, the two shuttle pilots floated below deck. Enright reached into one of the many equipment lockers covering the forward bulkhead from floor to ceiling. He retrieved two lightweight headsets. These were wireless communications carrier assemblies, CCA's, which enable intercom and air-to-ground communications without the necessity of plugging into cabin jacks.

Each flier placed his headset upon his bare head. In the mid-deck, they could remove their sweaty helmets since there were none of the flightdeck's ten windows vulnerable to laser emissions. In Endeavor's mid-deck, the only window is the circular, 11½ inch wide, triple-pane window in the side entry-exit hatch. With each of the inside and center panes 1/2-inch thick, and with the outside pane 3/10-inch thick, and with the mirrored, reflective sunshade still in place on the inside porthole, the hatch window was secure from LACE.

"Howdy, pard," the AC said, testing his headset.

"Gotcha, Will. You hear us, Flight?" Enright called, pressing his wireless unit's Push-To-Talk switch dangling at his chest.

"Five by five, Endeavor," the two headset earphones crackled. "With you another one and a half minutes."

Shuttle led Soyuz and LACE across Mozambique's eastern coastline for the black open ocean.

The AC slowly somersaulted until he was doing a handstand in the center of the mid-deck. He pulled up a handcrank seated in the floor which opened a small door in the floor. The open bay in the floor houses a rack for holding beer-can size canisters. The small cans hold lithium hydroxide pellets through which stale cabin air is circulated. The pellets remove carbon dioxide from the air exhaled by the crewmen. Activated charcoal, finer than talcum powder, in the same cans removes odors from the cabin air.

The upside-down airman took the mission's first two canisters from Enright standing rightside-up. The AC inserted the twin CO_2 absorbers into the floor bin's empty rack. After seating the canisters, Parker pushed the bay closed and returned its latch handle into the small well in the floor.

"CO_2 absorbers inserted, Flight," Enright radioed as Parker tumbled rightside-up. The two fresh cans would be good for twelve hours. They would keep the cabin air's concentration of waste carbon dioxide from exceeding 0.147 pounds per square inch partial pressure.

"LOS Botswana momentarily, Endeavor. At 03 plus 48. See you in twelve minutes. This is . . ."

Static followed by silence filled the CCA headsets as Africa fell quickly below the western horizon behind Shuttle.

"How about a burger, Jack?" the AC offered.

"Think my stomach is still a rev behind the rest of me. Maybe some soup."

"Pull up a stool, Number One. I'll build a fire."

Enright smiled rather listlessly. He floated across the compartment to the space between the biffy stall and the man-size, wall-mounted galley. Between the latrine door

231

and the galley unit is the side hatch. Enright wedged his space-suited body into the corner cranny by the latrine. His back rested against the stall door and his boots touched the shaving mirror on the side of the galley facility. As he rested, his weightless arms within his deflated pressure suit floated out in front of his body. Enright's orange arms looked like those of a sleepwalker. He rested as the mission commander hovered before the narrow galley which is secured to the mid-deck's portside wall.

The galley contains an oven, which in 90 minutes can cook pre-packaged hot meals for seven crew members. Parker pulled two plastic envelopes of freeze-dried soup from the forward bulkhead's lockers. From the galley, the AC pulled out a thin hose and nozzle which squirted hot water into each plastic bag.

The command pilot sent a soup bag floating over to Enright wedged into his corner.

As the two pilots kneaded their soup bags to moisten the dried contents, Endeavor coasted in the night sky above the South Atlantic's Isle Amsterdam at Shuttle's southernmost point of her orbital track, 38 degrees south latitude, about 3565 statute miles from the South Pole. Upstairs on the flightdeck, the mission clocks ticked past the fourth hour of the voyage.

"Endeavor, Endeavor," each headset crackled. "Colorado with you by Yarradee at 04 hours."

"Gotcha, Australia," the AC called through a mouthful of soup, which he sucked from a straw.

Parker floated motionless four feet off the floor. He levitated in mid-air like a magician's assistant with his helmetless head touching the side of the airlock at the center of the mid-deck's rear bulkhead.

"How's things in the basement, Will?"

Flat on his back in the air, the AC squeezed the last of his beefy soup into his mouth.

"Real cozy, Colorado. Just finishin' some soup. How's

232

things in the mountains?"

"Looking good, AC. We're waiting for radar lock-up on whatever your Angola traffic may be. Nothing yet, but we're listening. After your break, we would like you to charge the PLSS packs."

"Roger," the AC called as he shoved his body toward the floor by pushing his ungloved hand against the mid-deck ceiling. Enright watched from his corner.

Hovering upside down, the long AC hung like a bat with his face close to the floor. The Colonel's burly left hand held a handhold at the base of the airlock.

The cylinder-shaped airlock takes up a full third of the back wall of the mid-deck. Standing 83 inches high, the airlock is 63 inches wide on the inside. At the floor end of the airlock is a D-shaped hatch three feet across.

Grasping the handrail near the floor with one hand, Parker cranked the airlock hatch handle with his free hand. The hatch snapped open with a pop as the hatch seal released excess air pressure and swung open on its side hinges. Parker eased his inverted, floating body out of the way as the thick hatch opened outward into the mid-deck cabin.

Feet first, the AC floated into the airlock hatch. Still upside down inside, he inserted his boots into the foot restraints on the airlock ceiling.

"AC's in the airlock, Flight," Enright reported by his wireless headset.

"Copy, Jack. With you another three minutes."

The dark airlock illuminated with harsh, white lights as the AC flipped a row of toggle switches located at his upside-down eye-level by the open hatch.

In the five-foot-wide can, the tall command pilot easily somersaulted to put his head at the module's round ceiling. Only his boots were visible to Enright, who had floated to the open hatchway. The copilot floated on his side with his boots toward the mid-deck's access hatch on the portside wall.

Inside the airlock, the AC inspected the hoses, which ran from the airlock wall into two Portable Life-Support Systems, PLSS, backpacks which hung suspended upon the airlock's walls. Attached to each backpack was the top half of a thick white space suit.

"SCU's both secure, Jack."

"You copy that, Flight?"

"We heard him, Jack. Service and Cooling Umbilicals secure."

"I hear you from the can, Colorado," the AC radioed from the wide airlock.

The SCU lines charge the breathing oxygen and coolant water tanks within each PLSS backpack, which is permanently built into the upper torso of Shuttle's space suit for going outside in orbit. Two such upper torsos hung on the airlock's inside walls. Each helmetless upper torso and attached PLSS pack was half of Shuttle's extra-vehicular mobility unit, or EMU.

Slowly somersaulting, the Colonel returned headsdown to the control panel by the open hatch of the airlock. The AC worked the controls which sent a flow of Shuttle oxygen and coolant water into the two PLSS backpacks.

"Fillin' them up, Jack."

" 'Kay, Will," the floating copilot called into the open hatchway.

"One more minute with you, Endeavor."

"Uh huh, Colorado," Enright called.

"Backroom confirms a contact with your Angola sighting, Endeavor. NESS got an image of it through GOES-5. No doubt it was a missile, Endeavor."

From 22,300 miles high, the Hughes Aircraft Geostationary Operational Environmental Satellite monitored by the National Oceanic and Atmospheric Administration's National Earth Satellite Service had blinked its glass eye at the right moment. In synchronous orbit, the satellite

234

sits stationary in the sky as the Earth turns beneath it at precisely the same speed as the satellite's velocity across the sky.

"We hear you, Flight," Enright replied. "Understand a hot target alright."

"Losing you here, Jack, at 04 hours and 08 minutes. Sunup in 4 minutes. Begin Rev Four at 04 plus 20 plus 04. Next network contact by Hawaii in 18 minutes . . ."

The ground's voice from sleeping Australia trailed off as Endeavor led LACE and Soyuz across the arid Great Sandy Desert in the Western Territories of north-central Australia. Australia's Great Barrier Reef on the continent's eastern coastline of the Coral Sea lay 1,000 nautical miles and 3 flying minutes away. From Australia's coast, Shuttle would cross open water for 26 minutes and 7,800 nautical miles en route to California. Endeavor crossed a new time zone every 3 minutes and 45 seconds. But there was utterly no sense of motion within Endeavor's cozy climate of dry air smelling faintly of rubberized air ducts and sweat.

"Time to suit up," Enright called to Parker as the tall airman emerged headfirst from the airlock. As the AC steadied himself beside Enright, Shuttle sped through the darkness over the Australian desert, where only lizards and scorpions hunted in the darkness 90 minutes before sunrise on earth. For Shuttle, sunup would come in three minutes.

During the next quarter hour out of earshot of ground stations, the Crew Activity Plan called for the pilots to pry their bodies from their cumbersome, five-layer ejection escape suits. Each orange suit weighed 24 pounds.

"You first, Jack."

Four hours, ten minutes aloft, Endeavor flew over Australia's eastern coastline for the Coral Sea. As Shuttle crossed the shoreline, directly below lights twinkled faintly from the village of Ingham, Queensland, Australia.

Enright unzipped his heavy suit's belly. Behind him,

235

Parker had braced himself against the airlock. As the AC grasped both of Enright's shoulders, the thin copilot forced his sweating head down through the suit's helmetless, circular neckring. With a grunt of effort, Enright forced his head and shoulders through the suit's open chest. As Parker behind him held the copilot's suit, Enright floated out of the garment. Pulling his weightless legs behind him, Enright moulted, shedding his orange rubberized skin. In his long johns, Enright did a somersault as he flew out of his suit, which Parker held in his large hands. Enright's long-sleeved drawers were moist with perspiration and the little cans of charcoal filters in the mid-deck floor labored against the cabin's scent of a locker room at halftime.

Enright felt like doing a zero-G cartwheel in his new freedom without the bulky suit to restrain his movement. The AC read the rooky's face.

"Can't fly with your feathers wet, buddy."

Enright smiled.

Outside, at 04 hours and 12 minues MET, a new sun burst explosively over the eastern horizon a thousand miles away. The Earth below was still in darkness as the high starship entered daylight above the Louisiade Archipelago in the pre-dawn Coral Sea. A fiercely bright white ring seeped around the circumference of the mid-deck, hatch window's cover. The narrow band of daylight was brighter than the cabin's floodlights. Upstairs, daylight careened over the unshaded sills of the flightdeck's ten windows. Mother in her systems management mode felt the flightdeck warm to morning. She increased the flow of coolant water from the flightdeck's aluminum veins to the space radiators deployed on the open bay doors.

"Mornin', Skipper," Enright said in his long woolies. The AC nodded cheerfully.

Enright took his empty suit and floated with it toward the narrow bunk beds nestled against Endeavor's starboard

236

mid-deck wall. He pushed back the curtain hiding a narrow berth which resembled the sleep stations in a submarine torpedo room.

Enright stuffed his man-size suit into the top berth. From the same bunk he hauled out massive white trousers. He parked the bottom torso of his extravehicular mobility unit suit in mid-air. Then he secured his damp ascent suit into the berth where it reposed like a third crewman. Normally the bottom half of the EVA suit is stored in the airlock with the upper torso. There had not been time to put everything in its appointed corner before this flight. Four hours and fifteen minutes out, Endeavor flew in full daylight over the Solomon Islands of Guadalcanal and New Georgia. The tiny island of Bouganville lay 425 miles to the northwest, halfway to the hazy horizon. On the ground, it was morning twilight. On the three sleepy islands, the sun was half an hour from warming the silent fields of weathered crosses aligned in long, perfect rows. There in the sandy ground, fifty years earlier, Company B, 145th Infantry of Ohio's bloodied Thirty-seventh Division had left its youth forever behind, wrapped in green ponchos.

Endeavor cruised over the sea toward the Equator 1,500 miles of groundtrack to northward.

The heavy eight-layer trousers of Enright's EMU stood like half a man between the two floating pilots. Attached permanently to the thick legs of the half-suit were heavy boots. The section of EVA suit ended at its round waistring. The upper half of the suit hung with backpack attached upon the inside of the airlock.

Enright floated into the fetal position in mid-air as he climbed out of his long johns. He stood naked except for his jockey-shorts-style Urine Collection Device which covered his middle. The UCD shorts could collect and store a quart of urine.

Enright took his sweaty wet drawers, wadded them into

237

a ball, and sent his laundry flying directly into a sleep berth.

"Just like home," the AC grinned.

"That good bachelor life, Skipper," Enright smiled.

While Enright was crawling airborne from his drawers, Parker had retrieved another set of long johns. These were Enright's liquid-cooling garment—one-piece mesh long johns of Spandex material. The garment was high-necked with feet attached. The 6½-pound union suit contained 300 feet of plastic tubes through which coolant water would be pumped by the EMU's PLSS backpack.

Enright unzipped the coolant garment from throat to crotch and he climbed into it in mid-air while Parker steadied his shoulders. The thin copilot zipped himself into the mesh underwear from which the plastic tubes dangled.

Five minutes and 1,500 miles from Guadalcanal, at 04 hours 20 minutes into the flight, Endeavor sped northeastward over the Equator to begin her Revolution Four over Tarawa in the Gilbert Islands of the South Pacific.

With his hands pushing against the mid-deck ceiling, the copilot forced his weightless body into the EMU's lower torso, which stood stiffly on the floor. Enright grabbed the trousers' waistring and he pulled the thick pants up to his hips. With the massive pants doubling the size of his lower body, the small pilot looked ready to go wading and fly fishing. To Parker, his crewmate looked like a rodeo clown.

"Next," Enright said as he worked to steady his ponderous lower body.

"Right," the AC said dryly.

The mission profile hastily drafted by the Johnson Space Center's flight operations directorate called for Parker to don his own liquid coolant garment. Although Enright would walk alone in space, Parker would be ready upstairs on the flightdeck to go outside if Enright got into trouble. Wearing his liquid coolant underwear, the AC could climb into his EMU suit in five minutes to go to Enright's rescue.

With Enright holding the tall colonel's shoulders, the AC crawled slowly and painfully from the open middle of his orange pressure suit. Enright floated, braced against the galley unit where he held the AC's empty ascent suit by its shoulders.

"Damn, Will," Enright whispered.

The tall, lanky colonel floated with his long arms raised and touching the mid-deck ceiling. He said nothing as Enright squinted his space-puffy cheeks toward the AC's right leg. From ankle to knee, the AC's right calf was swollen to the size of his thigh. At the Colonel's right mid-thigh, a fist-size knot bulged against his long johns, stained brown with dried blood. The stain was the size of a silver dollar where a horse needle had pricked a surface vein.

"Our little secret, Number One," the Colonel said softly.

"Skipper," Enright began. He was checked in mid-thought by a blast of Parker's captain's-look. The AC's glare quickly melted away.

"Okay, Will."

"Thanks, Jack. It doesn't bother me much. Really." The tall pilot spoke firmly as his leg, thigh, and groin throbbed with new heat.

The AC floated stiffly to his berth below Enright's bunk. He dragged his orange pressure suit, which he tucked into his bunk after first pulling his liquid coolant garment from one of the mid-deck's 33 forward storage lockers.

The Colonel hung his coolant garment in mid-air as upon an invisible clothesline. Enright held Parker's arm as the tall colonel climbed out of his long woolies.

Enright said nothing as he frowned at Parker's naked purple right leg. The thickly engorged veins along the

239

swollen calf and shin resembled a road map of Los Angeles, printed in blue on blue.

The Skipper had to tug hard to pull the 6-pound coolant garment onto his swollen leg. The AC grimaced and the deep pilot's lines upon his weary face creased from his eyes to his ears.

"I got you, Skipper," Enright said quietly as his hands steadied Parker's shoulders.

The AC looked over his broad shoulder at his young, lean partner.

"I know that, Jack," Parker said softly with assurance absolute.

Tubes for the coolant water of the EMU suit floated weightlessly about Parker's waist. Behind him, Enright floated awkwardly in his 90-pound britches of eight layers of urethane-coated nylon, Dacron, neoprene-coated nylon, and aluminized Mylar, all within an outer shell of Gortex and Nomex cloth.

The EMU suits are built in Windsor Locks, Connecticut. With the gloves, helmet, and upper torso hanging in the airlock, and the PLSS backpack attached, the whole EMU suit weighs 225 pounds. Each suit weighed more than either flier.

Twenty-four minutes into their fourth hour aloft, Endeavor flew 720 nautical miles east of the Marshall Islands.

"After you, Jack," the AC smiled, gesturing toward the open airlock hatchway.

Enright held onto his waistring as he floated headfirst into the airlock hatch close to the floor. He stood up in the wide chamber. Outside, the AC donned his wireless headset to listen for Hawaii's call soon to come. Enright was bare-headed in the airlock.

The copilot examined the illuminated digital numerics on the small Display and Controls Module chestpack. The unit is affixed to the front of the hard upper torso of the

240

two EMU suits hanging on the airlock's inside wall. The gauges told him that the PLSS backpack on each upper torso was fully charged: In each backpack, two main air tanks held 1.2 pounds of pure oxygen pressurized to 850 pounds per square inch. Two reserve tanks in each PLSS held another 2.6 pounds of oxygen at 6,000 pounds pressure. The tanks of coolant water held ten pounds of water which the PLSS pumps will feed through the tubes surrounding the airman's body within the liquid coolant garment. The battery in each PLSS read 17 volts. With the tanks fully charged, each suit could sustain its flier for seven hours with another half-hour of reserve emergency oxygen.

The EMU upper torso hung on the airlock wall. Enright raised his arms over his head. His arms entered the upper torso with his body following. He pressed his hands into the suit's arms as his head peeked through the open neckring. With his feet secured to floor restraints, the pilot lowered his arms against the resistance of the thick suit. His ungloved hands reached for the space where the EMU trousers touched the waistring of the upper torso secured to the wall. Moving his hands around his hips, Enright locked the waistrings together and his suit became his private, 225-pound spacecraft. From the wall bracket where Enright hung like a bat where the PLSS was bolted to the wall, the flier took a set of huge gloves which he snapped to the arms of the suit. He twisted each glove to the arm wrist clamp until the gloves locked to the arms. A small cloth ring stretched from the sleeve of Enright's coolant underwear to each of his thumbs to keep the sleeves of his drawers from riding up his arm.

"Ready to go into the bubble, Skipper," Enright called through the open hatch of the airlock.

"Gotcha, buddy."

Enright pulled a soft Snoopy flight helmet over his

head. He snapped the neck strap under his chin and he adjusted the lip microphones under his nose.

"With me, Will?" Enright called after he activated the radio switch on the top of his small chestpack.

"Loud and clear," the AC confirmed over his headset in the mid-deck.

Enright pulled a tube from the inside of the EMU suit up through the neckring. He positioned it near his cheek. The tube led from the pilot's face to the drinking-water bag inside the suit. He had already connected the PLSS backpack to the tubes of his liquid coolant garment against his skin.

The pilot carefully placed a clear polycarbonate plastic helmet over his head. The fish-bowl helmet is translucent all around. Enright placed the helmet atop his suit's neckring and he locked it in position.

With his helmet double-locked to the suit, he activated the oxygen purge adaptor by attaching a hose to the top of his chestpack. The unit sent a blast of pure oxygen surging through the airtight suit to flush out the cabin's nitrogen-rich air mixture. Nitrogen in the suit would have been inhaled by Enright and could pose a lethal danger of nitrogen bubbles forming in his blood after he went outside the ship.

"Helmet lock and lock-lock, Skipper."

"Hear you, Jack."

Enright pulled a handle sideways at the front base of his chestpack. Instantly, he felt a rush of cool, pure oxygen surge out of the helmet vent pad behind his head. The suit circulation sucked the oxygen from his face down toward his feet where it was drawn back into the PLSS backpack. The PLSS recovered the oxygen at a rate of six cubic feet per minute to remove from the air water vapor, odors, and the pilot's exhaled carbon dioxide. The removed moisture was pumped by the PLSS into backpack storage tanks for recirculation through the liquid coolant

242

garment against the astronaut's body. As in farming, nothing was wasted.

Enright bent his head to view the gauges beneath his chin on the top of the chestpack. The bottom portion of his clear helmet was optically ground to slightly magnify the small meters on his chest.

"Oxygen at 4.3 pounds relative, Skipper."

"Super, Jack. Come on out."

Enright disconnected the backpack's service and cooling umbilical line, unsnapped the PLSS from the wall bracket which held the pilot fast to the airlock, and he floated free.

Carefully, Enright stuck his helmeted head through the yard-wide hatch of the airlock. Parker guided his shoulders like an obstetrician at the moment of birth to prevent Enright from snagging the awkward million-dollar suit or the thick backpack on the hatch rim. The PLSS barely cleared the hatch.

"Thanks, Will."

The suited copilot stood upright in the mid-deck. Sealed within his massive EMU, the pilot already panted from the effort of holding his arms down at his sides. The oxygen pressure in the suit, 4.3 pounds greater than the surrounding cabin pressure, made the arms rise, like blowing into an inside-out rubber glove pops out the fingers. Keeping the EMU's arms down required constant work by the pilot inside.

"Endeavor: Colorado with you via Hawaii at 04 plus 26." The AC in his liquid coolant long johns heard his headset crackle. His partner listened to the ground call from inside his airtight fishbowl. Shuttle's internal wireless audio system exchanged radio signals with Enright's backpack radios.

"Gotcha, Flight," the AC replied as he pressed his mike button. Both pilots floated with their feet slightly above the mid-deck floor. The stiff knee joints of his suit kept

243

Enright's knees bent.

"Okay, Will. We have a good lockup on you. We're up-linking your state vectors now. How you guys coming?"

The Hawaii station beamed to Shuttle exacting, electronically encoded statements of her velocity and position across the sky. In her Guidance and Navigation mode running on one of the ship's four primary computers, Mother received and digested the navigation update from Earth. Her warm, black boxes memorized the information for crosschecking the three inertial measurement units humming in Endeavor's nose.

"We're fine up here, Flight. Jack is suited and on pure O_2. He went internal on the PLSS at 04 plus 23. And I'm in my water pants."

Enright floated beside the command pilot. On Enright's chestpack, a digital timer ticked upward past 00:04 to keep the flier appraised of his oxygen time remaining.

"Will: We want you on the flightdeck right now, please. Give us a call when you're upstairs. No delay, buddy. Only with you another five minutes this pass."

Parker and Enright looked at each other. The AC shrugged. Enright held his ground by grabbing a ceiling handhold.

"Okay, Will. Go on up and leave Jack in the mid-deck. We want Jack to confirm placement of his EVA visor and to remove the sunshade from the mid-deck hatch. When you get upstairs, maneuver to minus-Z. Move out, guys."

The Ground Controller knew that Enright's EMU suit would not fit through the ceiling access hole to the flight-deck topside. The Spacecraft Communicator's voice relayed from Colorado Springs failed to conceal the urgency.

"On it, Flight," the AC called as he pressed his mike button. Parker floated headfirst into the airlock. Since his liquid cooling drawers had built-in feet like a child's sleeper, he was not uncomfortable in the cool cabin air. The AC floated out of the airlock. He carried another

244

large helmet. This one was white all around except for a rectangular face area. Enright took the second helmet from the Colonel and he placed it carefully over his clear helmet. He twist-locked the new helmet to his neckring. The face region of the outer visor was a mirror, laser-proof. Standing beside Enright, Parker saw his own lined face in the reflection from the mirrored visor.

"Jack has the EVA visor in place, Flight. I'm goin' up."

"Copy, Will. Call from upstairs," the ground called impatiently.

Parker flew on his side to his bunk on the starboard wall. He retrieved the helmet from his orange pressure suit. When he pulled off his light headset and pushed the damp helmet and its anti-laser visor over his head, a communications cable dangled from the neckring of the helmet.

"AC goin' topside, Colorado."

"Understand, Jack."

Until Parker plugged in his cables on the flightdeck, he had no link to Shuttle's four S-band, phase-modulated antennae.

Four hours and twenty-nine minutes aloft, Shuttle passed over the island of Kauai, Hawaii, in full daylight.

The AC gave Enright a thumbs-up as the tall flier hauled his grossly swollen right leg through the ceiling hole. He left Enright alone below decks where the copilot went to work on the window cover of the egress hatch by the galley.

"With you, Flight," the AC called from the upstairs, forward cockpit after he plugged in his communications cable. Drawing his lap belt across the waist of his liquid coolant underwear, he squinted into the fierce daylight of the flightdeck. "You with me, Jack?"

"On station down here, Will," Enright radioed from below, where he fiddled with the circular window cover.

"Rollin' over, Flight," the command pilot called from the

245

forward left seat.

Endeavor's Digital Autopilot held trim with the ship flying on her left side and her white, glass-covered nose pointing northwest perpendicular to the line of flight.

Parker pushed several square, white, lighted pushbuttons on the center console between his seat and the copilot's empty seat. He took over manual control of the ship's reaction control system thrusters.

"I have the con," the Colonel advised as he worked the rotational hand controller between his thighs.

"Understand," the earphones crackled inside Parker's helmet.

With the RCS jets in vernier mode, the thrusters popped only instantaneously no matter how far the AC torqued the control stick in his right hand. He maneuvered the 100-ton starship slowly to avoid excessive loads upon the open doors of the payload bay.

Slowly, the vessel rolled rightside-up as Mother chose the best combination of Shuttle's 44 RCS thrusters to obey the pilot's hand commands.

"Heads up," the AC confirmed when Shuttle's black belly faced the brilliantly blue Pacific. "Keep an eye on our Freon loop temperatures, Colorado."

"Will do, Endeavor."

With Shuttle flying rightside-up, the sun burned fully upon the open bay and upon the space radiators which require the cold shade of the inverted ship's shadow to do their work. Hence, Shuttle's normal belly-up attitude in space.

Without waiting for instructions, the AC cranked up the flow rate of the ship's freon coolant loops through which Endeavor sweats.

The ship's nose pointed northwest. Parker did not look over his left shoulder through the window where he knew LACE and Soyuz followed in tight formation. With Shuttle's port side toward their companion ships, Jacob

Enright in the mid-deck looked directly at their nearby traffic through the hatch window in the port side.

The AC had been too busy concentrating on the forward horizon 900 miles distant and on the attitude indicator ball before his face to look outside. He returned the ship to Mother's magnetic mind with instructions to hold automatic trim. Then the Colonel turned his face to his two left windows.

"Damn" was all the command pilot said. "You got the view out there, Jack?"

"Sure do," the intercom crackled from below decks.

The AC unconsciously touched his faceplate to confirm that his laser-reflective visor was down and locked.

"Who the hell is *that?*"

The Colonel's voice was not anxious so much as it was annoyed as he spoke privately to Enright over the intercom. He sounded like a man who had not merely blown a tire, but had done it in the rain.

"Gettin' a might crowded up here, Flight." This time, Parker depressed his mike button to energize the air-to-ground communications loop.

"Give us a visual, Will. Hawaii with you another minute only. Be advised we are on Channel B now and secure." No one but Mission Control, not even the press, could listen to the conversation. Ordinarily, Shuttle air-ground transmissions are public property except when the crew is working with secret military payloads or when the crew is making a regular daily medical report to the ground.

"Understand Channel B, Flight," the AC began. "Out Window Number One to my left, I have LACE maybe 120 meters off the port wingtip. Puts it about three points abaft the port beam, say 45 degrees behind me. Soyuz is out maybe 100 meters just left of our nose. And between Ivan and LACE is new traffic about 90 meters directly abeam of my seat. Soyuz is not between us and the new object . . . What the hell is it, Colorado?"

In Colorado Springs, the Space Command quickly digested the pilot's description to a triangle 300 feet on each side, with LACE, Endeavor, and the unidentified spacecraft each at one corner. Soyuz drifted 20 yards outside the triangular formation.

"Will: In twenty seconds, describe the contact."

"She's about the size of Soyuz. Very similar in fact: Spherical head module with a cylindrical afterbody behind. All black, no running lights that I can see. Short antennas—I see two—between the sphere and the afterbody."

"Okay, Will. You have your Angola bird. She's Chinese. Peoples Republic. Our people figure she went up on a Long March-3 booster. And she is manned. Keep Jack inside until we update you by California in four minutes. Losing you. . ."

The Long March-3 is the most powerful missile of the Peoples Republic of China. Standing 144 feet tall, the three-stage rocket returned the salvaged, U.S. satellite, Westar-6, back to orbit in April 1990. Westar had been retrieved from space by the shuttle in 1985. The relaunched communications satellite was renamed Asia Sat-1.

The Mission Commander sat in glum silence in his drawers with the dangling water tubes. He kept his visored faceplate close to the flightdeck's left side windows. With the sun already half up in the east, Parker had a dazzling sea behind three ships each barely three Shuttle lengths away.

"Can't be, Jack." The AC did not touch his mike pushbutton for the voice-activated intercom.

"I know," Enright radioed with his two bubble helmets pressed to the 12-inch-wide window in the mid-deck hatch. The round window was eight feet beneath the Skipper's seat upstairs. "They only launched—when was

248

it?"

The command pilot was already reviewing his orbital plot maps. He scanned the Mission Elapsed Time numerics which ticked away in little glass windows on Panel Overhead-3 above the forward window of the copilot's empty seat. The timer indicated that Endeavor was 00 days, 04 hours, 33 minutes, and 08 seconds out, over the north Pacific. The ship's position was about 30 degrees north latitude by 145 degrees west longitude, some 1,300 nautical miles from California.

"No more than 54 minutes, Jack. That makes their rendezvous in only 158 degrees. They sure as hell didn't carry any out-of-plane error under power. That's for sure."

"Like to go to their flight school, Skipper."

"Yeh, Jack. Probably have to bone up on your Russki to do it."

"How's the time-line, Will?"

"We're at 4 hours and 34 minutes, Jack."

"Nice. That gives us two hours before we skirt the Anomaly region on Rev Five. And they want me to stay put burning up my O_2, down here while Colorado plays air-traffic control. Real nice." The copilot in hard-suit floated close to his basement window.

"Reckon the backroom has its reasons, Number One. You'll get outside soon enough. 'Sides, they'll be on the horn in another minute."

"I'll be here, Skip."

Eleven hundred nautical miles due west of San Diego, the four vessels coasted in the perpetual freefall of orbit. Each ship was ever falling downward toward the blue-green December sea 130 nautical miles below. But so fast did they hurtle across the starless black sky of mid-morning that the curvature of the blue planet fell away over the horizon before the ships could plummet like meteors into the Pacific. As dictated by the laws of orbital mechanics, the Earth's far horizon, 1,000 miles to the east, fell away

249

just steeply enough that the four ships would miss it by 150 statute miles for years. Were it not for the infinitesimal drag against the ships from high, stray air molecules and the photon wake of the solar wind, the four starships would freefall in their orbits forever.

"I have traffic in motion at my twelve o'clock low!"

At Enright's shout from below decks, Parker turned his face to his left window where he squinted behind his helmet's closed faceplate.

The black intruder, scorched slightly by the air friction heating of its launch, slowly pitched its round head upward. The Chinese craft stopped its rotation with its blunt bottom pointed seaward.

As Parker and Enright watched from 300 feet abeam, the cylindrical afterbody of the Chinese vessel opened lengthwise. A dishlike device perhaps two meters across protruded from the hull. It pointed at LACE, which rolled slowly against the emerald sea off Shuttle's left wingtip.

"Don't do it!" Parker shouted. He pushed his transmitter button without any notion as to whether the intruder or the ever-silent Soyuz-T were listening on Endeavor's FM frequency band of 2287.5 megahertz.

The eyes of the American airmen concentrated upon LACE three shuttle lengths away.

At the upper end of the vertically positioned LACE, a hemispheric shroud—like the roof of an astronomical observatory—housed LACE's lasing equipment and focusing mirrors.

"Don't be stupid!" Parker shouted through Endeavor's antennae. His cry filled his helmet's closeness.

LACE slid back a wide panel on its shroud faring which covered its Large Optics Demonstration Experiment innards. In the ferocious daylight of airless space, Parker could clearly see LACE's works twinkle within the shroud under the fierce sun, like a diamond turning beneath a jeweler's monocle.

For an instant Parker and Enright were diverted to a yellow plume from a nose thruster on Soyuz. Slowly, the triple-module, 23-foot-long Soviet craft backed away from the tight formation. The high sun glinted blindingly from Soyuz's two solar cell wings, 35 feet from tip to tip.

The relentless sun, high and east of the four ships, washed out the details of each vessel's body. Parker could see a very faint green glow upon LACE's body in a direct line with the antenna-dish device protruding from the Chinese craft.

Endeavor's command pilot jerked reflexively in his long johns against his loose lap belt when a thick, blue-green beam burst out of LACE's open shroud.

The hair behind Parker's neck tingled where his helmet ended at his water-cooled drawers.

LACE's beam of light was faint with the sparkling Pacific behind it. But Parker topside and Enright below clearly saw the light strike and remain upon the manned Chinese ship.

In the instant between heartbeats, the Chinese vessel pitched forward toward LACE. The intruder's spherical head cartwheeled forward as if her thick body had been jerked backward from beneath her black, iron feet.

In the blink of Parker's wide eyes, the round head of the tumbling Chinese ship passed directly through LACE's steady, blue-green beam. The Chinese craft excreted a fine cloud of gas and glittering flakes of frost which she had carried on her cold side away from the sun. A huge teardrop cloud of gas, shining frost, and tiny bits of debris swelled around the craft. In the brilliant sunlight, the Chinese vessel was nearly invisible inside a gauzelike shroud which silently leaked from her ruptured hull. A ship was dying.

The round forward module of the doomed vessel bowed toward LACE. Within a spreading cloud of gas, the head

251

of the Chinese craft took LACE's lasing broadside for only three seconds.

In the instant before the dying ship exploded without sound, Parker sat frozen on the flightdeck as LACE's thick green beam reflected off the Chinese death ship.

LACE's beam bounced at a right angle off the Chinese hulk. Its reflected laser beam shot sideways silently into Endeavor.

As a reflex, Parker lifted his bootless feet off the floor under the instrument panel. He watched the beam of energy lie silently against Endeavor's glass body beneath his left side.

In an instant, the lased photons stopped.

12

"Jacob!"

The command pilot's voice over the intercom was shrill. Outside, Endeavor's six forward windows were covered with a cloud of vaporous debris. Parker momentarily paused to listen and feel for any impact upon Endeavor's fragile glass flanks. Shuttle was bedrock stable as Mother held the con in her firm hand.

"Jack!" the seated AC shouted into his faceplate.

The headset within the Colonel's helmet was silent.

In one motion, Parker pushed his seat back along its floor tracks as he pulled his communications plugs and released his lap belt. He floated from his seat, rolled over in mid-air, and soared helmet-first down the hatch hole behind his seat.

As the flier floated from the ceiling hole into the mid-deck, he turned his face toward the window of the side entry hatch. Where he expected to see Enright, he saw only the round window. Beyond the hatch window was a thick yellow cloud. For an instant, he recognized a pilot's recurring nightmare of the view when descending below minimums on short final.

Parker somersaulted weightlessly until he was right-side up. He held his position with his hands braced against the

253

basement ceiling. In his long underwear from which disconnected water tubes floated, the AC's stocking feet were a foot off the floor. When he whispered, "Jack," no one heard him. He was not plugged into a communications plug and did not wear a wireless headset.

Parker hovered in the air. He swallowed hard behind his closed faceplate.

Opposite the cloudy window of the side hatch, Jacob Enright stood rigidly with his face hidden by his silvered EVA visor.

Enright was right-side up with his PLSS backpack touching the sleeping berths on the starboard side of the mid-deck. The air pressure in his EMU suit forced his arms straight out at his sides. Floating with his boots and massive white legs two feet off the floor, the copilot hung motionless. He resembled a hard-suited Scarecrow waiting patiently for Dorothy and The Tin Man to cut him down.

"Jacob," Parker breathed inside his heavy helmet where no one could hear.

The AC pushed his helmet from his sweating head. The plastic container banged behind him against the latrine door. He swam to his partner.

Without his helmet, Parker could hear Enright's backpack softly humming as its fans, pumps, and condensers cooled and scrubbed the silent airman's claustrophobic world.

Parker placed his large hands on either side of Enright's small chestpack. He pulled his copilot down from where his helmet touched the ceiling. The AC could feel the rigidity of Enright's body inside the massive suit.

Parker carefully moved Enright to the center of the cabin where he eased the silent load sideways. Enright floated spread-eagle in the center of the mid-deck. Parker gently pushed him toward the floor until Enright hovered on his back with his PLSS backpack six inches off the floor.

In the perpetual freefall of orbit, neither pilot had any weight. But they did have mass. With one hand on the cabin's handrails which jutted from walls, floor, and ceiling, Parker's free hand was maneuvering a ponderous mass. He moved what on Earth would have been a 150-pound pilot inside a stiff 225-pound space suit. Although Parker had steered Enright's body to the floor in seconds, the command pilot had worked himself into a sweat. Each instant he pushed Enright, the force shoved Parker backward in his weightless state. Pushing Enright to the floor only sent Parker floating upward to the ceiling. The AC was panting with perspiration burning his eyes when Enright's back bounced lightly off the floor.

The AC straddled his rigid partner. He braced one foot through each of Enright's armpits. Bending well over, Parker wedged his bare, wet head against the airlock. Enright's silver outer helmet was between Parker's mesh-covered shins, one swollen twice the size of the other. Twice every second, the AC's right calf throbbed hotly in time with his pounding temples.

Crouching over Enright who did not stir, the pilot in command gently lifted off his partner's extra vehicular activity outer visor. The bubble visor floated out of Parker's moist hands toward the ceiling.

"Jack," Parker whispered.

Between the tall airman's knees, he saw Enright within the fishbowl, pressurized helmet. Will Parker did not recognize the face.

"Endeavor, Endeavor: Colorado with you by Goldstone at 04 hours and 36 minutes." Parker could not hear the ground's transmission, which stopped upstairs on the flightdeck at his empty earphone plug. Shuttle approached the California coast 800 miles away in piercing noontime sun.

"Jack," the kneeling pilot sighed. His breath fogged the outside of the clear helmet, chilled by the PLSS air blow-

255

ing from the vent behind Enright's head.

Jacob Enright's face was cherry red and swollen to twice its normal size. The puffy cheeks creased around swollen, thin slits of tightly closed eyes. Having lost its normal proportions, Enright's face looked like the face of a red and distressed newborn infant.

"Endeavor, Endeavor . . . We have PM downlink. Negative voice. Check your audio panels. Colorado standing by at 04 plus 39." The great dish antenna at Goldstone, California, beeped to no one as Shuttle crossed the coastline at Santa Cruz, 120 miles south of San Francisco.

Parker tightened his knees, which held Enright's stiff armpits to the mid-deck floor. Carefully, the AC laid a large palm on each side of his partner's helmet. With a quick, quarter turn of the bubble helmet, he broke the pressure seal of the neckring. The helmet's seal popped under its internal pressure with the sound of a pop-top beer can. A rush of cool air from the open neckring washed over Parker's face, wet with sweat. The chilly breeze which continued to blow from the back of the helmet smelled of sweat, rubber hoses, and cooked meat.

Parker grimaced as he disconnected the thin air tube which ran from the inside of the EMU suit to the helmet's vent pad behind Enright's head wearing the soft Snoopy communications helmet. Enright's thickly puffy lips pressed against the two microphone booms jutting from the cheeks of the Communications Carrier Assembly. The soft CCA had been dubbed "Snoopy helmet" back in Apollo and so it remained.

Parker sent the clear helmet floating toward the sleep station berths where it stopped against a reposing orange pressure suit which Parker had worn during launch. The AC moved a thick knob sideways at the base of Enright's chestpack. The rush of air in the depressurized EMU suit stopped and the digital timer at the top of the chestpack stopped at 17 minutes.

"Endeavor, Endeavor: Colorado by Goldstone broadcasting in the blind. Negative contact. Listening secondary frequency 2217.5. Over." Only the tense bunker of Mission Control in the Rocky Mountains heard the anxious call.

When Parker laid his ear over Enright's red and peeling nose he noticed that the facial swelling had opened the snap of the chin strap on the Snoopy comm helmet. The little strap floated upward toward Parker's sweating face.

"Thank God," the Colonel whispered as Enright breathed shallowly and rapidly into his captain's ear.

"Endeavor . . . Colorado at 04 plus 41." The Goldstone, California, dish pointed eastward, following Shuttle as she crossed the Colorado River over the northeast tip of Lake Powell, Utah. "Acquisition of signal by UHF-only through Northrop." The antennae at Endeavor's alternate landing site on the gypsum sands in New Mexico ached to listen to the silent purple sky of a winter afternoon in the desert.

A pilot learns to recognize many things: the gentlest buffet from a wing about to stall; the feel in the seatbones of a runway one foot from the wheels which cannot be seen from the cockpit but which can be felt by a pilot's special neurons. And flash burns. Any flier with friends who fly has logged time waiting for news from the burn ward. William McKinley Parker had looked too many times at this same puffy red face soon to fester into watery blisters. The Aircraft Commander winced, creasing deep furrows in his gaunt face.

"I'm here, Jack," the tall man sighed as he floated close to the charred face of his brother.

Parker rose and floated on his side toward the galley unit by the painfully bright window in the mid-deck hatch. Outside, the gas cloud had boiled away in the fearsome sun to a faint haze of yellow and glistening snowflakes. He did not linger there.

257

"Endeavor: With you by Kennedy at 04 hours, 44 minutes. Still negative contact voice." Shuttle flew 180 miles due south of St. Louis. "Please configure Number Two on your network signal processor. KSC listening."

Parker fetched a hand towel from the galley's accessories locker. He pulled out the cold-water nozzle which he buried in the little square of cloth. Floating upright beside the side window, Parker hovered with his knees flexed toward his middle. His feet were above the floor as he shot cold water into the towel. Bubbles of water rose and burst into tiny globules against the mid-deck ceiling beside the access hole which led upstairs to the flightdeck.

Returning to Enright, the AC found his shipmate levitating a foot above the floor. In his deflated EMU suit, Enright's motionless arms floated upward in front of his swollen face already oozing serum from dime-size blisters.

Parker straddled the prone copilot and he laid the wet rag gently over Enright's lips. He took care not to touch the open blisters and he waited and he perspired. His right leg up to his groin felt like Enright's face looked.

"Endeavor: With you by BDA at 04 plus 47." The antennae at Bermuda in the Atlantic listened to the western sky, where Shuttle cruised over the Great Smokey Mountains 200 miles northeast of Atlanta. "Negative contact. If you hear us, check your circuit breakers on Panel Overhead-Five, Row B, at signal conditioners Operational-Forward One through Four and Midships One and Two. Also check MDM breaker Flight Forward Three. Colorado listening by Bermuda . . ."

Parker laid a second wet towel upon Enright's lips. The copilot sprawled on the mid-deck floor moved his mouth against the cool water globules clinging to his lips.

"Easy, pard," the AC whispered. "Nod if you're with me, Jack."

The kneeling command pilot felt Enright's enormous, beet-red face move slightly against his fingers.

"Can you open your eyes, Jacob?"

The burned airman creased his swollen forehead. His eyes blinked half open and Enright labored to focus. Tears welled in the outside corners of his bloodshot eyes. The droplets formed a growing globe of salty water on Enright's blistered cheeks. In weightlessness, tears, like all liquids, do not run. Instead, the weightless molecules adhere to each other, held together by their surface tension.

"Welcome home, Number One," the big man sniffed.

Enright nodded.

The AC knelt beside his crewmate. Parker held his position with one hand braced against an airlock handrail.

"Endeavor: You are feet wet at 04 plus 49. Still negative voice. If you are upstairs, configure to Pre-amplifier Two at Panel Aft-A1A2 on your S-band modulation. With you another three minutes."

Shuttle crossed the East Coast over Wilmington, North Carolina, for blue water. It was nearly 3 o'clock down below on a chilly December afternoon.

Enright blinked the tears from his red hung-over eyes. His voice croaked dryly.

"Easy, Jack. You're a might sunburned, second degree from the looks of it. God knows what you would look like without that visor on when you got hit. Can you move?"

Parker watched Enright slowly lift his boots. The AC's free hand pressed his partner's chestpack to hold him from floating away.

"Try your arms, Jack."

Enright closed his thick eyelids as he slowly lifted his arms one at a time. When Enright felt Parker's hand upon his chestpack, he closed both gloves upon his captain's hairy forearm, which stuck out of his mesh woolies.

"Good, Jack. I want to move you, Okay?"

Enright nodded weakly.

Parker floated upright. He turned and for a moment fumbled with the sunshade for the hatch window. After he secured it to the round porthole, he returned to the dozing copilot. Gently, Parker pushed at Enright's backpack near the floor. The copilot slowly floated off the mid-deck floor and his red eyelids grimaced in pain.

"Another few seconds, buddy. Follow me through."

Enright nodded as the AC's pilot-talk sank into his parched brain.

"Endeavor, Endeavor. You're LOS by Kennedy. Bermuda still with you at 04 plus 52."

Shuttle drifted under the Digital Autopilot's firm hand 180 miles southwest of Bermuda Island.

The AC gingerly nudged the upright Enright toward the triple-decker sleep berths. He gently wedged the EMU-suited flier into a standing position against the bunk frame. From inside the middle berth, Parker pulled a long nylon strap used to restrain sleeping crewmen. He secured the long belt across Enright's chestpack. Each end of the strap Parker cinched to a post on the berth frame.

"That'll hold ya, Jack." Parker hovered close to Enright's face of oozing brown blisters.

"Don't wander off, Jack."

Neither pilot touched the floor with his feet.

"Thanks, Skipper," Enright whispered without opening his eyes.

The Colonel swallowed. "Jack: Do you know where you are?"

The AC watched Enright move his red eyes across the bright mid-deck of Endeavor.

"Frat house," Enright whispered hoarsely. "Goin' to bring in Daisy . . . Little Daisy." The copilot closed his watery eyes and a faint smile creased the corners of his swollen mouth.

"You got it, buddy," Parker smiled as he floated to the narrow front end of the cabin. From one of the lockers, Parker pulled a wireless Snoopy communications helmet. He covered his head with the soft CCA and snapped the chin strap. He slowly somersaulted in mid-air as he flipped a power switch clipped to his mesh long johns.

". . . in one minute. Try the malfunction protocol on the S-band antenna quadrants," Parker's headphones crackled as he steadied himself with a fist upon a ceiling handhold.

"Ah, I'm with you, Flight, from the mid-deck. Say again, please. Sorry we've been busy up here."

"Damn it, Will! We've held our breath down here for twenty minutes! We lost skin tracking on the PRC traffic at Goldstone. Soyuz has been in motion for ten minutes. And you guys have been out to lunch! We're LOS here in forty-five seconds by Bermuda. Next contact via Dakar in six minutes . . . What the hell is going on up there?"

The voice from Earth was shrill.

Clutching the mid-deck ceiling, Will Parker twisted with his stocking feet a yard above the floor. He looked between his mesh-covered legs toward Enright, strapped to the bunkbeds like Ulysses lashed to the mast.

"In 30 seconds, Colorado: LACE incinerated the Chinese ship. We took a reflected broadside from LACE's optics . . . Caught Jack in the face. He's alive but with second-degree flash burns to his face. Tending to him now. No apparent damage to the ship."

The AC could not resist smiling at the technicians below doing backflips at their consoles over his little status report delivered casually with Parker's very best "so how's things" voice.

"Copy, Will. If you can still hear us, use Kit Five in the medical locker. Kit Five. With you by Dakar in six . . ."

Endeavor sped over the horizon leaving Bermuda behind. The ground call gave Parker a mental fix of Shuttle's position over the middle of the Atlantic Ocean. A moment's thought told him he was but an hour and three-quarters from their near-miss of the South Atlantic

Anomaly on Revolution Five.

"Ground says to doctor you from Kit Five, buddy."

The copilot nodded although he appeared to sleep.

"Glad we have a horse doctor on board," Enright mumbled.

Parker flew headfirst and upside down to the forward storage lockers where he righted himself. From a locker drawer, he pulled a case labeled KIT FIVE: BURNS (THERMAL). He left behind kits labeled BURNS (CHEMICAL) and BURNS (ELECTRICAL).

A shuttle crew's years of training is equivalent to earning an Emergency Medical Technician certification. The AC knew the contents of Kit Five and what to do with it. As he swam toward Enright, he floated through a shaft of brilliant daylight raining down through the ceiling access hole from where the flightdeck above was filled with sunshine. Endeavor approached sunset six minutes and two time zones away.

Parker flew slowly toward his partner strapped upright to the berths. He aimed his stocking feet at Enright's sides just above the thick waist of the massive EMU suit.

The AC wrapped his legs around Enright's middle. Parker's calves closed lightly around the PLSS backpack. The command pilot floated with his mesh-covered chest touching Enright's chestpack. Enright opened his eyes when he felt the AC's breath upon his fluid-filled face.

"Little desperate, Skipper?" Enright smiled lamely.

"Grown particular, buddy?"

"Nah."

Straddling Enright's waist with his legs, the AC parked Kit Five by his shoulder. It remained motionless in the air at eye level.

Parker opened the small container from which he pulled pre-soaked towelettes which were orange with Green Soap antiseptic solution.

"Yell if this hurts, Jack."

"Not to worry, Will."

Gently, Parker washed the round and blistered face with the towel. Enright showed no discomfort.

After carefully dabbing at Enright with the soapy towel, Parker dropped the rag in the air where it hung motionless halfway to the ceiling. He opened another towelette soaked in isotonic saline solution. With this and two more, he rinsed the orange soap from Enright's edema-swollen cheeks.

After wadding the discarded rags into a ball, the AC carefully opened a gauze bag affair which resembled fine cheesecloth. It was soaked with penicillin cream.

"Close your eyes, Jack."

Parker slowly slipped the gauze mask over Enright's red face. It covered his head completely to his neck. The AC adjusted the eye, nose, and mouth holes on the antibiotic-soaked mask to fit Enright's features.

"Okay, Jack."

Enright opened his watery eyes and he peered at Parker's close face from inside his penicillin-drenched mask.

"Knew a stewardess I had to do this for," Enright whispered. "Only I made *her* wear the paper bag."

"I'll bet, Number One."

Enright wheezed a weak chuckle.

"Bottoms up, buddy," Parker said as he inserted into Enright's puffy lips a plastic straw from a squeeze bottle. The AC carefully pressed the soft container to force into the copilot's mouth an electrolyte solution of sweetened saltwater and sodium lactate. He timed each squeeze to Enright's labored swallows until the jug was empty.

"Still with me, Jack?" Parker released his leg-hold and floated back from Enright.

"Don't know who else would have you," Enright smiled behind his wet mask.

The AC unlocked Enright's waistring and he tugged at the EMU trousers. To keep from being drawn back to

Enright when he pulled, Parker braced his feet against the frame of the sleep berths.

When Enright's heavy pants came off, Parker directed them into one of the bunks.

"Feel better?"

Enright nodded. For half an hour, he had been without coolant water flowing through his liquid coolant garment which was damp with sweat.

"This will help, Jack," the AC said as he forced a long needle into Enright's thigh. He steered the hypo between the coolant tubes and through the mesh drawers. He discharged 50 milligrams of meperidine for pain. A second hypodermic entered into the side of Enright's other thigh where Parker fired 100,000 units of aqueous penicillin-G. Enright moaned slightly.

"That's it, Jack."

Parker floated away from Enright who was still strapped to the berth where he hung in half a space suit.

"Hope so, Will. I'm fresh out of legs."

"Oh? I can still roll you over, you know."

"Haven't been at sea that long, have you?" Enright managed to grin inside his damp mask.

"Not quite yet," Parker smiled as he stuffed the used towels and the empty syringes into Kit Five. He shoved the kit into a berth.

"Okay, Jack. Let's get the upper torso off. Can you help?"

Enright said nothing as he raised his heavily suited arms over his face and its new cheesecloth skin.

With a firm tug, Parker pulled Enright out the bottom waistring of the upper torso. The copilot floated in his liquid coolant garment from which floated water tubes and biomedical sensor cables.

"Feels much better," Enright sighed.

Parker directed one of Enright's bare hands to a ceiling handrail. With his eyes closed, the copilot closed his fingers around the handhold.

Parker coasted away toward the forward lockers. He fetched a set of baggy trousers from the forward lockers. These he pulled over the legs of Enright's long woolies. Shoulder straps from these pants held them in place upon the groggy flier.

The AC was worried about losing his shipmate to incipient shock. So he had dressed Enright in anti-G pants which looked like fisherman's waders.

During re-entry when Shuttle's return to Earth subjects the crew to deceleration forces of three times the normal force of gravity, all crewmen wear the rubberized, anti-G trousers. The pants have inflatable air bladders in the legs. Air pressure within the tightly inflated pants keeps re-entry's G load from causing the pooling of fluid in the crewman's legs. This loss of upper-body fluid could cause fainting during the critical approach to landing after prolonged weightlessness and its associated degeneration of blood vessels. The same inflatable pants would keep Enright's upper body from losing precious fluid as his burned face leaked plasma protein from damaged cell membranes.

"Thirsty, Jack?"

"No. Not yet, Skipper. I don't feel shocky. Just tired. And like I have God's gift to sunburns."

"I'll say. Let's get your legs blown up. Can you hang on here for a minute?"

"I'll be here."

Parker could hear in Enright's voice that he was coming around.

"Don't go 'way," Parker called as he went topside through the ceiling access hole. He soared to the front of the flightdeck cockpit. There, he locked tinted sunshades over the six forward windows of the cabin. He would protect Enright from the sun. Although quickly setting, the sun shone hotly through the windows from low in the

265

western sky. The cabin looked dusky with the shades over the windows. He did not bother to darken the two rear overhead windows or the two rear bulkhead windows facing the payload bay. These windows were already in shadows from Endeavor's hull.

"Okay to come aboard, Cap'n?"

Parker cast a surprised look toward the floor hatch behind the copilot's empty right seat.

"Sure," the AC replied with a faked, matter-of-fact voice.

"About done sunning yourself and takin' it easy, Jack?"

Parker watched the cheesecloth head float up from below. Enright carried the squeeze bottle of salty, electrolyte soup.

"Can't party all the time, Skip."

"Reckon not, Jack."

Enright strapped himself into his right seat. He plugged his outer pants into the cabin's portable oxygen system located on the back of each flightseat. The anti-G trousers slowly inflated to twice the size of Enright's thin legs.

The AC floated behind his own, empty seat. Looking over the center console, he studied his partner with the grossly swollen, masked face. The AC's face betrayed his concern.

"Now my legs look like yours, Will." Jack Enright was back.

"How you like it?" the AC smiled as he strapped into his left seat.

"I'd *really* rather be in Philadelphia."

"Me, too, Number One."

Out the tinted front windows, LACE hovered to the left of Parker's seat and Soyuz flew 50 yards off Enright's right shoulder. All but a wisp of debris had disappeared from the vaporized Chinese spacecraft.

"Down to just the three of us?" Enright asked.

"Yep."

"Wonder how many pilots she carried?"

"Don't want to know, Jack . . . Drink some water."

Enright pulled a squeeze bottle from beneath his seat and he forced the drinking tube between his painful lips behind his moist gauze mask.

"Endeavor: Configure AOS Dakar at 05 hours, 01 minute. Sunset momentarily. How's Jack?"

"Lookin' like the creature from the black lagoon, Flight. But we're both on station forward. Sunshade up on the windows forward."

"Real fine, Will. Do you have your visors on and locked?"

"Ah, negative, Colorado. Jack couldn't get into his with a crowbar. And I couldn't hear him if I wore mine. So we're a bit naked up here. Both of us still sweatin' in the liquid coolant skivvies." The AC spoke into the twin lip mikes of his CCA Snoopy hat.

Outside, the sun was flattening upon the western horizon orange and hazy. With Shuttle rightside-up and her nose parked toward the northeast, the low sun shone into Parker's leftmost forward window. The tinted shades cast a blue pall upon the cockpit. The Colonel's right hand reached up to Panel Overhead-Six above the forward windows. He turned five knobs which dimmed the floodlights of the cockpit and brightened the red back-lights of the instrument meters and pushbuttons. In a minute, the sun was gone.

"Pullin' the sunshades now."

The crewmen removed the six window shades to reveal the moist black sky west of the African coast. Outside, Soyuz 100 meters away had trained her intensely white arc lights upon LACE 50 meters from Endeavor's port side.

"Ivan is illuminating the target again. Any air-to-ground from him yet?"

"Negative, Will. Not a word."

267

Endeavor flew in pitch blackness halfway between Brazil and western Africa.

"With you another 2 by Dakar, Endeavor. We're not getting any bio from Jack. Check his plugs, please."

Before Parker could look sideways, the copilot pulled a cable from his coolant long johns and plugged it into a wall jack.

"Got Jack's vitals coming down now. Thank you."

Enright nodded. He could hear the ground over a wall speaker mounted in the upper right corner of the forward instrument panel.

"Will: We're looking at Jack's bio harness digitals. His pulse and pressure look stable. Doc wants you to keep close watch on both when you're out of ground contact. Pay close attention to his BP especially. If you see any sign of neurogenic shock, get an electrolyte IV into him immediately. We also recommend the anti-G pants for Jack for the rest of the mission."

"I'm ahead of you, Flight. Not to worry. Jack is doin' fine."

"Good news, Endeavor. Doc is right here if you need any assistance."

In the right seat, Enright fumbled with a CCA headset. Carefully, he put the Snoopy headgear around his neck like a scarf. Snapping the chin strap in front of his throat, the CCA floated upon his shoulders without touching his gauze face. He positioned the microphones to rest near his swollen lips.

"I'm with you, Flight," Enright said with a dry mouth. He spoke as through a mouth full of cotton.

"Super to hear your voice, Jack. Doc Gottwalt is at a Canaveral console listening if you need him. How goes it?"

"Afternoon, Mike. I'm uncomfortable but okay. Real stuffy in my nose. Skipper shot me up with the good stuff and I'm feelin' no pain. Could sell that on the street . . .

Safer way to make a living."

"Copy that, Jack. But you wouldn't get a room with such a view."

Enright looked through his wet and sticky eyeholes toward his right window. He saw the red-and-green running lights along the afterbody of Soyuz against a star field borrowed from a Christmas card.

"Guess not, Flight."

"Endeavor: At 05 plus 05, you're crossing the Equator. You are LOS Dakar and now AOS by Ascension Island."

"Roger, Flight."

Endeavor cruised southeastward 1,800 nautical miles west of Libreville, Gabon, on the west African coast. Missing the African mainland well beyond the eastern horizon, Shuttle would not make another landfall for 2,600 miles.

"For your burn pad, Will: Your next deorbit burn opportunities are coming up fast at 05 plus 33 plus 21 for Edwards and 05 plus 42 plus 11 for Kennedy landing. Can you set up for getting down that quickly?"

Parker glanced toward Enright at his right.

"Jacob?"

Enright raised his left hand. He gave an airman's thumbs-up.

"Ah, negative on that, Colorado . . . Ain't quite got 'em all in the corral yet. Jack and I are not done here yet." The voice of the Aircraft Commander was full of Go.

"Will, backroom says no joy with Jack. We want you down this revolution."

The tall flier's left hand gripped the glareshield overhanging the instrument panel. His free hand worked his microphone button.

"Tell your backroom to . . ." Parker felt a hand lightly upon his right shoulder. ". . . to put their re-entry plots away till a little later."

"Hear you, Will. Understand. But Jack cannot possibly

go outside."

The command pilot stroked his right leg, throbbing and swollen.

"Jack won't."

"Endeavor," the ground began.

"Stand-by one, Flight." Enright called softly over the microphones floating beneath his wet chin.

"Okay," the black boxes crackled.

"Skipper," Enright began without pressing the mike button of the air/ground channel, "you're not much better than me." Colorado could not eavesdrop on the cockpit conversation.

Parker looked glumly at his purple shin and knee, which he rubbed with long, hard strokes. Enright waited.

"Endeavor," the ground called. "One minute to . . ."

"Hold short, Flight," Enright insisted.

"Will?" The copilot looked at his long captain.

The big man in the left seat squinted his battered face out the left window toward LACE slowly rolling in the lights from ever-mute Soyuz. William McKinley Parker fogged the triple-pane window when he spoke softly but firmly.

"One final moment of glory: A man is entitled to that." The Aircraft Commander turned his haggard, pilot's face to his partner. "Jacob?"

The copilot furrowed his blistered brow within his cheesecloth mask.

"Flight," Enright radioed, "AC be going outside. I'll take the con."

The two airmen floated against their lap belts as they waited for the Flight Director 8,000 miles away to poll his controllers.

"We copy, Endeavor. You have a Go for EVA. Configure LOS Ascension Island at 05 plus 11. Botswana in 3 . . ."

Ascension Island fell off the western edge of the world

270

900 miles behind the starship.

"Can you handle the RMS, Jack?"

"Got two good hands, Skipper."

Parker nodded. Then the AC pulled his plugs and released his lap and shoulder harness.

"Stay put, Number One."

"Suit up alone?"

"Doin' it for years, Jack. Thanks."

Parker floated out of his seat and he touched Enright's left shoulder as he passed. He descended headfirst down the access hole behind Enright's right seat.

The Colonel soared through the lighted mid-deck to the sleep berths. Holding his position with his legs pointed toward the ceiling, he reached into the berth for the leg pocket on his orange ascent suit. He pulled a rumpled paper sack toward his face. From the bag, he retrieved a vile of phenylbutazone labeled "veterinary use only." Pausing, he contemplated the forward lockers stocked with powerful painkillers.

"Hell," he mumbled as he flew toward the zero-gravity latrine. Three hundred milligrams of anti-inflammatory horse balm were fired through his mesh woolies below his right knee swollen to the size of his thigh.

"In the can, Jack," the AC radioed topside as he swam into the airlock chamber.

"Take a magazine, Skipper."

Inside the lighted airlock, the upside-down pilot worked the airlock controls beside the yard-wide hatch. As he went through the ten-minute protocol for a solo suit-up, Endeavor cruised the nighttime South Atlantic toward Africa. He followed his checklists carefully: On Shuttle Five in November 1982, a spacewalk by two crewmen was canceled when a space suit failed inside the airlock. Someone somewhere down below had left a tiny but critical part out of an oxygen regulator in the suit. Parker steered his body through the waist ring of the EMU's lower torso

271

after removing it from its wall brackets. He winced as his right leg pressed into the pants. To his inflamed right leg, the suit's tight padding and insulation layers felt like hard fingers kneading raw dough.

Topside, Enright in the right front seat acknowledged Mission Control's call through the Botswana tracking station. Inside the airlock, Parker floated in his 225-pound, extra-vehicular mobility unit suit. After he had sealed and double-locked the airlock hatch, he had unclipped his PLSS backpack from its wall brackets. The PLSS chugged on his back. His inner helmet was locked to his neckring. The portable oxygen system continued to purge the heavy EMU suit with pure oxygen to flush out cabin air. The POS hose connected Parker's chestpack to the wall.

"Skipper: Flight wants you to do some vigorous isometric exercises when you're sealed to speed up your nitrogen withdraw time." Parker's soft Snoopy hat heard Enright but not the ground.

The medics on the other side of the planet were concerned about Parker going outside without first prebreathing oxygen for at least three hours to clean the nitrogen from his blood.

"Understand, Jack. With maybe a handstand or two for good measure."

"Don't hurt yourself, Will."

"Negative," the AC laughed. The throbbing heat in his right leg was retreating slowly before the horse medication which tasted slightly sweet in the Colonel's mouth.

"Where are we, Jack?" Parker called as he disconnected the oxygen purge hose from his chestpack.

"Road map says over Namibia. No exit signs for any truck stops."

Endeavor flew over sleeping southern Africa.

" 'Kay. Purge complete, Jack. Helmet locked and lock-locked. Puttin' on the outer visor. Real comfy in the suit." The AC's face within the plastic bubble disappeared inside

272

the white outer visor with the gold-mirrored, laser-proof faceplate.

"Copy, Skip. Don't forget your chin-ups."

The AC already had his heavily gloved hands gripping a wall handhold. With all of his strength, one arm pressed the handrail away as his other hand pulled it toward him. He felt his face flush and his pulse quicken. He sweated.

"Workin' out," the AC panted over the intercom.

Endeavor crossed the east coast of Africa at Port Shepstone, South Africa, twelve minutes after Parker had entered the five-foot wide airlock.

"Feet wet at 05 hours and 19 minutes, Will."

"Got my slickers on," Parker called, breathing hard of the cool, dry oxygen in the EMU suit pressurized to 4.3 pounds more than the inside of the bright airlock. The digital numerics on the top of the pilot's chestpack ticked up past three minutes of air time on the PLSS backpack.

"Ground says your bio looks fine, Will. They say you're working up a real lather. Hope you're not doin' anything that could make you go blind."

"Wish . . ." The AC blew hard into his twin lip microphones.

"Hear you, Will. We're LOS by Botswana at 05 plus 22. Radio silent for 15 till Australia. I'm real fine on the bridge."

Parker grunted his reply over the voice-activated intercom. He momentarily freed one hand to crank up the coolant water flow through the soft piping of his liquid coolant garment, which was sticky against his body. Upon his sweating face, he felt a cool wash of pure oxygen blowing from the inner helmet's vent pad behind his ears.

On the flightdeck, Enright in the right seat was feeling thirsty and vaguely lightheaded. He sucked at the plastic tube leading to a large squeeze bottle. He alternated sips of the tasteless, sterilized water with chugs of bitter electrolyte solution. The sweetner in the sodium drink could not dilute the aftertaste similar to warm sweat.

One hundred thirty nautical miles above the nighttime South Atlantic, Endeavor, Soyuz and LACE, all sped across a starry sky. LACE was bathed in the arc light from the silent Soviet ship. Shuttle had resumed her normal orbital attitude, flying upside down with her nose pointing into the direction of flight, now northeastward. Enright rolled the ship over while Parker was suiting up. Mother held trim. Facing Earthward, the space radiators secured to the open bay doors would be protected from the sun come daybreak in fifteen minutes.

"How goes it, Skipper?"

"Okay, Number One. Takin' a break to let the PLSS catch up with the heat load. Upstairs?"

"Same. Just finished running through a checkout of the fuel cells. They're purring away."

Enright took his foggy mind off his throbbing face by conducting test protocols of the electrical subsystems managed from the right seat.

"Roger, Jack. You got this watch." In the sealed airlock, Parker resumed his zero-gravity push-ups against the wall. He worked with his face close to the floor. As his bulky suit moved beside the hull of the round airlock, he tried out the EMU's urine-collection reservoir. A faint whiff of ammonia seeped into his helmet.

"Wish I had a creek," the working AC mumbled.

"Say again, Will?"

"Nothing, buddy."

Enright turned his attention outside. He reached over his head to Panel 0-8 where he dimmed the cabin lights in the forward cockpit. As the lights came down, he could see the green running lights on Soyuz through the far left window by Parker's empty seat. Straight ahead, he could make out the hazy horizon of the black ocean 1,000 miles away. He sensed the curving, inverted horizon where the star field stopped, blocked out by the dark planet. A few

274

bright stars were visibly growing brighter as they rose from beyond the eastern horizon and climbed through the Earth's gossamer atmosphere. When the points of light emerged from the thin veil of air close to the sea, their twinkling stopped. Concentrating to focus his bloodshot eyes out the thick window, Enright could distinguish cool blue stars from hot white ones. He made out one or two, faintly red suns where solar systems were in their final death throes. He felt no weight except for the pressure of his inflated, tight, anti-gravity pants.

"You are orange, Endeavor."

Enright was revived when the earphones floating upon his shoulders crackled. It should have been another two minutes before Shuttle was within range of the Australian Yarradee antennae.

"Say again, Skipper?"

"Didn't say nothin', Jack," Parker panted from below.

Outside, visible through the two square windows in the rear wall of the flightdeck, Shuttle's upside-down tail, 26 feet, 4 inches tall, glowed a neon orange as it plowed through stray oxygen ions loose in the vacuum of space 781,000 feet above the sea. Enright could not see the flickering energy 100 feet behind his bandaged head.

"Hello?" Enright called dumbly as he pressed the mike button to energize his air-to-ground FM radios.

"Hello, Endeavor! Your ion wake is quite brilliant."

Enright's swollen eyes blinked out the window beyond the Colonel's empty left seat.

The voice crackling through Enright's earphones carried a thickly Russian accent.

275

13

"Good morning," Enright radioed ship to ship. He was thinking of sunrise ten minutes and 3,000 miles away.

"Lieutenant Commander Enright? Your face is better, yes?" The thickly accented words crackled over the flight-deck speaker by the copilot's right shoulder.

"Yes, thank you . . . What is your status, Soyuz?" Enright got down to business after his initial surprise. His first hail from the black sky had sounded like a dream, like talking in his sleep.

"What's all the chatter, Jack?" Parker called from the airlock where he rested. He could hear Enright but not the Soviet transmission which was not multiplexed to the airlock by Endeavor's audio control electronics.

"Brother Ivan just dropped by to say hello, Will."

"Oh," the AC puffed below decks.

"The Colonel, he is preparing to go outside?"

"That's affirmative, Soyuz. Probably this pass across the

276

United States . . . What are your intentions? Are there two or three cosmonauts in your spacecraft?"

"Forgive my rudeness, Yakov Enright. We are two here. I am Alexi Karpov, commanding. Flight engineer is Uri Ruslanovich. We will provide whatever support you may require. We have been soft-suited and in oxygen five hours should you or Colonel need us outside."

Enright was taken aback by the cordial exchange 149 statute miles into the black sky.

"Skipper, they're Karpov and Ruslanovich. Here to lend a hand." Enright used the ship's intercom without pressing his air-to-air mike button. The circuit remained private.

"I'll bet, Jack. They were on Salut-7, weren't they?"

Enright looked outside toward Soyuz.

"You flew on the Salut space station, I believe?" Enright's puffy face moved abrasively against his moist bandages.

"Yes, Yakov. Thank you. We are pleased you follow our program."

"Well," Enright smiled uncomfortably, "you are the only other game in town."

Laughter followed from 100 yards away.

"I always enjoy what you Americans do with English."

"Any time, Alexi," Enright spoke around the water tube between his blistered lips.

"Endeavor, Endeavor. Configure AOS by Yarradee station at 05 plus 34. Your temperatures and pressures are stable. We see Will resting downstairs . . . Were we monitoring air-to-air?"

"Affirmative, Flight. Soyuz has broken radio silence on our primary frequency. They are Karpov and Ruslanovich."

"Copy, Jack . . . Soyuz: U.S. Space Command via Yarradee. Radio check, over."

"Loud and clear, Colorado. How me?"

"We have you, Soyuz. Welcome to the neighborhood, Major Karpov and Dr. Ruslanovich."

Enright raised a singed eyebrow at the ground's speed in shuffling dossiers.

"We thank you, Colorado," a second Russian voice replied.

"Endeavor's ion wake is still quite orange."

The second Soviet pilot carried fewer Slavic accents.

"Copy, Doctor. Thank you. Jack, ask Will for his PLSS time, please."

"Rogo." Enright released his mike switch over open water 900 miles west of the Australian mainland. "Backroom wants your pack time, Will."

"Ah, tell 'em 19 minutes used up."

"AC says 19 on the PLSS, Flight."

"Copy, Jack. Six until sunrise. Recommend you configure the sunshades."

"Will do."

Flying headsdown, Enright unfastened his lap belt. Standing out of his seat, he floated on his side across the center console toward Parker's empty seat. Bracing himself with a hand against the glareshield, he snapped three tinted shades into Velcro adhesive above the AC's seat. He took care to keep his floating legs close to his right seat and the air line to his balloon pants.

"You are in your underwear, Commander," an accented voice crackled over the radio. Enright waved toward the portside, visored window. Through the sunshade, he saw Soyuz blink her arc light which illuminated LACE in the darkness.

Returning carefully to his seat, Enright erected three sunshades on the windows around his seat. He floated against his lap belt when he returned his biomedical plug to the wall jack.

"Back with you, Flight. Six visors in place."

278

"Copy, Jack."

"Endeavor: Ruslanovich here. On Colonel's EVA suit, did he denitrogenate before entering the airlock?"

"Negative, Doctor. We have been depressurized to about 10 psi in the cabin for a few hours. The AC has been hyperventilating in oxygen for about half an hour now. We hope that should purge him."

"Understand. Watch him closely. We can go outside if he saturates."

"Thank you, Doctor." Enright did not know what else to say.

At 05 hours, 39½ minutes into Endeavor's mission, the three craft crossed the western coastline of Australia over Carnarvon. Enright returned to running his systems check of Shuttle's three fuel cells. He worked the instrument panel at his right elbow as he followed the checklist printed upon the 6-by-9-inch television screen on the forward panel. The left and center screens were blank.

"Jack: We see you running down the electricals. Confirm Auto Trip in monitor position on AC Bus Two, Panel Right-One."

"Monitor it is, Flight."

"Understand, Jack. Your cryogenic pressures and quantities are nominal. LOS and sunup in one minute."

"Rog . . ."

Below in the airlock, Parker rested in his EMU suit. As he floated in the can, his heavy boots pointed upward toward the flightdeck.

The AC felt vaguely uneasy inside his iron can, which became suddenly small. The sensation was familiar: first, the prickly discomfort between his shoulder blades. Then the moistness in his palms and the quickening of his pulse. He could feel his heart high in his neck. Parker's mouth was suddenly dry and he licked his lips. Claustrophobia: the dread predator. And it was with him, breath-

279

ing upon him in the can, in the stiff suit close to his wet face inside his two, doubled-locked helmets. The AC's ears hummed.

The Colonel closed his perspiring eyelids and he forced his arms down to his sides. Wincing with effort, he worked to send his mind downward. His disciplined brain plunged through space, through the night without air, to an unseen and faraway rail fence white in morning sunshine and to air heavy with the smell of fresh cut Timothy hay. Parker's nostrils flared as he sniffed new grass tasting wetter and sweeter than his first love.

Slowly, the beast retreated, gaining speed as Parker backed away. His heart descended from his throat as his white, wet hands relaxed their death-grip on the waistring of his suit. He opened his eyes, which immediately burned with sweat.

"I'm ready to go outside, Jack."

The strange urgency in the Colonel's voice distracted Enright from sunrise, which comes furiously in orbit. Endeavor plunged into daylight like a train erupting from a mountain tunnel at noon. Shuttle, upside down in broad daylight over the King Leopold Mountains of northern Australia, flew over ridges still in darkness. Endeavor would fly in harsh daylight over an Earth still in nighttime for five more minutes. So high did she fly.

"Understand, Skip. Hang loose a while longer. We're in daylight now at 05 plus 42. LOS Yarradee a moment ago."

"Hangin', buddy. Hangin'." The AC was anxiously calm in the can which had shrunk visibly in upon him.

Enright continued his fuel cell checks and Parker labored to levitate his mind elsewhere for the 2½ minutes required to overfly north central Australia toward the sea. At 05 hours 45 minutes out, Shuttle left Australia behind for the fourth time. In broad daylight, the ocean below was still dark as the starship crossed the 250-mile wide Arafura Sea between Australia and the island of New Guinea in 50 seconds.

Over New Guinea, Enright saw the lush green island become illuminated by morning twilight. The island's tropical rain forests, 420 nautical miles wide, were crossed in daylight in 90 seconds. Enright, flying upside down, watched the land recede over the upper sill of his inverted window. Five minutes after losing contact with Australia's antenna, Endeavor left New Guinea in her wake as she made for blue water stretching unbroken for 7,200 statute miles and 24 flying minutes toward San Francisco.

"Skipper: At 05 plus 49, we're into Rev Five," Enright called by intercom as Endeavor crossed the Equator for the eighth time over the Admiralty Islands in the brilliant Coral Sea.

"Endeavor: Configure AOS by Guam station. With you four minutes."

"With you, Flight," Enright acknowledged 900 miles south of Guam.

"Five-by, Jack. Your vitals are Go. We would like the AC outside by California acquisition in 19 minutes."

"Okay, Colorado."

"Also want to remind you that after your Atlantic Ocean transit and after you lose Botswana station at 06 hours 53 minutes, you will be out of ground contact for half an hour . . . Sunset this pass in 41 minutes at 06 plus 32. Sunrise follows at 07 plus 11."

"Got it, thanks," Enright said with fatigue in his voice as he scanned his own Crew Activity Plan text secured to a small cranny on the center console at his left.

"How do you feel, Jack?" the ground asked gently.

"Oh, okay. A bit tight in my face. Dry mouth, too. Takin' both the water and the sodium solution PRN-PO."

"Copy, Jack. Must be a nurse in your sordid past somewhere . . . Soyuz on the phone?"

"Listening, Colorado," a thick Russian accent crackled.

"Roger, Major. We remind you to watch your attitude thruster plumes when we go outside."

"We understand. We use only cold gas jets during the Colonel's work outside."

"Excellent, Alexi. Thank you."

Endeavor cruised upside down over the Caroline Islands.

"After we lose you, Jack, you are cleared to maneuver to the target and to power up the RMS. Rockwell people say your air line for the pressure pants should reach from the portable O_2 to the aft station, if you don't do any backflips."

" 'Kay. No danger of any aerobatics just now," the copilot at the helm replied with his dry mouth. Behind his clammy face mask, his blistered face was sore.

"Losing you, Endeavor. Back with you in nine by Hawaii. Good . . ."

Shuttle went over Guam's horizon above the Truk Islands at 05 hours 53 minutes, MET.

Enright completed his evaluation of the ship's triple electrical lines. After disconnecting his biomedical and communications cables, he unbuckled his lap and shoulder belts. Slowly, he floated out of his seat. Tucking his legs toward his chest, Enright drifted over the center console. With a gentle push off the ceiling, he guided his body into the left seat, the captain's position on every flying machine since the days of white scarves and goggles and iron men on wooden wings. He plugged his cables into their wall jacks on the left side of the cockpit.

"With you from the left seat, Skip."

"So how does it fit, buddy?" the AC drawled over the intercom.

"Too big," the thin copilot replied seriously.

"Not to worry, Jacob. I know for a fact they come in 37 short."

"Hope so, Will."

Although both forward stations have a rotational hand controller for changing Shuttle's position in-place, only the left seat has a translational hand controller, THC, for changing Shuttle's orbit.

Any orbit for any spacecraft is an ironclad rail in the black sky. Although Shuttle, Soyuz, and LACE flew only fifty yards apart, each cruised in its own private, orbital energy state as peculiarly unique as a fingerprint. For Endeavor to move only one foot closer to her target requires a complex change of Shuttle's delicate orbit. Otherwise, the starship would simply veer off on a new trajectory leaving LACE and Soyuz behind.

Enright could not merely point Endeavor toward LACE and fire his RCS engines to push his ship toward LACE. Even the slightest maneuver requires meticulous budgeting of fuel and kinetic energy within the balance of the laws of orbital mechanics.

A perfectly horizontal burst from Shuttle's engines would not propel her in a horizontal direction. Orbital physics is more demanding. Instead, a forward thrust in the direction of the orbital track (called the Velocity Vector) would send the ship not forward and faster, but upward into a slower orbit. And a horizontal thrust backward against the direction of the orbital path would send Endeavor not backward and slower, but downward into a lower, faster orbit. The higher the orbit, the slower the speed.

So Enright commanded Mother to consult her warm black boxes to sort out the most fuel-efficient course to be flown toward LACE.

Working his computer keyboard, Enright ordered Mother to prepare to use her RCS jets to maneuver closer to LACE in such a way that Endeavor and LACE would assume tandem orbits.

"Stand-by for maneuvering, Skipper."

"You got the helm, Number One. Okay down here. Don't bend nothin'."

Mother winked her READY light and Enright depressed the illuminated EXEC key on his little keyboard.

Instantly, Mother popped a battery of Endeavor's small Reaction Control System thrusters. Enright did not know which RCS jets were triggered. The two heavy OMS rockets in the tail are used only for more massive maneuvers.

Slowly, Shuttle closed in on LACE as Enright watched his Range and Range-Rate displays on the forward television screens. Through his tinted sunshades, he watched as LACE approached the upside-down starship. As the range-to-go ticked down from 40 to 10 meters, Mother fired combinations of her 38 primary RCS thrusters and her 6 tiny vernier thrusters.

Ten meters from LACE, Mother brought Endeavor to a stop. Using his square-handled translational hand controller in his left hand, Enright pushed the ship a few feet closer by eyeball. Mother still flew the jets with him. Using the rotational hand controller between his knees in his right hand, he kept Shuttle on an even keel, belly up in the piercing sunshine. Though the pilot handflew both control sticks, Mother rode shotgun over his shoulder.

"All stop," Enright sang out over the intercom.

"Then shorten sail, Jack, and bring her into the wind." Four minutes past Guam and four hundred miles west of Wake Island, the AC was full of GET IT UP—GET IT DONE—GET IT DOWN.

"Done, Will. Eight meters and sitting pretty."

The copilot returned the helm to the Digital Autopilot with computer instructions to roll Shuttle a quarter turn until she flew with one wing straight up and the open payload bay facing LACE 25 feet away. The 100-ton ship rolled automatically and stopped dead on station, frozen one-fourth way through a snap-roll.

With Endeavor's starboard wing pointing upward, the space radiators took direct sunlight as the sun moved swiftly across the sky where each orbital day is only 90 minutes long, half of it in darkness and half in unrelenting sunshine. Enright increased the flow of freon coolant through the two radiator loops to carry the extra heat upon the sunlit bay doors.

Outside, Soyuz executed her own movement to the far side of LACE. With less fuel on board than Shuttle, the 7-ton Soyuz moved slowly. The Soviet ship approached LACE to put LACE between itself and Endeavor. When aligned, the three vessels would freefall eternally like three cars on the same train: Endeavor leading toward the forever receding eastern horizon, LACE tumbling slowly behind, and Soyuz following as flagman in close pursuit.

"Soyuz in motion, Will."

"Wish I had a real window in here, Jack." The outer hatch of the airlock leading into the payload bay has only a four-inch window.

"Soon, Skip."

"Endeavor: Hawaii for one minute at 06 plus 02. Status?"

Six hundred nautical miles northwest of Honolulu and 720 miles east of Midway Island, Shuttle brushed the northern limits of the range of Hawaii's antenna. Although the last revolution carried Endeavor directly over Honolulu, during the intervening 90 minutes the planet had turned on her daily axis 1,552 statute miles to eastward. The Earth's spin had carried the Hawaiian Islands with it out from under Shuttle's ground track.

"With you, Hawaii. We're in position 8 meters out. Attitude in X-POP with Y in LV. I'm ready to go aft to power up the RMS. AC be downstairs bangin' on the door."

"Copy, Jack. Understand X-body-axis perpendicular to orbital path; Y-axis in local vertical. Go to unstow the RMS. Will is cleared to depress the airlock for egress after contact via GDX. Keep the AC inside till radio contact by Goldstone in 5 minutes. Data drop out at . . ."

"We're LOS Hawaii, Will. I'm going aft now. You have a fat Go to depress the can."

"Super, Number One! Startin' to smell like my laundry bag down here. Ready to walk!"

Parker, floating upside down, cranked the airlock relief valve down from 10 to 6 pounds per square inch. He would reduce the pressure by 2-pound increments every few minutes and hold it there long enough to check his EMU suit for its pressure integrity.

Topside, Enright was already on station on the portside corner of the rear flightdeck. Through his wet gauze which covered his painfully swollen face, he scanned the Toronto-built controls for the remote manipulator system arm reposing on the portside sill of the payload bay. He braced his stocking feet in the floor restraints. Behind where he stood in his sweaty, liquid coolant garment, Enright's anti-gravity pants stood empty with the disconnected air hose coiled limply about the floating legs. The air line was to reach to Enright's position. It did not.

Although the flier at the rear of the flightdeck had inserted sunshades on the two overhead windows and on the two windows in the aft bulkhead before his face, the copilot could not squeeze his helmet over his swollen face. He floated before the open bay without his laser-proof faceplate. By leaning toward the aft window, he could see LACE close to the bay. By raising his face to the ceiling window overhead, he could see the sun reflecting fiercely

286

from the solar cells of Soyuz.

"RMS ready for you, Will."

"Okay, Jack. Down to four pounds in here."

Enright's communications headgear still floated on his shoulders. The headset was plugged into the wall jacks for the radios to maintain air-to-air contact with Parker when he went outside. Radio communications were essential. The EMU suit with Parker inside would fly free of Shuttle without being tethered to a safety and intercom umbilical line.

"Down to 2 point 5 pounds, Jack. No leaks in the EMU. Got your air pants on upstairs?"

Enright looked over his cloth mesh shoulder to where his deflated britches floated in a lump.

"Sure, Skip. Just like the doctor ordered." As he spoke, Enright sipped from the plastic jug parked in mid-air beside his left arm.

"Good, Jack. Takin' it down to one here."

" 'Kay."

Endeavor, Soyuz, and LACE sped eastward 480 nautical miles west of San Franciso. The terrible afternoon sun was nearly overhead.

"Endeavor: California by Goldstone with you at 06 plus 08."

"Howdy, Colorado. RMS is powered up. AC down to 1 pound in the airlock. We're set up here."

"Understand, Jack. Your digitals look fine. Will is Go for EVA."

"With pleasure." Enright's voice energized the ship's intercom. "Clear for EVA, Skipper."

"Super! PLSS time now 51 minutes . . . Down to zero point five psi . . . Point 3 . . . Point 1 . . . Apparently holding there."

"Okay, Will. Stand by . . . Flight: AC is down to one-tenth pound. That alright to crack the hatch?"

"Endeavor: Backroom says Go for egress."

"Thanks . . . You're Go, William. Take your time. I gotcha covered from here." Enright sounded anxious and serious as his partner prepared to do the job for which Enright had trained for months. Both pilots had trained for going outside into the bay to close the payload bay doors should they fail. But Enright had logged most of the simulated EVA time as the space-walker.

"On my way." Parker's voice brimmed with Go.

"Soyuz, radio check," the Colorado Springs bunker called through the California antenna dish.

"Soyuz is with you. Keeping clear but ready if needed."

"Thank you, Major," the ground called. "We are remoting your transmissions to your center at Kaliningrad."

"Thank you, Colorado," a Russian voice replied. "Hello, Natalia!"

"And Hello, Natalia, from the good ship Endeavor! You got modulation?" Enright asked as he powered up the RMS arm. He had raised the arm's shoulder joint enough to free the arm's wrist nearly sixty feet from Enright's bandaged face. With the wrist and the end effector unit cranked toward the forward flightdeck, the wrist television camera was aimed at the sealed hatch of the airlock forty feet from the end effector. The outer hatch of the mid-deck airlock was at the base of the aft bulkhead eight feet under Enright.

"Good picture, Jack. We see Bulkhead 576 clearly. Don't change the zoom any."

"Understand, Flight." Enright watched the closed-circuit television, CCTV, monitor by his right shoulder.

The bay's floodlights were brightly illuminated to fill in any shadows caused by Endeavor's body although the sun burned with excruciating glare from above and south of the vertical starboard wing. The mid-winter sun was well below the celestial equator even at noon.

Over the sill of the downward facing portside wing, San Francisco Bay passed under scattered clouds at 06 hours 10½ minutes, Mission Elapsed Time. Just east of the city, Shuttle's orbital path began to arc southeastward en route to the Gulf of Mexico.

"Hatch swinging open," Enright called as he saw the door open slowly on the television screen. From the rear, double-pane, 14-by-11-inch window, Enright could not see the floor of the open bay closer than 29 feet behind the rear bulkhead. Nor could he see either of the bay doors well below the bay walls. Parker would be in the rear half of the 60-foot-long payload bay before Enright could see him out his aft window.

The command pilot hung heads-down inside the airlock canister. Parker turned the outer hatch crank through a 440-degree arc which required thirty pounds of muscle pressure to break the seals. With 1/10 pound of air pressure inside the airlock, the 40-inch-wide hatch popped when the Colonel yanked it inward into the airlock. Parker faced upward as he floated on his back out of the floor-level hatch. He took great care not to snag his precious PLSS backpack on the bottom sill of the hatch. The thick backpack reached from his suit's waistring to his helmet.

"Like the miracle of birth, Jack," Parker called as his boots followed his bulky EMU suit outside. Enright watched on the television monitor as the AC slowly floated to his feet and locked his boots into the restraints on the bay floor 13 feet below the lower sill of Enright's bulkhead window.

"In the foot restraints, Jack. I've closed the airlock hatch. Hope I remembered the key! . . . God, what a sensation, Jacob. This is really flying!"

". . . 'Where never lark, or even eagle flew.' " Enright sighed the words from the pilots' benediction: John Gilles-

289

pie Magee's air poem, "High Flight." Magee had written the poem for his mother while the young American pilot flew with the Royal Canadian Air Force during the first months of World War Two. In his purple sky, he was killed in action.

"Amen, Brother Jacob . . . You got me on PM downlink, Flight?"

"Loud and clear, Will," Colorado replied. "Your telemetry looks fine. Super FM modulation down here."

Ninety seconds east of San Francisco, Endeavor flew over Las Vegas.

"Real dry down there," the AC observed over Nevada.

"Not much of a white Christmas," the earphones crackled inside Parker's two helmets.

"Still seven days to go," the AC called. "Maybe you'll get some," the tall flier added as he stood in the lethal vacuum of his black sky.

"Radio check, Will. UHF through White Sands at 06 plus 14."

"Loud and clear, Flight. I'm in my golden slippers out here." The flier referred to his foot restraints covered with gold foil to reflect sunlight. "Backin' up into the MMU . . . Easy does it."

"A tad to your left, Will."

"Thanks, Jack."

With Enright spotting for him by the television monitor, the AC leaned backward into the wide nook of the Manned Maneuvering Unit from Martin Marietta. The MMU was mounted on the bay's inside brackets close to the sealed airlock.

The MMU was carried aloft in the bay secured to the bulkhead which separates the bay from Shuttle's cabin. The MMU hung sideways on braces protruding from the bulkhead such that the front of the MMU faced the port side of the bay by the centerline. With Endeavor flying on

290

her left side, Parker looked straight down 149 statute miles to the Earth.

Parker carefully eased his wide PLSS backpack integrated into the upper torso of his suit into the MMU.

The AC wedged his body backward into the MMU. Latches on the secured MMU engaged his PLSS backpack.

"Contact . . . Latch and hard-latch."

"Copy, Skipper."

Endeavor traveled beneath the sun over Shamrock, Texas, 95 miles east of Amarillo at 06 hours 17 minutes.

Parker reached down to his massively padded hips, where he grabbed each of the MMU's arms. He pulled each armrest upward where they latched rigidly out in front of his sides. Each metallic arm draped in thermal insulation locked under the pilot's arms. He rested his forearms atop each MMU arm as upon the arms of a chair.

"Arms up and locked, Jack."

"I'm watching it, Will."

The AC was now part of the 4-foot-high, 300-pound manned maneuvering unit locked to his backside over the PLSS backpack.

The spaceman perspired lightly inside his two helmets. He checked the MMU systems as Endeavor flew on her left side over Dallas at 06 hours 18 minutes, MET.

"Colorado listening by MLX."

"Okay, Kennedy . . . I have MMU arms in place. Let's see: Left nitrogen tank at 2-9-9-0 pounds pressure. Right N_2 at 2,850 psi." The nitrogen tanks, each pressurized with 1630 cubic inches of cold gas, fuel the MMU's 24 thrusters. Each tiny jet shoots only 1½ pounds of cold thrust. "Battery in the green. Looks ready to fly, Jack." The pilot had checked the MMU's two silver-zinc batteries each holding a 16.8 volt charge.

The all-white MMU hugged Parker. Short wings jutted from the MMU at his back on either side of his face. A similar wing projected just ahead of each of the pilot's bent knees.

"Comin' forward, Jack."

Parker flexed his legs to pull his body well forward. A wracking pain wrenched his right leg. Leaning forward, he moved closer to the portside sill of the open bay. Over the bay wall, he looked straight down 149 statute miles to a brilliantly clear New Orleans at 06 hours 20 minutes.

"Stupendous view, Jack!"

"From here too, Will." Enright could see the ground out his aft, sunshaded window in front of his face. But he could not see his partner except by television relayed from the flexed remote arm.

Endeavor, Soyuz, and LACE made for open water en route to a momentary landfall over southern Florida one minute and 300 miles away.

The AC pulled a release ring which silently freed the MMU from its retention brackets. It took even more leg strain for the tall airman to bend his body forward. Although the 300-pound MMU and the 225-pound EMU suit had no weight, their combined mass was ponderous. Parker's throbbing right leg provided the metabolic energy for torqueing forward the backpack and suit combination, which weighed three times more than the pilot inside.

The Colonel pressed his body forward until his small chestpack between the MMU armrests touched the grapple fixture latched to brackets in front of him. When the wedge-shaped fixture contacted his chest, Parker had to apply constant leg pressure to lean against the device long enough to close its latches by hand. He was panting from work and pain as he locked his body to the flying grapple fixture. The AC let the secured fixture hold his body bent forward while he rested. With sweat burning his eyes, he turned up the chestpack coolant controls. The flow of cool water increased through the 300 feet of tubing within his liquid coolant garment against his moist skin.

Enright could hear Parker's heavy breathing when the AC's breath triggered his voice-activated helmet microphones.

"Take five, Skipper."

"Sure, Jack," the AC panted. One minute southeast of New Orleans, Endeavor crossed western Florida over St. Petersburg.

The pilot outside rested against the grapple fixture as the glass-covered starship crossed the Florida peninsula from St. Pete to Miami in forty-five seconds. Below, the Merritt Island antennae at Cape Canaveral listened to Parker's telemetered pulse rate just this side of tachycardia.

"Take your time, Will," Colorado called through the Kennedy Space Center antenna.

"He is, Flight," Enright advised so his captain could catch his breath.

"Just like Gemini, Flight," Parker radioed over his backpack transmitter. "Everything in Zero-G outside takes a little longer." Parker hoped the strained calm in his voice would pacify ground medics. With his wet eyes closed, he thought of Gemini Nine. Then, unexpected stress during a space-walk by Astronaut Eugene Cernan in June 1966 overtaxed the space suit's coolant loops. His helmet faceplate fogged so badly that he had to come inside his cramped, two-man ship early.

"No rush, Will," the ground offered. "Give the coolant loop a break."

"My pleasure," the slowly recovering pilot breathed.

"We're listening by Bermuda now at 06 plus 22, Endeavor."

"Hear you," Enright acknowledged. They flew southeast-

293

ward over open water toward the easternmost tip of South America 13 minutes and 3,900 flying-miles distant.

"With you another 3 minutes by Bermuda, Endeavor."

"Okay," Enright called from his aft station upstairs on the flightdeck.

Over the Atlantic, very blue in the long sun angles of late afternoon, the three ships sped southeast.

"Grapple fixture free," Parker called as he stood upright in his foot restraints. He now carried 300 pounds on his back and 50 pounds upon his chest, all wrapped around his 225-pound suit. Although weightless, he felt like a piano mover at work.

"Great, Will," Bermuda radioed. "Hold short a moment . . . Jack: We want the PDP recorders running now."

"Done," Enright said behind his moist and sticky facial bandages. He leaned to his left and threw a switch beneath the starboard rear window. He turned on instrumentation in the Plasma Diagnostics Package berthed in its pallet at the tail section of the bay. The PDP would record LACE's electromagnetic wake and any leaks from the target's gas-laser generator.

"Two minutes to LOS, Jack. Run the PDP program as soon as possible."

"Copy, Flight . . . Stay put a second, Will. RMS in motion."

"Be here, Jack." Parker floated free except for his golden slippers, which held his boots to the payload bay floor.

The television image of the AC resting by the sealed airlock hatch disappeared as Enright flexed the 50¼-foot-long, 900-pound remote arm. A fully automatic program steered the RMS arm and its end effector unit toward the berthed, plasma-sensing PDP canister. The arm carried its wrist camera and the end effector camera away from Parker, who was now invisible to every human eye in the universe save for the four Russian eyes in Soyuz fifty yards away.

The arm stopped automatically a foot above the PDP's grapple probe post.

"Endeavor . . . ground is losing you at 06 plus 26. Back with you in 13 via Ascension Island. Sunset in 6 . . ."

Enright did not bother to acknowledge as Shuttle went over the Earth's edge above San Juan, Puerto Rico. Running the arm manually with Mother's help, he guided the EEU down to the PDP with his television monitor at his right shoulder. The end effector unit grabbed the package and Enright squeezed the EEU snare trigger in his right hand. A RIGIDIZE light flashed on the Canadian console. Throwing another switch freed the PDP can which rose at the end of the RMS arm out of Shuttle's bay.

Enright lifted the ion-sniffer ten feet high. It hung above the open bay with the sea behind it. The sun low in the west glinted off the canister suspended from the arm. The sun swiftly approached the western horizon behind Endeavor and its white globe burned directly into the bay. Parker's gold plated, outer visor glared like a strobe light.

"Looks great, Jack."

"Feels real smooth, Will. Wrist now in motion."

Enright commanded the arm's furthest joint to lower the PDP until it hung from the arm 90 degrees below the forearm of the RMS. This movement dropped the PDP can away from the elbow joint's television camera. In fully manual mode, Enright torqued the arm's joints individually until the outstretched mechanical arm aimed its elbow camera back toward Parker.

Slowly, the Colonel's glaring helmet came into view on Enright's second television screen below the TV monitor which showed only the top of the PDP can.

"Got you and the PDP, Skip."

"Good cameraman, buddy!" The Colonel's helmet

glowed like a small sun atop his huge white suit.

Six and one half hours aloft, Endeavor was 300 nautical miles east of eastern Venezuela's coastline, hazy in the gathering gloom of swift sunset in space. The sun began to flatten in the west where it sank through the blue atmosphere at the planet's cloudy edge.

Although the sun dipped below the port side of the payload bay as Shuttle flew southeastward on her left side, the six arc lights in the bay covered Parker with harsh light.

At 06 hours 32 minutes, the sun disappeared for 45 minutes of night. The sea was gone except for tiny patches of fluorescent plankton glowing on the black Atlantic 600 miles north of the Equator.

Soyuz on LACE's far side guided her powerful floodlight upon the target rolling slowly at one revolution every six minutes.

"PDP in place, Skipper. RMS oscillations dampening out."

Two of Endeavor's tail thrusters showered an instantaneous, fiery orange plume into the vacuum as Mother and the Digital Autopilot kept trim. Enright had disabled the 16 RCS jets in Shuttle's nose by which LACE hovered and where Parker was bound.

"Okay, Jacob?"

"Pull your chocks, Will." Enright momentarily shut off his voice-activated intercom, which dangled from his neck. He added softly, "Godspeed, old friend."

Parker rested his gloved hands on each handle at the end of his MMU armrests.

With his right hand, Parker pumped the MMU's rotational hand controller. The right hand RHC controlled his attitude in-place. He commanded the cold nitrogen jets by his face and knees to thrust. His body pitched slightly forward as he held his position in the foot restraints. Tweaking the RHC in the opposite direction, tiny jets of 1½ pounds of thrust eased him backward. To protect the EMU suit, the backpack had no hot rocket thrusters. Enright watched by television as Parker checked his MMU jets. Next, the AC's left fist moved the translational hand controller. The THC handle fired the MMU jets which squirt fore and aft, up and down, left and right. These jets push the MMU and its pilot through space between the black Earth and the moistly starlit sky. The full moon was in the eastern sky well up but blocked by Shuttle's vertical right wing.

"Thruster run-up complete, Jack. Ready to roll."

The AC's voice, now rested, was full of Go.

At 06 hours 34 minutes outbound, the starship flew southeastward across the Equator for the ninth time 420 nautical miles east of Macapa, Brazil.

"You're number one for takeoff, Will. Watch your feet, buddy."

Enright saw Parker in the greenish television as the AC briskly saluted with his thick arm. He returned his right hand to the hand controller.

A brief jerk on the THC in his left glove sent Parker rising slowly toward the lighted window in front of Enright's face. Pushing the THC handle downward the instant his helmet reached Enright's window, the AC floated freely and motionless at his partner's bright rear window. The thrusters above and behind the Colonel's helmet fired an upward burst to bring Parker to a halt before Enright's face on the far side of the double-pane porthole.

"You look like the creature that time forgot," Parker radioed to Enright's bandaged face, where only puffy eyes were visible. "What was that you were saying yesterday, 'Who was that masked man?' "

"Maybe I'll become a prophet. You look a bit Jules Verne yourself, Skipper."

297

"Keep the coffee hot, pard," the AC smiled inside his mirrored helmet visor. He well knew that he was stealing his best friend's moment of glory, for which Enright had lived and breathed for a year. Enright could not see the Colonel's face behind the gold-leaf visor. "Wait up for me, Jack."

"Count on it, Will."

William McKinley Parker knew he could take that to the bank as his MMU thrusters shoved him upward and away from Enright's bloodshot eyes.

From Enright's aft window, the white figure of the command pilot appeared to ascend straight up. Seconds after the AC's feet lifted beyond the rear window before the bandaged face, Enright saw his shipmate drift slowly into view outside Overhead Window Eight directly above the copilot's upturned face. But in his weightless freefall, Parker felt as if he slid out of the bay on his left side. Shuttle lay upon her port side in the frigid darkness 275 degrees Fahrenheit below zero. Parker jetted from the bay with his face toward Enright and with his back toward Shuttle's tall tail. As the AC's boots cleared the bay and the deployed RMS arm, he could see to his right the star Menkar in the constellation Cetus on the Celestial Equator directly above Endeavor. To his left was the black ocean which changed from mid-winter into a Latin American summer at the microsecond when Shuttle darted south of the Equator.

As Parker flew ten feet beyond Enright's ceiling window, the glare of the arc-lighted bay fell dryly upon the white EMU suit and the bulky, white manned maneuvering unit. LACE floated in the light thrown by Soyuz as the tight formation crossed the momentary landfall of the easternmost point of Brazil at 06 hours 35 minutes, MET.

In the arid light of the open bay illuminated garishly as a stage, Parker drifted as in moonlight. He looked ghostly

298

with his one side shining a cold white, while his other side was black against the black spacescape. Parker's boxy, shadowy figure so close yet so far from Endeavor sent a tingle down Enright's sweating neck.

The AC's left hand twitched on the arm of his MMU. Invisible nitrogen jets fired upward behind his head and he stopped above Shuttle's blunt nose fifteen feet from the open bay.

"You look like a man wearing a bookcase, Skip." Enright needed to hear his partner's voice from Out There.

"Feels like I left all the books in it," Parker chuckled over static. Although the cold in nighttime space is so intense that even atoms cease to resonate, the AC was comfortable inside his stiff Beta cloth water-cooled suit.

From only three Shuttle lengths above the flightdeck, Parker could clearly see Jacob Enright through the 20-inch by 20-inch, triple-pane window in the aft flightdeck ceiling. Parker studied his starship, his glass-shelled home away from home.

Like the three satellites dead motionless around him, the AC was in an orbit of his very own, governed independently by the dictates of orbital mechanics. Without the cold jets strapped to his backside or Shuttle's hot RCS thrusters, Will Parker would never close the short distance back to his ship. Never.

Hanging directly above the flightdeck, Parker could see the cabin lights behind the two ceiling windows and the six forward windows wrapped around Endeavor's nose. He thought of the nighttime glow of a mountain cabin casting warm, solitary firelight from its windows upon new snow.

"Surely looks cozy in there, Jack. Real cozy."

"I'll deck the halls for you, Skip." Enright's two hands worked to keep the remote arm's elbow camera aimed upon Shuttle's wandering son.

299

"Thanks, Number One. I can see the whole ship from here. Breathtaking! The thermal blankets in the bay are brilliant. A sixty-foot-long reflector with the bay lighting around it. The PDP pod is maybe 40 feet from me."

The plasma-sensing package automatically sniffed and electronically logged Parker's invisible cloud of nitrogen molecules from the MMU jets.

"Oh! And I have a full moon just peeking above your starboard wingtip. Awesome! High tide somewhere down below tonight."

Enright could see the white moon reflected off Parker's golden visor. The moon's face was slightly washed out by the lights from the payload bay.

"I'll bet," the shipbound copilot called as warmly as he could to his friend making a walk which was to have been Enright's.

At 06 hours 37 minutes, Endeavor ended her two-minute landfall over South America. The three ships and Parker left Recife, Brazil, behind for the dark South Atlantic. Endeavor and her small human satellite would be over open sea for the next 38 minutes and 11,400 statute miles of darkness.

"Endeavor, Endeavor. Configure AOS by Ascension at 06 plus 39. With you for 3. Downlink looks fine. All MMU digitals and bio are nominal. We see the AC stopped. You can turn up the TV gain a notch in the artificial light . . . Much better, Jack. Thanks . . . Radio check, Will?"

"Five by five, Flight. What a night for a moonlight stroll!"

"We copy that, Will . . . Jack: Could you configure DAP loop Alpha to deadband zero point one."

". . . Autopilot, loop A, to point one, Flight."

"We see it, Endeavor. Leave it there. We also want you to forget about the IMU alignment this pass. Your stable

300

member matrix is solid enough all balls."

"Okay."

"Soyuz: Comm check by Ascension Island." Colorado hailed through the mid-Atlantic antenna.

"Soyuz is with you, America. We see Colonel at about 40 meters. Soyuz standing by."

"Understand, Major. Thank you."

"We will be with our tracking ship for a minute, please," a Russian voice called into the darkness at sea.

"Frequency change approved," Colorado acknowledged, sounding like Departure Control.

"Thank you," Soyuz replied as if the Soviet craft required Center clearance. The United States Space Command and the NASA tracking network were tuned to the FM radio spectrum. Colorado was not privy to the Soviet dialogue over blue-green laser between Soyuz and her trawler off nighttime Brazil.

Parker did not speak directly with the ground. Instead, his MMU radio signal was absorbed by Shuttle which multiplexed his voice to Earth over Endeavor's antennae.

"Endeavor, you are Go to affix the grapple fixture to the target. Slow and easy, William. We remind you that your Anomaly proximity pass begins in 6 minutes at 06 plus 47 and lasts one minute. We will look for your post-proximity status report by Botswana 3 minutes later. Losing you . . ."

"Okay, Flight. I'm right and tight out here. Movin' out to the target."

"Copy, Will. Watch your relative rates. At 06 plus 42, data dropout . . ."

"Guess we're on our own again, Skip." Enright felt throbbing in his face as he craned his neck upward to Parker fifteen feet above the flightdeck ceiling. He also felt slightly lightheaded either from the burn-induced fluid imbalance in his body, or from acclimation to weightlessness.

301

The latter process usually requires two days, five for sure.

Shuttle flew on her side 1,035 statute miles south of Ascension Island in darkness. Below, exactly midway between Sao Paulo, Brazil, to the west and Windhoek, Botswana, to the east, each 2,000 miles from Endeavor, the brass clocks on unseen ships upon the black sea read 2043 local zone time on a clear December night. Below, it was summer.

"See you in motion, Will."

Parker's left hand directed the MMU's tiny, cold jets to push the flier toward his target. Through his overhead window, Enright watched the white-suited figure move away slowly. Although no ground station was within radio range, the pilot in the cabin steered the RMS elbow camera to keep it upon Parker. The television would be ready when the network made contact from Africa in seven minutes and 2,000 miles.

Within ten feet of LACE, Parker jetted to a stop. He still floated on his side with the black water to his left. To his right, the bright star Acamar shone dryly in the southern constellation Eridanus. The corner of the southern sky above Endeavor had few bright stars. The bright star Achernar in Hydrus hung in the south. And Canopus, the heavens' second brightest star, glowed brilliantly halfway between the horizon and the sky overhead to the southeast. In the sparsely starlit sky of the South Atlantic, most other stars were washed out by the brilliant full moon.

Parker and Endeavor were both on their sides relative to the ground. But in the arc light from Soyuz, LACE hung vertically with its long, narrow body perpendicular to the sea. LACE's base pointed toward the center of the Earth in the satellite's "gravity gradient" stabilization. Because LACE was ten feet long, the planet's gravity tugged on LACE's Earth-facing bottom with a force infinitesi-

302

mally stronger than the gravitational attraction exerted upon LACE's top end, ten feet farther from the center of the Earth. As result of this minuscule difference in gravity, the target had become stabilized by gravity's weak grip with the close end down and the far end up. LACE slowly rolled about its long axis, an imaginary line joining the two narrow ends of the 5-ton satellite.

Parker's right hand on the MMU armrest fiddled with the rotational hand controller. Combinations of jets on opposite sides of the MMU fired to push the pilot's feet out from under him until his helmet pointed skyward and his boots pointed seaward. The AC arrested his rotation when his backside faced Endeavor. From Enright's overhead window where Shuttle rode sideways among the few stars, Parker appeared to float upon his back twenty feet above the flightdeck. Only the MMU was illuminated from below by the lighted payload bay. LACE spun slowly, close to Parker in the light from Soyuz at Parker's side.

"What kind of flying you call that, Skipper?" Enright could only see Parker's back in the overhead window and only his side in the television from the RMS arm deployed at Parker's left.

"As Saint John put it, Jack, this is 'lighter than air.' "

The Colonel quoted a comment from space made years earlier when the Mercury spacecraft Friendship-7 had carried John Glenn into orbit in February 1962.

"Makes sense, Will."

"Okay, I'm two meters out now. Eyeball to eyeball with the target . . . How's the timeline?"

Parker looked small as he hovered motionless beside LACE twice his height and twice his breadth. The target was upright relative to the horizon as was Parker two arm-lengths away.

"Ah . . . Comin' up on 06 plus 47, Skipper. I guess we're there." Enright's mouth was dry.

The three ships with Parker inside their tight triangular formation now skirted within 80 nautical miles of the magnetically volatile South Atlantic Anomaly.

"Ten seconds in," Enright called. He had one gauze eye-hole on Parker above and the other on the event timer ticking away on the panel in front of his chest.

With a start, Parker clearly saw from the corner of his eye that Endeavor's tail grew orange against the backdrop of black starless sky and moonlit sea. Even in the harsh glow from the payload bay, Shuttle's tail looked like a neon tube as it cleaved through isolated oxygen atoms.

"Twenty seconds inside, Will."

"Jack, I'm lookin' at one orange tail! I can see it getting brighter even against the bay lights. The SAA must some-how affect the valence electrons of our ion wake . . . Hope that's all it stirs up."

Enright copied the Colonel's parting remark.

"Forty inside. Stay put, Will."

"I'm sittin' here."

Both airmen glued their eyes upon LACE as they ended their close transit of the Anomaly zone. The target did not twitch. Over his left shoulder, Parker saw the eerie or-ange glow fade around Shuttle's tail fin.

"And . . . 3, 2, 1, sixty seconds. Made it." Enright sighed audibly behind his moist mask.

"Kinda hairy, aye, Jacob?"

"Yeh. How's my tail now?"

"Dark as far as I can tell. No glow at all . . . Movin' in."

"Easy, Will." Enright guided the remote arm's camera in anticipation of radio contact 2½ minutes away.

Parker laid both gloved hands upon the grapple fixture attached to his chestpack which controlled his EMU suit. The fixture was the size of a hatbox. The pilot's heavily gloved fingers made out two clamps on the fixture's far side opposite the pilot's chest. Each clamp was open and felt to Parker's fingers like two hands joined in prayer but with open fingertips.

"Latches open."

"Copy, Will. Slowly now."

"Ah huh."

Working his hand controller in his right glove, the AC made certain his body was parallel to LACE. With an instantaneous press forward on the left translational controller, and a quick jerk back on it, he closed to within a foot of LACE and stopped. With a push up on the THC in his left hand, he slowly ascended LACE's body like a steeple jack. A press down with his left hand tweaked upward-firing jets behind his head. He stopped with the grapple fixture's jaws six inches from a thin, projecting ledge, a metal seam, which girded the 13-foot circumference of LACE's center like a belt.

"All stop." Parker's voice was subdued, almost reverent, as his words entered the flightdeck ten yards behind his back.

"Copy." Enright held his breath.

From Earth, the stars overhead move slowly westward one-quarter degree of arc every minute. The faint southern stars above Parker moved sixteen times faster.

The AC was perfectly motionless beside the towering LACE which revolved very slowly before his face. He floated transfixed by the awesome, black, and utterly silent machine. Although it was night all around him, Parker's backside was in the daylight glow from the payload bay and his side was brilliantly illuminated by Soyuz's floodlights only twenty yards away. The Soviet ship hung motionless beside Shuttle.

For a long moment, Parker watched LACE turn slowly from left to right. He watched the titanium rivets on the midline seam come out of the darkness at his left. The

305

tiny heads entered the artificial light, passed into the shadow between Parker and LACE, and very slowly moved over LACE's edge back into the darkness beyond Parker's right side. Each rivet head, the size of a dime, rose into the light from the left and set in darkness on his right. They were a tiny, silent solar system of cold metal one foot from the pilot who breathed bottled oxygen smelling faintly of sweat, urine, and rubber fittings. Parker did not blink his weary, hollow eyes as he watched the rivets move hypnotically like the white lines on a highway beneath headlights deadheaded from nowhere to nowhere.

"You awake, Will?"

"Sure," the AC whispered.

With a press forward on the THC grip, Parker moved toward LACE until he felt the flying grapple fixture touch the target's hull. He looked down his nose over the inner helmet's neckring to see the fixture's jaws open on either side of the protruding ledge. With a touch to the lever atop the grapple unit secured to his chest, the stainless-steel clamps closed without sound upon LACE's middle. Instantly, the panels and rivets before the AC's face stopped their transit. The white-suited pilot became part of LACE, and with it, he turned slowly to his right.

"Endeavor: Colorado by Botswana at 06 plus 51. We see the AC going for a ride."

The ground called from the darkness where in Africa it was nine minutes before midnight. Shuttle flew over the sea 100 miles southwest of Cape Town, South Africa. Since Shuttle's last revolution 90 minutes earlier, the entire African landmass had moved eastward out from under Endeavor's path and no landfall would be made.

"Only way to travel," the Colonel radioed as he revolved with LACE latched to his chest. He slowly approached the edge where he would roll out of the artificial light for his

306

own private sunset of sorts behind LACE's shadow.

"Copy that, Will. Any observations during your SAA proximity pass?"

"The AC reported quite a bit of ion wake activity when we were close. Hope the PDP registered something."

"Understand, Jack. You can dump the plasma data by OI loop over the States."

Colorado would review the recorded plasma data when Shuttle's operational instrumentation radioed the memorized information to the ground.

"Rog."

Shuttle was directly below a brilliant full moon which moved westward across the sky well north of Endeavor's extreme southern latitude.

"We would like to see the target stabilized as soon as you can, Will. Only with you another 90 seconds."

"I was just startin' to enjoy the ride, Flight. About to drop in another quarter."

"Believe you. But please get to it." The ground sounded impatient.

As the ground spoke from the darkness, Parker rolled behind LACE and out of view from either Enright's overhead window or the television screen beside Enright.

In the icy darkness behind LACE, the revolving flier could feel his aloneness. LACE's body blocked his view of both Soyuz and Endeavor. His left hand pushed the translational thruster handle and he held it in firing position. Four cold gas jets on the right side of the manned maneuvering unit squirted continuously against the direction of LACE's rotation.

"Firing!" the AC called. A shoulder and then a mirrored, gold visor emerged very slowly from behind LACE.

"Gotcha now, Will."

"Still thrusting."

"Not much visible reduction in your roll rate, Will.

307

Watch your consumables."

"I'll be here."

"Will: Colorado here reporting your roll rate is down from one point one to point seven degree per minute. You're braking well in rate. Continue thrusting. You're Go from here at 06 plus 52. One hour 36 minutes on your PLSS. Losing you momentarily. We remind you that your next 28 minutes will be out of ground contact."

"We'll stay on the job anyway, Flight."

"Hope so, Jack. Configure . . ."

As Shuttle lost the network over water, she rounded Port Elizabeth on Africa's southern tip. The ship began an 8,500 statute mile run without radio contact over the Indian Ocean. This revolution, Shuttle would miss the west coast of Australia by 1,100 miles since that continent had moved eastward with Africa out from under Endeavor's path.

Enright watched Parker for the 2½ minutes he was in view until he disappeared behind LACE for the second time. During that period, Endeavor covered a thousand miles and passed the southernmost point of her orbital path 2,622 statute miles south of the Equator.

Enright continued to monitor the temperatures and the voltages within the remote arm's six servo power amplifiers which held the plasma sniffer pointed toward LACE. The PDP was recording LACE's radiation signature for later relay to the ground.

"Still thrusting," the AC called as he rolled back into the bay lighting and into the view out Enright's overhead window.

"Okay, Will. At 07 hours even. You are definitely slowing down out there. About one more circuit should do it. Pace it to stop with the grapple fixture facing me if you can."

"No sweat . . . You with me, Soyuz?" Parker glanced to

is side. His gold faceplate shone brilliantly in the arc light from the Soviet craft.

"Watching closely, Colonel. Estimate one-tenth degree per minute in roll rate now."

"Thank you . . . Still thrusting, Jack."

At 07 hours 02 minutes, Endeavor cruised over the dark Indian Ocean on her northeast course 3,500 miles west of Australia.

LACE rolled ever slower. Parker attached to its midline required two minutes to come around the corner. In the artificial daylight cast by the lighted bay, he reached the halfway point of his slow roll.

At 07 hours 04 minutes, Endeavor rode the black sky into 2 a.m. local time, one day ahead of Cape Canaveral where it was 5 p.m. on a cool and clear day.

"All stop," Parker called with his back toward Shuttle. Damn, that burned a lot of gas, Jack."

"What are your N_2 reserves?"

"Maybe a thousand pounds psi."

"Should get you home, Will."

"Hope so."

As the AC floated latched to the perfectly motionless LACE, a stabbing pain in his right knee reminded him of his hotly throbbing leg. He closed his eyes in the light between his helmet and LACE which came from Soyuz to his left.

"Sunup in 5, Skipper," Enright noted at 07 hours 06 minutes, MET. Endeavor had already logged 117,540 statute miles across the sky.

"Comin' home," the AC called with his back to Shuttle. His gloved right hand pulled the release ring on the side of the grapple fixture clinging to himself and to LACE. At the same instant, his left hand pulled back on the THC handle. His small thrusters shot forward, one by each ear and one beside each of his bent knees. He waited to push off from LACE leaving only the flying grapple fixture attached to the target.

"Damn."

"Say again, Skipper?"

"Said no joy on the disconnect . . . Stand by."

Enright's bare right hand fine-tuned the zoom lens on the remote arm's elbow camera. Parker's backside and MMU filled the closed circuit television screen.

"Once more, Jack."

This time, as the AC pulled the release mechanism ring, his left hand pushed hard against LACE's black and frigid side.

Instantly, pain pierced Parker's left elbow and left shoulder. The pain felt like acute tennis elbow, only his shoulder felt the same way. He remained a white fixture upon LACE. When he tried to close his left fist upon LACE, his fingers only trembled. When he tried to open the grapple fixture's jaws which held LACE, they also failed to budge.

"Ah, Jack . . . I'm still attached out here. Negative separation at either end of the grapple unit . . . And I think I may be startin' to saturate a little . . . Crap."

Parker slowly lowered his sore left arm to the MMU armrest. He had to use his right hand to wrap his left fingers around the THC handle. He breathed hard. Each warm breath activated the lip microphones which filled Endeavor with his distress.

"William?" Enright spoke as calmly as his painful lips and cottony mouth would permit.

"Gimme a minute, Jack."

"Okay, Will. No rush. Got five hours left in your PLSS."

Like a weary stockman resting against a fencepost at day's end, the AC gently laid his outer faceplate upon LACE's freezing side. Had the pilot laid bare skin against he motionless satellite, he would have been burned crisp by the terrible cold of space without sun.

Cold sweat beaded upon Parker's upper lip and upon his forehead below his soft Snoopy helmet which held his earphones and twin microphones. The pain in his left arm crept downward into his left knee and ankle. The sensation was the prickly pain of a limb awakening after having gone to sleep. His left foot felt full of gout.

William McKinley Parker was paralyzed.

In the glare of the lights from Soyuz, the Colonel floated in the nighttime sky, alone. At 07 hours 09 minutes, over Parker's left shoulder toward the west, the solitary faint star Puppis-ro sped westward directly above Shuttle. The few stars in the southern sky's constellations Puppis and Vela, directly overhead, were obscured by the white moon which glowed as coldly as statuary marble. The brilliant moon was above and north of Endeavor.

In Parker's joints, from his toes to the cervical joints of his sweating neck, microscopic bubbles of nitrogen gas surfaced in his blood. Throughout his body, his circulation carried a fine frothy head which exerted exquisite pain against capillary walls.

The Bends.

The nightmare of fliers and deep-water divers tightened its grip on the pilot. Parker would have cried were he not afraid of the pain in his temporo-mandibular joints in his gaunt face in front of his ears. His anguish confirmed that his pre-breathing of pure oxygen in the airlock had failed to purge his body of nitrogen before he ventured outside.

Except for his massive EMU suit, Will Parker was naked ten yards from home and 149 statute miles from his mother the Earth. The weakening pilot longed to reassure his partner who waited anxiously in Shuttle.

"Help me, Jacob."

311

Parker did not feel his blue lips move. But inside his bubble helmet he recognized his own voice.

Enright's swollen eyes blinked moistly behind his gauze mask.

"Dr. Ruslanovich!"

"We are listening, Yakov. Major Karpov is already in our orbital module relieving cabin pressure. I am now closing to three meters."

The Soviet pilot flew his ship from the center section, the re-entry module of Soyuz.

"Understand, Soyuz . . . Hang on, Will." Enright's transmission was followed by labored breathing coming from outside over the radio. "Soyuz in motion to your left, Will."

Soyuz eased closer to LACE. The 7-ton ship required a minute to stop ten feet from Parker bolted to LACE's flanks. The Russians' arc lights filled the American's mirror faceplate. Parker could feel its radiant heat upon his face.

Soyuz is bulbous and her long rendezvous antennae give a look of metallic clutter, akin to a spacefaring oil rig. She is three modules bolted end to end. Her maneuvering rockets—small compared to Shuttle—and her stores and tankage are in the 9-foot wide afterbody. Attached to this service module is the 3-ton, funnel-shaped, re-entry module. In this center module, the crew of either two or three cosmonauts rides into orbit and home again. This compartment houses the flight controls and instrumentation. It is cramped, spartanly appointed, and all business. And attached to this is the forward, spherical, orbital module which is the on-orbit workbench and experiment station. Only the middle, re-entry module returns to Earth.

The Soyuz-TM is the final generation of the vehicle which through over 40 flights and 25 years aloft is the work horse of Soviet manned spaceflight. She had come a long way since the first manned Soyuz flight killed Cosmonaut Vladimir Komarov on April 24, 1967.

If to the naked eye Soyuz appears boxy and primitive beside Shuttle, which is fourteen times heavier, she remains the object of her crews' affection and of her American competitors' respect. Like sitting an aged B-17 Flying Fortress beside a supersonic B-1 bomber: one may shine with sensual sleekness, but one exudes a heritage which brings a fine mist to pilots' eyes. Like the old bomber with a generation of oil stains blackening her weathered cowlings, Soyuz is a proven ship of the line with a proud past which could be trusted. Enright did.

"Brother Ivan on station, Will."

The AC cranked his stiffening neck to his left where Soyuz hung motionless against black sea and black sky. In the light from the payload bay, he could see frost sparkling on the service module of Soyuz's afterbody.

"Got 'em, Jack." Parker's voice was breathless.

Enright felt obliged to keep the command pilot talking.

"Looks like 3 or 4 meters, Skip."

"Ah, ah . . . Yeh, Jack. Maybe ten feet."

"He's dumping cabin. Can you see his hatch on the orbital module forward?"

"I'm awake, Jack. No need to walk the patient." The AC's voice was annoyed and very tired.

"Sure, Skipper."

"Sorry, buddy . . . I hurt, but I'm on duty, 'kay?"

"Copy, Will."

"Colonel? Karpov here. I am in hard suit. Cabin depress completed. Hatch in motion."

Enright trained the remote arm's cameras on the Russian ship. In the glow from Shuttle's bay, he saw in his television monitor that the Soyuz orbital hatch swung inward toward their cabin. Enright made a mental note:

313

Perhaps an inward opening hatch was designed to prevent a seal rupture as had killed three cosmonauts in June 1971 when Soyuz Eleven became a deathtrap on the long ride back into the atmosphere.

A large round helmet emerged from Soyuz's open hatch on the side of the orbital module. In the glare from Shuttle's bay lighting, Enright could read "CCCP" stenciled across the white helmet above a gold, mirrored visor.

"Cavalry comin', Will."

"See 'im, Jack."

"I am outside." Thickly accented words filled Parker's helmet with slow and labored English. The Russian's transmission went to Endeavor which multiplexed the traffic out to Parker.

At the end of a thick, tether umbilical secured to his space-suit middle, the Russian floated out of Soyuz at Shuttle Mission Elapsed Time 07 hours 11 minutes.

As the boots of the Soviet flier cleared his hatch, the far eastern horizon behind Endeavor exploded with red and orange. The horizon's curvature glowed a deep purple as the white sun seared through the atmosphere close to the sea.

Shuttle flying on her left side, Soyuz, LACE, Karpov and Parker outside, all plummeted over the horizon of the Indian Ocean into fierce daybreak. Below, the sea remained black for five more minutes. Overhead, the stars were erased in the black sky between the high moon and the low red sun.

"I am coming, Colonel," the Russian panted.

"I'll be here, Alexi," Parker sighed into his fifth sunrise in seven hours.

Cosmonaut Karpov's umbilical tether was covered with a thermal-protection wrap of aluminized insulation. In the low sun, the Russian's safety line glowed brilliantly.

Alexi Karpov wore the Soviet's new, Orlan-DMA space

314

suit. But he was not strapped to the Russians' new manned maneuvering unit. Their MMU, much like Will Parker's rocket backpack, was first flown in space, manned in February 1990 on a spacewalk from the Mir space station. the MMU is too bulky to fit through the narrow, 1967-vintage hatch on the Soyuz-TM spacecraft. The Russian MMU remains a fixture inside the Kvant-2 research module which docked with Mir in 1989. The larger hatchway on the Kvant allows the MMU to be flown from Mir, but never from Soyuz.

Karpov carried a hand-held airgun of stainless steel which glistened brightly in the sunshine above the sea still dark. The cosmonaut fired a burst of compressed gas which pushed him slowly toward LACE and Parker who rode it. The gas gun was similar to the handheld thruster carried by America's first spacewalker, Astronaut Edward H. White on board Gemini Four in June 1965. Two years later, Astronaut White and two colleagues were incinerated on the Cape Canaveral launch pad. White, Virgil Grissom, and Roger Chaffee burned alive inside Apollo spacecraft No. 201 atop its Saturn 1-B rocket.

"Halfway, Colonel." Karpov dragged his wrist-thick tether toward LACE and Parker. His voice went by hardwire from his large white helmet over the umbilical to Soyuz where Russian black boxes converted the intercom to FM transmissions.

"I see you, Alexi." Parker's voice was weakening.

"Not long now, Will." Enright gritted his teeth in his rear station of Endeavor's flightdeck. Light-headedness tormented his ability to concentrate. He squinted through his gauze mask at the empty jug of electrolyte which floated near his left shoulder.

"Finally got dirt underfoot, Jack."

Endeavor flew over the narrow strip of Java, Indonesia, where the sun had reached the planet below at 07 hours

315

15 minutes. Java passed between Parker's boots in seconds, followed by specks of rosy ground. Dawn warmed the Kepulauan Kangean Islands southeast of Borneo. The Equator was only 600 miles and two flying minutes to the north.

"Good morning, Villam."

"And to you, Alex-yeh." Parker labored to properly pronounce his brother's name.

The Russian laid one thick glove against LACE where the low sun had warmed its shiny black side to the boiling point of water. Parker felt Karpov's other glove firmly upon his shoulder.

The Russian floated very close to Parker. Karpov's white knees touched the left side of the American's MMU backpack.

Karpov and the immobilized American were so close that their helmets gently touched without sound in the airless dawn. The Soviet pilot released his grip upon his airgun. It floated motionless behind Parker. Carefully, Karpov wedged both of his massively padded arms between LACE and the Colonel.

"Try it now, Colonel."

Parker nodded inside his double helmets. Neither flier could see the other's face behind his mirrored faceplate glowing like burning magnesium in the rising sun.

When Parker jerked the grapple fixture release ring on his chest, Karpov pressed his left gloved hand against LACE. His right hand forced Parker away from LACE. The American felt Karpov's arm pressing against his upper chest between the small chestpack and his neckring.

Parker did not move off.

"No joy, Jack," the AC sighed.

"Got lots of time, Skip," Enright mumbled.

The two Americans waited high above the tropical isle of Celebes 100 miles due east of Borneo as a brief flurry of Russian dialogue filled the vacuum.

"I try something else, Colonel."

"Sure." Parker closed his eyes. His knees, elbows, and shoulders moved in joint capsules which felt filled with sand.

Karpov eased back a foot from Parker. In the ferocious daylight, the Russian adjusted his snakelike tether, which had coiled about his boots. After pushing the umbilical out of his way like a bride adjusting her train, Karpov floated up LACE's broiling side.

At the top of LACE, six feet above Parker's head, the Russian slowly somersaulted taking care not to tangle in his lifeline. He stopped upside down along LACE's body.

Above the brilliant sea dotted by tiny islands, Parker and Karpov floated head to head. The Russian's feet pointed toward the sky. Parker's boots were framing the blue-green ocean. With their helmets touching, both men waved away the coiled mess of Karpov's tether line.

"Okay," the Soviet airman panted from the exertion of keeping his body from floating away from LACE.

The Russian flexed his thick legs until he appeared to kneel against LACE just above Parker's helmet. He braced a gloved hand on each wing of Parker's boxy maneuvering unit on each side of Parker's sparkling helmet.

"You pull release device. I push."

"Sure, Alexi . . . You with us, Jack?"

"Here, Will. Looks like you both will make the Bolshoi for sure. At 07 plus 18, we're Rev Six."

Beneath Parker's feet, the Kepulauan Sula Islands of Indonesia crept toward Soyuz off Endeavor's long tail. Radio contact with Guam was two minutes away.

Parker could feel the pressure of Karpov's hands against the MMU backpack. The American's body flexed backward.

At the instant Parker pulled the grapple fixture's release

317

lever, Karpov pushed off LACE with his knees while his forearms gripped Parker's helmet. Had Parker's MMU backpack not fit him behind like an old chair, his spine would have ruptured his stomach.

"Skipper!" Enright shouted hoarsely into empty space.

14

Parker was held in a headlock by Alexi Sergeovich Karpov, twice decorated Hero of the Soviet Union. The pilots rolled end over end through the sky toward Shuttle. Where no wind blows and where no bird flies, the Siamese airmen joined at their visored faces tumbled toward a white sun against a black sky at the leading edge of Endeavor's right wing.

Although Karpov had kicked mightily off LACE, he had worked against the mass of 1,200 pounds of pilots, pressure suits, life-support packs, and tether cable. His leap had heaved the pair slowly into the vacuum.

"Thrust, Will! Thrust!" Enright's cry was joined by a torrent of Russian from a shouting Uri Ruslanovich in Soyuz.

As the two shipbound airmen shouted to their soaring partners, Parker furiously fired his MMU jets to stop the tumbling and the flight of the two pilots who pitched slowly toward Endeavor's right wing. Like a wall of white, the glass-covered wing pointed straight up. Parker and Karpov tumbled slowly through space in an orbit of their own directly above the Equator and Pulau Obi Island east of Borneo.

The starboard wing of Endeavor is 60 feet wide where its root joins Shuttle's body and 5 feet thick. Its trailing edge behind is 26¼ feet long. Covered by inch-thick aluminum skin beneath its heat-resistant glass tiles, the four-spar wing is built by Grumman, the old Ironworks on Long Island.

When Karpov and Parker slammed into Endeavor's starboard wing, Shuttle's 100-ton mass did not twitch from the collision. Shuttle budged no more than the windshield of an 18-wheeler absorbing the impact of an insect.

Enright stood at the aft flightdeck station in the portside corner. He looked through the rear window across the open bay toward the starboard wing pointing skyward. Because Parker and Karpov had slammed into the thick inner wing where the bay door drooped over the sill, Enright could not see them on the far side of the 13-foot-high wall of the payload bay.

"Skipper!"

Parker did not reply. In his pain-wracked arms, he clutched Alexi Karpov, who did not move.

As Enright held his breath, he floated off the floor to put his swollen and blistered face close to the rear window.

"Will?" he repeated. Enright watched the coiled, shining, umbilical tether of the Russian float above the bay edge. Like a cobra rising, the end of the lifeline floated upward.

The tether line was attached to nothing. Air rushing from the open end made the umbilical sway like a loose fire hose.

"Endeavor: Configure AOS by Guam at 07 plus 20. We do not have the AC on the television. And we see his pulse at 140. Status, please! . . . Standing by." The voice

320

radiated from Guam to Shuttle 966 statute miles south-west of the island antenna.

"Stand by one, Flight!" Enright demanded breathlessly over the Sonsorol Islands. "Will!"

Enright was already steering the remote arm across the bay to peek over the edge with the RMS elbow camera.

Loaded with the heavy plasma diagnostics package, the arm moved slowly at its loaded rate of 2½ inches per second. Pilots earn their pay by making pilots' decisions. Enright made one.

With a squeeze on the pistol-grip trigger in his right hand, the arm's end effector let go of the 350-pound plasma package. The expensive experiment from the University of Iowa spun free twenty feet above the sunlit bay into its own lonesome orbit. Its inertia carried it past Endeavor and upward. There, the PDP's systems would die by suffocation where it would circle the planet. Instantly and automatically, the whole arm stopped against its emergency brakes. Mother felt the arm lighten when the PDP can veered away. The computer stopped the arm to await the end of the limber arm's oscillations induced by the sudden loss of the heavy canister. Immediately, Enright assumed full manual control of the mechanical arm, ordering it to continue toward the bay wall. The arm's Caution and Warning lights—DERIGIDIZE and RELEASE—both illuminated red, and the computer's television screen flashed RATE LIMIT ALERT to demand the pilot's attention to the bending moments straining the fragile arm. Enright ignored the alarms.

"Jack, Colorado has rate C and W on the RMS, a high-rate alert on the plasma package, and a derigidize indication on the end effector . . . What's up? Over!"

"I dumped the PDP and rammed Will and Karpov. Stand by, damn it!"

Enright fumed through clenched teeth behind his bandages as he steered the twanging arm over the edge of the bay. Colorado Springs waited quietly as stunned controllers watched their television monitors. They saw Endeavor's starboard bay wall grow larger as the arm's camera approached the white wing.

Enright steered the remote arm by hand. He flew it by reference to the view from his window and from the elbow camera.

Over the island of Ulithi, 600 nautical miles north of the Equator, the television by Enright's right shoulder was filled with two white-suited figures. The figure nestled within the manned maneuvering unit moved his thick arms.

"Thank God," Enright sighed. "I have you, Will! Wave if you read me."

Will Parker delivered a stiff salute against his mirrored, faceless visor.

"Gotcha, Skipper. Negative radio. Ground is with us by Guam . . . Flight? You got the video?"

"Affirmative, Jack. We're at 07 plus 23. With you another 5. We do not see Karpov's umbilical."

"Yeh. He lost it. Went out to pry Will from the target. Think the AC saturated out there. We had no joy on separation of the grapple fixture. When Karpov pushed Will off the target, they pranged into our starboard wing, just beyond the deployed door. I dumped the PDP to get the arm out there."

"Roger that, Jack. We concur with the PDP jettison."

"And we're negative reception on the AC, Flight."

"Copy." Guam was only 100 miles east of Endeavor's ground track at 07 hours 23 minutes. "Ask Will the status of Major Karpov. We have Kaliningrad on the line here."

"Skipper? Is Karpov alive?" Enright watched the two pilots in the monitor screen. The Russian floated in a ball in Parker's lap, touching the wing. Karpov's gloved hands

322

pressed against his suit's belly inlet where the tether had been torn loose.

Parker gave a slow thumbs-up sign.

"Copy, alive, Will . . . You got that Soyuz?"

"Yes. Thank you. The suit inlet valve automatically seals when the hose is disconnected. He should have maybe five minutes of oxygen trapped in the suit. You must get the Major inside immediately." The voice of Uri Ruslanovich was anxious.

"We have lots of room, Doctor . . . Did you catch that, Will?"

Enright saw another thumbs-up on his monitor screen. "Can you move, Will?"

Enright's question was answered by Parker's left hand, which moved the left hand controller on his MMU backpack. As Parker slowly climbed upward from the vertical wing, Karpov appeared to hug the American's neck. The legs of the Soviet pilot trailed limply.

"Two in motion, Colorado."

"We're watching it, Jack. So is the Soviet center. Do you see any wing damage?"

Enright had not thought about the wing. As Parker and Karpov ascended to the level of the bay sill, Enright focused the zoom lens past them toward the wing. In his monitor, he saw a foot-wide section of the wing which was black in the midst of the otherwise white glass tiles. The dark area was bare skin covered only by the heat-resistant glue which holds the tiles in place. Perhaps a dozen tiles, each the size of a bar of soap, were missing.

"You see that, Flight?"

"Affirmative, Jack."

"Goin' back to Will on the CCTV."

"Copy."

Enright cranked the arm slowly around until the distant, elbow section camera found Parker's backside in the forward bay close to the closed airlock hatch. Because Enright had been watching the wing in the monitor, he missed the two fliers when they drifted under his rear windows.

"Goin' downstairs, Flight. I'm leaving DAP in loop B."

"Roger on the autopilot. Plug in at earliest opportunity in the mid-deck, Jack. After we lose you in 2 minutes, we'll be with you by California in 16 minutes. Before you leave the flightdeck, advise if grapple fixture is still on the target."

"That's affirmative, Colorado. Target still real tight in gravity gradient. No motion of any kind."

"Good news, Jack. Go below and get Will and Alexi inside. Moscow indicates no more than one minute of breathable air in Karpov's suit."

Enright pulled his plugs. He left the remote-arm television trained on the airlock hatch so the ground could watch. As he swam toward the floor hatchway, his pounding and swollen head felt dizzy and congested. He ached for sleep. When the thin pilot's stocking feet followed his sweat-soaked body into the square hole behind the left front seat, Mother held the bridge. Outside, Parker's ten-million-dollar manned maneuvering unit floated up past the rear windows of the flightdeck. No pilot was attached to the MMU as it tumbled slowly out of the bay.

Enright executed a slow somersault in the bright mid-deck. He floated beside the large airlock can as he plugged his communications plug into a ceiling jack.

"With you from below, Flight."

"Copy, Jack. Our video has the airlock hatch closing. Both the AC and the Major are inside. No apparent movement from Major Karpov that we could see from here. LOS in 2 minutes this station."

"Understand . . . Will?"

Enright squinted and he blinked his blurry eyes to focus

upon a control panel on the outside of the airlock. The air-pressure meter slowly climbed past five pounds, halfway to mid-deck pressure.

"Here, buddy." Parker's voice was mainly air, heavy with fatigue and pain.

"One beautiful sound, Will! . . . You got a copy, Colorado?"

"Sweet music, Jack. He must be plugged into the intercom. We hear him."

"Ah yeh, Flight. Comin' to you by hardwire. I'll crack my visor when I get to niner pounds. Karpov is out of it just now."

"Hear you, Skip," Enright acknowledged as the pressure meter pointer showed seven pounds per square inch in the airlock. Soyuz was silent.

"You with us, Soyuz?"

"Yes, Yakov. The Major is time-critical on air by now."

"Working on it, Doctor . . . Will: You're up to 8 point 7 psi."

"Uh huh. Gettin' Karpov's helmet now . . . Ah, ask 'im if it's a left or right twist as I look at it?"

"Anti-clockwise," a Russian voice interrupted from Soyuz.

" 'Kay, I hear him . . . And helmet is off the Major . . . He's out, Jack. Breathin' though. Barely . . . He's definitely cyanotic."

"Nine and a half, Will."

" 'Kay . . . Upper torso waistring open here. Climbing the wall now." Parker panted over the intercom as he floated to the wall-bracket housing for his PLSS backpack and the upper half of his EMU suit. ". . . Okay, Jack. Upper torso stowed . . . And . . . I'm free!"

Inside the five-foot-wide airlock, Parker's PLSS backpack was locked to the wall. The AC eased himself downward and out of the upper torso of the EMU. He had not bothered to remove his inner bubble helmet which remained attached to the suit. When he raised his arms to slide out of the suit, the pain in his shoulders was blinding. Since the suit carried his communications cable, the AC was disconnected from the intercom when he slid weightlessly from the upper torso. He still wore the massive EMU lower torso and his soft Snoopy headgear around his wet and wasted face.

"Will? You're at 10 point 1 . . . Will? Will?"

Enright's voice rose in pitch. He felt faint and his face throbbed like a broken ankle.

"Easy, Jack." The Colonel was plugged in again as he wrestled in the airlock with his heavy pants. He labored to avoid floating into the unconscious Karpov who dozed bare-headed upside down.

"Endeavor?" A Russian voice pleaded over the audio electronics.

"Stand by, Uri," Enright said softly as he tried to keep his eyes open inside his facial bandages.

"Thirty seconds," the ground called as Shuttle approached the northeast limit of Guam's radio range 780 nautical miles west of Wake Island.

"Comin' out, Jack."

As the airlock hatch opened with a slight pop close to the mid-deck floor, Enright's feet were well off the deck. He was close to losing consciousness and his dry mouth was full of tongue.

Karpov's tranquil face emerged slowly across the floor from the open hatch. His lips were blue and deep creases contorted his wet, ashen face where the cheek pads of his helmet had pressed tightly.

"Major Karpov is out of the airlock," Enright radioed. He felt as if someone else's lips had moved inside his gauze mask soaked with penicillin and cold sweat.

"Understand, Jack. Guam is losing you at 07 plus 28.

326

Next network contact by GDX in 16. Advise when . . ."

The limp Russian floated on his back in his deflated white pressure suit inches off the floor. Parker steered the Major's legs from inside the airlock.

After Karpov's heavy boots cleared the hatchway, the AC floated headfirst from the airlock. Halfway out and wearing only his soaked, liquid coolant drawers, Parker rolled over. When his long johns and socks were through the hatch, he floated into a kneeling position beside the reposing Russian. The AC lifted his face toward Enright's grossly swollen head. The copilot hovered dopy-eyed in mid-air beside the airlock. Enright blinked lazily at his captain. He hardly recognized the tall pilot's face.

Like Moses when he descended from the sacred mountain with his hair newly white, Parker had aged visibly while outside.

"Afternoon, Jacob," the AC smiled feebly. He held his long arms close to his wet chest to ease the pain in his shoulders.

"We make quite a pair," the burned copilot said wistfully as he fought to navigate back from the warm, soft edge of dizziness.

"Don't call us 'the icemen' fer nothin', Jack." Parker licked beads of perspiration from his upper lip. His face was moist, gray, and weathered like a retired cowboy.

The Russian moaned beside the AC.

"O_2, Jack."

Enright shook the haze from his brain. He found an oxygen mask from the mid-deck's portable oxygen system.

Parker took the yellow airlines-type mask which hissed softly and he pressed its soft cup against Karpov's face.

As the kneeling, floating AC held the mask to Karpov's face, Enright rolled forward until his stocking feet touched the mid-deck ceiling. He carried a long cable which was plugged into a ceiling audio panel. With his hands work-

327

ing under Parker's chin, he disconnected the Colonel's intercom cable which stretched into the airlock. The copilot gently pressed the cable he held into the soft CCA headset worn by the Colonel. When the plug snapped into the jack near the AC's throat, Parker was again part of Shuttle's black boxes.

In Parker's arms, Alexi Karpov stirred and pushed the oxygen mask from his face.

"Easy, Alexi," Parker smiled. A weak exclamation in Russian mumbled from the Major's lips.

"English, Alexi."

"We are alive?" The Soviet pilot blinked his eyes where he floated close to the floor.

"Yes, my friend. And you are our prisoner," the AC grinned, cracking deep fissures in his tight face.

Major Karpov tried to sit up.

"Take your time, Alexi. You're in Endeavor. We'll be giving you a ride home."

The Russian nodded as he collected his wits. His gloved hand rested on Parker's shoulder.

"Soyuz?" Enright called over Parker's head.

"Here."

"Alexi is coming around. Looks fine. You copy, Doctor?"

"Yes. Thank you! Very good news. Tell the Major it is very lonesome over here."

"Will do, Uri . . . Soyuz says he misses you, Major."

The Russian aboard Shuttle sat up without weight. He braced against Parker's arm as the Colonel gripped a handrail on the outside of the airlock.

"You have room for one more?" the Russian asked as he floated upright.

"Got a ticket?" the AC replied as he stiffly straightened his legs beside the airlock.

"You take American Express?" Karpov smiled weakly.

"You're on, Alexi," the tallest of the three airmen laughed.

Floating in the bright mid-deck, Karpov unzipped his pressure suit and he squeezed through the opened chest area. As he hovered above the floor of the mid-deck, Parker regarded his Russia-red long johns.

"Just as I expected, Major."

"Yours are blue, yes?" Karpov grinned.

"You betcha," the AC drawled.

Swimming to the forward lockers, the AC found a set of orange beta cloth coveralls for the Russian. Both Americans steadied the stocky Soviet flier as he floated upside down and pulled the lightweight intravehicular constantwear garment over his body. As he zipped up the front, he patted the American flag sewn upon the sleeve.

"I could lose my pension for wearing this!"

"Who has a pension?" Enright chuckled. The thin, masked copilot handed a communications headset to Karpov, who pulled it over his head and adjusted two, lip microphones.

"How are we on time, Jack?" The command pilot of Endeavor felt much better as the lethal gas bubbles in his joints went back into solution in Shuttle's pressurized cabin.

"About seven and a half hours by now. Gonna be real tight on the Anomaly transit, Skipper." Enright still felt woozy and his face felt ready to explode. But having Parker home was medicine.

"Yeh." The AC stood by the round sidehatch window full of daylight in the cabin wall. "You go topside with the Major. I'll stop in the biffy first. And, Jack, don't forget your pressure pants. 'Kay?"

"Sure. This way, Alexi."

The Americans, in their mesh woolies, and Karpov, in his flightsuit, pulled their communications plugs from the ceiling jacks. Karpov floated behind Enright up through the ceiling hole to the flightdeck.

When they flew through the ceiling, the AC floated on his side to his sleep berth. He rooted inside behind the privacy curtain for a crumpled paper sack. With the little bag in his hand, he backed carefully into the tiny stall. As he closed the latrine curtain, he rubbed his right knee, which bulged like a softball inside his mesh liquid coolant garment.

At 07 hours 34 minutes, Shuttle Mission Elapsed Time, Endeavor, Soyuz, and LACE hurtled northeastward across the Pacific. Although two revolutions earlier they had flown directly over the Hawaiian Islands, they now were 1,200 statute miles northwest of Hawaii and 500 miles beyond the radio range of the Hawaii antennae. Hawaii could not contact the ship this pass.

Alexi Karpov stood with his stocking feet ten inches above the flightdeck floor beside Enright. The copilot was curled into a ball in mid-air as he climbed into his inflatable pants. After donning his air trousers but before he plugged in the air line, Enright flew to the rear station. There, he directed the RMS arm to flex. He pointed the arm's built-in camera toward LACE which hovered motionless beyond the open payload bay.

Cosmonaut Karpov blinked at the flightdeck filled with instrumentation. He had been inside Houston's shuttle simulator during a Glasnost tour. And he was rated to fly the Soviet Buran space shuttle on its massive Energia booster rocket. But he had never seen a working shuttle — American or Russian. The great ship was alive with blinking lights, humming fans, the clutter of business, and the blinding daylight filling the flightdeck's ten windows.

"She's something, huh?" Enright called as he eased into the forward left seat. He gestured to Karpov to take the

330

right, copilot's seat.

"Something," the Russian said with awe. He buckled into the right seat, where he tucked his hands behind the shoulder harness crossing his chest. He feared that his floating arms might touch the switches which wrapped around his corner.

At Karpov's left, Enright pulled the air hose from beneath the seat. He plugged the line into his rubber pants which inflated tightly from his ankles to his waist. This done, his left hand worked the side panel, where he activated the cabin pressure controls. He raised the air pressure from the pre-EVA level of 10 pounds to normal flight pressure of 14.7 pounds per square inch. The two seated airmen forced themselves to yawn to clear their ears as cabin pressure slowly increased. The command pilot did likewise below, where he rubbed his throbbing leg, newly inoculated with horse medication.

As Parker floated upward to the ceiling access hole, the pain in his joints had abated, leaving in its place a dull ache throughout his body. To the AC, whose head rose through the access hole behind Enright, his long body felt like the morning after of his long-gone rodeo days.

Parker floated toward the front cockpit, where he stopped at the center console between the two seats. With his legs flexed off the floor, he balanced with his left hand on Enright's right shoulder. He glanced above the center windows to the digital timer ticking up past Day 00: 07 Hours: 40 Minutes. Nothing but blue water and a vertical horizon glowed beyond the six forward windows, each pane the largest piece of heat-resistant, optical quality glass ever forged. Still on her left side, Endeavor in tight formation with LACE and Soyuz passed the sixth revolution's northernmost declination of 38 degrees north latitude, 1,600 miles west of San Francisco. Their ground track bent southeastward from there. When they made landfall over North America this pass, they would overfly only San Diego and the southern corner of California. This revolution would take them across the States for only one minute. On the next revolution—if Endeavor survived its direct entry into the South Atlantic Anomaly—they would miss North America altogether.

Enright had requested a ground track plot which glowed green on the center of the three forward televisions. A fly-size Shuttle winked three inches to the left of the graphic coastline of California.

"How long to SAA transit, Number One?"

"Thirty-six minutes. Real tight, Will."

"Yep. Target looks stable." Parker scanned the left television screen which Enright had tapped into the deployed arm's camera.

"Let's go in, Jack."

"Want the wheel, Skipper?" Enright looked over his right shoulder.

"Your bird, Number One."

As Parker spoke, Enright felt his blistered face rub painfully against his antibiotic-soaked bandage. He was smiling as he energized the control stick between his knees and the translational hand controller at the upper left corner of the forward instrument panel.

"We're moving in, Soyuz. Can you move back ten meters?" Enright released his mike button on the control stick between his thighs.

"Soyuz in motion," a Russian accent called. Through Endeavor's forward windows, the three pilots could see Uri Ruslanovich back the Soviet ship away from Shuttle's tail. The Russian, who flew alone, wore Enright's smile as the Soviet flight engineer assumed his own first command.

Parker pushed off Enright's seat back. The AC floated on his backside to the rear of the flightdeck. With his back facing the flightdeck floor seven feet below him, he stopped with his face close to the starboard overhead window. His stocking feet were against the ceiling behind Karpov's head.

"Soyuz still moving," Parker called from the rear. "She's all-stop now, well behind us, Jack. You're clear."

Parker pushed off the ceiling and he righted his long, thin body at the remote manipulator system station at the rear wall. His back faced Enright up forward in the commander's seat.

There was an audible pop from Endeavor's front end as a thruster on each side of Shuttle's nose fired together with downward-firing jets in each of the two tail pods. With Shuttle on her left side, the jets fore and aft firing downward pushed the ship horizontally to close the distance to LACE. At Enright's hand commands to the THC handle, Mother chose the jets to fire, each with 870 pounds of thrust. Small vernier thrusters, each with only 24 pounds of force, fine-tuned Endeavor's slow trajectory toward LACE.

"Endeavor, Endeavor: With you at 07 plus 44 by Goldstone," the ground called by the California antenna just over Shuttle's eastern horizon. "Good downlink here. We'll be updating your state vectors momentarily. We show you in motion. Status please?"

"We're Go here, Colorado," Enright radioed. His tight pressure pants had revived him. "I'm in the left seat, our guest is in the right seat, and the AC is on the RMS. We're sealed at 14 point 6 on the ARS. And we are inbound on the target."

"Understand, Jack. We'll be with you by the States another fourteen minutes, including a UHF pass via Northrop. We remind you of SAA transit in thirty-two minutes. You are time-critical . . . Will? Watch your arm rates while Jack is in motion here."

"On it, Flight," Parker called from his aft post. He

333

watched through the rear window and the overhead window as the remote arm flexed with each pop of Endeavor's thrusters. On the top center of the Canadian console which controlled the arm, a PORT TEMP light was illuminated yellow. The arm's three motors strained to absorb the thrusters' forces, which made the 50-foot-long arm twang with each firing jet. Mother's green television also flashed a SYSTEM ALERT warning. The AC anxiously looked upward as LACE approached with a glaring, blue-green sea behind it. The arm wobbled as a battery of upward-firing jets ignited in Endeavor's nose and tail. Karpov jumped reflexively against his lap belt as twin plumes of orange flame erupted before his forward window.

"All stop," Enright called with LACE only fifteen feet beyond the open bay. Parker watched the arm's far end sway through a foot-long arc.

"She's really dancin'," the AC called.

"We see it down here, Will. Doesn't look critical . . . Jack, do you have room to roll left ten degrees to put the arm in the shadow of your starboard wing?"

"Ah," the AC interrupted. "Let's just sit tight and let Mother work."

"We're sitting," Enright acknowledged before Colorado could protest.

"We copy, Endeavor," the ground replied formally. "Please dump your PDP data by OI downlink when you can."

"Comin' at ya now," Enright radioed as he reached over his head and over Karpov to the rows of toggle switches and circuit breakers on forward panels Overhead -14, -15, and -16.

As Enright checked his payload signal conditioners, the AC floated at the rear starboard panel arrays with his back toward Alexi Karpov.

334

"Okay, Flight," the Colonel began from the rear. "At Panel A-2, payload data interleaver power off; payload encryptor power on; encryptor on; coding transmitter on; network signal processor transmitting bit rate to high; S-Band mode high by transponder Number Two; S-Band power amplifier Number Two on; and, S-Band pre-amplifier Number Two on. Moving on, Flight: OPS recorder Number Two, power on; Number Two recorder to playback in Maintenance Loop One; recorder speed set at three; and, we're running."

Parker glanced at the mission timer ticking up through 07 hours 45 minutes.

Before being jettisoned overboard by Enright, the Plasma Diagnostics Package had sniffed LACE's electromagnetic wakes much like the wake of a ship underway. The PDP fed its electronic sniffs to one of Endeavor's two operational instrumentation pulse code modulation master units. Simultaneously, the Operational Instrumentation system's Master Timing Unit had slipped time tags into the stream of recorded information to identify each sniff later on. PCMMU Number Two then routed the data to Network Signal Conditioner Number Two. The steady flow of PDP sniffs then flowed at the computer speed of 128,000 data bites per second into Operations Recorder Number Two. In the recorder, the PDP information was stored, awaiting the command from the crew to beep the recorded data to the ground. At Parker's order, the recorder let its encoded sniffs flow into Endeavor's FM Signal Processor. The signal processor fed the time-tagged data to one of Shuttle's FM transmitters which directed the computerized plasma sniffs at a frequency of 2250 megahertz to the ship's S-band antenna quads. Mother automatically selected the best antenna for beaming the signal to the great dish antenna at Goldstone, California.

"Your S-band downlink looks real clean, Endeavor. We

335

hope to digest it for you before we lose you in thirteen minutes."

" 'Kay. The AC is with the RMS and we're station-keeping at the target."

"We see it, Jack. You are Go to deploy and affix the PAM to the target. We remind you that sunset is coming up at 08 hours and 01 minute. SAA follows in darkness at 08 plus 16 . . . You're up against the wall on time-line, Jack."

"Then let us get to it, Flight," the AC interrupted from the aft flightdeck.

"We'll let you work, Endeavor, as we review your downlink. We are still feeding your state vectors to you. Your REFSMAT looks remarkably close on guidance. And, Will, we're getting real fine modulation on the payload bay television. Leave the lens setting as is."

Endeavor arced down her ground track toward San Diego three minutes and 1,500 miles away to the southeast. The fierce sun hung high to Shuttle's left and burned ferociously into the open bay. Below, it was 2 o'clock on a North Pacific winter afternoon.

In the rear of the flightdeck, Parker set the remote arm to its fully automatic mode. The AC's shoulders still ached and the throbbing pain in his right leg had not been seduced to sleep by another injection. He was beyond the therapy even of horse medicine.

As the unloaded end of the mechanical arm was steered by Mother toward the rear of the open bay, the arm repeatedly stopped automatically at memorized pause points. Parker punched the PROCEED button at each rest-stop. His eyes darted between the view out the windows and the panel meters which read out the position of the end effector fifty feet out at the end of the half-ton arm.

Up front in the captain's seat, Enright worked Shuttle's

coolant systems to manage the high heat load. Seven hours of flying with the open bay's radiators exposed to unrelenting sunlight for half of each 90-minute orbit taxed the radiators to their limits. With so much time spent flying on her side instead of upside down for passive thermal control, Endeavor's glass brow sweated and her hot black boxes complained at last.

"We're getting a temperature C and W from the forward avionics bay and from midships instrumentation, Skipper." Enright called Parker by the voice-activated intercom without pressing his microphone button, which would have radioed his alert to the ground.

"Can you manage it, Jack?"

"Think so, Will. But I'm on high flow rate Loop Two already. Watching it."

"Endeavor: We're getting a Systems Alert on your freon outlet temps."

"We have a handle on that, Flight. But keep an eye on it while you have us."

"Copy, Endeavor . . . Will, we show the end effector passing 930 inches X_0. Halfway there."

"Ah, yeh, Flight," Parker called weary from the fire in his right leg. The AC assisted Mother's control of the arm which stretched toward the rear quarter of the bay.

Over the port sill of the bay as Endeavor flew on her side, the California coastline passed beneath Shuttle, LACE 15 yards away, and Soyuz twenty yards behind Shuttle's silent main engines. At 07 hours 48 minutes, the white highways around San Diego were visible as fine spider webs 149 statute miles below.

"Afternoon, California," the AC radioed.

"And to you, Will. You'll be feet-wet this time next rev."

"Hope not too wet," chuckled Parker with his hands full of RMS.

"Roger that, Endeavor."

"And so long, California," a tired AC sighed without pressing his mike button. Thirty seconds after passing San Diego, Shuttle was over the narrow strait of the Gulf of California half a minute from landfall over the Sonora region of western Mexico.

"We see the end effector at Keel Three, X_0 at 1003 inches, Will. Be losing you here at 07 plus 52. Configure UHF for Northrop station."

As Endeavor flew over Monterrey, Mexico, out of radio range of the California antenna, Enright turned on the UHF radio otherwise only used for landing. Compared to the clarity of normal FM radio traffic, the UHF air/ground was grainy and full of static like old Mercury days.

"Shuttle listening UHF," Enright called.

"With you by Northrop," Colorado replied via the White Sands, New Mexico, antenna. "LOS in 55 seconds. Advise when you are PAM rigid, Will."

"Almost there, Flight. How's our time?"

"Looks like . . . ah, 24 minutes to SAA transit."

" 'Kay. Thanks."

Nestled in the rear quarter of the payload bay, the boxy Payload Assist Module rocket, the PAM, was locked in its cradle. Built by McDonnell-Douglas, the three-ton PAM was packed with 5,325 pounds of solid propellant in its single Thiokol Star-48, rocket engine. The PAM booster first performed on the Shuttle Columbia in November 1982. One PAM was then attached to the Satellite Business Machine SBS-3 satellite, and one to the Telesat Canada Anik-C bird. Each PAM flawlessly launched its satellite from the Shuttle Five bay.

With his eyes glued to the television monitor at his right shoulder, Parker handflew the end effector the last six inches to the PAM grapple probe. A squeeze to the trigger on the pistol grip in his right hand closed the wire

nare of the end effector unit around the spike sticking up
rom the PAM.

"Rigidize," the AC called.

"Copy, Will . . . Jack: Configure AOS by MLX."

"With you, Canaveral. Sounds much better."

"Believe it, Jack. We have good CCTV modulation
rom the arm camera."

At 07 hours 53 minutes, Shuttle spoke with the Space
Command in Colorado through the Kennedy Space Cen-
er as the ship crossed Mexico's east coast over Tamaulipas
or the Gulf of Mexico.

"With you for five, Endeavor. We would like to have
PAM ejection before we lose you here. Backroom advises
our PDP data dump was very dirty during the Anomaly
roximity pass last rev. You plowed through knee-high
lux for a good two minutes. Garbage everywhere, guys.
Let's get the PAM deployed and you out of there."

"Tryin', Flight," the AC grumbled as sweat beaded on
is face. In zero-G, perspiration sticks and it does not
un.

The remote arm's EEU held tightly to the PAM probe
top the five-foot-high, three-foot-wide rocket pod. Work-
ng the arm's panel, Parker configured its electronics to its
rm-loaded logic. When Mother was told by the AC that
a three-ton mass was dangling from her 50-foot-long re-
note arm, she adjusted the arm's gears within the joint
notors to bear the burden.

At 07 hours 55 minutes, Shuttle led LACE and the
Soyuz-TM across the Yucatán Peninsula leaving the Gulf
ehind.

"Load secure, Jack. Ready to cut loose."

"Whenever, Will."

"Okay . . . PAM latches arm; RMS logic loaded; eject
rogram running; READY light on . . . And the PAM is
ree."

The PAM did not move to the command pilot's eye 14 yards away. But the arm twitched as the end effector lifted the heavy package an inch out of its mooring cradle. The remote manipulator arm automatically stopped at its first programmed Pause Point.

"We see PAM free, Will," the ground confirmed. "With you another 2."

Eight minutes from San Diego, Endeavor flew over Belize, British Honduras.

"Running in Manual Augmented. Movin' her out."

Slowly, making only two inches per second, the loaded arm lifted the PAM unit upward as seen by Parker at the rear window of the flightdeck. Since Shuttle still flew on her left side to keep the bay's reflective blankets toward LACE, to Uri Ruslanovich in Soyuz the arm appeared to pull the PAM sideways, parallel to the hazy, late-afternoon horizon. Endeavor crossed Honduras in twenty seconds.

"Endeavor: At 07 hours 56 minutes, you're LOS in 90 seconds. Shuttle then out of radio contact for 39 minutes. Sunset at 08 plus 01 in 3 minutes. SAA transit in 18 minutes . . . Jack, watch your coolant loop temps. You're yellow-lined both loops. As soon as possible after your evasive maneuver, shoot an IMU alignment. Then configure headsdown, PTC, for the duration. After we lose you here, you're AOS by Botswana for a one-minute status report at 08 plus 26 after SAA transit. And we show your downlink breaking up already . . . Godspeed . . ."

"RMS in motion, Flight," Parker called as he and Mother lifted the PAM higher. "You there?"

The pilot's headset was full of static two minutes before their eighth hour in the fretful sky. South America and the black starless sky of daytime filled the flightdeck's ten windows.

Outside, the low sun two minutes from plunging over the western edge of the world highlighed the lush green

340

highlands of Columbia.

"We're on our own, Will," Enright said quietly over the intercom. "Our show here on out."

"Reckon so, Number One."

15

Nicaragua below was already dark although Endeavor flew in daylight into her eighth hour aloft.

Through his rear and overhead windows, Parker saw the end effector swing the heavy payload assist module to within two feet of LACE.

LACE's glass sides with thousands of blue-black solar cells glowed brilliantly where the sun burned very low in the west. Fist-size globules of melted silicon and glass cluttered LACE's sides. Hundreds of electricity-generating cells had melted from the intense sunshine. Until Parker had arrested LACE's slow rotation, the satellite's constant rolling had protected the delicate cells from prolonged exposure to the blistering sun of airless, cloudless space. With LACE at a standstill, the vicious sun broiled her fragile flanks during the daylight half of every 90-minute orbital "day."

With an explosion of now familiar orange-and-red bands along the western horizon, the sun flattened, gave one burst of crimson protest, and conceded to the frigid night.

Shuttle was engulfed in freezing blackness at 08 hours 01 minute, MET. The floodlights brilliantly illuminated the payload bay and bathed LACE in coldly white glare.

In the artificial daylight, Parker could see LACE's seams and titanium rivets where the view was not obscured by the PAM canister which hung from the flexed remote arm.

"You should see this view, Jack!"

The Aircraft Commander studied LACE. To his surprise, tiny craters were opening silently all along the satellite's body. During its pass without spinning for passive thermal control through 45 minutes of merciless daylight, hundreds of half-dollar-size blisters had risen upon LACE's skin of thin solar cells. Now in the sudden, atom-topping cold of nighttime space, the little glass blisters were imploding—exploding inward. Silently, ragged holes opened over LACE's entire body. Her once sleekly black and shining skin erupted into silicon acne.

"Whatcha got, Will?"

"LACE's skin is popping all over the place. The solar arrays must have blistered after spindown. Looks like she's being machine-gunned."

"Let's hope not . . . Thirteen minutes to the Anomaly, Skip."

At 08 hours 03 minutes, Shuttle crossed the Equator southbound into summer over Rio Negro in northern Brazil.

Forward, Enright in his balloon pants felt much recovered. He sipped a fresh jug of electrolyte solution. He watched the coolant temperatures decrease in the radiator loops, and he adjusted the freon flow within them to avoid overcooling the delicate plumbing.

Over nighttime Brazil, Parker steered the PAM to within one foot of LACE. As Shuttle flew on her left side with her flat black belly facing southeast, Parker faced northwest through his rear and overhead windows aft.

343

The PAM canister with LACE almost touching was just below the vertical horizon. Out the rear window, Shuttle's vertical tail was parallel to the horizon, seen very faintly against the dayglow of South America. The weightless AC had the feeling of lying on his side. He was. In the western sky behind LACE, the satellite moved swiftly across the six-star group of the constellation Corona Borealis visible on the far northern side of the Equator. The bright star Nunki in Sagittarius was directly above Endeavor. To the AC's weary mind, the death ship outside, with her pitted and ragged skin, looked sadly forlorn and beaten against the icy backdrop of black Brazil, black sky, and faint stars.

"Ten minutes to transit, Will."

"Okay. Goin' in . . . Easy now . . . Easy, babe."

Running the remote arm in fully manual mode, Parker used both bare hands to lay the heavy PAM alongside LACE.

On the side of the boxy PAM, a grapple fixture protruded. The arm's end effector unit held the PAM at a right angle from the mechanical arm. The PAM appeared to dangle by its narrow end from the end effector's snares.

The arm gently touched the side of the PAM to the side of the weathered LACE. The AC saw an instantaneous blue spark erupt behind the PAM unit.

"Damn!" Parker whispered.

"What's up, Skipper?"

"A static discharge. No apparent activity by the target . . . I don't need these little surprises, Jack."

"Yeh . . . Niner minutes."

Shuttle was ten degrees south of the Equator still over Brazil in darkness at 08 hours 07 minutes, MET. They were four minutes and 1,200 miles from the sea.

"Radio check, Endeavor," a Russian voice crackled.

"With you, Doctor," Enright called as he worked the coolant controls. "The Colonel has made contact with the target."

"Yes. I saw the spark. Soyuz standing by."

Parker watched the PAM lie against LACE in the light thrown from the open bay. The elbow camera on the arm could not peer over the top of the PAM to where the two bodies touched. The AC commanded the arm to pull the PAM slowly along the side of LACE until the unseen grapple fixtures engaged, one on the payload assist module and one on LACE which had been left by Parker.

The PAM climbed LACE's midsection. Parker watched intently for the twitch in the long arm which would signal a hard latch of the grapple fixtures.

"Damn it, Jacob. Nothin'."

"Again, Will. Eight minutes to SAA transit."

Parker pushed the PAM down LACE's motionless side. At LACE's mid-line ridge, the end effector stopped abruptly. An audio tone from the RMS arm's Caution and Warning sensors rang in the AC's headset as a yellow CHECK CRT light flashed on the Canadian instrument console. Parker consulted the CRT screen, where green letters flashed CHECK MCIU. The sudden inertial resistance from picking up LACE's mass—unexpectedly to Mother—had triggered the alert alarm to check the arm's computerized manipulator controller interface unit. Parker's fingers on Mother's keyboard reassured her that all was well and that her 100-million-dollar arm had not banged into a wall.

"Hard latch, Jack!"

The man-size PAM with a rocket nozzle at its base was firmly latched to LACE's mid-line grapple fixture.

"Super, Will! Let's arm the thing and begin our pitchup . . . Soyuz? We're positive rigidize on the target. You can back off at earliest opportunity."

"Soyuz in motion, Endeavor. Thank you."

Enright and Karpov up front, flying on their left sides, could not see Soyuz off Endeavor's tail section. But Parker

345

through his overhead windows could see the Soviet vessel behind Shuttle.

In the moistly black sky over Brazil 20 degrees south of the Equator, Parker saw the orange flash of thrusters on Soyuz as she slowly backed away from Shuttle and LACE close to Endeavor's open bay.

"Rotating," Parker called as he commanded the arm's wrist joint to flex. The end effector slowly twisted to lay the upright, 10,000-pound LACE on her side.

"Five minutes, Will. Feet wet," Enright called. At 08 hours 11 minutes, Shuttle left Vitoria, Brazil, behind as Endeavor, with LACE in tow, and Soyuz sped past the coastline for the South Atlantic and 11,000 miles of open water.

The remote arm gently laid LACE on her side. A full minute ticked by as the target with the PAM attached assumed a horizontal position with the PAM rocket nozzle pointed toward Shuttle's tail. LACE's ten-foot-long, blistered body was parallel to the open bay.

"Ready for pitch program, Number One."

"Okay, Skip. Four minutes . . . Soyuz: Endeavor rotating. You clear?"

"Clear!"

Major Karpov in his coveralls watched Enright disengage the digital autopilot and energize the control stick steering.

"CSS alive, Will."

Parker floated at his aft window. Outside, the moon was directly over Mali in central West Africa, halfway between England and the Equator. As Shuttle flew on her side with her nose pointed northeast, Enright and Karpov had the cold white moon in their center forward windows. It looked brilliant but small without air to magnify its face.

Enright pulled back on his rotational hand controller. Mother chose the best thrusters in Shuttle's twin tail pods. Parker saw orange plumes erupt upward in the darkness

346

on each side of Endeavor's tail fin.

Shuttle pitched upward. Since she lay on her left side, her motion as seen from the sea was a flat, counterclockwise maneuver as her body's longitudinal nose-to-tail axis remained horizontal.

Enright stopped his rates when his green television told him that Shuttle's tail pointed toward the direction of flight, southeastward. Endeavor moved backward toward the South Pole. This aimed the PAM motor against LACE's orbital path. PAM's rocket engine would thus brake LACE's speed.

When Shuttle stopped her maneuver, her nose faced South America far to the northwest.

"Three minutes, Skip!" Enright sounded anxious. "Dump it!"

"Pre-arm electrical bus armed." The AC carefully read the PAM ignition checklist printed on the aft television screen. "Signal interface unit disabled." He turned off the PAM electronics left in its bay cradle to prevent electrical interference. The AC sent his commands to PAM by radio when he tapped out coded instructions on the aft computer keyboard. His moist fingers moved slowly. He had to get it right the first time. "PAM guidance on." PAM's own liquid-fueled attitude thrusters would hold LACE's horizontal position when Shuttle disconnected from the PAM.

"Two minutes, Skipper!"

"PAM motor armed." The command pilot had triggered the PAM's internal firing mechanism. The braking rocket would ignite automatically in 180 seconds, ready or not.

"Damn," Enright sighed. "Puts us a minute long, Will."

The payload assist module engine would fire in three minutes, but LACE and Shuttle would enter the SAA zone in two.

"Yeh, Jack . . . Okay to release our babies. Get ready to fly, Number One."

347

Enright had his left hand poised on the translational hand controller and his right hand gripped the attitude control stick between his thighs.

The Crew Activity Plan had called for LACE and PAM to be freed at least half an hour before PAM ignited. That would give Endeavor ample time to back away from PAM before ignition. Now, PAM's rocket would go in their faces, and go well within the South Atlantic Anomaly. At their velocity of 17,500 statute miles per hour, the mission time-line was an immovable object. LACE would be one minute and 300 miles inside the Anomaly when PAM's rocket fired to drive LACE into the sea.

Parker squeezed the pistol grip in his right hand to release the end effector's hold upon PAM.

The three snare wires did not move.

A yellow PORT TEMP caution light on the RMS panel flashed as a warning tone wailed.

"No joy, Jack!" Parker pumped the release trigger in his large right hand like a .44-40 at high noon.

"One minute to transit, Will. Two minutes to PAM ignition."

Jacob Enright spoke very calmly. He could have been in the Singer Mission Simulator with a cup of cold coffee on the center console between himself and Alexi Karpov. The pilot's reflexes inside the Russian inspired him to tighten his seat belt.

"Damn," the exhausted, sore Aircraft Commander sighed. He had not bent his metal in a flying machine for ten years. He hesitated with his tired face close to his rear window.

"Forty-five seconds to transit, Skipper."

"Okay, okay!"

Parker reached for Panel A-14 by his inflamed and throbbing right thigh.

"RMS shoulder guillotine to jett!" the AC shouted.

Explosive charges silently ignited in the remote arm's

shoulder mount, where the arm joined Shuttle's portside sill under Parker's nose. He saw the expensive elegant arm, still attached to the PAM, separate from Endeavor in a tiny cloud of insulation scraps and severed wire bundles. The 100-million-dollar mechanical arm was space junk.

"Hit it, Jack!"

The open payload bay faced LACE with PAM and the crooked arm dangling from it.

Enright's left hand jerked the THC handle. Upward firing thrusters in Endeavor's nose and tail pushed the starship back from LACE. The jets fired for ten seconds and stopped. Aft, Parker anxiously watched the amputated arm as it cleared the bay sill while Shuttle backed off ponderously.

"Bay clear! Roll, Jacob!"

"Clear, Soyuz!" Enright shouted as he backed blindly away from LACE.

Above the forward windows, the event timer ticked down the seconds until Shuttle, Soyuz, LACE, and PAM pierced the invisible electromagnetic wall of the Anomaly in the middle of the South Atlantic.

. . . 5 . . . 4 . . . 3 . . .

Parker stared at the timer in front of his sweating face.

. . . 2 . . . 1 . . . Zero.

Making five miles per second beneath the untwinkling stars, Endeavor entered the South Atlantic Anomaly, 2,000 miles east of Porto Alegre, Brazil, 30 degrees south of the Equator. The small television on the panel to Parker's left ticked down through 55 seconds to PAM automatic ignition.

Forward, the left of Enright's three televisions showed the horizontal situation display blinking out the distance from Endeavor to LACE. The kinetic energy imparted to Shuttle by her momentary thruster firing carried the manned starship sideways away from LACE. The green

349

numerics climbed slowly through 10 meters, 20 meters, 30 meters.

"Roll initiated!" Enright called. He commanded Mother to choose her best reaction control system jets to roll Shuttle over until her black belly faced LACE and PAM's rocket, now 40 meters away.

Slowly, Endeavor's wings rolled over in the eternally silent nighttime sky.

Parker gritted his teeth at the slow roll rate Mother maintained to prevent snapping off the great, open doors of the empty payload bay.

"Thirty seconds to ignition. Fifty meters," Enright chanted as Shuttle flew momentarily upside down with her wings horizontal. The wingover continued slowly as the flightdeck rolled away from LACE.

Parker turned off the bay floodlights as Shuttle rolled over. When the last arc light went dark, the AC squinted into an orange neon tube.

Endeavor flew inside ball lightning.

"Jesus have mercy," William McKinley Parker whispered. At his left beneath the orange rear windows, the small television blinked -20 . . . -19 . . . -18 . . .

"All stop!" Enright recited over the intercom activated by his rapid breath.

Shuttle flew with her portside wing pointing seaward, her starboard wing aimed at the black sky and her tail pointing southward into the direction of flight. Endeavor's black underside and its thousands of fragile glass tiles faced LACE and the fury of PAM.

Since Shuttle's tail flew into the direction of flight, it cleaved the magnetic flux of the South Atlantic Anomaly. The 26-foot-tall tail and rear bay glowed orange as she plowed through ionized oxygen atoms. The outside of the six forward windows did not glow.

Through the orange wake of ions aggravated by local magnetic disturbances, Parker could see Soyuz faintly, two

350

hundred yards farther along the flight track. Uri Ruslanovich had maneuvered his vessel around so only the round, blunt bottom of his service module faced Shuttle and LACE.

"Ten, nine, eight . . ."

In his sweat-soaked headset, Parker heard Enright's calm voice. The copilot sounded very far from where the AC floated. Parker braced his weightless, pain-weakened body with a ceiling handrail in his left hand and a wall handhold in his right. He looked blankly out the rear window by his face.

"Five, four, three . . ."

To Parker, the voice of his burned and bandaged brother had the faraway sound of being hailed by a distant voice through a thick and silent snowstorm.

"Two . . . One!"

Parker tensed his grip on the handrails.

Nothing.

No sound. No vibration. No debris in the windows or clanging against the glass hull. No flash of fire through the shimmering orange night.

Parker's sweating face scanned Mother's green face. The little screen flashed "IGNITION PAYLOAD ASSIST MODULE. TVC NORMAL. ATTITUDE HOLD, PAM."

"Ignition!" Enright called. Only his television told him that PAM's engine with 17,630 pounds of molten thrust had begun its 83-second burn to push LACE to a flaming death dive through the atmosphere. She would slam into the air in 25 minutes over the desolate Indian Ocean a thousand miles from any land.

"Ignition plus 20 seconds. Thrusting. Range 2 miles." Enright calmly read his television numerics, which confirmed Endeavor was pulling away from LACE as PAM's engine continued to slow LACE's orbital velocity fatally. A telemetry transponder in PAM beeped engine and ranging

351

signals to Mother.

Shuttle was bedrock solid as PAM blazed against the black sky. If the rocket was scorching Endeavor's underside, her crew could not feel it. They would rely on Soyuz to make an eyeball inspection of Endeavor's belly tiles and wheel wells. Significant tile loss would jeopardize Shuttle's return to Earth.

"One minute. Still burning . . . Four miles behind now. Slant range two miles, Skipper."

"Ah huh." Befuddled with horse medicine, Parker's mind was elsewhere.

PAM's attitude thrusters were programmed to keep the braking rocket horizontal for maximum deceleration and to hold a slight sideways tilt to the thrust vector. This off-center component of the rocket burn would push LACE both downward and away from Shuttle.

"At 70 seconds, 6 miles behind us, 3 below, 3 point 9 miles cross-range."

The AC released his grip on the handrails. He had held so tightly that his long fingers ached. Flexing his knees, he floated three feet above the aft flightdeck floor.

"Shutdown! LACE delta-V at minus 897." Enright's television confirmed in feet-per-second that LACE's orbital velocity had slowed by 612 statute miles per hour. Her death dive had begun. "Range 9 miles behind us. Cross-range 4 point 3. She's on her way now, Skipper!"

"Guess so, Jack."

Nineteen minutes into the eighth hour of Endeavor's long day aloft, the command pilot was not ready to relax. His right leg pounded hotly, his joints ached, and Shuttle had six minutes left inside the Anomaly zone with LACE's laser well within striking distance.

In the darkness broken only by Shuttle's orange tail glow, Endeavor flew 35 degrees south of the Equator bound for the southern tip of Africa. The glass starship flew on her left side, tailfirst. Outside, the dark payload bay glowed orange only ten miles above the descending LACE.

Parker could feel a distant uneasiness. The fighter pilot in his bones could taste the killer satellite out there in the darkness.

"Range, Jacob?" The AC kept his face close to the overhead window which faced the distant South Pole. Somewhere in the blackness, Soyuz was 400 yards away. The tone of Parker's voice made Enright feel the hairs on the back of his neck.

"Twelve below, 10 cross-range, 07 behind . . . And *closing.*"

There was surprise in Enright's voice over the intercom. His blistered and swollen face had pushed from his fuzzy mind the subtleties of orbital mechanics: LACE had been *slowed* by the PAM engine. But by braking LACE's velocity, the death ship had been pushed down into a lower orbit designed to intersect the atomsphere in twenty minutes. Enright's mind slowly wrapped around the grimness in Parker's voice: In its lower, steeply elliptical orbit, LACE must actually speed up. Kepler's law of orbital physics demanded as much. In her doomed descent, LACE was accelerating and was closing upon Endeavor from below. LACE would overtake Shuttle from underneath and would pass her in the night — with five more minutes to go within the Anomaly.

"Six behind, 15 below, 18 cross-range." Enright was intense.

"I know. What say we roll over and give her our reflector blankets, Jack?"

Before the AC had finished, Enright was firing Shuttle's RCS jets to roll the ship until she flew headsdown with the open bay and its mirrorlike blankets facing the invisible LACE somewhere behind and below and off to the side.

Although Shuttle's RCS thrusters popped like howitzers,

353

Parker could not feel them where he floated at the aft station. Nor could he feel the ship's slow roll. Only the rolling of the spherical, black-and-white Eight Ball in the attitude director indicator confirmed that they were coming about. The ADI on the upper left wall of the rear bulkhead told the AC that he was standing on his head over a black ocean, 1,200 miles this side of the edge of the Anomaly.

"Five and a half behind and closing, 18 below, 21 cross-range, Will. You got him?"

Parker floated toward the rear overhead window. Through it, he squinted into the darkness toward the sea below. From the ceiling of the aft flightdeck, he could not see the tail's orange wake.

"Negative, Jack."

"Endeavor, Endeavor. Soyuz here. I am 450 meters out. You want I should approach?"

"Negative, Uri. Parker here. We are monitoring LACE coming in from the northwest. His track is about 22 miles north of us and 6 miles behind and overtaking. Hold short with your service module in minus-Z until he passes."

"Understand. Will hold blunt-end-down. Soyuz standing by."

"Okay, Uri . . . Jack?"

"Three behind, 21 below, 23 cross-range. Anything?"

"Still zip. Makes me itchy like the old days, Number One."

"Yeh. I feel it, too. He's 02 behind, 24 below, 25 outside."

On a great circle of longitude joining the North and the South poles, the full moon was on the same meridian as Shuttle. The moon's cold face cast its fuzzy reflection on the nighttime ocean well north of Endeavor. Parker caught a distant glint outside his overhead window against the black water.

354

"Wait one," the AC called. He reached toward the rear panels and then spun slowly in mid-air to each side wall. He turned the knobs which dimmed the rear flightdeck lights. In the cozy gloom illuminated only by the red backlighting of the instruments, he returned to his ceiling windows.

"One behind, Skipper, 26 below, 27 out."

Looking straight down from the ceiling window, Parker caught a faint white star twinkling beneath and well to the north side of his ship.

"Contact! Your ten o'clock high, Jack!"

Enright and Karpov both looked high to their left as they flew headsdown with Shuttle's tail leading the starship's nose across the dark sky.

"Have traffic!" Enright glanced at his television. "One-half behind, 29 below, 30 north . . . And there she goes!"

LACE sped under Shuttle well to the inverted portside off Enright's left shoulder. The copilot in his captain's seat looked to the north.

"He's really hauling the mail, Will."

"Yeh. I got him by overhead. Movin' behind us. Time, Jack?"

"08 plus 24. One minute to go in here."

Parker moved to the rear window facing the dark bay still orange around the tail and aft OMS pods.

"On your six!" The fighter pilot in the rear cabin watched LACE illuminated by moonlight as it disappeared behind Shuttle's boxy stern, which housed the dead three main engines and the twin orbital maneuvering system pods. Each pod on either side of the tail contained a third of the ship's reaction control system jets and the large OMS engines needed to bring Shuttle out of orbit.

"I have it, Jack!"

Parker's deep voice filled the darkened flightdeck.

The AC facing aft grabbed the attitude control stick located in the center of the rear instrument arrays between

355

the two rear windows in the wall.

"I got it!" Parker shouted hoarsely.

The command pilot violently jerked the rotational hand controller. Instantly, Mother fired a battery of jets in the two OMS pods sending out fiery plumes on each side of the inverted tailfin.

Outside, the long vertical tail was no longer orange, although the rear walls of the bay still glowed. The tall tail was a flat, faint blue-green: the color of high-intensity, laser light.

The tail thrusters pushed Shuttle's hindquarter skyward and the inverted nose dipped toward the sea.

"What the . . ." Enright craned his neck to look back at Parker.

"We're hit! We're hit, Jack!"

The AC steered the tail out of the eerie green glow which lasted five seconds.

"Damn!" Enright shouted as warning horns blared and lights flashed on the Caution and Warning panel on the upper center of the forward instrument panel between him and Karpov.

"Left OMS! APU temp!" Enright read the two flashing caution lights.

The Colonel worked his attitude hand controller. Slowly, the heavy ship came to a stop with her body vertical. Out the rear window, Parker saw the tail fin move slowly across a faint starfield visible with the cabin lights dimmed. With Shuttle's rear end pointing straight up, the square stern of the open payload bay moved southeast across the bright, southern constellation Canis Major at 08 hours 24 minutes. Just northeast of the upright tail, Sirius, the heavens' brightest star, moved like a brilliant white beacon.

"Hittin' the lights, Number One."

Parker cranked up the flightdeck lights. Enright glanced at the mission clock under his forward windshield.

356

"08 plus 25, Skip. We're out."

Endeavor darted vertically out of the Anomaly over open water 550 statute miles southwest of Cape Town, South Africa.

"There it is, Jack."

The AC had powered up the payload bay lighting. He looked through the harsh glare in the bay to the tail section. To the port side of the tail's base, the left OMS pod was enveloped in a brown cloud of vaporous monomethyl hydrazine and nitrogen tetroxide escaping from laser-melted and ruptured fuel tanks. Within the thickening cloud were chunks of heatshield tiles. A tangled mess of pipes and tubing protruded from the left OMS pod.

"That's all she wrote on the left OMS, Jacob."

The Aircraft Commander's voice was very calm, very matter-of-fact. The consummate aviator: "Ah, ladies and gentlemen, this is your captain. We're circling Newark in this little thunderstorm up here. Ah, Number One is feathered and Number Two is running a little hot. But, ah, we'll be at the old gate right on time. Thank you for flying with us tonight. Hope to see you all again real soon."

"Yeh, Will. Goin' to zero-zero on Left OMS consumables." Enright squinted through his bandages at the glass meters above the right-center window above Karpov's anxious face.

"Check on Brother Ivan, Jack."

"Right . . . Soyuz, Soyuz. Endeavor has sustained maneuvering system damage aft. No cabin damage. Status there? Over."

Enright, Parker, and Major Karpov waited.

"Soyuz, Soyuz. Endeavor. Over?" The voice was Parker's as the lighted bay filled with brown gas which glistened with sublimating frost in the frozen nighttime vacuum.

"Uri!" Alexi Karpov pressed his mike button. Perspiration beaded upon his face round and puffy from twenty hours of weightlessness.

"Endeavor, Endeavor: Configure AOS by Botswana at 08 plus 26. With you for 45 seconds only. We show you zip on Left OMS tanks with two hot APUs. LACE is well inbound now, 90 ahead of you, 70 cross-range, 37 below. Good work, guys! . . . Advise status. LOS in 20 seconds."

"AC here, Colorado . . . We took a broadside from your blackbird. I dumped the RMS arm . . . Left OMS up in smoke . . . Suspect internal damage aft fuselage with APU damage . . . Negative contact with Soyuz. This is Endeavor."

"Oh . ." The ground was lost in static as Shuttle rounded the southern tip of Africa over water. Another 25 minutes of Indian Ocean out of radio range lay ahead.

"When's sunup, Jack?"

"Ah . . . in 14, Skipper."

" 'Kay. Try Soyuz again."

"Soyuz, Soyuz. Endeavor. Over?"

As Enright spoke, Karpov leaned forward to look up under the top sill of his windows. He saw only darkness.

"Could be antenna damage, Alexi." Enright's voice was unconvincing.

"n'Da . . . Yes. Could be," the Russian pilot sighed at Enright's right.

Endeavor's downward pointing nose drifted to the left as seen from the front seats. No RCS jet had fired. Parker in the rear saw the tail slowly tilt to his left against faint stars overhead.

"She's venting from the left OMS, Jack. Bit of a lateral movement from the outgasing. Real garbage pile out here."

"Yeh, Will. I see us yawing to portside . . . Soyuz, do you read Endeavor?"

"Maybe come around. Get the bay lights on him." Parker watched the brown cloud dissipate in the payload

358

bay.

"In motion, Skipper. Left OMS idle-cutoff."

Enright threw a battery of switches on a center ceiling instrument cluster. He closed whatever propellant lines remained in the left tail pod.

The copilot turned Shuttle on her nose by using the nose jets and the right-only OMS pod's RCS thrusters. Endeavor rolled clumsily with a slight wobble. She was not designed to fly without half of her tail thrusters.

The vertical tail rolled with the ship still upright. Parker squinted into the black sky beyond the bay's brilliant arc lights.

The payload bay slowly came around to face southward in the Indian Ocean 35 degrees south of the Equator. Parker peered through his aft overhead window behind Karpov to the position of Soyuz and her lone pilot, Uri Ruslanovich, Doctor of Medicine and Doctor of Mechanical Engineering.

All three pilots in Shuttle exhaled at the same instant the bay's harsh glare fell silently upon an enormous cloud of white gas, bent scrap metal, and frozen liquid globules, barely visible in the nighttime distance 600 yards from Endeavor.

16

Will Parker had seen the same yellow cloud of rubble exactly four hours earlier. His mind recognized it before his heart had time to absorb the ugliness.

Having rounded the southern tip of Africa, Endeavor sped northeast toward the Equator 2,000 nautical miles away. In the darkness over the Indian Ocean, the crippled starship flew alone. First there had been three vessels among the stars, then four, then three again. Now there was one ship badly mangled and a cloud of wreckage a quarter mile from Shuttle.

"Alexi, I am truly, truly sorry." Enright broke the sullen silence where he floated against his lap belt at Karpov's side. "So very sorry."

In the aft section, Parker blinked his moist eyes which looked into the brightly lighted bay. The sixty-foot-long cargo hold still carried a brown cloud leaking from Shuttle's ruptured tail. An airman feels his ship's pain, like a mother for her child. The haggard Colonel ached inside.

Major Alexi Karpov turned his wet eyes toward the large window at his right shoulder in the copilot's seat. "They will issue a proper statement, of course: 'The Soviet Union has lost a brave son.' Our governments are so good at that."

"A brave son," Parker sighed into his voice-activated mi-

360

rophone at his lips.

"My country has lost a son," Karpov said slowly, fogging the window with his anguish. "But I have lost a brother."

"All of us have, Alexi," Enright offered.

Endeavor, alone, flew through the darkness 540 nautical miles south of Madagascar a thousand miles east of Port Elizabeth, South Africa.

"How long to sunup, Jack?"

Enright looked at his mission clock: Day 00: 08 Hours: 3 Minutes.

"Eight minutes, Skip."

"We have to shoot an IMU alignment . . . We must carry on, Alexi."

"Yes, Colonel. Fly your fine ship."

"Rollin', Skipper."

Enright put Shuttle into a slow roll. She came about until her wings were level. Flying heads-up, Enright yawed the nose around laterally until Endeavor flew rightside-up with her nose pointing northward. The starboard wing pointed eastward along the direction of flight.

The two star-trackers under Enright's left window searched the heavens for navigation stars. He laid his swollen, bandaged face close to the silver-dollar-size reflecting mirror at the base of the crew optical alignment sight. The COAS tube protruding from the cabin ceiling scanned the southern sky's few conspicuous stars.

Squinting into the COAS sight at eye level, Enright found the bright star Regulus in the constellation Leo about 0 degrees above the horizon to Shuttle's northeast. Into the computer keyboard at his right knee, Enright tapped in Star Number 26. Moving Shuttle's nose with his control stick to search the sky to the northwest, Enright found brilliant Sirius about 60 degrees above the planet's black horizon where the faint stars stopped. Enright plugged in Star Number 18.

Mother digested the star sights automatically made by the

361

two star-trackers in the ship's nose. Her mass memory unit which had memorized the sky, compared the star-trackers' sight reduction to Enright's eyeball observations. Mother re solved her sights at the speed of light by mental haversine functions. Satisfied that she knew her bearings and that she knew which way was up, Mother adjusted her three inertial measurement units for precession error. Mother worked with her Reference Stable Member Matrix.

"IMU aligned, Will. REFSMAT nailed down."

Parker swam from the aft payload specialist station toward the forward cockpit. He stopped to float at the center knee-high console between Enright and Karpov.

As the AC reached the back of Enright's left seat, the co pilot was already rolling Endeavor onto her back to protect the radiators latched to the open bay doors from sunrise seven minutes away.

The AC scanned the third green television near Karpov. A video ground track displayed the bug-shaped shuttle over the southern Indian Ocean 700 nautical miles southeast of the great island of Madagascar. Radio contact was still 18 minutes away. On the television, their next network station was a circle one inch across with Okinawa at its center. At the bottom of the screen, numerics read REV 6 and MET:00:08:34:21.

"Next daylight landing window, Jack?" Shuttle can land only at fields equipped with microwave landing systems for instrument approaches. Such facilities with critically needed support vehicles are located only at Cape Canaveral, Edwards in California, White Sands in New Mexico, Hawaii, Okinawa, and the military field in Rota, Spain.

Enright tapped his small computer keyboard.

Immediately, the television displayed a new ground track two revolutions in the future.

"Okinawa at Kadena field, Skipper, during Rev Eight. Deorbit burn at 09 hours 55 minutes during Rev Seven. That's an hour and 20 minutes from now. Wheels on at 10

362

hours 46 minutes. That's 9:46 a.m. local time. Plenty of daylight. Gonna be tight on the time-line. But no sweat."

Parker furrowed his sweating, pale brow. They had thundered into a purple winter sky a very long eight and a half hours ago. They had gotten it up. They had gotten it done. But not without cost. One Russian had been vaporized and Endeavor had been hurt badly, perhaps fatally.

"Let's go home, Number One."

"I'll work up the digitals, Will."

"Good. We'll run a look-see at the APU's and the right OMS. Guess it's about time to try a single-OMS re-entry anyway."

"Seems so, Skip."

"Yeh . . . While you're pullin' the checklists, I'll fetch Alexi's seat. You about ready to hang on the feedbag, Jack?"

"Starved, Will . . . You be stayin' for dinner, Major?"

The depressed Russian smiled weakly.

"Three for dinner, Skipper. Window seats, if you can do it."

"Done."

Parker descended headfirst through the floor hole behind Enright's back.

It pained Parker to think of food so soon after a brother had smothered. But both he and Enright knew the imperative of taking in liquids prior to the physiological stresses of re-entry. Beginning with the tenth shuttle flight, Mission 41-B in February 1984, "fluid loading" was part of the Shuttle re-entry routine during which orbiting crews forced themselves to consume fluids 90 minutes before coming home. The "fluid loading" now known as "Hypersomatic Fluid Countermeasures" was a project of the medics who hoped to increase human adaption to spaceflight. So the command pilot went below decks to satisfy the flight surgeons; but he felt the awkwardness of planning a weightless wake topside.

As the AC somersaulted into the mid-deck below, Shuttle stopped her slow roll. With his feet close to the floor, the AC stood with his head pointing seaward as Shuttle flew upside down 20 degrees south of the Equator at 08 hours 40 minutes aloft.

The mid-deck galley can cook up to seven meals simultaneously. But that requires 90 minutes. So from the pantry Parker pulled three containers of peaches and three plastic pouches of freeze-dried tea. The fruit was packed in small tins irradiated for sterilization and in thick syrup to keep the sliced peaches from floating away when the tin was opened. The AC floated to the galley by the round window in the side egress hatch. He inserted the hot-water nozzle into each plastic container. The hot water revived the dehydrated tea. From a large forward locker, he also retrieved a portable flightseat and a set of anti-gravity, balloon trousers. With his hands full, Parker rose through the ceiling hole and emerged behind Enright.

"Three Beef Wellingtons with a hearty but vaguely tempestuous Burgundy." Although still in pain at his right leg from his ankle to his groin, the Colonel felt invigorated by the prospect of soon getting down to doing a pilot's business. He struggled to ease the cabin tension.

Enright was busy working with Mother's four primary computers in her Maintenance Loop mode of operation.

"Hi, Skipper. Right OMS looks stable. Helium and propellant pressures and quantities in the green. We may yellow-line on quantities with a single-OMS deorbit maneuver. Right RCS could get tight, too. And Auxiliary Power Units One and Two seem okay. Three is shot."

"Okay, Jack. Have some chow."

Parker handed a tin of peaches and the hot squeeze jug of tea to Alexi Karpov. Beyond Karpov's right seat, the world remained dark over the Indian Ocean.

"Thank you, Colonel. In my country, we drink it out of a glass with a sugar cube held between our teeth."

364

"This must be your first drive-in?" The AC smiled.

As Parker hovered at the center console, he handed Enright two fruit tins and two teas.

"Hold mine, Jack, while I set up Alexi's seat."

"Sure. But hurry before I gobble yours, too."

The command pilot rolled over and flew down to the floor behind Karpov. He stopped beneath the starboard overhead window in the rear. After unfolding the collapsible jumpseat, he inserted its four short legs into a floor track. The portable flightseat sits $14\frac{1}{4}$ inches from the floor and its backrest can be moved back ten degrees from vertical for comfort. The flightdeck has room for two rear seats behind the forward seats. Six more can be installed below in the mid-deck for space rescue operations or for flights when the European Spacelab is carried in the payload bay as was first done in Columbia on Shuttle Nine in December 1983. With the new seat erected aft, Parker sat down behind Karpov and buckled in.

"Ready, Jack."

Enright looked over his right shoulder as he aimed the sealed fruit tin at his captain. The AC caught the sailing tin with a hand between his knees.

"Low and inside, Number One."

Parker caught the tea container with his outstretched left hand.

"Outside. I'll take my base."

As Endeavor flew at five miles per second into the forty-first minute of her eighth hour aloft, the white sun exploded into Enright's portside window which faced east as Shuttle cruised upside down over the ocean 1,600 miles south of the southern tip of India.

Enright stopped sucking the plastic tube in the tea. He inserted the tinted, transparent sunshades on the frames of his forward window and two side windows. His fruit and tea floated motionlessly over the center console while he worked. Karpov pulled three sunshades from beneath his right seat and snapped them on his center and two starboard window frames.

"We have—had—these in Soyuz, too."

The two Americans said nothing.

Below, overhead as seen from the headsdown ship, the sea remained night as the white sun rose swiftly taking the stars with it.

Parker floated out of his rear seat toward the forward cockpit four feet away. The seated pilots handed him their empty containers. Stuffing the trash into a small bag, the AC went down the floor hatch to the mid-deck.

Below decks, the AC floated to the forward lockers where he put the garbage and then to the sleep berths along the starboard wall. His bunk looked inviting to his weary body and to his brain fogged by horse medication which no longer worked.

Parker leaned into the top bunk and his mesh-covered legs floated well off the floor behind him. He tightened the bunk straps around his reposing orange ascent suit. He did likewise to Enright's pressure suit worn during launch. From there, he floated to the nearby airlock against the mid-deck's aft Bulkhead No. 576. With a slow flip, Parker turned upside down such that his stocking feet were close to the ceiling, 6 feet 8 inches high. With his face near the floor, he pushed the inside hatch of the airlock closed. With one hand on a hand rail, his other hand cranked the hatch seal tightly closed. The hatch inside the airlock leading into the payload bay was already locked.

Still upside down, the command pilot surveyed each corner of the mid-deck: Storage lockers closed, galley switches off, ascent suits and helmets secured, biffy door and privacy curtains closed.

As the AC popped through the access hole, he flipped off the mid-deck lights on a ceiling panel. His mother raised him right.

Topside, flying headsdown at 08 hours 47 minutes 39 seconds, Endeavor approached her first landfall in 11,000 miles over Sumatra, the 150-mile wide principal island of Indonesia. Early-morning daylight warmed the island which Shuttle crossed in half a minute.

"Ascending node, Rev Seven, Skipper. Home stretch. Secure below?"

"All set, Jack."

Endeavor in burning daylight sped over the South China Sea with Malasia out the inverted right window to the north and Borneo to the south.

"Let's get the doors, Number One."

" 'Kay."

Parker floated to the aft station. Up front, Enright powered up the crackling UHF radios for a call to the network on Okinawa in five minutes. The island itself would not come under Shuttle for another eight minutes. After this pass, the next time they would see the island they would be parked there at the end of Runway 23, and its 12,000 feet of concrete.

Parker floated to the aft Mission Specialist consoles on the starboard side wall behind Karpov. He plugged his headset into the wall jack.

"Comm check."

"Gotcha, Will. Flash evaporators on-line."

Enright in the forward left seat worked the controls on Panel Left-1 near his left elbow. He powered up the evaporators to cool the ship's two freon loops during the descent down to 140,000 feet on the re-entry. He also activated the warm-up plumbing and electronics for the two ammonia boilers which would cool the ship below 120,000 feet. The water spray boilers for cooling the two surviving Auxiliary Power Units in the damaged tail would be activated for re-entry shortly before the de-orbit OMS firing an hour away.

Parker floated upright behind Karpov at aft panel Right-13.

"Radiator latch control, System A to release. Radiator

367

control to stow." The AC scanned television screen Number Four at chest level. "Six radiator panels in motion, Jack."

"I can see it." Enright watched his center television as green video graphics depicted the radiators on each bay side rising from the open doors.

"Got 'em by eyeball." The AC looked over his right shoulder to the aft wall windows. In the sunlit bay, he could see the radiators climbing over the bay walls. The units slowly rotated upward over the rim and then downward toward the inside walls of the payload bay. He could not see the bay doors below the sides of the bay.

"Colorado, Endeavor by Kadena." Enright called the ground as Endeavor crossed Manila. Her next landfall was 13,000 miles away over South America.

Flying nose forward pointing northeast, Enright and Karpov had an upside-down Philippine Sea out the front windows. Beneath the inverted open bay, Parker could see a dazzling South China Sea through the overhead window above his face.

"Endeavor: Colorado with you by Kadena at 08 plus 54 . . . What the hell is your situation up there? We've been holding our breath worldwide for 25 minutes down here!"

"Enright here . . . We're bent, but right and tight. AC been packin' it up in the bay. We're burning-in this rev. Alert Okinawa for company. We aligned the IMU's 20 minutes ago. We'll do a single engine de-orbit burn this rev. Port OMS and RCS stack are dead. TIG at 09 hours 55 minutes 12 seconds at about 38 degrees south by 007 degrees west. Wheels on the numbers at 10 plus 47 . . . Radiators now stowed. Evaps on-line and in the green. We don't foresee much problem running the re-entry on the forward RCS and right-only RCS aft. Have the backroom run a sim on partial, aft-RCS stabilization. Figure we can go to control surface, aerodynamic steering a bit early on the descent." The thin airman paused and he sighed so deeply that his breath activated the ship's intercom. "And, Flight, Soyuz

368

has been destroyed by the same laser burst which crippled us up here . . . Negative survivors. Please advise Kalinin Control Center. It has been such a very long day, Colorado."

"Understand, Jack. Get back to you on elevon evaluation. Try to do a complete data dump by California in 26. We'll only have 3 minutes with you after California via Botswana at 10 plus 01. That means your brief California pass will be it for a pre-burn status call. At least Botswana and Indian Ocean Ship at 10 plus 13 will both be solid acquisitions before the comm blackout inbound. We would predict entry interface at 10 plus 17. Should be able to pass along reliable state vectors and approach trajectory data."

"Countin' on it, Flight."

"Roger that, Will. One more minute here . . . We copy the loss of Soyuz . . . And our deepest condolences to Major Karpov. Uri was one good man, a credit to we who fly . . . That comes from all America, Major."

Shuttle flew with Okinawa 300 nautical miles to the northwest. Although the island was only one-third of the distance to the horizon, Enright and Karpov could not find it in morning fog.

"Endeavor: Kadena WX will be scattered clouds at 30,000 with wind out of 220 at 08 knots. Visibility 12 for the approach. Runway 23 is the active—12,000 feet with displaced threshold. At final approach, sun will be about 36 degrees high at bearing 153 degrees True."

"Okay, Flight . . . Ready on the doors, Jack. Radiators stowed and latched."

"All yours, Skip."

At the starboard wall instrument consoles, Parker energized Bay Mechanical Power, System One.

"Doors lever-locked closed, Jack . . . In motion left and right."

"See it, Skip."

Slowly, silently, the motors lifted the great doors upward

369

from the wings. With the inverted bay facing the dawn sea 900 miles east of Okinawa, Parker watched the two doors seal out the brilliant ocean beneath the sixty-foot-long chasm. Like huge white clamshells, the bay slowly closed over Parker's right shoulder.

"Two feet to go, Jack."

"Endeavor: Coming up on LOS by Kadena. With you by GDX at 09 plus 20 . . ."

At one minute before Shuttle's ninth hour aloft, Okinawa fell over the edge of radio range as the ship overflew the Bonin Islands. To Endeavor's south, 150 miles away, a tiny green dot was visible in early-morning daylight out Enright's inverted side window: Iwo Jima.

The blue sea disappeared behind the overhead seam of the bay roof. With the bay floodlights burning brightly, it was still daylight inside the closed payload bay.

"All green latches, Will."

"Okay, Jack. Takin' my look-see."

Parker set up a small, telescopic theodolite much like a surveyor's instrument. With it, the AC focused the optics through the rear window. Carefully, he conducted a slow, meticulous inspection of the bay ceiling seam. The instrument at the AC's squinting eye scanned the length of the closed roof seam one inch at a time.

"Not a ripple, Number One. Bay seal is secured . . . Lights off."

Parker extinguished the six lights inside the bay. Outside the two rear windows, the payload bay was black and ready for the fiery plunge homeward.

"Fifty minutes, Skipper."

The mission event timer at Enright's eye level ticked down the time remaining to the de-orbit ignition of the one surviving OMS engine in the broken tail section.

In the rear of the flightdeck, Parker floated from panel to panel where he powered down systems and rear lighting. When he had finished, he floated toward Karpov.

"Time to play musical chairs, Major."

The Soviet pilot released his lap belt and floated over the center console. Like tandem swimmers, Parker and the Russian floated to the rear jumpseat.

"For the re-entry G-load, Alexi." The AC handed Karpov his rubber, inflatable pants which had been stowed under the jumpseat. The Russian in his American flightsuit hung upside down in the rear of the flightdeck. Parker held Karpov's shoulders while the Major pulled on his anti-gravity pants. "Prevents grayout during the re-entry G spike which we take headsup. The inflated pants stop blood pooling in the lower body."

Wearing his balloon pants like fisherman's waders, the Russian buckled into the jumpseat. Floating beside Karpov, Parker touched the large overhead window above the Major's head.

"Escape hatch, Alexi. If you pull here, the whole window frame opens inward like a trapdoor. If we get bent or wet, crack the window seals and punch out. We'll be right behind you, I promise."

The sole surviving Russian nodded.

"Enjoy the ride, my friend." Will Parker's gaunt and deeply lined face smiled. So did the Major.

As the AC floated forward, Enright had already moved into his right seat. His anti-gravity pants covered his mesh drawers. Parker pulled his inflatable waders from under his seat. He pulled the pants over his own sweat-soaked woolies. He winced as the tight trousers squeezed over his grotesquely swollen right leg. Then he eased his long body over the center console and into the left front seat — the Captain's Seat. The AC plugged in his communications cable for the soft headset. An air tube went from behind his seat to his rubber pants. Karpov behind Enright plugged his communications line into a wall jack as he plugged his pants into the Portable Oxygen System outlet behind Enright's seat.

Above the sunshaded windows, the forward event timer

371

ticked down past minus 44 minutes to de-orbit ignition.

Will Parker pushed a floating, three-inch-thick procedures manual down into his lap. For a moment, the Aircraft
Commander took the measure of the forward instrument
arrays and the brilliant, inverted ocean outside against the
flatly black, starless sky.

"I have the bridge, Number One."

"Aye, aye, Cap'n."

Enright smiled behind his sticky, hot face mask.

"Tell me again, Cleanne. Please?"

The beautiful young woman with the eyes of a frightened
child looked intently at the small woman by her side. The
sun of a clear Texas evening shone brightly through the
window.

From the setting sun, soft daylight glowed crimson upon
the rumpled auburn hair of the younger woman. As they
sat on the bedside with their backs to the window, the short
blond hair of the older woman glowed warmly. On the
nightstand, a round clock showed twelve minutes after six
o'clock.

The square bedroom was bright with a child's stuffed animals and with piles of colorful books about talking animals,
fairy godmothers, and trains. In a corner, a short green
Christmas tree stood within a pile of brightly wrapped
packages. All the little boxes bore "TO MY GIRL" in
thickly printed letters.

"Your daddy and Mister Enright are getting ready to
come home, Emily. They will start down real soon. And we
can watch them get out of their spaceship on television in
just an hour and a half."

The blond woman looked tired. The angular beauty of
her face and her softly dark eyes were heavy with the strain
of sounding cheerful.

"That's my daddy!"

372

The red-haired, child-woman pointed happily to a Houston newspaper on the floor. Smiling photographs of William McKinley Parker and a youthful Jacob Enright looking like an Eagle Scout were side by side under a banner headline: "SHUTTLE PURSUES INTELSAT-6." And under that in letters an inch high: "RUSSIANS READY TO ASSIST."

"What does it say, Cleanne? Tell me again."

The gentle physician with slumped shoulders tried not to choke upon her words.

"It says your daddy and Mister Enright will be home after dinner."

"Can we go watch the TV now? Sister Lisa said it's starting real soon. Oh, please?"

"Emily, I think we should wait until the airplane is really coming home. I mean until we can really see it. Okay?"

The younger woman became serious. Her great eyes studied her happy little tree and its pile of treasures.

"Will Daddy be here for Christmas in this many days?" The red-haired girl worked her hands together to hold up seven fingers. She licked her upper lip as she got her fingers up. "This many?"

The blond woman gently laid her arm upon the girl's thin shoulders.

"I'm sure of it." The physician sniffed once, softly.

"Daddy said Mister Enright would take care of him." The young woman raised her happy face to the exhausted physician who turned her wet eyes away.

"Mister Enright promised, didn't he, Emily?"

"Left air data probe lever-locked stow."

"Right air data probe, ADTA Two, circuit breaker, Main bus B, Overhead Panel-15, Row E, closed."

"Closed."

"Air data transducer assembly Four, Main C, Overhead Panel-16, Row E, closed."

373

"ADTA Number Four, closed."

"Overhead Panel-6: MDM at FF-2, on."

"Multiplexor-demultiplexor, Flight Forward Number Two, on."

"MDM, FF-4, Overhead Panel-6, on."

"Flight forward, Number Four, on."

"ADP Right, lever-locked, stow."

"Air data probe, Right, lever-locked stowed."

"And, ADP stow to inhibit."

"Right ADP inhibited," Enright confirmed as his left hand touched the center console between himself and Parker.

Karpov intently watched the two serious pilots cover page after page of pre-descent checklists. Depending upon which pilot was closest to the switches and circuit breakers being checked off, one airman challenged the item while the other read back and touched the switch. The two armed air data probes were stowed within the cabin walls. They would deploy into the slipstream outside after Endeavor was well within the atmosphere.

Endeavor flew upside down over the north Pacific 1,436 statute miles due west of San Diego. The mission clock ticked up through 09 hours 18 minutes and the event timer ticked down past 37 minutes to de-orbit ignition of the right orbital maneuvering system rocket.

Inside Mother's four primary General Purpose Computers, re-entry program OPS-3 was running. The fifth backup computer rode shotgun on the four main computers. Computer program Major Mode 301 supervised the de-orbit preparations.

"TACAN, Jack."

The crew flipped to the checklist page for warming up the three navigation beacon receivers which would listen for the Okinawa instrument landing signals. The TACAN receivers would give the pilots range-to-go vectors when Endeavor acquired Kadena Air Base's beacon 500 miles from Runway

23 about 19 minutes after hitting the atmosphere.

"Breaker AC-1, Panel Left-4, Row P," Enright read aloud.

The AC touched the round black circuit breaker at his left elbow.

"Closed, Jack."

"MDM, Flight Forward One, Overhead Panel-6, on."

"On."

"Channel select flight control system, set."

The AC turned four thumb-wheels to bring a four-digit code into tiny windows.

"Flight control system channel set, set, set, and set."

"TACAN Number One, mode select, Overhead Panel-7, to GPC."

"Number One to General Purpose Computer."

"Antenna select, Overhead Panel-7, auto."

"Automatic."

"Overhead Panel-7, tone ident off."

"Identifier off . . . TACAN Number One ready."

The crew repeated the TACAN receiver protocol for receivers Number Two and Three.

"Endeavor, Endeavor: Configure AOS by Goldstone at 09 Hours 20 Minutes."

"With you, Flight."

"Copy, Will. We remind you of sunset in 10 minutes. We want you to shoot a final P-52 alignment after sundown. And you can dump the OI data now. We'll update your state vectors in 2 minutes. For data dump, use high bit rate, please."

"Rogo, California. Operational Instrumentation comin' atcha. We'll get the balls aligned at about 9½."

As Parker spoke, he could see the inverted Pacific outside as Shuttle cruised a thousand miles west of Baja California. The AC could not see land on the hazy western horizon. The ship flew heads-down, tailfirst, ready for the OMS burn. Enright double checked his side of the cockpit to confirm that Shuttle's three main engines remained slightly retracted within the square tail section for protection from re-entry's searing fury.

"Okay, Jack. MLS Number One: Breaker Main A, Panel Overhead-14, Row E, closed."

"Closed."

"MLS One to off, Overhead-8."

"Off."

"Channel select, Overhead-8."

"Set, set, set, and set."

The three receivers for the Microwave Landing System were checked. These instrument landing beacons guide the 100-ton glider's final approach when the ground's beacons are picked up by Mother 12 miles from the runway at an altitude of 18,000 feet. The crew checked out MLS receivers Two and Three.

"Next, radar altimeter, Number One: Breaker, Main A, Overhead-14, Row E, closed."

"Closed, Skipper."

"MDM, Flight Forward One, on, Overhead-6."

"On."

"Radar altimeter One, off."

"Number One, off."

The routine was repeated for radar altimeter Number Two. These two ground-sensing beacons come on when Endeavor descends below 5,000 feet. These C-Band radio signals are vital to the last 100 feet of the final approach to landing.

"Endeavor: Your data dump is in. Your state vectors are now coming up. Colorado standing by through GDX."

"Rogo, Goldstone . . . Aerosurface amplifiers, Jack. Number One ASA."

The aerosurface electronics receive and generate computer commands to guide Shuttle's aerodynamic control surfaces: the elevon-ailerons on the back edges of each wing for roll control and pitch control, the tail's vertical rudder for side-to-side, yaw control and turn coordination, and the tail's speed brakes. ASA black boxes also work the body flap under the tail for center-of-gravity, trim control during descent. Four separate flight control system channels work the four aerosurface activation loops.

"FCS, Number One, channel select, lever-locked auto, Panel Center-3."

"Auto," Parker replied as he touched the center console under his right arm.

"MDM, Flight Forward One, Overhead-6, on."

"On."

"MDM, Flight Forward Two, Overhead-6, on."

"On."

"Flight Forward Three, Overhead-6, on."

"On."

"ASA, Loop One, on."

"Overhead-14, Main bus Alpha, ASA Number One is on."

Aerosurface loops Two, Three, and Four were readied for coming home.

"Coming up on the edge by California, Endeavor. With you after de-orbit burn by Botswana in 36 minutes. Keep your feet dry and keep your airspeed up, guys."

The starship's final Stateside pass ended in static as Shuttle left the range limits of the Goldstone, California, antenna. The mission clock showed 09 hours 25 minutes and the event timer began the last 30 minutes of counting down to de-orbit ignition command. Endeavor's ground track never touched the continental United States, home. She would not make a major landfall until Peru in 3,300 miles. The winged spacecraft arced down the North American western coastline, barely visible on the far purple horizon to the east of the inverted ship.

"Landing gear brakes, Jack. Main bus A, Overhead-14, on."

"Main Alpha, on, Will."

"Main bus Bravo, Overhead Panel-15, on."

"Main B, on."

"And, Main Charlie, Overhead-16, on."

"Main C, on."

"Your side, Jack, Panel Right-4, brake heater hydraulics A, on."

"Alpha, on."

"Brake heater hydraulics B, to on."

"Bravo, on." Enright touched the cluttered panel at his right elbow.

"And, heater C, on."

"Charlie hot, Skipper."

" 'Kay . . . Nose wheel steering: Circuit breaker, Overhead Panel-14, Row E, Main bus A."

"Bus Alpha, closed."

"And my side, Panel Left-2: Nose wheel steering, mode select to GPC."

"My side, Will, Right-4: Landing gear hydraulics isolated valve Number One to GPC; Number Two to GPC; and, Number Three also to General Purpose Computer."

"Check, check and check."

"Your side, Will, Panel Forward-6: Landing gear PBI to armed. And my side, Panel Forward-8, gear pushbutton indicator also armed."

"Armed, Jack. My side, Left-4, Row P: Circuit breaker, landing gear sensors One and Two, closed and closed."

At 09 hours 27 minutes, Mission Elapsed Time, Shuttle darted headsdown over the small speck of Isle de Revillagigedo, 730 nautical miles west of Mexico City. Only Alexi Karpov aft saw the little brown island through his window above his head. The sea 150 statute miles below was in deepening twilight although Endeavor had a broiling white sun low in the west out the front windows.

The AC turned up the forward flightdeck lights and he pulled off the tinted sunshades from his one front and two side windows. Enright did likewise.

"Horizontal Situation Indicator, Jack, my side and yours,

378

select entry mode."

"Entry logic loaded, Skip."

The 6-inch-square glass instrument in front of each pilot's chest would display side-to-side trajectory errors during descent.

"And my side, Jack: Entry roll mode select lever-locked yaw/jet rudder."

"Yaw/jet rudder, Will."

The clock above the center windows on the cabin ceiling showed 09 hours 30 minutes and the event timer above Parker's right knee ticked down past 25 minutes to de-orbit ignition.

"Won't see that again for a while, Will." Enright blinked through his moist mask toward his right.

"Guess not, Jacob."

Outside, to the southwest, the sun flattened against a dazzling orange horizon. The inverted ocean below was already black as Endeavor carried her three wards into Shuttle's seventh sunset in 9½ hours. A thin red band stretched above the brighter orange band for the full length of the slightly curved, upside-down horizon. With a rapid change from orange to bright purple, the red flat sun winked out leaving the starship in her last frigid night in orbit.

"I got her," the AC called as he pushed the illuminated CSS pushbutton on the glareshield overhanging the forward instrument panels. He energized Control Stick Steering to powerup the rotational hand controller between his thighs. The pilot in command wanted to feel his ship live in his hands. He twitched the control stick. Mother instantly chose the best combination of RCS thrusters in her nose and ruined tail to roll the starship rightside up for one final star sight in darkness. A cold, alabaster-white moon hung low in the northeast sky above the dark horizon as Endeavor executed her slow, wobbly wingover in the eternal silence.

Three minutes after sunset, Shuttle headed south across the Equator for her last transit of the Southern Hemisphere and her last summertime aloft. Directly below, the darkness swallowed the Galapagos Islands 600 nautical miles west of Ecuador.

"Ready on the Auxiliary Power Units—what's left of 'em."

"Ready APU Two and Three, Skipper."

"Okay, Jack. Let's do 'em both together. We're gettin' short here . . . Your side, Panel Right-2: Controller power lever-locked on."

"Two and Three, on and on."

"Fuel tank valves, lever-locked open."

"APU, Two and Three, open and open."

"Ready."

"Two and Three, barber-polled ready to start, Skip."

"Speed select . . . Let's go with high on Two and normal on Three."

"Two high; Number Three normal speed."

"Hit it, Jack."

"Number Two APU, Ignition! RPM and exhaust gas temp okay."

"Number Three, Jack?"

"Number Three APU, Ignition! . . . Nothing, Will. Going to override-start . . . And Three is running. RPM and EGT are Go."

"Super, Jack. Hydraulics circulation pump, Two and Three, on."

"On and on . . . Pressures green."

"Main hydraulic pump pressures, lever-locked normal."

"Two and Three, normal and normal, Will."

"APU auto shutdown, enable."

"Automatic shutdown, enable Two and Three."

"APU Number Two: Fuel pump valve coolant, Loops A and B, auto."

"Valves A and B, automatic . . . At least we can steer her."

The Auxiliary Power Units are essential to move Shuttle's wing surfaces for airplane-steering in the lower atmosphere.

"Star-trackers running, Jack. P-52 running."

Mother and her two sensors scanned the dark southern sky.

"Make it a good one, Skipper."

The AC moved the control stick between his legs to shift Endeavor's nose to the northwest. Peering into the COAS periscope tube, he found the bright star Altair in the constellation Aquila 15 degrees above the black horizon on a magnetic bearing of 280 degrees True.

"Star Number 51, mark!"

Enright entered Altair into the computer at 09 hours 36 minutes, MET, over Peru.

Since the COAS cannot swing across the sky on its own as can the automatic star-trackers in Shuttle's nose, Parker turned the ship heads up to the southwest. High in the sky, almost overhead at 60 degrees high, he found the bright star Fomalhaut in Piscis Austrinus at a compass bearing of 220 degrees True. High Fomalhaut with faint Al Na-ir in Grus constellation 20 degres lower and Peacock in the constellation Pavo 15 degrees closer to the southern horizon formed a three-star line from Shuttle to the South.

"Fomalhaut, mark!"

Enright tapped Star Number 56 into the computers.

"One more for good measure, Skipper."

Parker steered Shuttle's nose toward the northeast. He squinted into the COAS sighting-mirror as Capella in Auriga slowly crossed the COAS crosshairs 10 degrees above the horizon and 40 degrees east of north. Capella was faint below and left of the brilliant moon.

"Number 12, mark!"

"Got it, Will. Let Mother chew on that."

Mother reduced her own star sights from the two star-trackers and Parker's sights. While she worked, the AC removed the COAS tube from the ceiling brackets and stowed the little sextant away.

"IMU aligned all balls. Well, Jack. Mother knows where we are anyway."

Over nighttime Bolivia, Endeavor was commanded to roll over until she was flat on her back for the OMS burn only 15 minutes away. The ignition of the single OMS rocket from the ship's crippled tail feathers was all that stood between Endeavor and home.

17

"They are now in darkness over the mountains around Sucre, Bolivia. Revolution seven. Retro fire in 14 minutes."

The big man raised an eyebrow as he scanned the wall plot board beyond the glass greenhouse suspended above the floor. A tiny bug followed a curved line across the video projection of the Earth's middle latitudes 40 degrees above and below the Equator. Above the large screen, one clock displayed 00:41 GREENWICH, another, 19:41 EASTERN STANDARD, and the third digital clock read 00:09:41 MISSION ELAPSED TIME.

Four tired men in open, rumpled collars were at table with large, grim Admiral Michael Thomas Hauch.

An afternoon nap had revived the sailor who looked less worn than the men around him. By the vault door to the basement bunker, two young Marines stood rigidly like pillars of salt.

Admiral Hauch was elegant in his dress blues which carried seven inches of ribbons and gold wings upon his heart. He only broke out his blues for audiences with the Chiefs or with the Old Man himself.

The Admiral rose and walked to the glass wall of their chill cage. His spit-shined shoes glowed five feet above the concrete floor under the floor of clear glass. Standing erect by the glass wall, the Admiral gripped one huge fist in the other behind his back which faced the men behind him. As he gazed at the wall charts, he cut every inch the image of the flag ship commander upon his high quarterdeck.

"Well, Doctor. Your impressions now?"

"Admiral." The little man with the squirrel face fumbled with a stack of green computer paper as he addressed the Admiral's ample backside. The technocrat perspired under the ceiling lights.

"We've run a full re-entry simulation. Assuming an operational right OMS pod with its RCS capabilities, Endeavor can shoot a successful re-entry profile. They will experience lateral trim imbalance flying with only half their aft RCS capacity, but they should still be within the attitude deadband limits of the flight control loops. Endeavor will have to fire the one remaining, OMS engine for a full five minutes to do the work of two normal engines. Our real concern is the tile loss on the aft fuselage."

"Fatal?"

"Don't think so, Admiral. We may lose some structural integrity from soak-back heating, maybe even one of the two, surviving auxiliary power units. But I vote for survival."

The standing Admiral sighed audibly.

"We build them pretty tight, Doctor."

"Yes. And you have two of your best pilots up there."

"My best. I know."

"Any word from Moscow, Admiral?"

"Yes, Colonel." The big man did not turn to face the table. "It's Sleep Tight."

"But they have their own man in there."

"Yes they do, Major. But LACE was and is to be a totally . . . antiseptic operation. With extreme prejudice if necessary."

"If I may: I cannot believe that the Kremlin would advocate such a senseless waste."

384

"I agree, Commander." The old fatigue crept into the Admiral's deep voice. "They have their 'upstairs' and we have ours. I imagine the Kremlin knows as little about this operation as our own government. Even the President has not been briefed on all these little details."

"Admiral, I cannot support assassination."

The tall sailor turned to glare coldly and wearily at the small assembly.

"None of you were invited here to vote! The votes are all in. You are here to help your country out of her worst embarrassment since the Bay of Pigs in '61 . . . Doctor, will your Programmed Test Input Seven do the job?"

"Absolutely. With the left aft RCS pod disabled, the shuttle has lost one-third of her total Reaction Control System impulse for precision attitude control. The key here is attitude rates: She will be slow in attitude changes. The PDPU maneuver of PTI-7, that's push-down pull-up, will crack her spine . . . just like that."

The Admiral winced as the little man snapped his fingers.

"Major? Will the crew run the PTI if they have doubts about it with partial RCS capacity?" The Admiral spoke slowly.

"That is their job . . . Of course they will run it, Admiral."

"Then I shall relay the go ahead to the network feed."

"Mike, you can't!"

"That is *my* job."

The large man in his dress blues turned away. He looked up at the small video insect which crawled across eastern Brazil toward open sea and its local midnight darkness. Then the old dragon of the Tail Hook Club closed his tired eyes tightly.

"Nine minutes, Skipper."

385

The mission clock ticked up past 09 hours 46 minutes. Endeavor flew upside-down and tailfirst through the night. Below, it was almost midnight. The starship left Porto Alegre, Brazil, and the coastline behind as she made for open water and Okinawa, now 15,400 statute miles away. There would be no more major landfalls until wheels-on, except for a brief glide over Southeast Asia.

"Feet wet." Enright studied the television on his right side of the forward cockpit.

When Endeavor crossed the coast, she entered a 5,130-statute-mile stretch of the South Atlantic Anomaly. Now it did not matter. An ionic orange glow warmed Shuttle's inverted 26-foot-long tail which led the way southeast making 300 miles per minute. That made no difference to the crew, either.

"Entry attitude hold, set." The Aircraft Commander read his checklist. "Ten degrees up bubble on the bow . . . Yaw right 007 degrees. Set."

Shuttle's nose was lower than her tail section from the local horizontal as she flew backward. But since the crew was oriented headsdown, the nose appeared to them higher than the tail. The computers directed the nose to hold slightly off center. This side drift would help the single OMS engine deliver its 6,000 pounds of thrust in a thrust vector through the ship's center of gravity. The single right orbital maneuvering system rocket can also swing from side to side through an eight-degree arc to direct the line of fire.

"Looks fat on propellant, Will. Good news."

Enright had run a check of the OMS propellant tanks in the single right pod in the tail. The OMS pod was loaded with propellant for 1,250 seconds of firing. Only 190 seconds worth of fuel and oxidizer were burned during the two firings of the OMS pod to insert Endeavor into orbit 9½ hours earlier. Very little had been consumed during the first-orbit rendezvous with LACE. Ordinarily, with both OMS engines firing to slow Shuttle for leaving orbit, the

386

de-orbit burn lasts 150 seconds. With only one OMS pod to fire the 77-inch-high, 45-inch-wide Aerojet General rocket engine, the burn would take a full five minutes to jar Shuttle from her circular orbit 149 statute miles high.

"OMS prep, your side, Jack."

Enright looked up through his bandages at the panels of switches and pushbuttons on the ceiling. The AC challenged and Enright readback.

"Overhead Panel-8: Helium pressure vapor insolation valve, Loop A, to General Purpose Computer."

"Alpha to GPC."

"Loop B to GPC."

"Bravo to GPC."

"Propellant tank isolation valve, Loop A, talk-back open."

"Alpha, open."

"Loop B, talk-back open."

"Bravo, open."

"Right OMS crossfeed, closed, Loop A."

"Alpha, closed."

"Right crossfeed, Loop B, closed."

"Bravo, closed, Will."

"Panel Overhead-16, engine valve, on."

"On."

"Engine lever-locked arm." Parker checked the toggle switch on the center console by his right elbow.

The clocks reached 09 hours 50 minutes, MET, and the event timer ticked down through minus five minutes to OMS ignition.

Endeavor flew on her back, tailfirst, over the black water below and with the faint star Acamar in the southern constellation Eridanus above. In the west, 1,400 nautical miles away, Montevideo, Uruguay, slept away a summer night. Below, it was midnight, six days before Christmas.

"State vectors loaded," the AC confirmed. "Major Mode 302 running and Mother likes it."

On the center of three television screens, the plots were

387

up for the de-orbit maneuver. At the base of the green screen, numerics counted down in tandem with the event timer near Parker's painful right knee.

"Jack: ADI to inertial mine and yours, ADI error and rates to medium. And DAP to auto." The crew set their round attitude director indicators for the final plunge home.

"Four minutes, Alexi," the AC called over his right shoulder.

The Soviet survivor nodded to the back of Enright's bandaged and blistered head. Then he tightened his lap and shoulder belts.

"Let's do it, Jacob."

"Think I'm old enough, Will?"

Dozens of greasy hands reached into bowls of popcorn on the floor. The large hands belonged to adults but their voices and their eyes were those of children.

"Told you it was already on TV."

"You were right, Emily. Let's just remember that the television people don't know everything."

"Oh, I know that, Cleanne. I wish everyone would shush so we could hear about my daddy."

The two women leaned toward the television in the airy, institutional family room. Outside, it was a dark winter evening.

"Dan, the day has certainly taken on a tone far different from this morning."

"Yes indeed, Walter. There was that magnificent launch of the Shuttle Endeavor from Florida this morning. Even though we have seen Shuttle ride that pillar of fire other times, it is still awesome and the crowds still line Coco Beach to watch her go. Then that first-orbit rendezvous with the lost Intelsat-6 satellite and with the Russians sent up for this first truly international space repair operation . . ."

388

"And then, Dan, it became unglued this afternoon. Somehow, the whole thing just unraveled. And we know very little tonight. First we had Astronaut Parker going outside instead of Jacob Enright who was injured, mysteriously, inside Shuttle. Barely two hours ago, we were told that Parker's spacewalk had failed to secure Intelsat-6 to Shuttle. And then an hour ago: that terse announcement from NASA in Houston and from Moscow that Intelsat-6 had been destroyed, that a Russian cosmonaut was dead, and that a Soviet survivor was picked up by Shuttle."

"Unraveled is the word tonight, Walter. From the day's dramatic turn of events, the sparse air-ground communications which NASA has relased to us, and then this sudden announcement less than thirty minutes ago that Shuttle is coming home at this very moment—all these events suggest that someone will have some explaining to do in the days to come."

"Indeed, Dan. And Endeavor is coming down damaged, perhaps fatally . . . Eric?"

"Yes, Walter. Dan." The white-haired retired journalist with the elegant Mount Rushmore face spoke with his wonderful voice. His upper lip never moved as his words flowed like warm honey.

"I think that the worst part of this strange day in space is the brevity of this mission not yet ten hours old. The suddenness of this flight and this now, life-threatening crisis announced with so little real information coming out of Houston has somehow cheated us, I think.

"The nation simply has not had time to get to know our brave men up there: Parker and Enright. Who even remembers that Colonel Parker flew the two-man Gemini spacecraft and then Apollo so long ago, back when we still called their tiny craft 'capsules.'

"Before yesterday, no one really knew about this sudden rush to Intelsat at all. And I cannot help but wonder if anyone is even following this flight at home with us now?

"It's funny, you know, how an old reporter's memory works, Walter. Dan was too young, but you and I covered the state funeral for Franklin Roosevelt a lifetime ago. And all three of us covered the national pageant at John Kennedy's death.

"I just cannot stop thinking about the demonstration which would follow the tragic loss of those three men up there in Endeavor: Parker, Enright, and Karpov. At least the Apollo One astronauts who burned on the launch pad in 1967, Mercury astronaut Gus Grissom, and Roger Chaffee and Ed White, America's first spacewalker, all received a hero's funeral. The country had the sense of really knowing those three men. But no one knows Parker and Enright.

"Remember when the seven bodies were plucked out of the sea after the Challenger explosion? They could have gotten the national funerals on television. All seven of them, and especially the schoolteacher from New Hampshire. But they really did not. Almost as if NASA wanted everything to go quietly away — quietly into the ground and into fading memory.

"And, strangely, it is not the sadness which this old warhorse remembers, not the feeling of loss, not the mournful tattoo of muffled drums. I remember, instead, the saddest and the most austere sound of all: horses' feet falling crisply upon the street. That cold, stark sound. Even now when a Manhattan or Boston mounted policeman rides by, I hear again that terrible sound, that sadly grand, manful sound which brings the chill to the back of the neck. Like Shuttle herself thundering into the sky, the sound of six great grays plodding slowly before a gun carriage is a sound which has flesh and which becomes a part of the flesh and the bone of all who hear it."

The great stoney face frowned.

"Yes, Eric. Let us hope: Not again. The crippled ship Endeavor is out of radio contact now. She will remain so for about six more minutes. Out there, in the darkness, Parker

Enright, and Karpov, the Russian, will be firing their only maneuvering system rocket in one minute. As we have noted, they cannot fire Shuttle's three main engines, since the fuel for them left when the external fuel tank dropped off after the launch this morning. On our monitors here in New York, we can see Mission Control in Houston. We understand that the new United States Space Command in Colorado is also helping to bring Endeavor safely home to Okinawa, one of her secondary landing sites. As we look in on Mission Control, everyone looks rather quiet."

Tristan Da Cunha, a tiny group of three South Atlantic islands, were dots on the large video plot board. Above their image, a little bug crept along its curved track line. At the base of the screen, digital numerics read TIG -30 SECONDS.

The big man in dress blues sat alone in his glass house. Sitting in his high-backed chair with his back to the erect Marine sentries, the Admiral slumped with his head bowed. As the clocks reached twenty seconds to single-engine ignition, the old sailor looked down at his thick hands folded in his lap.

"Fifteen seconds, firing command is in." Parker pressed the EXEC key on the computer keyboard on the center console.

The AC's voice was calm. After all, he had returned to Earth from Out There three times before this moment.

"Proceed light!"

Enright's voice was brimming with excitement. As the launch 9 hours and 55 minutes earlier was his first ride of the sacred fire, so this was his first homecoming from the great silence.

Mother's green faces showed the first re-entry trajectory

391

plot as her warm black boxes hummed confidently with computer program Major Mode 302.

"PAP at 360! Ten, nine . . ." Enright called.

The television in front of Enright's swollen face confirmed that the Pneumatic Activation Pressure in the gaseous nitrogen, firing mechanism in the OMS engine's propellant valves was at ignition pressure.

As Endeavor flew headsdown, tailfirst, and 10,520 statute miles southwest of her Okinawa target, the two fliers read aloud and together the seconds winking on the event timer.

"Four . . . Three . . . Two . . . One . . . Ignition!"

"Fire in the hole! Looks good." The copilot's voice was ecstatic.

As the 6,000 pounds of thrust from the single right OMS rocket fired against the momentum of the 200,000-pound starship, the deceleration was only a gentle nudge of the flight seats against the backs of the three airmen.

"Go, babe!" Enright shouted. "One minute down, four to go. NTO flow rate right on." The nitrogen tetroxide oxidizer utilization was nominal on Mother's television.

"Much gentler than I expected, Skip."

"Should have felt an SPS burn in Apollo. A real eyeballs-in maneuver." Will Parker once rode Apollo's Service Propulsion System engine out of lunar orbit. In all the world, only 24 men could say that. Three more moon men in their crippled Apollo 13 mothership had no SPS engine after a near fatal explosion. They rode their Lunar Module engine home, instead, in 1971.

"Sorry, Will. I wasn't old enough then."

The AC chuckled.

"Got a little out-of-plane building. Anything, Jack?"

The single engine on the far right corner of Shuttle's upside-down tail labored to compensate for the off-center forces of its three tons of thrust. The flight director needles on Parker's instruments displayed a slight side-to-side error in trajectory.

392

"Negative, Skipper. Still fat inside the cross-range envelope. Hang tight. PC at 125. Oh, sweet, sweet bird!"

The OMS engine combustion chamber pressure was normal. Shuttle's cross-range landing capability allows her to land at a site nearly 1,000 miles on either side of her ground track. Any reasonable, cross-range error will be adjusted as she steers through the upper atmosphere at a velocity of twenty times the speed of sound.

"Three minutes; one to go, Will. OMS mixture ratio 1 point 65. Right on!"

The single OMS rocket continued its 298-second firing. The engine burned 14 pounds of nitrogen tetroxide oxidizer and 9 pounds of monomethylhyrazine for each one-foot-per-second change in Endeavor's speed. Gaseous, high-pressure helium forced the caustic propellants into the engine. Inside the engine's combustion chamber, the propellants burned at 2,300 degrees Fahrenheit.

"Seventy seconds to go, Will . . . 68, 67, 66. Positive nose RCS, now!"

Enright noted that with 66 seconds left in the OMS deorbit burn, an early OMS shutdown would not be fatal. After this moment, the additional rocket power needed to leave orbit could be provided by turning Shuttle around and firing the three, forward-firing, nose thrusters for 150 seconds. This is the maximum allowable continuous thrusting time for the reaction control system jets in the ship's nose. A 2½-minute burn of the three RCS engines firing together has the same impulse as one OMS engine firing for 66 seconds.

"Twenty seconds to go."

The pilots watched Mother's green faces tick off the final seconds to automatic engine shutdown. They read the digital numerics from the screens together. Parker had his finger poised to manually give the stop command if Mother failed to pull the OMS plug herself.

"Five . . . Four . . . Three . . . Two . . . One . . . Auto shutdown."

"Thank you, Mother," Enright said with reverence as he patted the glareshield above the instrument panels.

The instant the OMS engine stopped automatically, all three fliers floated out of their seats as far as their lap belts. They were still in orbit, still weightless. All the OMS engine did was lower their 130-nautical-mile-high orbit to a low point some 12,000 miles on the other side of the planet. Were there no atmosphere, Endeavor would remain in this new, very lopsided orbit for centuries. What would bring her home was the air which they would now intersect in another twenty-two minutes at an altitude of 76 statute miles.

"Looky there, Jack. Delta-V of minus 269. Right smack on the nose! What a lady!"

Mother's face told the crew that the five-minute OMS burn had slowed Shuttle's forward velocity by 269 feet per second. Slowing Endeavor by this 183.4 statute miles per hour would cause her to strike the solid wall of air in another 6400 statute miles of flight.

"And we're speeding up. Amazing, Will. So Kepler was right after all."

At the moment the hot OMS engine stopped, Endeavor's reduced speed began to increase. The rearward firing of the rocket, by inserting Shuttle into a lower orbit, dictated that the ship's velocity must accelerate. Written three hundred years ago, Kepler's laws of orbital mechanics argued that bodies in lower orbits must travel faster than bodies in higher orbits.

"Endeavor: Configure AOS by Botswana. Doppler ranging confirms your de-orbit burn. Digitals look very close to nominal."

Still headsdown, Shuttle flew over open sea 120 miles southwest of Cape Town, South Africa.

"With you, Flight. Good burn."

"Copy, AC. Great news!"

"Okay, Colorado: Burn on time. TIG 09 hours 55 minutes 12 seconds. Burn time 298 seconds. Delta-V 268 point

394

3 plus point-2 left. We have nulled the residuals. Stable trim. And we aligned the balls a while back. Jack is now purging the OMS plumbing."

From his right seat, Enright directed gaseous nitrogen through the outer nozzle cone of the OMS engine to clean out the fuel which had been circulated through it to cool the engine bell during the rocket firing.

"And Flight, computer Major Mode 303 now running for descent. We'll do the thermal conditioning in a minute for the aero surfaces."

"Copy, Will. With you another 3 minutes."

"Understand."

Enright was directing warm hydraulic fluid into the movable control surfaces of the wings and tail. He warmed the complex plumbing to ready it for the re-entry heat load.

"Conditioning in progress, Flight. Vent doors closed."

"Copy, Will."

Mother had sealed the ten vent doors in the aft fuselage and payload bay to protect the closed bay from re-entry. Four vent doors in the cabin section, one on each wing and one in each of the two OMS pods also closed.

"Forward RCS pod not disabled. We'll dump forward propellants further inbound."

"Understand."

Ordinarily, this would be the time when the 16 thrusters in the nose should be turned off for re-entry and their propellant reserves dumped overboard. But the crew elected to use these jets to help the remaining 14 jets in the one surviving OMS pod aft. The RCS jets were only needed until the ship glided below 339,000 feet 2 minutes 41 seconds after slamming into the atmosphere. From there, the wings' flying surfaces would begin to take over the burden of steering.

"Traj One is up, Flight."

"Copy, Will."

The first of a series of re-entry plots was now on Mother's

televisions. The object of the computers and the crew is to steer a graphic Shuttle-bug down the curved graphs. To fly ahead of or behind the power curve would be fatal.

Underneath Shuttle at 10 hours 03 minutes, Port Elizabeth in darkness passed for a final 45-second landfall as the ship rounded South Africa for her last time.

"Endeavor: Sunrise in 7 minutes at 10 plus 10."

"Okay, Flight."

The ship was over water again.

"And preliminary tracking and ranging put Entry Interface at 10 hours 17 minutes 04 seconds, MET. We'll refine that for you by IOS in 8 minutes."

"Roger, Colorado. Twelve minutes to The Wall."

"Your state vectors look real tight. You're Go for pitch program to entry Alpha angle."

" 'Kay."

Endeavor still flew upside down, tailfirst. On Parker's hand commands to the control stick between his thighs, the RCS thrusters fired to pitch Shuttle's tail up toward the nighttime sky for a half-circle cartwheel. The huge ship's nose passed beneath the tail as she pitched around until her nose pointed toward Okinawa. Rightside up, nose forward, Shuttle's nose was 40 degrees above horizontal for re-entry.

"LOS in 20 seconds, Will."

"Okay, Flight. We are finally flying right: Heads up and feet down. Alpha 40 degrees up bubble. All set here."

"Roger, Will. With you in 7 . . ."

"Okay, Jack. Panel Overhead-8, OMS safing: Helium pressure vapor isolation valve, closed. Tank isolation open and cross-feed closed."

"Done, Skipper."

"And, computer Major Mode 303 running with attitude Item 24 Roll, and Item 25 Pitch, and Item 26 Yaw." The AC tapped the EXEC computer key after tapping in each Item number into the computer keyboard. "Digital Autopilot set manual. And, my side, Panel Left-2: Cabin pressure relief, systems A and B to enable. Nose wheel steering to off; entry roll mode to off; speedbrake handle closed full forward. My side and yours, Jack: Air data probe set navigation. Speedbrake set auto. Guidance and Navigation, Panel F-2, Pitch to auto, Roll/Yaw to auto, and body flap to manual."

After a ten-second nighttime landfall over Madagascar island, Endeavor flew headsup with her nose riding 40 degrees above the horizon. As the mission clocks passed 10 hours 10 minutes out and homeward bound, the orange sun exploded over the eastern horizon a thousand miles away.

"Won't see that for a while, Will." Enright spoke softly as he reached beneath his seat for the windows' sunshades.

"You will, Jack. You'll be in line for the left seat within eighteen months. You got lots of uptime left in you, buddy."

"Hope so, Skipper."

Outside the six forward windows, the low sun was brilliant where it climbed in the southern, mid-summer sky a week before Christmas. As Endeavor descended in the dawn toward the atmosphere seven minutes away, the television screens showed 6056 nautical miles to Runway 23, Okinawa. As the AC called up computer program Major Mode 304 for the first phase of the re-entry, Enright configured the electrical system switches at his right for the final plunge into the morning sky.

Parker was moving the control stick between his thighs for a final check of the ship's aerodynamic control surfaces. With each twitch of the stick, pointers above the forward center television showed the amount of deflection generated in each surface by Endeavor's four Aerosurface Amplifiers. Alexi Karpov looked over Enright's left shoulder at the instrument displays.

"ASA ready and willing, Jack. Back to automatic trim."

"And fuel cells One, Two, and Three, all set my side, Will."

"Endeavor, Endeavor: AOS by IOS at 10 hours 16 minutes. With you for three."

"Morning, Indian Ocean Ship," Parker drawled. Outside, the sea was now daylight and dazzling.

"Will, Okinawa weather remains clear. Your temperatures and pressures are all Go. We see right OMS inerted. Ready with your inbound pad?"

"Ready to copy, Flight."

"Okay . . . Entry Interface at 10 hours 17 minutes 01 second at Mach 24 point 6. Thermal control until EI plus 02 minutes 41 seconds; elevons on-line at EI plus 03 minutes. Deactivate RCS roll jets at EI plus 04 minutes 40 seconds at Mach 24, altitude 280,000 feet. First roll reversal at 4 pounds dynamic pressure. You are guidance internal at 263,000 feet. And you come out of S-Band communications blackout at EI plus 18 minutes 47 seconds. Wheels-on at 10 hours 47 minutes 43 seconds. Your ground track is still off a tad but well within the descent envelope."

"Roger, Colorado. Got it. We're right and tight in the sky and ready for a few steaks and taters — don't forget to set a place for Alexi."

"Copy, AC. And, Will . . . backroom says you are Go for PTI-7. Repeat: Go for PTI-7. Acknowledge."

Parker and Enright traded glances.

"Ah, Flight, we're single-aft RCS up here. Not to mention tile damage aft portside. We bent our metal a bit. You sure on the PDPU maneuver?"

"Affirmative, Endeavor. Go for PTI-7."

"Alright, Colorado."

"Be LOS momentarily. Next contact at Kadena field by UHF on approach. Chase planes are now airborne for intercept at 40,000 feet when you're Mach zero point 8 at 22 miles range-to-go . . . Will, Jack, Major Karpov: Keep your feet dry, my friends. Configure . . ."

"See ya, Flight."

Endeavor left her last network station behind over the dozen small islands of the Chagos Archipelago which glistened in the early-morning sunlight 90 miles beneath the descending starship.

"Coming up on one, Skipper . . . mark! One minute to Entry Interface."

"Yeh . . . About PTI-7, Jack."

"I know."

Mother's re-entry plot showed 4,700 nautical miles to Okinawa still invisible 3,800 nautical miles on the far side of the hazy, blue horizon ahead.

Endeavor cruised closer to the upper, feathery wisps of the blue planet's breath. At Entry Interface, the starship would plow into the atmosphere at her velocity 24 times the speed of sound and eight times faster than the muzzle velocity of a .30-06 rifle bullet. One minute after that, Shuttle would cross the Equator for the fourteenth time in ten hours aloft to begin Revolution Eight.

The friction of hitting the wall of air at that speed would heat Endeavor's 34,000 pure glass tiles until they glow cherry red at 2,500 degrees Fahrenheit. The heat of re-entry is twice as hot as the melting temperature of Shuttle's aluminum skin behind the one-inch- to five-inch-thick glass tiles.

"Fifty seconds to EI, Skipper. About PTI-7?"

On the computer keyboard above the AC's swollen and throbbing right knee, the EXEC pushbutton blinked, awaiting the touch which would execute the program for the Push-down Pull-up, Programmed Test Input Number Seven.

William McKinley Parker floated against his lap belt. His deeply lined face looked out the window beside his left shoulder. Behind his gray pilot's eyes, he was somewhere better. The exhausted Aircraft Commander was home.

In Houston by the bay, all the clocks on all the walls read 17 minutes past 7 o'clock on a crisp, clear evening. Inside the tall airman's home close to the cold sea, no light shined. The last of evening twilight waned in the western sky beyond the dark windows.

Exquisite paintings and photographs of lighthouses hung in a neat row along the dark walls. Each stone tower beneath its solitary light stood alone upon a rocky shore.

The pilot in command was there. His long, tired body floated against his lap belt. But under his stocking feet he could feel the floor, his floor in his home on his Earth.

Will Parker could see the lighthouses standing mutely to warm the hearts of hard men unseen, who braced their salty bodies upon pitching decks.

"Thirty seconds, Will." Enright's voice sounded like a question.

The AC blinked at his window filled with black sky, morning sunshine, and glaring sea beyond the tinted sunshades.

Enright was surprised to see Parker's large right hand open above the center console between their seats. The thin pilot with the bandaged, burned face reached over with both of his hands to grasp his captain's hand firmly.

"I am proud to have flown with you today, Jacob. You did good."

The AC smiled and the deep lines in his face cracked. Jacob Enright blinked behind his gauze eyeholes.

Will Parker pulled his hand from Enright's and he placed his hand above the small keyboard of the computers.

On Mother's green face, digital numerics ticked down through 12 seconds to the searing Entry Interface, the wall.

"We are pilots, Jack." The Mission Commander spoke quietly but firmly. His fingers were poised above the execute key on the computer keyboard which flashed EXEC, EXEC, EXEC.

"That we are, Will. And the icemen, too."

The Aircraft Commander nodded as he pressed the pushbutton near his right knee. Mother's green face blinked "PTI-7 PROCEED."

Parker wrapped his right hand around the control stick

400

between his legs. His left hand held the T-shaped handle of the speedbrake controller on the left side of the cockpit. The speed brakes would open the long flanks of the vertical tail fin to slow the ship by air drag a little further inbound.

Together as one voice, the two airmen called out the countdown flashing on their television monitors. On the far side of the numbers was re-entry's wall of fire. And 4,390 nautical miles and thirty minutes beyond Entry Interface was a tiny green island with a ribbon of concrete pointing into the wind beneath blazing Pacific sunshine.

"Four, Three, Two, One . . . Interface!"

18

The little boat pitched in rough gray seas. A brilliant sun low in the west made the old boat's white hull glisten in the salt spray which stuck coldly to the faces of the two boatmen. The sailor at the wheel in the open cockpit cuddy was as old and weathered as his boat, the *Rebekah Sara*. On the lobster boat's open stern, hardly thirty feet from the rolling bow, the younger of the two men stood awkwardly braced against the heaving sea.

The captain pointed the boat's bow northward into the mouth of Frenchman's Bay on the far eastern shore of rocky Maine. In the bay of Downeast Maine, the boat stood dead in the water between Mount Desert Island and its Bar Harbor resort to the west and Schoodic Point, just south of Winter Harbor, to the east. To keep from being dragged out to sea by the retreating tide, the boatman at the helm kept his old diesel engine chugging softly against the tide to hold his position just off the lighthouse on Egg Rock Island in the bay. The two cold sailors had waved to the great Blue Nose ferry minutes earlier as the fine old ship plowed the heavy sea on her daily run from Bar Harbor to Yarmouth, Nova Scotia.

On the *Rebekah Sara*'s stern of peeling green paint, Jacob Enright gulped back nausea as the foaming water challenged his 18 years in his country's Navy. Only Jack Enright knew that he had taken up flying from the decks of aircraft carriers just to get his feet off the pitching ships which made him sick. But today, he would lose his lunch rather than abandon his mission in Frenchman's Bay. He had gone to sea to keep a promise to a friend.

The Shuttle Endeavor was wrapped in a plasma bubble of white-hot gas. The seething heat generated by the 100-ton glider plowing 23 times faster than the speed of sound into the atmosphere had boiled the upper wisps of the blue Earth's air. In the inferno hot enough to melt steel, the ionized vapors engulfed the Shuttle in a blanket of electrically charged fire so tightly that fragile radio waves could neither exit nor enter. The traditional "black out" of re-entry sinks every returning shuttle into 16 minutes of absolute radio silence. Once the ship slides out of orbit and down to 400,000 feet above the ground, the pilots on board could not be more isolated from ground control if they were on the back side of the Moon.

Command Pilot William McKinley Parker sat watching his three CRT television screens on the instrument panel. Jacob Enright at this right side blinked watery eyes at his own consoles. Copilot Enright was still inside his moist mask of drug-soaked gauze which stuck painfully to dime-size blisters raised hours earlier by the laser jolt from LACE. Colonel Parker's face bathed in the cherry light of re-entry's glow was puffy and sweating from the ordeal of decompression sickness which had nearly blown his body apart during his spacewalk. The lethal phase of his case of the bends had subsided, but the pain lingered and clouded his weary brain.

"Down the old kazoo, Skipper," Enright mumbled as he scanned his instruments reading out Endeavor's rate of descent, cross-range error along the ground-track which had to dog-leg well sideways to hit Okinawa, and angle of bank as the ship's computers automatically rolled the shuttle wingtips up and down to bleed off energy for a precise landing at the emergency shuttle landing strip at Kadena Air Force Base.

"Yeh, Jack," the Mission Commander croaked. "The PTI ought to kick in at about 350 K."

"At three hundred fifty thousand, Will. Lookin' for the son of a bitch in twenty seconds." Enright squinted his bloodshot eyes at the large "eight ball" attitude indicator in front of his face and a bit below shoulder level. The Flight Director, a round black ball with yellow indicator needles, would show the ship's gentle pitch-up when the Programmed Test Input was executed by the humming memory banks in the four primary computers. The fifth computer watched the other four to keep them honest during reentry's blinding firestorm. A steering error of a gnat's eyelash could reduce the already wounded ship to a ball of molten aluminum.

"She's got the wobbles, Jack," Will Parker stammered. His own eight ball showed a very slight instability in the ship's glide caused by its ruptured tail section.

"Still within the deadband envelope, Will."

"Seems so, Number One. But if I get a rate C and W, the PTI goes into the dumper." Colonel Parker watched the bank of Caution and Warning lights for the first flicker of an indication that the ship's parallel attitude-control loops could not handle the PTI maneuver. The forty-degree, nose-high attitude of the ship used the flat side of the massive, black wings to deflect the scalding slipstream away from the damaged tail area. Endeavor literally rode down her own shock wave like a surfer's waxed board skimming over a curl at Malibu. Only the shuttle rode a wave of ionized gas more than 3,000°F hot.

"About now, Skipper," Enright said loudly. Neither he nor Parker wore their helmets, since Enright's face was bandaged and Parker would not be able to hear his copilot if Parker had donned his own helmet. They spoke over the roar of air slamming into the windshields at 22 times the speed of sound.

Just behind the exhausted flier, Soviet cosmonaut, Alexi Karpov, leaned forward from his backseat position on the upper flightdeck to look over Enright's shoulder at the arrays of instrument panel displays.

"Bastard" was all Will Parker said when the ship's nose simply dropped out from under him. He did not shout. The word came softly and heavy with disappointment instead of anger at their sudden peril.

When the bogus PTI-7 maneuver pushed Endeavor's nose downward, the view outside the forward windows changed quickly. After five minutes of black sky illuminated by the red wall of ionized plasma, the windows filled with red gas and blue ocean. The sparkling Indian Ocean off the coast of Thailand shimmered as if viewed through a piece of cranberry stained glass.

"Runaway AP!" Jack Enright called. His pilot reflexes instantly propeled his hands toward his panel of circuit breakers and the buttons which would cut the electrical power to the ship's autopilot now on a rampage of its own.

"Command override!" Parker called. "I got it!"

With a copilot's inbred training, Enright let his left hand drop away from the control stick between his knees. When the pilot in the left seat says "I got it," the copilot, even if his logbook boasts 10,000 hours of jet time, immediately becomes the student pilot. Enright's right hand continued to grope for the switches to disable the brain-dead automatic pilot.

"DAP inhibit," Enright stammered. He had pulled the plug on the twin digital autopilot systems. It had taken him no more than three seconds. He could do it in his sleep.

While Enright had put DAP's lights out, Will Parker had wrapped both hands around the control column between his thighs. He did not blink for the ten seconds he wrestled with his doomed ship.

The instant Endeavor dropped her black nose, she poked her face into the molten shock wave. The nose-high angle had kept the firestorm well beneath her wings where thousands of heat-resistant black tiles of pure glass insulated her soft belly.

The cabin claxon droned loudly as the red master alarm light illuminated before each pilot's face. In the center of the instrument panel, the red CABIN DEPRESS light flashed.

Enright, now on his own internal autopilot, instinctively checked the cabin-pressure gauges for confirmation that perhaps a window seal had melted a bare heartbeat before the forward windows blew out to let in hellish death by incineration.

"No sweat, Skipper," Enright shouted, sweating. "Ride her out!"

When Endeavor's nose went down, the sudden heat pulse over the forward cabin had heated the outside shell of the ship just enough to make it expand. When the cabin skin stretched in the heat, the inside cabin became imperceptibly larger. The cabin environmental-control sensors felt the inside air expand to fill the wider flightdeck and the low-pressure alarm was triggered by the air molecules seperating for an instant to fill the suddenly larger vessel. The ship's mechanical lungs refilled the cabin immediately, and the red light blinked off. Enright then turned off his red master alarm light. He reached in front of his captain's sweating face to press Parker's master alarm light as well.

By the time the alarms silenced, Parker had gently pulled Endeavor's charred nose back up toward the black sky still red in re-entry's glow. His pilot's steady hand had prevented his initial panic from allowing his hands to jerk Endeavor's nose skyward in a back-breaking loop. Parker did not consciously caution himself against such a lethal recovery. As a professional pilot, he understood that half of real flying is trained reflex; the rest is simply magic.

With Endeavor now down to 35 miles above the Pacific, she again flew safely nose-high. The center of the three television screens on the forward panel filled with warning alerts. The attitude-control systems were baffled by the runaway autopilot. The electronic brains which picked their way at light speed through the re-entry computer program looked toward their two human helpers for relief.

"You got it, Number One," Will Parker said through clenched teeth. His hands slipped forward of the control stick. The three negative "G's" of slowing down made all three airmen lunge forward against their seat belts and shoulder harnesses.

"I have the con, Skip," Jack Enright said breathlessly. Still in intense facial pain and too tired to die, Enright gripped his hands around the control stick. Endeavor would have to make the program's first completely hand-flown re-entry and landing. Make it or die. Even though the digital autopilot had been strangled to death by Enright, the computerized flight director indicator system still generated flying instructions. The pilot had only to follow its needles: pull up to catch a needle rising; bank left to catch a needle drifting leftward. "Turn to the needle," Enright's numb brain mumbled into his buzzing and burned ears.

"You got it," William Mckinley Parker had said. Something in the command pilot's voice reached deeply into Enright. He took the stick and did not look to his left at his captain and his friend. Enright simply studied the gauges. Independent of conscious thought, he felt his hands do what they had trained for a lifetime to do. They flew to where every pilot since Orville and Wilbur longed to fly: "I'll take her home, Will."

Admiral Michael Hauch sat alone in his Pentagon bunker. Beside a single red telephone, a radio squawkbox hissed at the center of the massive table. The last word from the United States Space Defense Operations Center at Colorado Springs had been a weary flight controller's status call, "Downlink data dropout."

The television monitors in the Operations Center's consoles had been flashing "S-S-S-S-S-S" for 16 minutes to signify that nothing but static was being received from Endeavor through the tracking and relay network during the radio blackout of the fiery re-entry plunge.

The lone commander watched his wall clocks monitoring Mission Elapsed Time. When the MET clock ticked up to the time for the PTI-7 automated death maneuver, Admiral Hauch closed his eyes. In his sudden solitude, he did not wipe away the tear which rolled down his pale and stubbled cheek. He knew that his old friend, Will Parker, had just been incinerated. A lifetime with Will Parker of flying and drinking together, and standing stiffly in dress blues beside open pilots' graves, had just ended in a Mach 23 fireball of molten metal and melted glass tiles. The big man sagged into his high-backed chair.

On the glass wall of the Crystal Room, the MET clock counted up while next to it the AOS clock counted down to predicted time of acquisition of signal when the re-entry blackout should end 17 minutes after it began. When the second hand wound through 5-4-3-2-1, Admiral Hauch rubbed his sweating forehead with both palms.

"Endeavor, Endeavor," the squawkbox crackled. "Space Ops by Kadena. Over." The controller's voice sounded tired and anxious. He knew that Endeavor was limping home on a ruptured tail section and a prayer. "Endeavor, Endeavor. Over."

Admiral Hauch sighed deeply, leaned forward, and reached for the button on the top of the little monitor. His moist finger paused for a heartbeat before turning off the telltale receiver. No good news could come from the static in the awful purple sky halfway around the world above the

Pacific Ocean.

"With you, Flight," a strained but youthful voice stammered from 165,000 feet above the sea and 200 miles from the Okinawa coastline.

The thick hand poised above the squawkbox slammed down hard on the mahogany tabletop.

"Good for you!" Michael Hauch bellowed. His blond head rolled back and he pounded the table in bone deep pleasure. "My sweet sonsobitches!" The big man wiped rolling tears from his haggard face.

"Good news, Endeavor!" the faceless voice from Cheyenne Mountain radioed out to sea. "Status, Jack? Over."

"Okay, Colorado." Jacob Enright's voice was a hoarse whisper barely audible above the static. "We're a bit wobbly but stable. Rates are pegged in the green, all vectors. But we had one hell of a ride when that damn PTI kicked in out here. She did a hammerhead stall or something, pitching down like nothing I ever saw in a nightmare. Will recovered with full manual while I took the whole DAP off line . . . ."

"You say a runaway digital autopilot, Jack?"

"Must have been. Don't know and don't care." Enright's Mach 8 sigh could be heard above the distracting static. "We're still holding together, but definitely unstable about the lateral axis with all that trash hanging out the OMS pod damage. Alexi and I are okay, but . . ." The voice hesitated. Michael Hauch looked hard at the squawkbox. "But Will is out cold. I can't take my eyes off the FDI to check him out. You got any vitals on him?"

"Okay, Jack. Understand you're flying the flight director indicator. Are you still full manual control?"

"Affirmative, Flight. What about Will?"

"Sorry, Jack. Nothing by way of medicals on any of you. Sure you're plugged in?"

"Damn," the voice from the fringe of space radioed. "Guess not."

"Is the AC moving at all, Jack?"

409

Enright turned quickly to look at the slumped Aircraft Commander. Will Parker's bare head gently bumped sideways into his wide window at his left shoulder. His soaked hair left a round grease mark on the glass. The deceleration forces generated by the ship's speed reduction in the thicker atmosphere forced all three men to strain forward against their restraint belts. Parker's hard hands banged against the base of the forward instrument panel above his swollen knee. His eyes were closed. Enright squinted through his sticky gauze mask. His burns hurt furiously.

"Just can't tell you, Flight. He's moving around from the G load, but that's all I can see. I'm going to be hand-flying the ruptured duck down to the deck, I'm afraid . . . God, I really hurt."

"We know, Jack. Just hang on for ten minutes, buddy. You're almost home and the beer at Kadena is cold and waiting."

"Sure, Flight. Thanks. Just hand me off to Kadena and get us home." Enright fought back nausea as the sky outside slowly turned from dull red to dark purple. The blue of real air was only minutes away. "Please, Flight."

Hauch remembered his mission, if only for a moment. He was glad that Endeavor was aimed for Okinawa instead of the more public Edwards base. At least landing at a distant military reservation would ensure security and ample opportunity for the G-3 boys to "sterilize" the press release explaining the damaged shuttle, the Russian's death, the injuries—or worse—to Will Parker and Jack Enright's burns.

Admiral Hauch looked wasted. The week of high-level discussions, the mission to LACE, the Russian's death, and Endeavor's return from the dead had drained him. He had nothing left inside except fear for his unconscious friend and sheer joy at Endeavor's return. But the joy was tempered by his knowledge that no shuttle had ever come home without an automatic pilot to steer the huge glider onto final approach. Only on short final do shuttle astronauts take the hand controls for the last five minutes of the descent. And no pilot ever did it solo. Burned, dehydrated, and in pain, Jack Enright would have to do it all.

The Admiral forced his finger to turn off the radio. He had simply borne too much to endure listening to Enright roll Endeavor into a ball on a flyspeck island near Japan. Michael Hauch, Naval aviator, had spent ten years at Edwards Air Force Base, California. There, the rock-hard surface of Rogers Dry Lake was pockmarked by permanent smears of oily black where two generations of test pilots had bent their metal in unproven flying machines and rocket planes. The other proud pilots who knew that they were too good to blow up would then attend what they called "the slow walkin' and sad singin.' "

Clicking off the radio, the seaman mumbled, "Keep the shiny side up, Jack."

Then the tall man laid his large hand upon the red telephone.

Jacob Enright never cried. Not when the medics at Kadena had removed his medicated facial bandages. Not for the two days at the military burn center in San Antonio. There, Air Force physicians had peeled away the burned and blistered skin from his face like layers of an onion to expose the pink and oozing baby skin underneath. And he did not cry when he sat holding Emily Parker's hand when the President spoke sadly of the high cost of exploring the heavens.

Emily Parker had looked radiant in the Houston sunshine of an unseasonably warm day when the President stood beside William McKinley Parker who heard none of it.

"Mister Enright, why is my daddy in a box," Emily had pleaded softly into his ear. "When will he get out?"

Emily's red hair glowed and the grown woman's beautiful face was full of the eyes of a terrified little girl. Her child

411

mind made her wet eyes look like a wounded animal's eyes and Jacob Enright could say nothing. He could only look away toward the President who stood surrounded by grim faced NASA technocrats.

The President spoke of the irony that Will Parker should have survived a lifetime as a test pilot, an orbital mission in a tiny, two-man Gemini spacecraft over twenty years ago and one trip to the Moon, only to die coming home from a routine shuttle flight to fetch a damaged communications satellite.

The medics said that Will Parker's brain had quietly ruptured from a stray nitrogen bubble which slammed into a blood vessel during the forces generated by re-entry. The bends had killed him after all. But not before he had saved his battered ship and had handed the bridge over to his devoted and trusted First Officer.

The medics on the ground had swarmed over Endeavor when Enright gently set her down on the little island and had rolled to a stop on the concrete. The men in white worked on Colonel Parker for fifteen minutes while Enright and Karpov watched silently. Everyone knew all along that Will was gone.

"No!" Jack Enright had protested when the Kadena people wanted to carry Will Parker's limp body in long woolies out of the flightdeck first. "No. The skipper leaves last." Enright was coughing fluid which was slowly filling his lungs now that gravity was working on his burned body after eleven hours of weightlessness. The Air Force people did not argue. They gently eased the bandaged Enright from his sweat soaked seat upstairs and helped him down to the mid-deck and out the hatchway to fresh air. Alexi Karpov followed silently.

Two Air Force sentries held Enright upright, one at each arm, as the medics carried Will Parker down the portable stairs rolled to Endeavor's charred side. In the ship's nose area once glisteningly white glass tiles, the whole cockpit

412

was blackened by the fierce heat of the PTI-7, roller coaster ride. And the OMS pod in the left tail section was rubble.

Jack Enright freed his right hand from the sentry's welcome grip when the body of the command pilot was carried past Enright and Alexi Karpov. In unison, the swooning Enright and the grieving Russian survivor saluted their captain as he passed.

William McKinley Parker had been the last man to leave his ship.

"When will my daddy get out of the box?" the woman asked again.

"I'll tell you later, Emily," Enright whispered dryly while his President spoke with deep emotion.

The President remembered the seven dead heroes of the destroyed shuttle Challenger. And he movingly spoke of the British poet John Masefield and about tall ships and stars to steer them by.

But Jack Enright did not cry through the eulogy to his friend, nor when the haunting strains of Taps echoed down the Johnson Space Center concrete campus, nor when the T-38 jets screamed overhead and one little plane peeled off from the others to make the Missing Man Formation.

Then the Air Force Band struck up "My Old Kentucky Home" in slow, dirge cadence in honor of the Blue Grass State's dead son. Only then did Lt. Commander Jacob Enright lower his freshly wrapped face and wet his bandages with tears. Between him and Dr. Cleanne Casey, Emily Parker softly whimpered.

"I think you better do it," the pilot of the *Rebekah Sara* called in his clipped Mainer accent. "Tide going out fast now, Mr. Enright."

In the three weeks since Will Parker's memorial service in Houston, the bandages had been removed from Enright's face. His new skin looked bright red, raw, and painfully

413

sunburned. His cheeks were covered with a ghastly paste of sunscreen and zinc oxide.

"Thanks, Fenton," Enright shouted over the sea's noise off Bar Harbor. Enright braced himself on the lobster boat's rolling and open stern.

Before the funeral, Dr. Casey had taken him aside to inform him of Will's strange phone call the night before the launch. She spoke of how he longed to be buried at sea if he were killed in space. At that instant, Enright resolved to honor his captain's last wish at any cost—even his career.

Enright was stunned by the ease with which his request for Parker's body had been granted. First he had called Will's old pal, Admiral Hauch, only three days before the memorial pageant. But the Defense Department had informed Enright that the Admiral was TDY—on temporary deployment outside the country. Where, they refused to say. So Enright went to the NASA brass. The personal assistance people in Houston immediately granted Enright's request on condition that the body be present for the memorial service. Later that day, Will Parker had been reduced to a jug of ashes, tiny bone fragments, and silver dental fillings.

Government men with no humor and narrow neckties had gently suggested that Enright not answer any public questions about the alleged accident. After the Challenger disaster's treatment by the press, Enright did not have to be told twice. Besides, he had seen his Earth from heaven once—and he wanted to see it again.

The world media accepted the press releases and the spokespersons who lamented the unforeseen collision between the Soyuz spacecraft and Endeavor's tail end which had killed Will Parker and one Soviet flyer and had burned Enright. An American delegation of astronauts led by the Secretary of State and the Vice President had attended the Moscow memorial for the Soviet pilot killed in Soyuz. Moscow declined to demand a formal board of inquiry. Glasnos had prevailed serenely.

With one hand on the little boat's rail and his other arm stretched over the side, Enright dumped the can of oily powder into the high gray sea. Two passing whitecaps, and William McKinley Parker was gone.

"Rest well, Skipper," the thin airman whispered to the cold and receding tide. "Rest well."

"Are we done?" the Mainer asked anxiously in the rising swells of Downeast Maine. To the east, the gray surf pounded against the granite boulders of Schoodic Point.

"Take us home," the pilot said above the salty wind.

PINNACLE'S FINEST IN SUSPENSE AND ESPIONAGE

OPIUM (17-077, $4.50)
by Tony Cohan

Opium! The most alluring and dangerous substance known to man. The ultimate addiction, ensnaring all in its lethal web. A nerve-shattering odyssey into the perilous heart of the international narcotics trade, racing from the beaches of Miami to the treacherous twisting alleyways of the Casbah, from the slums of Paris to the teeming Hong Kong streets to the war-torn jungles of Vietnam.

LAST JUDGMENT (17-114, $4.50)
by Richard Hugo

Seeking vengeance for the senseless murders of his brother, sister-in-law, and their three children, former S.A.S. agent James Ross plunges into the perilous world of fanatical terrorism to prevent a centuries-old vision of the Apocalypse from becoming reality, as the approaching New Year threatens to usher in mankind's dreaded Last Judgment.

THE JASMINE SLOOP (17-113, $3.95)
by Frank J. Kenmore

A man of rare and lethal talents, Colin Smallpiece has crammed ten lifetimes into his twenty-seven years. Now drawn from his peaceful academic life into a perilous web of intrigue and assassination, the ex-intelligence operative has set off to locate a U.S. senator who has vanished mysteriously from the face of the Earth.

Available wherever paperbacks are sold, or order direct from the Publisher. Send cover price plus 50¢ per copy for mailing and handling to Pinnacle Books, Dept. 17-459, 475 Park Avenue South, New York, N.Y. 10016. Residents of New York, New Jersey and Pennsylvania must include sales tax. DO NOT SEND CASH.